KT-174-526

THE Single Mum's WISH LIST

'What fabulous, confident writing! One of the freshest, funniest, most exciting new voices I've read for a long time.' Jane Fallon

'A warm and insightful debut with a clever, funny and totally relatable heroine.' *Sunday Express*

'Very funny and delightfully relatable – this was a real treat.' Trisha Ashley

'We've all been a "Martha Ross" at some point, so we loved this hilarious and moving novel about starting afresh.' *Take a Break*

'Fresh and funny and REAL . . . Martha really spoke to me. She will steal everyone's heart!' Veronica Henry

'Beautifully written and emotionally intelligent. I rooted for Martha from the start.' Sara Lawrence, *Daily Mail*

www.penguin.co.uk

THE Single Mum's WISH LIST

Charlene Allcott

CORGI BOOKS

TRANSWORLD PUBLISHERS
BAINTE DEN STOC, London W5 5SA
www.penguin.co.uk

FROM DÚN LAOGHAIRE RATHDOWN
Transworld is part of the Penguin Random House group of companies
whose addresses can be found at global.penguinrandomhouse.com

Penguin
Random House
UK

First published in Great Britain as *The Reinvention of Martha Ross*
in 2018 by Bantam Press
an imprint of Transworld Publishers
Corgi edition published as *The Single Mum's Wish List* in 2019

Copyright © Charlene Allcott 2018

Charlene Allcott has asserted her right under the Copyright,
Designs and Patents Act 1988 to be identified as the author of this work.

This book is a work of fiction and, except in the case of historical fact, any
resemblance to actual persons, living or dead, is purely coincidental.

Every effort has been made to obtain the necessary permissions with
reference to copyright material, both illustrative and quoted. We apologize
for any omissions in this respect and will be pleased to make the
appropriate acknowledgements in any future edition.

A CIP catalogue record for this book
is available from the British Library.

ISBN 9780552175791

Typeset in 10.75/13.5pt Sabon LT Std by Jouve (UK), Milton Keynes
Printed and bound in Great Britain by Clays Ltd, Elcograf S.p.A.

Penguin Random House is committed to a sustainable
future for our business, our readers and our planet. This book
is made from Forest Stewardship Council® certified paper.

MIX
Paper from
responsible sources
FSC® C018179

3 5 7 9 10 8 6 4 2

To Graham, for believing in me before
I believed in myself

1

I THINK IT'S APPROPRIATE to begin at the end. People say it's best to start at the beginning but I've never been a believer. I'm loyal to endings; I skip to the final page of every book I read. The end is where the truth is, and the end starts when Jacqueline opens her door.

I've never seen Jacqueline looking anything less than glamorous and even with sleep still clinging to her eyes and a silk robe replacing her starched, navy shift dress, she looks like an off-duty Marilyn Monroe. I feel inadequate in my workwear 101 outfit of black T-shirt, black trousers and flats.

'Martha,' she says carefully, 'are you OK?' Jacqueline says things like, 'Are you OK?' when what she really means is, 'What the fuck are you doing at my house at eight thirty in the morning?' That's why I need her. Jacqueline is my therapist.

She asks me in. 'Asks' is a strong word; she makes a gesture close to a shrug and steps to one side. I can't afford the luxury of socially acceptable behaviour, so I go through. Jacqueline ushers me past her magnolia-coloured therapy room and into a light, open-plan kitchen. I know this is her way of saying 'this is not official' but I don't mind because I've always wanted to see what goes on behind the velvet rope. I spend 40 per cent of every session with Jacqueline wondering who Jacqueline actually is – what she does at weekends; if she does Pilates; if she still has sex with her husband; if her husband is in fact a wife. I am not disappointed; the room looks like something from the pages of *Homes & Gardens*. I am transfixed by a huge, tartan-print three-seater. I have always fantasized about having a kitchen large enough to house a sofa. I take a few moments to imagine a sofa-kitchened life but then Alexander wanders into the fantasy with his bare feet and his ripped Diesel jeans, and I remember why I am there.

'I need you to tell me to split up with Alexander,' I say. Jacqueline shuts her eyes briefly and then gestures towards a high stool next to a granite-topped island. My mouth is dry but she doesn't offer me a drink and it doesn't seem appropriate to ask for one. Jacqueline doesn't sit, which I think is her way of saying she's only tolerating my visit, but why become a therapist if you don't want to invite crazy into your life?

'You said to contact you whenever I needed and I really need an answer today.' I don't know why today; today is no more significant than any other day: a Friday morning, mild with a threat of rain, no major events in the calendar. It is sinister in its mundaneness. Jacqueline makes a face that I have seen many times and previously taken to mean she is absorbing the significance of my words, but now I'm wondering if it means 'you are very irritating'. Perhaps it's the facial equivalent of one of those words that can mean two completely different things, like beat or tender or leaves. I've forgotten the name for those sorts of words. Alexander would know; perhaps that's another reason I should stay with him.

During the pause in which Jacqueline is thinking or

praying or whatever she is doing, I try and predict what she will say. I am thinking: 'Why do you believe this is an issue for you?' Or maybe: 'Would it help if I reflected back to you what I just heard?' Or her favourite: 'I'm more interested in why you've posed the question.' She really loves that one; my money's on that.

She says, 'Yes, you should.' And I feel nauseous. I immediately understand that I came here because I thought she would not be allowed to give me the answer my heart already knew.

'Thanks,' I say as I stand. 'Sorry, I have to go to work.'

Jacqueline continues, 'We've spent a great deal of time discussing your relationship and it is obviously very flawed. In addition, your demeanour today suggests you may need some time to focus on yourself.'

'Thanks,' I say again.

'Also, before you go,' says Jacqueline, and I take a deep breath. She clears her throat. 'I can't see you again. I think some boundaries have been crossed here. I can recommend someone very good . . . very firm.' She turns and writes something on a handily placed book of notelets on the island and passes it to me. I have an urge to sniff it but I put it in my trouser pocket.

'Thanks,' I say and leave. This is the end.

Actually, this is not quite the end. The end is twelve minutes later when I'm on the bus rumbling along the Brighton seafront towards the concrete prison that serves as my place of work. I send Alexander a text terminating our six-year marriage. It reads, 'WE ARE OVER.' Less than thirty seconds later he replies, 'OK.'

2

WHY I STAND by endings – beginnings are bullshit. Let me tell you about the start of Alexander and me. We were best friends but we weren't really best friends; I was the dumpy chick he tolerated hanging around. Everyone knew I was hopelessly in love with him but anyone with eyes could see I wasn't his type – I'm slightly above average height and more than slightly above average weight; I'm mixed race without any of the exoticism it claims to offer. My face is fine but forgettable. The only thing that stands out about me is my uncontrollable hair and I have spent a lifetime experimenting with products that might stop that being the case. So, I sat on the sidelines and I watched Alexander go through a series of petite, striking blondes, my favourite part being when they broke up and he would take me to the Twisted Yarn for a debrief. I would sip my dark ale (which made me gag at the time but now I actually quite like) and I would get to tell him all the things I had been secretly storing for a week, a month, or on one occasion, an entire year. To be honest, I was happy with that. OK, I was on the outskirts of happy; I could certainly catch the scent of happy if the wind was blowing in the right direction. And then one of the blondes broke his heart.

Her name was Jenna. She was impossibly and impractically posh. She was one of those chicks that's done everything, but really how much can you experience in a rural, all-girls boarding school and then a small, top-tier university and then a cushy job, handed to you on a gold platter by your father? Still, when she spoke, Alexander listened. He was like a Labrador when he was with her. He looked at her the way I imagine I looked at him. Anyway, Jenna ended the relationship with very little explanation. I heard a rumour she had joined a bloke called Tristan on his boat in the Caribbean for the summer but I kept that nugget to myself. Jenna always seemed to have one eye on the lookout for something better, so the break-up came as no surprise to anyone but Alexander. I'm assuming he had been dumped before but on this occasion, it consumed him. I waited by the phone for him to arrange our usual post-break-up pity party, but the call never came. When I tried to contact him, he wouldn't answer and his voicemail message said he was 'taking time out from life'.

After a few days of this I did what any friend would do and went to his flat. I let myself in using a key I knew he kept hidden in a pot of dying lavender. The first thing that hit me was the smell – it was two parts gym locker room, one part that weird odour that haunts kitchen cupboards and always turns out to be rotting potatoes. Alexander was in bed and it looked like that had been the case for several days. The debris around him told a story – a broken photo frame, an overflowing ashtray, three empty wine bottles and a pizza box.

'Alexander,' I said gently. 'Alexander, you have to get up.' He continued staring into the distance, so I quietly set about filling a bin liner with rubbish. When I had finished he was asleep and I gave the kitchen a thorough clean and then made soup out of the selection of sad-looking veggies in his fridge. When I walked in to tell him the food was ready he was awake but still huddled under his duvet.

'What's wrong with me?' he said.

'Oh my God, nothing,' I reassured him.

'It was different this time,' he said. 'I was gonna give her this.' He let his hand fall on to the bedside table, where lay a green velvet box.

'Is that . . .'

'Look,' said Alexander. I walked towards the box slowly, as if it might detonate. I picked it up carefully and checked if Alexander was watching me; he was not. Inside, safe in its satin nest, was an antique ring. Not exactly my style, except for the bold emerald stone – a unique rock for a one-of-a-kind girl. Much later I would get that ring and, fool that I am, instead of seeing it as some other woman's cast-off, I thought it meant I had won. At that point I didn't want it anywhere near me. Without saying anything I placed the box in Alexander's sock drawer.

'You have to try.' I sat on the edge of the bed and with some effort hauled him into a sitting position. 'See, not so hard.' Alexander gave me a weak smile.

'Not so hard with you,' he said. There was a pause in which I assume the room was silent but in my head I was screaming, 'Kiss me! Kiss me! Kiss me!' And he did.

When huge things happen, it feels like everything should change. The sky should turn purple and the laws of gravity should no longer apply. It's almost offensive how very much the same everything seems when I arrive at work. How can the security guy, Darryl, still be playing Candy Crush when I feel like every cell in my body has been altered? I'm thinking about this as I power up my computer and put on my headset.

Oh yeah, I work in a call centre. I never actually say I work in a call centre; I say I work in customer services. Not that there's anything wrong with working in a call centre, if that's what you want to do, but from my experience no one does. We're all waiting for our big break; even Darryl has shared his movie script with me. I want to be a singer. Slight problem – I've never sung in front of anyone. Well, I've sung in front of Moses. Moses is my son. Our son, mine and Alexander's. You wouldn't know it from their interactions. Alexander always looks mildly surprised when he sees him in a room – 'Oh, you again? Well, I guess you can stay for dinner.'

Moses is beautiful, though. I know that all parents are supposed to think their kid is beautiful but Moses actually is. When I was pregnant we played a game where we each got to pick the features we wanted our unborn baby to have; Alexander said he hoped he wouldn't get my chin and he didn't. He has my crazy black curls and his father's startling green eyes – eyes that I know from experience will bestow even the most mundane utterings with an intoxicating intensity. Women stop me in town and tell me he'll be a heartbreaker when he grows up, which is a creepy thing to say about a toddler, but I believe them.

I thought being a mother would make me a grown-up, that I would have no choice but to grow up. It was only after he was born that I realized how little adulting I had got around to doing. I watch other mothers carefully for evidence of how to stay calm and keep a child vaguely clean but I always end up Googling 'the dangers of eating cat food' or fishing electronics out of the toilet. Sometimes I share these anecdotes with people around me, in order to gauge exactly how close I am to becoming a *Daily Mail* headline. Like Greg, who sits next to me at work. He has two girls; I know this because he has a gigantic picture of them on his desk – pretty, blonde things with lopsided bows and the promise of mischief in their eyes. When I tell him my mishaps he always chuckles or says, 'It's like that.' Or, 'Tell me about it, buddy.' So I think I'm kinda on the right track.

I took the job at Fairfax Financial Services because Alexander said I needed to think about my future. I'd left a temp job to have Moses and had nothing to go back to. I told Alexander I was thinking about retraining and might start to do some singing auditions, but he told me he couldn't fund a dream-chasing lifestyle. The call centre had two advantages – it offered shift work, so I would be able to fit it around childcare and singing gigs; and it was hellish enough that I wouldn't stay too long, six months tops. That was nearly a year ago. Now I wonder if even this job will fit my new life. Everything's fallen apart and it all needs to be put back together like a sadistic game of Jenga.

I try and make a start on constructing an image of what this new chapter will look like; I have a lot of time to do this because most of my job entails directing customers to yet another call centre where presumably someone will do something useful, by which I mean I say, 'Putting you through now . . .' two million times a day; it doesn't take much mental energy.

We're allowed two breaks a day, one short and one long. Sometimes I would use the opportunity to call Alexander, not always but often. I feel bereft of this; it's like when I gave up smoking – it wasn't the nicotine I missed so much as the ritual of it, the way the process punctuated time.

'Do you smoke?' I ask Greg.

'Nah,' he says. 'It's bad for you.'

'So I've heard,' I say.

'I didn't know you smoked,' says Greg, as if we are life-long friends and I have intentionally kept this fact hidden.

'I've got a lot on my mind,' I say. He doesn't turn away.

'You OK, buddy?' he says. Every office has a Greg – you might know him as Steve or Dave, but they all share the same affable nature and inoffensive brand of charm. They're usually found offering to make the older women strong cups of tea or having intense debates about football team managership with the lads in the post room; their strength is in their consistency, and as I look at Greg's gentle, ex-boyband-member face, I'm hit by the fact that he is probably more reliable than the man I had pledged my life to. I nod my head. If I speak I will cry and if I cry I will be 'woman who cries at work'.

My phone rings and it's Alexander, as if he knows I need him. My break is officially over, and I'm not even supposed to have my phone on my desk. The lines are automated and if I'm not available the customer calls will go unanswered, but I accept his call anyway. I give Greg a hand signal, one that I hope he understands as, 'Cover for me, this is very important.' He seems to comprehend because he winks at me.

'Hello,' I say, as I scuttle out of the room to the only place of sanctuary in the building – the disabled loo.

'Thanks for answering,' says Alexander.

'Yeah, you too,' I say. 'I mean, thanks for calling.' I realize this is the only time he's called me during the day; he almost always sends a text and even then its content is of the practical, almost always instructional nature: 'Buy milk', 'Can you pick up dinner?', 'Where's the gas meter?' Nothing personal or intimate. Perhaps by forcing space on him he has realized that proximity is what he needs.

'It's brave of you to say what had to be said.' Alexander

stops; I'm not sure if he's waiting for me to speak or over-come with emotion but then I hear someone ask if he has a loyalty card and I realize he's in a supermarket. 'I've packed some of your stuff and I'll drop it at your mum's before you finish. Given that Moses has a room there, it makes sense if you both stay with her for a bit. I called and asked her to pick him up from nursery tonight.'

I lean against the wall. 'Alexander, I—'

'Don't worry,' he says. 'We can have a chat in a day or two, when the dust has settled.' I have a sudden urge to laugh, but instead I end the call. Then I don't feel like my legs will hold me, so I sit on the floor. I squeeze myself between the toilet bowl and the sanitary towel bin and sob.

I don't know how long has passed when I get up and brush myself off. My eyes in the mirror remind me of those of the white gerbil I had when I was seven – small, sad and pink. I try and make my face presentable with a blast from the hand dryer, and when I check myself again, my eyes fall on my rings. I wrench at my wedding band until it comes away, leaving a red, raw mark. I slip it in my pocket but I can't make myself do the same with the emerald. I tell myself it's too pretty but I think I'm not ready to let go of the knowledge that, at least one time, he chose me.

As I'm walking back to my desk Greg stands. He's on a call but he does a series of stretches, as if he's preparing for some sort of office-based sport. As I get closer his gestures become more involved; it's almost like a dance. I wonder if he's unstable – the secret lives of call centre workers, eh? Too late I see that the title of Greg's contemporary piece is 'the boss is coming, stay out of sight for a minute' and the second I make it to my desk I am besieged by Bob.

Bob demands that I come to his office. I might be in serious trouble but I might not be as Bob demands everything. He manages to make every interaction feel aggressive; I swear even his sneezes are threatening. I don't know why Bob feels the need to be so macho about everything – he's tall, fit (on account of an apparent gym addiction) and he's good-looking if you like that artificially bronze, extra-from-*TOWIE* vibe, but obviously something has gone awry at some point. Rumour has it he's not even called Bob. He briefly dated Danielle in HR and after their break-up she revealed that he had chosen the name Bob because he 'did not feel his given name suited his present mindset'. Bob vowed never to date within the organization again following this indiscretion. He told me so during my interview: 'I don't shit where I eat, so don't get any ideas.'

Bob doesn't invite me to sit, so I end up standing with my hands in front of me like a kid being called before the headmaster. Actually, these days I bet the kid would be allowed to sit down; we're all so invested in children's welfare and treating them with respect. Bob is not a bedfellow with respect, so he leaves me hovering. He tells me I have dropped 36.5 calls over the past forty-six minutes and wants to know why. I want to know how it's possible to drop half a call but I'm not sure he would appreciate the question. I think about telling him the truth, saying, 'My heart feels like it's been ripped from my body and shredded on the fine side of the grater,' but then I look at Bob's impassive, possibly Botoxed face and say, 'I've been bleeding for twenty days.' Bob gives me the rest of the day off with strict instructions to 'find something to plug that up' by my next shift. I leave the office and head to Leanne's house.

3

LEANNE OPENS HER front door. She's wearing leggings covered in a brightly coloured geometric pattern and a long-sleeved top made out of shiny black material. 'Not that you aren't welcome,' she says, 'but this is a surprise.' Leanne takes Fridays off to spend 'quality time' with the kids and catch up with what she calls 'home admin'.

'Are you busy?' I ask. She pauses but says no.

'I was just about to take Lucas out with the running buggy.' Leanne heads to the kitchen and puts the kettle on, without needing to ask if this is the correct course of action.

I follow her and sit at the table. I start about twenty sentences in my head and go with, 'It's over.' And then, 'Oh God, it's really over. It's actually over.'

Leanne shoos her youngest, Lucas, from the room – she's clearly desperate to protect her children from legitimate human emotions for a couple more years. When he's safely out of earshot she says, 'What has he done?'

'It's not him, it's me!' I slap my hand against my breastbone as if there's another contender for the title of me.

'What have you done?' Leanne asks patiently.

'I ended it. I had to end it. Jacqueline told me I should end it. Everyone knew it wasn't working, everyone. Oh God. Oh God.' Leanne stands up and pulls my head into

12

her chest. I can feel my tears creating a damp patch on her top and I try and pull away but she just tightens her grip.

'It's OK,' she whispers. 'It's OK.' We stay there in silence, both waiting for my breathing to return to a steady rhythm. Eventually my pace matches hers; there's something soothing about the synchronization of our exhalations. 'Martha,' says Leanne, 'who's Jacqueline?'

Leanne lets me hide within the bustle of her home. I follow her around like a puppy as she continues her daily routine. As we fold laundry and prep dinner, I play a canny game of avoidance – I avoid her gaze, I avoid my feelings, I avoid fourteen missed calls from my mother and a text message that says, 'CALL ME NOW!!!' After the fifteenth call, I text her: 'I AM FINE. WITH LEANNE. PLEASE PUT MOSES TO BED.' Then I turn my phone on silent. I know that if I hold my son I'll crumble; he'll have to watch his mother fall to pieces and won't understand why. And in addition, I don't need to hear 'All the Ways Martha is an Epic Failure: Volume 78' from my mother. Not today.

I accompany Leanne and Lucas to collect my god-daughter, Millie, from school. When she sees me at the gates she breaks into a spontaneous little tap dance and it is almost, but not quite, enough to lift my spirits. 'Auntie Marfa!' she cries when she reaches me. 'The truth came out!'

'It always does, beautiful,' I say.

'Look!' Millie carefully extracts a wad of tissue from the pocket of her pink coat and unwraps it carefully to reveal a tiny, white tooth.

'Well done, chicken,' I say. 'I'm so proud.' I pull her into a hug. 'I'm so, so proud of you.' Millie wriggles out of my arms and carefully places her treasure back in her pocket.

*

When the kids are in bed and Leanne's husband James is back from work and pottering about in that way only men can, it is no longer possible to avoid Leanne's slightly overwhelming concern. She makes me tea and then seats me on her sofa, where she paints my nails a shade of pearly pink. This is a throwback to our teenage years, when we would spend Saturday evenings getting beautified for parties to which we would never receive invites. We speak very little as she carefully coats each fingernail, although she gently probes into some of the pertinent details: Do I need somewhere to stay? (No.) Do I have enough money? (I don't know.) Do I need a good solicitor? (I hope not.) When she has finished she instructs me sternly not to smudge her work and then makes us both another brew.

'Is this definite?' she asks. I nod. 'When did you know?' 'Yesterday . . . Always,' I say.

'Will you go back to "Ketch"?' Leanne asks. I am yet to give this thought but the answer arrives quickly.

'No. No, I'm still Martha Ross. I want to have the same name as Moses.' Also, I need the reminder – not of Alexander but that, at one time, I belonged to someone. Leanne sips her tea. I suspect she is filling her mouth to prevent further comment. 'You can say it,' I continue, 'you can say whatever it is you're thinking.' For some reason, I think she's going to admit she thought I was too fat for him.

'I'm sorry,' she says.

Without introduction, my friend Cara walks into the room and falls heavily on to the sofa. Leanne must have sent a text requesting back-up. 'What do I need to fix?' she asks.

'How did you get in?' asks Leanne. A bird tweets from within Cara's bag and she ignores Leanne's question, retrieves her phone and starts stabbing at it violently.

Leanne narrows her eyes at Cara as we both watch her scarlet-tipped fingers move deftly across the phone face. When it's apparent that Cara is oblivious to her silent judgement, Leanne switches back to concerned mode. She pats me on the thigh and tells Cara, 'Everything's under control. Martha's had a shock. It's over between her and Alexander.' Cara puts her phone away, tucks her spike-heeled ankle boots up beside her and pushes the sunglasses she's wearing on to her thick, inky head of hair.

'Thank fuck for that,' she says. 'He's a prick.'

'That's not helpful,' says Leanne.

'He is a bit of a prick,' I whisper.

'He's a lot of a prick,' says Cara. 'He could very easily go by Alex, but he forces everyone to say two pointless, extra syllables. Do you need him hurt?' she asks. 'I know a guy in Rochester.' I'm not sure if she's serious. Leanne pushes Cara's feet off the sofa cushions.

'Martha doesn't need anything like that,' she says. 'She needs some space and she needs us to listen and be *here* for her.' Cara flares her nostrils and places her feet on the coffee table. Leanne lets her eyes rest on them for a second and then asks, 'What happened?' And so, I tell them.

You know those couples who are so perfect they look like performance art? Alexander and I were one of them. If you came for dinner, we would make two courses and offer you mid-priced wine and finish each other's jokes and wave you goodbye at the door. Then it would be curtains down. Alexander would retreat to his office and I would hang out with my lover, Netflix. Slowly we spent less and less time with each other and soon, I was no longer sure I wanted to spend time with him at all. The saddest thing about a relationship that ends in this way is the nagging feeling that it could have been saved. It's like when you move into a house and there's a crack in the wall and you say, 'How ugly, we'll get that fixed right away,' but of course you don't. There are far more interesting things to do – tables to buy, prints to hang, housewarming parties to host. For a few weeks, your eyes fall upon that crack and you promise yourself you'll address it but soon you grow accustomed to it. The crack becomes a part of the home; you don't even see it any more. Except occasionally, in the middle of the night, you can't sleep, and you think, I must deal with that crack. And then one day you're standing in your living room with a bloke called Mike and he's telling you that you have to give him five grand to stop your house from caving in. I don't know who Mike is in this analogy but I do know that the house fell down.

'I knew something was going on,' says Leanne. 'It was like you were getting smaller. He was extinguishing you. You're so brave. I have so much admiration for you.' I'm spared from saying anything by James walking into the room.

'I thought you might need this,' he says, and places three glasses and a bottle of wine on the coffee table before shuffling out backwards like some kind of geisha. I can tell Leanne is attempting not to beam with pride and I find myself resentful. Why does she think she can be so smug? I wouldn't go out with James if he were the last man on earth. OK, if he were the last man I would but only because if he were the last man and willing to date me, I would officially be the hottest woman on the planet. Other than this unlikely scenario, he would be a no. He's nice but wears terrible shoes and has too much gel in his hair and his mouth is too small for his face, which in my opinion gives him a slightly ratty appearance. It would be like being married to a devoted dormouse. Alexander is hot.

Not movie-star hot, unless the movie was a low-budget, independent drama about a man reconnecting with his ailing father, but general-population hot. Cara leans forward and pours three large glasses of wine. She hands Leanne and me a glass each and then downs half of the third before topping it up again.

'To freedom,' says Cara, raising her drink. Leanne smacks her on the leg.

'To hope,' she says.

'To the hope of freedom,' I say, and we clink our glasses together.

'What are you actually going to do, though?' asks Leanne. I take a large mouthful of wine.

'Find someone new,' I say, 'something better.' Leanne places a hand on top of mine.

'I think it's a bit soon,' she says.

'It's not soon enough,' says Cara.

I can see Leanne gearing up to protest, so I say, 'I'm ready, I deserve to be happy. I want what you have, Leanne.'

Leanne colours a little and sips her drink. 'OK,' she says, 'what do you want? What wasn't Alexander giving you?' My mind is flooded with so many things – a kiss goodnight, a smile in the morning, a sense of safety.

'I don't know,' I say. Leanne stands and walks over to her solid oak bookcase. She pulls a notepad and pen from one of the shelves.

'If you're not clear on exactly what you need, you will never get it,' she says. Leanne sits back down and opens the pad to a clean page. 'My business coach got me to do one for work but I don't see why it wouldn't be the same for a bloke.'

'Totally did this last year,' says Cara, 'and the next day I met Rico.'

'What was on your list?' Leanne asks. Cara ticks the items off on her fingers: 'Young, fun, not in town long and most importantly a really massive co—'

'The universe will receive your message and manifest it for you,' interrupts Leanne, turning her back on Cara's mockery, 'but you need to focus on what you want.' Cara crosses her eyes as she tips her head and lets her tongue fall out of her mouth. Sometimes I think Leanne and Cara don't like each other.

I met Leanne at school and we spent many Saturdays crying over Leonardo DiCaprio and perfecting our acne-camouflaging techniques. We drifted apart after university – Leanne worked hard, settled down quickly with James and pursued a parent-pleasing career path in accounting; I was mostly drunk. It was only when I was planning my wedding and realized that I couldn't trust any of my drinking buddies to rock up to the right place on the right day that I reached out to her and asked her to be my bridesmaid, and we rekindled our friendship. She has taught me a lot about being a wife and a mother, mostly about the stuff I'm doing wrong.

Cara, I met at a temp job. I was an admin assistant and she was the receptionist, or at least I think she was, but I never saw her do any work. She left suddenly amid rumours (which she has never confirmed or denied) of a mysterious pay-out. Then one day she called to ask if I would accept a package that was arriving at the office for her. When she came to collect it (thirty minutes late) I asked her what was in the box; it was very large and had taken some effort to conceal.

'Toys,' she said. 'You know, cock rings and such. You're a superstar. I need them for tonight.' She must've seen the shock in my eyes because she tutted and said, 'Not for me,

18

for the talent.' The shock shifted to confusion and she sighed and said, 'Come on, I'll show you.' And she did.

'She's right, you know,' says Cara. 'You're not very good at focusing.'

'Remember the novel?' says Leanne.

'Which one?' says Cara, and they both snort-laugh simultaneously. I remember that even if they don't like each other they are united in the cause of trying to prevent me from continually fucking up my life.

With the aid of another bottle of wine we pull together a list, the summation of my hopes and dreams and values in human man form. It takes some time and negotiation but an hour or so later we are confident we have succeeded.

The definitive, non-negotiable – approved by Leanne, Cara and the universe – perfect man for Martha Ross official guidelines:

1) <u>Must have blue eyes and red hair.</u> (I have always had a predilection for redheads and I once heard that this combination of features is one of the rarest in the world. This man needs to be one in a million.)

2) <u>Must be intrigued by me.</u> (I never really felt I held Alexander's interest.)

3) <u>Has to work for himself but not be in it to make money.</u> He's got to do something useful to society. He has to spend his free time doing something inspiring; not just inspiring but also worthy, e.g. deworming African orphans or similar. He can have little to no interest in developing strategies to excel at Championship Manager.

4) <u>Must be spiritually aware.</u> Not necessarily religious but have values and a belief system. He

has to have done work on himself and be able to evidence that.

5) <u>Must be close to his family.</u> Not in a creepy way. He cannot under any circumstances live with his mother, but he must understand the importance of familial relationships (Alexander hates every last member of his family; Jacqueline had a field day with this).

6) <u>Has to like kids, but can't have kids.</u> He can't be childless because he can't commit or has some huge flaw that has prevented anyone wanting to breed with him. He has to have a legitimate reason for not having become a father, preferably tragic.

7) <u>Has to be confident in all senses of the word</u> – socially confident, sexually confident but especially confident about the fact that he's crazy about me.

8) <u>Has to be tall</u>, in exceptional health, has to like reading and long conversations.

9) <u>Has to like animals</u> and will have a cat called Hendrix.

10) <u>His name will be George.</u>

Cara tries to talk me out of George. 'George is a dead uncle name,' she says. I like George, though. George is solid; he sounds reliable. 'And why the cat thing?' she asks. 'You don't even like your cat.'

'I love my cat,' I say. 'As soon as I get a place for me and Moses, I'm gonna go get Moxie.' I don't love my cat that much – he's cranky and he pisses under the sofa when it thunders – but I don't see why Alexander should get everything. Leanne rips the page out carefully and hands it to me.

'There he is,' she says. I read it again. I already feel like I know him better than I know the man I married.

I didn't need a list when I met Alexander. I saw him, and I knew. The first time we met we were at a party in a pub garden on the edge of town. A girl called Petra was leaving for a three-month trip around South America; I remember I almost didn't go. I thought it was excessive to hold a party to mark such a short absence; I keep cheese in my fridge that long. As I walked into the room I whispered to myself, 'Why am I here?' And like an answer to my question, he fell into view. His sandy hair was longer then and when he laughed, as he was doing as I watched him, it fell forward, and he would push it back with his long, slender fingers. He had on black-rimmed glasses; somehow, I knew they were not prescription and this fact made him seem a little vulnerable. I asked three separate people who he was, and no one seemed to know. To my relief after about an hour Petra pulled him over. Embracing her role as fabulous hostess, she placed him in front of me.

'Hey,' she gushed, 'you having fun?' Without waiting for an answer, she patted Alexander on the shoulder. 'This is Alexander, he was a freelancer on a project I did at work. He's so much fun. Alexander, this is Martha,' she said, grabbing my wrist to pull me closer. 'We go way back. We were in the Scrabble club together at uni.' As I silently thanked Petra for that little gem she rushed away to do more introductions.

'Hey,' said Alexander. I was conscious of the fact that I had to look up to make eye contact with him, something that doesn't always happen when I meet a guy.

'Hey,' I replied. It wasn't love at that point, but I had this visceral feeling that I needed to be near him.

'You have a bit of guac on your chin,' he said. I felt a

21

heat build in my chest and rise steadily. I knew it would produce a colour on my cheeks so vivid even my tan skin wouldn't mask it. He smiled, reached out and gently swiped his thumb across a spot just under my lips. Then it was love.

If I had had a list back then, it wouldn't have mattered. I was a kid; I thought love was enough. Alexander has taught me that love is only the start. A man needs more than a cute smile and an endearing way about him. Even in my wine-and-adrenaline-fuelled haze I can see that if Alexander was what I wanted, *this* man – the man from the list – is what I need.

'He's amazing,' I say. 'Where the hell am I gonna find him?' Cara reaches towards the coffee table and picks up my phone. Her thumb moves purposefully across the screen.

'What is this thing,' she mutters.

'An iPhone,' I say.

'Maybe it was five years ago, darling.' After a couple of minutes she passes me my phone. 'Here you go.' On the screen is a photo of a man I do not know.

'What do I do with him?' I ask. Cara rolls her eyes.

'Jesus, don't you have wi-fi under your rock? This, honey, is Linger. All the available totty in a ten-mile radius. You swipe left for no and right for the shag-worthy. Welcome to twenty-first-century dating.'

The man has a nice smile, but his eyes look cold. I swipe him left and he disappears and is replaced by a new face. I look to Cara and she nods encouragement. I swipe the next guy left and the next. No, no, no, not Alexander, not Alexander, not Alexander. I throw my phone on to the carpet.

'This isn't going to work,' I say. I can feel a tightness

22

building in my chest. It's as if something is pressing down on me and even if I wanted to I don't have the energy to push it off. The girls are both silent for a few seconds and then Cara claps her hands together. She retrieves her tote from the floor and begins rooting around in it.

'I see we're going to have to do this the old-fashioned way,' she says. 'Ladies, we're going out.' She holds up a bottle of tequila triumphantly.

'Why in God's name do you have that?' asks Leanne.

'Because,' says Cara, 'as this situation has just demonstrated, you never know when you're gonna need it.'

By the time our cab pulls up outside the Freaky Funk club, Cara's rejuvenating pep talks and lubricating tequila shots have convinced me that, if I cannot find the one, I can definitely find the one for tonight and sometimes the one for tonight can become the one. That totally happened to my cousin's best mate's sister. As we stand in the doorway of the club, Cara makes a sweeping gesture with her arm.

'Welcome to the land of the easy and the home of the desperate,' she says, and as if by celestial intervention, at that very moment the DJ drops 'It's Raining Men'.

4

As leanne gets the first round in I give the room a quick survey. There's a stag party, or at least I hope that's their excuse for the T-shirts emblazoned with penises; what appears to be a quiet after-work drink that got away with itself; and a few stray groups of people who obviously have a penchant for sticky floors and eighties hits. I decide to approach the stags – they're all giving it some welly on the dance floor – and whilst the tequila means I don't need encouragement to join in, they offer it.

One of them, a short guy with unnervingly animated eyebrows, has a cowboy hat on. As I shimmy towards him he tips it and I accept this invitation and allow him to take me in his arms. He's not tall but he's solid and I feel safe enough to relax into his chest. There's something wonderful, yet slightly irritating, about how good his presence against me feels – despite all the finger waving and carping on about independence, it feels so delightful to have a man just hold you upright. As we're swaying vaguely rhythmically someone comes in behind me and so I reach back and place a hand on the unidentified hip. I'm really getting into being the ham in my man sandwich when Leanne comes over with a drink. I shuffle out, leave the two guys dancing together, and down the drink in one.

'Slow down,' says Leanne. I assume she's talking about the booze but she's looking at the men.

I say, 'I've been slow for a decade, I need to catch up.' I'm not sure that's exactly how it comes out because Leanne just stares at me from below knitted brows.

'I'm gonna go get you some water,' she says. 'Dancing Queen' comes on and I re-join the stags. I love this song. OK, right now I love every song but in this moment it feels like Benny and Björn and Agnetha and the other one are speaking directly to me. My body is the slightly saggy shell of a thirty-something woman but my soul, my soul is seventeen.

One of the cutest stags is watching my performance with quiet interest. He has lovely eyes, really warm and thoughtful, but when I wink at him he smiles and his smile is nothing short of wicked. His smile says, 'If you give me half a chance, I will ruin you' – and I love that. I walk slowly towards him and drape my hands over his shoulders, still moving my hips along with the jaunty beat. He leans in and whispers, 'We're all attached, love.' My hips halt. 'Well, all except Bryan.' He points to a chair at the edge of the room where Bryan, I assume, is asleep. Someone has scrawled the word 'BANTER' on his face. I thank the man and his smile and head to the bar.

'I will have three of your cheapest sambuca please, bar man,' I say.

'Sure thing,' he says, and lays out three glasses.

'And might I say you are quite handsome,' I say, and as I say it, I realize he is. Like me, he's obviously of mixed parentage but he's not from common or garden black and white parents, as I am. I wonder if he has Asian heritage.

I lean over the bar in order to ask and he says, 'That's nice but I am so, so gay.' I stand up straight and bolt down one of the shots.

'I'll have another,' I say, and he pours out another sambuca.

I pay, drink a second shot, and then take the others and push past the revellers to find the girls. Leanne is standing close to the entrance, looking like she was just beamed down from her spaceship and is hoping that someone will help her phone home. 'I got you a drink,' I say, pushing one of the glasses into her hand. 'It might help dislodge that stick from your arse,' I add in my head. She places it on a table next to her and carefully wipes some escaped alcohol from her hand with the corner of her cardigan. She then offers me a glass of water, at which I shake my head vigorously.

'Do you wanna come home, honey?' she asks. I hate that voice she does. That 'I know what's best for you' tone. As she speaks she smooths an invisible crease out of her dress. Her outfit is cute but screams 'I'd rather be home with my husband'. I bet it's from Boden; it has to be from Boden.

'Where's your dress from?' I ask.

'Joules,' says Leanne. Same thing.

'I'm not ready,' I say, and give her my best 'I'm fabulous and I'm having a fabulous time' smile. 'Where's Car?'

Leanne nods in the direction of a dark corner where I see Cara on a sofa, perched on the lap of a gentleman who appears to be in his late sixties. When I reach her Cara is telling him he reminds her of her father.

'Is that a good thing?' he asks eagerly.

'No,' she says.

'I got you this,' I say, handing Cara the shot. She drinks it without breaking eye contact with her new friend.

'I'm striking out,' I tell her. Now I think of it, I do kinda wanna go home, I just don't have a home to go to. Cara turns to me.

'If you want to have sex, just go and have sex.'

'I don't just want to,' I say, 'I have to. I have to extract Alexander from my soul. I need to know that I haven't completely fucked up my only chance to have sex again.'

The man looks at me with open curiosity. Cara sighs and says, 'Sex for validation, so healthy.' And then a bit more kindly she says, 'So you need an orgasmic cleansing. We've all been there but you're not going to get it talking to me, so go.' She waves me away like I'm a puppy. 'Carpe dickem!' she calls as I walk away.

I pick the guy because of his shoulders, broad shoulders that make me think he could hold me up against a wall, although I would never let a guy hold me up against a wall because what if he couldn't take my weight? I would die of shame on the spot. Also, that's about all I have to go on as his back is to me while he talks to his companion. Just before I reach him, Leanne stops me.

'I was just outside on the phone to James. Apparently, Lucas woke up and couldn't find his blankie and I had to remind him that we gave it to the blankie fairy like three weeks ago.' She shakes her head in the way married women do when they are expressing how adorable but hapless their husbands are. 'I should probably get back, come jump in a cab with me. We could stop for pizza?'

I want to say, 'That's all good for you. You go home to your comfy house and have lacklustre sex with your mouse-faced husband; I have to find my self-esteem in someone else's orgasm,' but instead I say, 'Sorry, there's someone I have to say hello to.' And I step round her and continue across the room. When I reach Broad Shoulders, I tap him on his equally broad back and he turns around. His face does not quite match his shoulders in that his body says man and his face says little boy lost but it's a friendly face, one that doesn't erode my nerve to say, 'Hi.'

'Hi,' responds Broad Shoulders.

'Do you want to have sex?' I ask. Broad Shoulders makes the kind of face one makes when an air steward asks if you want chicken or fish before saying, 'OK.'

We leave almost immediately; there's a slight kerfuffle over the fact that the cloakroom attendant has lost my coat before I remember that I wasn't wearing one but soon we're standing awkwardly together on the street. The cold air is almost but not quite sobering.

'Where do you live?' I ask. I hope this makes it clear that the 'your place or mine' discussion is unnecessary.

'Not far,' he says, and starts to walk. I have to trot a little to catch up with him, but he doesn't protest as I fall into step beside him. Isn't it strange how the same act, depending on the context, can become something entirely different – walking in silence on a dark night with someone you have dated for some time is intimate, romantic even; doing the same with a man you have just met falls squarely into the category of sinister. Also, 'not far' is very subjective. I mean, Guatemala probably doesn't feel that far when you're flying in a luxury private jet; Broad Shoulders lives extremely far on a frigid, dark night. Far enough to make my nose run and my legs start to ache; far enough to make me lose all the courage I have, Dutch or otherwise. I'm about to bail; I'm literally considering how I will explain to Cara that I could not pull in a club where sex is so available they should offer the morning-after pill as a bar snack, when I realize Broad Shoulders has come to a stop.

'This is me,' he says. We're outside a row of stunning mansion flats. I used to walk Moses in his buggy along this road and try to peek through the windows at a life beyond my imagination. Broad Shoulders jogs up the steps to the building and puts his key in the door. Before he pushes it open I ask him his name.

'Rupert,' he says. He doesn't ask mine. Inside he asks me if I want a drink.

'Yes please,' I say.

'Water or squash?' he asks. I pick squash.

He leaves me standing in the hallway as he goes to prepare it. From the sounds that emanate there is a lot of work that goes into the process. He returns with a pint glass and a mug and hands me the mug. 'This way,' he says, and guides me gently towards a room I assume is his bedroom, although only a mattress on the floor signifies this. There is no other bedroom apparatus – no wardrobe, no photos, no throw cushions. I suddenly miss my throw cushions. I got them from Homesense. They have navy stripes on them.

I'm trying to work out how to sensually mount a mattress on the floor when I notice that Rupert is taking off his clothes, all of them. Naked, he has strange proportions. His impressive upper body contrasts dramatically with his thick, short legs. Rupert gets into the bed, lies back and puts his hands behind his head. I put down my drink before taking off my shoes and joining him and it is then that he kisses me. The kisses are not exploratory or even sexy; he pecks away as if he thinks I have an access code. I let him think he has unlocked it and reach down to grab his penis. It is sort of hard but weirdly cold and damp. He makes a noise of encouragement, although I'm not really doing anything. I can't help but think about Alexander's penis. His penis was, and I assume still is, perfect. I actually gasped when I first saw it. He laughed so hard that he lost his erection but neither of us cared. Rupert's penis is not perfect but it is here, and I am told that beggars cannot be choosers. He shifts his body on to one side and undoes my trousers with his free hand. Without further introduction, he shoves his fingers under my pants. I have a flashback to a party in Year 10. Adele Healey's mum went to the Canaries and I spent half the night with Kieran Nuttall in her younger brother's bedroom. He asked me if I knew that my lips were uneven; it took me a week to realize he wasn't talking about the ones on my face.

I'm not liking whatever Rupert is trying to do so I try and encourage him to move past the trailers.

'Do you have a condom?' I ask. He jumps up and leaves the room, still naked. I'm left feeling like I'm halfway through a particularly inept smear. I wiggle out of my trousers and knickers and leave them at the bottom of the bed. I'm thinking about removing my top when he returns. I can't stop imagining where he might have had to go to get the rubber. I picture the places one puts things to keep them safe – an empty Quality Street tin, an overfilled shoe-box. This turns out to be a good thing because it distracts me for the half a minute Rupert spends wrestling with the johnnie before returning his attention to the jabbing. I make a noise that I hope sounds positive but not too enthusiastic; I want the prodding to stop but I'm not sure what I want him to replace it with. In response he readjusts, straddles me and pushes himself inside me. It doesn't hurt. It doesn't feel good. It doesn't really feel like anything. It feels like exploring an ear canal with a cotton bud, only less satisfying. I feel my tears before I understand what they are. I've never been a silent crier – excessive snot production is the cause, I suspect. It takes around five strokes for Rupert to realize what's happening. He stops, puts a hand to my cheek and says, 'Is it all right if I finish?'

5

I SPEND THE NIGHT, more for convenience than anything else. When I wake, Rupert is snoring gently; the little puffing noises he makes remind me of Moses. I roll on to my back and grab my breasts; I'm relieved to find my key and debit card still stashed in my bra. I locate my trousers under the covers and get out of bed and slip into them before stepping into my shoes. My phone lies on the carpet and I notice several missed calls before I put it in my pocket. I forgo my knickers because I'm scared I'll wake him whilst rooting around for them. I convince myself this is sexy, a lacy calling card, although I'm pretty sure I left a panty liner in them. As I make my way through the flat it becomes apparent that Rupert's home is in fact a squat. Under the spell of alcohol and anticipation, I had failed to notice some of the apartment's less charming features, specifically a life-sized mural in the hallway depicting Margaret Thatcher preparing to breastfeed what appears to be a bonneted Tony Blair.

When I get outside the crisp morning seems to magnify my own internal dankness. I speed-walk a few metres down the road, eager to put some distance between myself and the night before. How could I be a respectful wife and mother one day and a walk-of-shamin' hussy the next? I look at my phone and the calls are from Leanne. I know James usually gets up with the kids on a Saturday, so it's safe to say she's not trying to reach me for a casual catch-up. I let my thumb rest on her name and she picks up after one ring.

'How the fudge could you be so irresponsible,' she says. 'I'm nearly dead with worry.' I love how even in the wake of trauma Leanne is mindful of innocent ears. Her concern hits me somewhere around my throat and I gasp for air.

'Can you come get me, please?' I ask.

'Where are you?' she says softly.

'I don't know,' I say.

'What can you see?' asks Leanne.

'A post box.'

Leanne finds me outside a Costa Coffee a couple of roads away from the squat. The bag that I left at her house is waiting for me on the passenger seat. She drives me back to my new but old home, in silence. It's a classic mum move, so much worse than the lecture I was prepared for. When we pull up at my parents' house she says, 'It will get better, you know. If Alexander wasn't the one, you'll find him.'

'Yep,' I say, and move to get out of the car.

Leanne grabs my hand. 'You deserve the one. Someone fit for the list,' she says with a smile. I give her a kiss on the cheek and climb out.

The energy of my mother's home – the hum of the fan oven; the enriching chatter of Radio 4 – makes me realize how hungover I am. Hungover doesn't cut it; my head feels like it's encased in amber. I just want a litre of Coke and a hole to crawl in and instead I get my mother.

Mum is in the kitchen with Moses. Despite the fact Ivy Ketch hasn't worked a day of my lifetime, she is dressed as though she is fresh from the office in slim navy trousers and a cream blouse. Her rich, brown skin is make-up free, aside from an ever-present coat of Fashion Fair's 'Ruby Plum' on her lips. I stand in the doorway watching her hold up a flashcard with a picture of a strawberry on it. Moses is in his high chair and has a plate of fruit in front of him. He is laughing at my mother's efforts, revealing the two little teeth that sit alone in the lower half of his mouth. 'Can you find the strawberry?' says Mum, enunciating each syllable carefully. She then shouts, 'Martha?!' As if I am not an only child and anyone else would be letting themselves into her quiet semi-detached home on a Saturday morning.

'I'm here, Mum,' I say – well, croak. 'Hey, baby,' I say to Moses. He scrunches up his fists and waves them in the air in excitement. I kiss him on the cheek and he makes a smacking sound in return. I can feel my mother's eyes on me.

'Good night?' she says.

'Not exactly,' I say, walking to the sink to get a glass of water. I lean against the counter to drink it; the cool liquid feels amazing in my mouth but seems unsure of itself in my stomach. Moses reaches out to me and I pull him from the high chair.

'Eskimo kiss,' I say, and he rubs his nose on mine, smearing crushed fruit on me in the process. His smile takes the edge off my hangover. If a man ever looked at me the way he does, it'd be game over.

'What will you do today?' I say, manoeuvring him so that I am holding him under each armpit. Moses wriggles in anticipation. 'Will you go up?' I say, lifting him in the air. He shrieks and kicks his legs. 'Will you go down?' I let my arms fall and Moses's eyes open wide. 'Will you go round and round?' I spin us both in a circle and Moses giggles throatily. Upon completing it I regret the sudden movement and I sit down on one of the kitchen chairs with Moses on my knee.

'Don't excite him, he's due a nap,' says Mum, taking my son into her arms. 'I take it you had a bit to drink then?' I don't answer and avoid her enquiring eye. 'Do you think this is an acceptable reaction to your marriage ending?'

I don't say anything because this is a rhetorical question. Almost all my mother's questions are rhetorical because for them not to be she would have to consider the possibility that someone knows more than her. Mum shakes her head almost imperceptibly; obviously not imperceptibly because then it wouldn't have the required effect of making me feel worthless. Mum then rubs at her right temple. This is her tell – this is the sign that she is about to deliver her killer blow. 'No wonder he ended it, if this is what he has to deal with.'

I love my mum – I mean, I would run into a burning building to save her life, even though I know she would scold me for not waiting for the fire service. I love my mum, but I don't like her. I don't dislike her because she is judgemental, and I don't dislike her because (particularly since the onset of menopause) she is unnecessarily spiteful; I dislike her because I will never become the daughter she wants me to be.

It started with ballet. Mum enrolled me when I was

34

seven. I was many things as a child – spirited, inquisitive and uncontrollably talkative – but graceful I was not. I was curved where I should have been straight and stiff in places where the other girls bent easily. I did the work, though. I had a cassette tape that I would play on my Sony Walkman, practising the steps for hours at a time in our garage. On the day of my first recital I was so full of hope that I could be the type of little girl a mother would be proud of. I was faultless during the performance; around halfway through the butterflies escaped from my stomach and for a minute and a half I really believed I was a dancer.

After the show I waited backstage for my parents, watching as other children flew into the embrace of their mothers, waiting patiently for my turn. When Mum appeared, tears spontaneously came to my eyes. She stopped short of me; she had a look on her face I had seen many times before, one that seemed to say, 'Is this really my child?'

'Why did you keep picking your knickers out of your bum like that?' she asked, and I feel like I have been picking my knickers out of my bum ever since. I want to tell her this. I want to tell her that all I have ever wanted is her love; all I have ever needed is for her to tell me just once that everything will be OK.

I'm not sure I convey this when I say, 'Fuck you, Mum.' I leave my mother sitting with her mouth open and head towards my bedroom. On the way I stick my head into the living room. My father is sitting on the armchair, to which I'm starting to wonder if he's surgically attached.

'You all right, love?' he asks, his gaze not shifting from the golf on the TV. His long, thin legs are stretched out in front of him and his hands rest on the small belly he has cultivated since his retirement.

'No, Dad. I'm pretty crap actually,' I say. He looks at me

then, his hazel eyes full of questions that I know he will never ask me.

'I know, love,' he says, 'I know.'

I go to my room, which is no longer really my room but a spare room. My pale pink walls have been replaced with a hotel room grey. The bed is the same though, an antique piece with a wrought-iron headboard – Mum had insisted I would want it when I moved into a home of my own, but I didn't. Alexander favoured a more minimalist look; he was obsessed with Scandinavian chic.

From the bed, you can see into several of the upstairs windows of the houses across the quiet, tree-lined street, but the only one that ever concerned me was the house on the right-hand corner. That room, in that house, was the bedroom of Joseph Henchy, and Joseph Henchy was my first ever love. People often say that young people don't understand love, but I don't agree. Free of responsibilities, they have nothing to think about but love; I had whole weekends at a time when all I had to do was conjugate a few French verbs and be in love.

Joseph and I started out as buddies – well, young children aren't really friends; they just kind of occupy the same space and time – but Joe was a kind lad and, although I was a couple of years younger than him, he would often invite me to be one of the victims in whatever massacre he was re-enacting for the afternoon. Things changed abruptly when he went to secondary school. I guess he was too distracted to notice me, or maybe his growing independence allowed him to expand his social circle beyond our leafy avenue. Whatever the case, he was always friendly and polite, but he never again included me in his war games or brought me out a glass of Ribena and a slightly soggy rich tea biscuit. I imagine hormones played some part but it was at the moment of his withdrawal that I recognized the depths of my affection for him. On this bed I would watch the house for hours; I started to understand his patterns. He would arrive home from school at four, except for Thursdays when he would be given a lift home by someone at around seven. On Saturday mornings he left early, wearing shorts, and returned home late, later and later as the years went on. On Sundays I might catch several glimpses of him; he would nip to the sweet shop on the main road or sit on the front step and chat to his mother as she weeded the front garden.

Once I had entered secondary school myself, I grew braver. We were not at the same school, but I ensured that he would see me in my uniform and perhaps once again view us as equals. There are only so many excuses to find for loitering around in the front garden of a family home and after a couple of years of casual waves and unmet gazes, I thought that perhaps I should make a move. One Sunday I waited until he stepped outside and then bolted into the street.

'Are you going to the shop?' I called. 'Me too.' Joseph smiled and paused to let me catch up to him. 'Long time, no see,' I said, super casual like. 'What you up to?'

'Nothing much,' said Joseph.

'Have you got a girlfriend?' I asked, looking at my shoes whilst trying to suppress the hope in my tone.

'Yeah,' he said. 'You know Claire Baycock?' I did. Everybody did. She lived in the flats next to the park; from what I knew of her she was a rebellious redhead with a big fringe and an even bigger mouth.

I had one question: 'Why?' An abbreviation of the full question, why her and not me?

Joseph looked to the sky before saying, 'She's got big tits and a fit body.' It was so reasonable and so true that I couldn't really fault him.

'I forgot my money,' I said, and ran back to the safety of my bedroom, from where I continued my adoration until he left home at eighteen. I thought unrequited love was the saddest thing I would ever have to go through and I was right but I didn't yet know how right. Unrequited love when you have been promised absolutely nothing is painful, but unrequited love from someone who has promised you the world is a slow death.

I fish the list from my handbag. It's crumpled and smeared with something a little greasy but, even now I'm sober, it still makes a lot of sense. If I had kept it in mind I would not have ended up hungover and humiliated in Hove this morning; if I had written it earlier, I might not have a failed marriage. One thing is for sure: I can't rely on my own improvisation. I need a blueprint. I don't know how Joseph would have measured up to this list; I was so uninterested in details back then. All I wanted was to feel something; I had so much passion to give and no one and nothing to give it to.

I saw Joseph a few years ago, in a restaurant in London. Alexander and I had been to the theatre and Joseph was in the Pizza Express that we had stopped in for a quick bite. It took a few moments for him to connect me to the child he once knew but when he did he broke into a smile so genuine, I almost forgave him for the years of torment. He was eating with a woman I assumed to be his wife. He asked after my parents and talked animatedly about the crust of his pepperoni pizza. He spoke with such enthusiasm about his uninspired dish that I suddenly felt very sad.

When I was young, I would play incredibly maudlin indie music as I watched Joe from the window. Sometimes I would write embarrassingly overwrought love songs, which I imagined I might develop when I 'made it'. My CD player and discs are still stashed in a cupboard and so I plug it in and put on Radiohead. The haunting opening bars of 'Creep' take me to a familiar, lonely place. I turn to watch myself in the full-length mirror as I duet with Thom Yorke. I imagine Rupert seeing my album in a supermarket and trying to convince his companion that he once slept with me in a squat on the south coast. I see Broad Shoulders blend into the crowd at my intimate East London gig; I feel the band behind me and I open my arms to allow space for my chest to expand and the sound to flow from the bottom of my lungs. I see more and more faces in the crowd; it's full of all the boys and men that have ever let me down and all the girls with big tits and fit bodies and every teacher that has poked holes through my dreams and every cab driver that's driven past me in the rain and my mum and my mum's stuck-up friends and in the centre, at the very front, is Alexander. When I sing the final lines, I'm singing just to him and he's seeing me, really seeing me, as if for the first time.

My mother bangs on the ceiling with a broom just as she did twenty years ago. I turn off the music. I crawl under the lavender-scented duvet, in the clothes I have been wearing for a day and a night. I have the sense that I want to cry but I can't. I am completely empty.

The sleep I have is dense and dreamless. When I wake it is dark and I'm disorientated for a few moments. My father is knocking on my door. I know it's him because the rapping is so tentative. I sit up in bed and shout, 'Yeah, Dad!' He opens the door a few inches and seems to slip in the room through the gap.

'Your phone's been making little noises,' he says. I must have left it in the kitchen. He hands it to me like it's a bird with a broken wing. 'Do you think you could come and sort it out with your mother?'

'Sure,' I say.

'Moses has been asking after you.'

'Yeah,' I say. My head still throbs but now I think it's from guilt. From what I understand every working parent feels as though they're on an eternal quest for balance; I can say conclusively that sambuca doesn't help. I sit up and try to look as if I'm ready to engage with the world. 'I'll be down soon,' I say. My father nods his head and retreats. I redo my ponytail so my curls look a little less chaotic and decide I'll make us all smoothies. Moses loves them and it might help replenish some nutrients for me. I'm about to get out of bed when I see an unfamiliar notification on my phone. It's from Linger and reads, 'You have a match!' I have a very broken memory of swiping wildly in the cab on the way to the club, the girls cackling gleefully and the driver watching us apprehensively in his rear-view mirror. For a few moments, I think about deleting my account and all the potential for heartbreak it holds within, but curiosity gets the better of me. I open the app; it takes a few seconds for my match's face to appear but it's worth the wait. He has such an easy smile; it's like he's not just smiling at me but sharing something between us too. He's looking straight at the camera and his eyes are a truly dreamy shade of blue. His hair is mostly cropped out of the photo but from what I can see it's the perfect shade of strawberry blond. It's electrifying, it's mystifying; it's *him*. Below the picture is a message.

> Undeterred83: I'm sorry. I haven't used this before and I can't think of anything to say but I had to contact you because I was so intrigued by your profile.

It's not clever or funny but that makes it better because it's real. He's real. The man of my dreams, and on my list, may have been within ten miles, all this time. I don't reply right away because I want to savour the feeling, a jittery light-headedness I have not experienced in many years. It's a complicated mix of thrill and comfort wrapped in a soft, warm blanket of expectation.

6

ALTHOUGH I SPEND Saturday doing my best impression of a pious daughter – being on hand to facilitate channel changes and offering weak teas hourly – the atmosphere between my mother and me remains slightly frosty. To avoid the chill and try to re-establish an image of responsibility, I offer to do an extra shift at the call centre on Sunday. I've never worked a weekend before – I've always reserved this time for poorly playing happy families – but I'm pleasantly surprised by how relaxed the atmosphere in the office is. Generally, there's a constant stream of people to pretend you have an interest in interacting with; today my whole bank of desks is empty apart from Greg and a girl called Tashi, a part-time worker also studying for a degree at the local university.

'Hello, stranger,' says Greg as I sit down.

'I saw you on Friday,' I say.

'Feels like longer, buddy,' he says. 'What you doing here on a Sunday?'

'I need the money,' I say. It's not until I say it that I realize it's true. I am officially a statistic: a poor, single mother in a dead-end job.

'Sorry to hear that,' says Greg, 'but it's a nice surprise.'

'What are you doing here?' I ask. 'Isn't there some sort

of Disney On Ice you should be seeing?' Greg is always emailing me discount vouchers to tedious-sounding children's events. After each one he tells me how much his girls enjoyed it and asks me what I ended up doing with my weekend; I always lie and say I was visiting friends as opposed to watching *Come Dine with Me* reruns.

'I work weekends when I don't have the girls,' he says. His words are like a glass of ice-cold water in my face. This hadn't occurred to me, that Alexander and I will need to split our time with Moses. It is heartbreaking and also exhilarating.

Bob is in the office too. When he sees me, he throws me a quizzical look and waves his hand around in front of his crotch. I give him a thumbs up in return. Greg looks at me with concern.

'Don't,' I say firmly. Tashi eyes me over the partition between us.

'I'm feeling there's a lot of stuck energy within you,' she says.

'It's probably the dodgy breakfast burrito I had,' I say.

'No,' she says brightly. 'You have this kind of cloud over you. I'm going to this retreat in a couple of weeks – it's an aura-cleansing camp, based on this wonderful meditation practice developed by my guru. I'll send you the details.'

'Please don't,' I say.

'It's run on donations and I'll drive, it won't cost you anything. Just think about it. Before I found Tula Shiki I was closed so tight, just like you.' I look at Tashi with her beaded hair and I decide I'm happy being closed. I yawn.

'I'm just tired,' I say, and I am. I was up late messaging my match.

Marthashotbod: Where did you go to school?
Undeterred83: Everywhere really. We moved about a lot

43

when I was a kid. Even spent some time in Singapore. I
moved to Brighton three years ago and it might be the
longest I've been anywhere.

Marthashotbod: That's so interesting. It must have been
an exciting childhood.

Undeterred83: It was actually kind of lonely a lot of the
time. Always felt like I was on the outside looking in
but it made me interested in people. What makes us
different, what makes us the same.

Marthashotbod: What does make us the same?

Undeterred83: I think we're all trying to work something
out.

Marthashotbod: What are you trying to work out?

Undeterred83: At this moment, you.

It was so wonderful to talk to someone clever and funny
and curious, especially when most of that curiosity is
about me. He asked me where I was born and what books
I loved; he admitted that his favourite novel is Margaret
Atwood's *Cat's Eye*, even though it's a female coming-of-
age book.

Undeterred83: I sometimes tell my mates it's Catcher in
the Rye. I do like it but I think Holden just needs some
therapy and a talking to.

I felt that delicious wave of pleasure you experience when
someone just gets you. When someone seems to reach in
and access a private part of who you are. I am not alone in
having overdeveloped feelings about fictional characters; I
might never be alone again.

'It helps with tiredness too,' says Tashi. 'It helps with

everything.' Bob walks past and gives an artificial cough so we all return to our calls.

After work I stop by Leanne's and give her a bouquet of lilies to apologize for being an even hotter mess than my usual level of hot messiness. 'You shouldn't have,' she says as she accepts them on the doorstep, but we both know I needed to. 'Come in,' she says. 'We should talk properly.'

'I can't,' I say. 'I want to run back to the flat.' Alexander did a decent job of packing my stuff but failed to include any knickers. Also, I want to see him. I'm not entirely confident about why this is. We have practicalities to discuss; I have questions I deserve answers to; but also I need to see him, because seeing him every day is natural. Not doing so feels like suddenly deciding not to brush your teeth – odd, rebellious, but also a bit gross. My marriage with Alexander had started to feel like a slowly shrinking box but now I was beginning to wonder if freedom was over-rated. Spending the night with Rupert made me think that perhaps one shit husband is worth a sea of unattached morons.

'If you're sure,' says Leanne. 'I'm sorry I let it get out of hand. We should talk things through.'

'You didn't let it get out of hand; that was Cara.'

Leanne laughs and then stops and nods her head.

'Actually, Cara and I had a chat and we thought we could go to the spa at the Queens Hotel after work tomorrow.' I'm both excited and perturbed by the idea of Leanne and Cara interacting without me as a buffer. I had considered them as the friend equivalent of two violently reactive chemicals, only able to coexist with me present to neutralize them. 'You should have a little chill-out and some self-care,' says Leanne. 'If your mum can't have Moses, I'll get James to stay in with the kids.'

'Sure,' I say, 'that would be nice.' Although I'm not sure it will be nice – self-care to Leanne means spending loads of money and I find it really hard to relax in spas; I never know when and where I should be naked.

'I'll call you tomorrow then. I hope it goes OK with Alexander.'

'Thanks. I'm sure it'll be fine,' I say, because I'm hoping the universe will hear me.

I walk to the flat slowly. The roads feel unfamiliar although I know it's me and not the streets that have changed. I'm surprised that I have to take a few fortifying breaths before I knock on the door, an alien act in itself. As I hear foot-steps approaching, I curse myself for not putting on some make-up before coming over but then I think it might be better this way, for him to see me looking broken and drained. If men are visual creatures, perhaps Alexander needs to set eyes on my despair to comprehend it. It's not Alexander that answers the door, however; it's Poppy. Poppy with her low-waisted dark denim skinnies and then metres and metres of taut white skin before the hem of her cropped T-shirt. Poppy is Alexander's part-time PA and even though she knows who I am she looks confused to see me standing there.

'Is Alexander in?' I say. She doesn't speak so I walk past her and into the kitchen where Alexander is standing at the counter preparing two mugs of coffee.

'Martha,' he says when he sees me, 'what are you doing here?'

'This is my home,' I say.

'I mean, why didn't you say you were coming?'

'Do I have to?'

Alexander takes a sip of coffee and rage floods through me. How can he be casually concerned with topping up his caffeine consumption when this is the first time we have laid eyes on each other since our break-up?

'I'm not really in a head space to talk about stuff,' says Alexander.

'What's stuff?' I ask. 'Our marriage? Our child? Little stuff like that?' Alexander folds his arms and appraises me.

'You look tired,' he says.

'Yeah,' I say with forced lightness. 'I won't lie, I've had better weeks.'

Alexander makes a noise crossed between a scoff and a laugh. 'Can I remind you that you sacked me off,' he says.

'But you didn't have to take it so well.' At this point I notice Poppy hovering just outside my eyeline, all twelve pounds of her. She's like the world's most ineffectual bouncer. I turn to tell her to fuck off out of my flat and crawl back to her grubby little house-share and drink cheap rosé with her disillusioned twenty-something friends, when I notice her feet. On Poppy's feet is a pair of beige fluffy slippers – my slippers. I turn back to Alexander.

'Are you even gonna ask about your son?' I demand.

'Your mum's been texting me,' he says. Fucking treacherous bitch.

'And what about us? Did you not even want to ask why?!'

'I know why,' says Alexander, 'because I suck at being married, *we* suck at being married. You're clearly not happy.' I take a step towards him; he flinches as if I'm going to strike him and I stop.

'You never even tried to make me happy,' I say, but the last syllable gets caught up in a burped sob.

Alexander rubs the bridge of his nose before saying, 'No one can make someone else happy, Martha.' I want to believe he believes this. It feels a little less traumatic to think that he saw our break-up as a hurtling train that even James Bond and all the X-Men couldn't stop. And then I see Alexander gaze over my shoulder. I follow his eyes to Poppy's reddening face and I can take it no longer. I fall to my knees and grab her right foot. After a couple of mortifying seconds, I am holding a slipper. Poppy removes the other one and hands it to me. I stand and clutch them to my chest.

'These are *my* slippers,' I say.

'I . . . I'm sorry, I just found them. Alex said it was cool.'

'Alex*ander*,' I whisper, and then more loudly I say, 'I'm gonna go.' I can buy knickers.

7

LEANNE CALLS ME ten seconds into my lunch break the next day. She skips the verbal canapés and gets to the meat.

'I've booked us in the spa for half six and I'm getting you a pedicure – no arguments. I called Ivy and told her we wanted to treat you, so she's picking up Moses.' Leanne has always been the only person able to tame my mother. I drank too much cheap vodka at our end of school prom and Leanne got me home and somehow managed to convince Mum I had eaten undercooked chicken; after that I started calling her The Ivy Whisperer.

'I haven't brought my swimming costume,' I say. Leanne makes an odd little noise – half sigh, half groan. Even when she's trying to do something nice for me I manage to make things difficult.

'Don't worry,' she says, 'you'll be given a robe. See you there.'

Fifteen minutes before the end of my shift, Bob corners me and tells me to induct a new member of staff. I've already tidied up and packed my bag and I'm reading an article Tashi left on my desk, about the benefits of meditation (weight loss!). Bob can clearly sense my resistance and reminds me that it's part of my job description. I have to show some bloke Jake how to log on to the system. Jake may be an intelligent fellow but, if so, he has chosen this day to keep it deeply hidden. I have to show him the set-up half a dozen times before he makes any indication he has retained even the slightest crumb of knowledge. Thirty minutes after the end of my shift, I lose patience and tell him he seems to have everything under control. Jake thanks me effusively before putting his headset on backwards.

Bob doesn't react to my words when I tell him I'm leaving. He's staring at his phone, biting his lip in concentration. I take a few steps closer. On his screen is a video of a well-endowed woman on a Space Hopper. 'Bob,' I say sharply. He slips his phone into his pocket.

'Yeah, thanks for that,' he says. Bob doesn't do thank yous – he even said that in a team meeting once – so his gratitude makes me suspicious.

'I don't remember it saying in my job description that I have to induct new staff,' I say.

Bob inspects the cuticles of his left hand. 'Yeah, it does at the end. You know, "any other tasks your manager assigns you".' I want to tell Bob exactly where he can shove his job description. The feeling gives me a thrill; I could do it. I could tell Bob exactly what I think of his job and his tan and never return. I could leave now and never say the words 'putting you through now ...' again, but I haven't had much luck with endings recently, so I don't.

When I find them at the Queens Hotel, Leanne and Cara are the best part of the way through a bottle of prosecco.

'We would have waited ...' says Leanne.

'But we didn't want to,' finishes Cara. I pour wine into the empty glass waiting for me and Leanne lifts hers in a toast.

'To our beautiful, brave friend,' she says. I drink deeply; the alcohol immediately loosens my muscles. 'How did it go?' asks Leanne. I shrug and drink again. Cara stretches out on the white sofa and appraises me squarely.

'Leanne tells me you had a crap shag.' I cough into my glass and look behind me. The spa is ridiculously chic and very quiet, not the sort of place you should say 'shag', unless discussing home decor. There's a woman folding towels but if she noticed Cara's lack of discretion she hasn't let on. Cara doesn't wait for me to confirm or deny. 'We need to get you drilled again – a bad lay will have you going back to A-hole.'

Leanne laughs in a manner that I know is forced. I keep drinking to stop myself from telling the girls how accurate Cara's assessment is. I can see now that going back to Alexander isn't an option. Even if we tried, it couldn't be a return. It would be a relaunch and a lifelong race away from the shadow of our failure.

'I'm not sure I want to have sex again for a very long time,' I say. Cara puts her glass down so heavily for a second I fear it will break.

'This is what I mean,' she says. She seems genuinely cross. 'You can't let one dickhead and his little dick send you into hibernation.'

'It wasn't actually little,' I say. I gaze up to the ceiling as I pull together a hazy image of a naked Rupert. 'It was average-sized, I guess.'

'Little dick is a state of mind,' says Cara as she taps the side of her head knowingly.

'Martha's got to do what she wants to do,' says Leanne.

She says this to Cara but she's smiling at me, a weak sympathetic smile, the kind you would give to a dog wearing a cone. Cara dismisses this with a rueful shake of her head.

'She's gotta do what she *needs* to do. My aunt Nina did that whole waiting-for-the-right-time shit. Died a couple of years ago with a cooch full of cobwebs.'

Leanne's dog smile collapses and she reaches out to pat Cara on the hand. 'I'm sorry about your aunt,' she says.

'S'all right,' says Cara. 'She was a bitch. Probably because she needed to get laid.'

Leanne's eyes narrow. 'It's not all about sex,' she says.

'Yeah, but it is,' says Cara. 'All of it – film, music, the fact that we're here to have our toenails painted primary colours. Everything is about sex.'

Alexander and I haven't had sex in one hundred and nineteen days. I know this because when I realized it had been two weeks I made a note in my diary. I thought that when we did the deed I could tell him the number and it would surprise him, perhaps shame him a little. I guess I can stop counting.

'Get on Linger,' continues Cara. I think of my match and am about to say something but she continues, 'Everyone's on there for sex, even if they pretend otherwise. That's why I advertised your wares in your profile name.' And like that another man has let me down, before I've even met him – a record. His messages seemed completely sincere and the realization that he could have other motives makes me feel exposed and I start to blush. I'm so focused on my own embarrassment that I miss the debate that has sparked between Cara and Leanne.

'He's great. He barely speaks English,' says Cara, 'so he *couldn't* upset her.'

'Sorry, who?' I ask. Leanne readjusts her robe; its thick folds drown her slim frame and for a second she looks incredibly young. When she speaks, however, it's clear she's a woman, one who knows her own mind and apparently mine.

'Cara has kindly offered to set you up with a personal trainer named Igor, but *I* was just saying that, *if* you're going to date, you should start as you mean to go on. In fact, I was telling James about your . . . uhm . . . encounter and he reminded me there's this guy he works with. He's called Tom. I met him at the summer barbecue and he's kinda cute. He's very polite. I think you could do with someone who will treat you like a lady.'

I wonder why Leanne has to share every last detail of every last thing with James? Someone needs to tell her he's her husband, not her journal. I'm unsurprised she has a solution to a problem I was yet to voice. Whenever I call her to say something's gone wrong, I can hear a shiver of pleasure in her voice. I'm a good friend to her in that regard, always flooding my kitchen or trying to work out how to get a new passport within forty-eight hours. When we were teenagers and I found myself distraught because I had completely forgotten about the existence of an exam she would arrive with sweets and flashcards and drag me through it. The thing is, I always slightly resented her for it; sometimes I just wanted to be her friend and not her renovation project. It didn't occur to me that I could resolve this by simply saying no.

'I don't know . . .' I say.

'Of course, it's up to you,' says Leanne.

'Yeah, but cobwebs,' says Cara sagely.

A woman in a white tunic approaches us.

'Martha?' she asks. I raise my hand. 'Are you ready?' I finish my drink before standing up.

'Yes I am,' I say.

Leanne approaches the set-up of the date with the same attitude she does most things in life – methodically, thoroughly and extremely efficiently. Phone numbers and photos are exchanged; Tom looks happy and approachable in his picture, if a little stylistically challenged. Leanne also sends me a bit of background – almost exclusively his career achievements, but she also includes the fact that he ate a whole plate of king prawns at the barbecue. A few days later, Tom sends me a sweet message asking me to dinner the next evening and after waiting a couple of hours I reply positively; then I think about cancelling approximately every six minutes. Mainly because I think that even if Poppy, eater of men and destroyer of souls, has got her claws into Alexander I shouldn't settle for being courted by some desperado from the East Sussex council drainage department. But also because of this:

Marthashotbod: This isn't about sex, is it?

Undeterred83: No, not at all. I find you fascinating. I mean I'm sure I would like to have sex with you but I'm looking for much more.

Marthashotbod: I'm really pleased to hear that.

Marthashotbod: BTW my friend Cara picked my username :/

Undeterred83: I'm sure it's fitting :) Don't get me wrong you're gorgeous but I already know that's just the start.

Marthashotbod: You do?

Undeterred83: I know what I like and I like you.

Marthashotbod: I like you too.

Undeterred83: I really love talking to you. I can't believe the timing. I want us to meet but I'm leaving the day after tomorrow. Working on a children's project in Uganda for twelve weeks! We'll set something up the second I'm back though?

Marthashotbod: Of course. Your trip sounds amazing, so worthy. Do you mind if I ask if any of the kids have worms?

Undeterred83: Ha ha! I don't know if I'd call it worthy but I find it really inspiring. They do occasionally have parasites but we give them a treatment.

3) <u>Has to work for himself but not be in it to make money.</u> He's got to do something useful to society. He has to spend his free time doing something inspiring; not just inspiring but also worthy, e.g. deworming African orphans or similar . . .

My match tells me he's a freelance researcher and the things he examines – health, birth rate, education – they make a difference. Not in a casual, transient way but significantly and permanently. And the fact that he seems to possess so many of the qualities I need makes me believe that he can make that sort of difference to my life. I'm a romantic of sorts – I'm a fan of chocolates and love letters; my ultimate fantasy is that someone will race across a bustling city to stop me boarding a plane – but I have never believed in the concept of one great love. Even when I was mooning over Alexander for all those years, I didn't think he could be my one and only potential soulmate. How could it be logical, with over seven billion people in the world, that my one true love would happen to live in the same seaside town? No, I believed that there were dozens of people with whom I could build a life. Until I wrote that list.

I do wonder if I'm descending into madness and then I ask myself if the questioning of my sanity is a sign of my lack of madness and then I wonder if that thought is in itself mad. Would it be possible that, caught in the storm of grief, I have conjured up this man? It certainly wouldn't be beyond me to imagine a guy who represents everything I need; didn't I do that with Alexander? I re-read the list, forcing myself to appraise the situation objectively. It's undeniable – he's making the grade. I send a silent prayer to the universe that this person is simply a long overdue karmic refund.

So, I'm standing in my jeans and bra, to-ing and fro-ing between meeting Tom and slipping into my onesie and calling the whole thing off, when I decide I have to ask.

> Marthashotbod: I can't believe I haven't asked you your name! I assume your parents didn't name you Undeterred83?
> Undeterred83: :) No, it's Nathan but my friends and family sometimes call me George, because I was always asking questions when I was a kid.

George?! Fuck. Fuck, fuck, fuck, fuck, fuck.

I go on the date with Tom because I know now that there may be some truth in the concept of one true love and I will definitely need a dummy date before I meet mine, and also because there's still a chance I'm certifiable and crazy people don't go on dates.

I sneak into Moses's room to kiss him goodnight before going. He's still awake and pulls the covers over his face when I come in. I pull them down and tuck them around his body. 'It's not playtime, silly,' I whisper. He reaches out and I hold his hand. I stand in silence and after a minute I can feel his grip relax. I let his arm fall and watch him as he loses the battle to keep his eyes open.

As I leave, a floorboard creaks and Moses stirs and says, 'Mummy.'

'Shhhh,' I say. 'Mummy will be back soon.'

I try to get out of the house without my mum seeing me. I told her I was going to yoga with Leanne. I shout goodbye from the hallway but just before I can get out she calls my name. 'What time do you think you'll be back?' she says.

'Not late,' I say quickly. 'We might go for a drink afterwards.' I can feel her behind me and turn my head to say bye as I open the door.

'You're wearing heels to yoga?'

'You don't wear shoes, Mum, and like I said we might get a drink afterwards.'

Mum takes the door from me. 'Be careful,' she says.

'Yep, promise,' I say, as I walk away.

Tom picks Côte; this is good. Tom arrives wearing burgundy cords; this is bad. Tom pulls out my chair (despite my feminist protestations); this is good. Tom clicks his fingers at the waiter; this is very, very bad. I decide it's unfair to compile a catalogue of Tom's flaws before the first course and so channel my energy towards the story he has been telling me since we got settled. It's something about how you can work out how many people can fit on a boat by multiplying its length by its width, so I know that now.

Tom orders us both steaks, insisting they're divine. I don't really like eating steak – it feels like cardio – but I decide that I should save our first disagreement for dessert at least. I ask Tom how he knows James and he tells me that they both attend the same monthly meeting about sanitation and I think, so you don't really know him, and then I start to panic about how this date came to pass. Did James send out some sort of company-wide memo imploring anyone with a little time on their hands to take out his wife's crazy, loser friend?

'What do you do?' asks Tom, which is of course the question that everyone hates. What the hell does it even mean? The real answer is almost always, 'Barrel through life attempting to function as a semi-responsible human being and read the *Mail Online* more than I should.' The reason the question is so disconcerting is because it appears so innocent, but in reality it's quite aggressive. It's the small talk equivalent of folding your arms, leaning back and saying, 'Impress me.'

'I work in finance,' I say.

'Ah, that's cool,' says Tom. 'My uncle works in finance. Where do you work?'

'In Hove,' I say as I pick up the drinks menu. 'Another glass of wine?'

'Yes, but who do you work for?' asks Tom. I drain my glass.

'It's a small company, you wouldn't know them. We're basically the client support team.'

'So that means you do what?' asks Tom. What is this, a police interrogation?

'I answer the phone,' I say.

'I don't understand,' says Tom.

'Customers call and I take those calls,' I say.

'Right, so it's like . . .'

'A call centre. It's a call centre.'

Tom clears his throat. 'That must be . . . interesting.'

The waiter arrives with our steaks. 'Well done?' he asks.

'Here,' says Tom.

The waiter places the meal in front of him before putting the other plate down in front of me. 'More wine?'

'Yes,' I say.

As the waiter leaves Tom says pointlessly, 'Well, this looks well done.'

We eat our food in uncomfortable silence. After a few minutes Tom asks me how my steak tastes. It tastes like dead cow but I make some agreeable noises.

'Yeah, it's great here,' says Tom. 'My ex discovered it.' I want to tell him Côte is a chain, that his ex discovered Google, but he looks so pleased that I just nod. 'Yeah, she loved eating out. One of these girls that always wants to go places. To be honest it was exhausting. After a hard day's work the last thing you want to do is go dining . . . Sorry.'

I'm not sure what he's apologizing for – for bringing up his ex, for revealing himself to be a rubbish partner or for being terminally boring.

'Why did you break up?' I ask.

'I don't know,' he says. 'I think maybe we stopped trying.'

I catch his eye and we share a smile, one that says, we may hail from different planets but some things remain the same. I think this moment is what resuscitates the date – no longer restricted by the pressure to present a flawless facade, we commiserate about our overbearing mothers and swap stories about the not-so-hilarious-at-the-time bullying we endured at school. There's one uncomfortable moment when Tom discloses that he voted UKIP but he takes great pains to make clear that it was a protest vote. I think it helps that our waiter keeps the booze coming, perhaps sensing with his professional intuition that these two very out of practice thirty-somethings would need a helping hand.

I insist we split the bill since Tom didn't really ask me

out and he tells me that that sounds 'very reasonable'. As he walks me to the bus stop he says, 'I would ask you to come for another drink but I think we've had enough.'

'I'm OK,' I say, but he doesn't ask again.

'I'm here,' I say at my stop.

'OK. I'm just round the corner so I'm going to walk back.'

'OK,' I say. He kisses me then and it's surprisingly nice. I could stand there for hours snogging under the gaze of all the passengers making their way home on the 21A.

When I get home I feel really positive for the first time in weeks, if not years. Perhaps I should not concern myself with a hypothetical future with a guy from the internet I have yet to lay eyes on, when I could be enjoying the here and now with a man who wants to kiss me goodnight in the moonlight. I can't help it; as I brush my teeth I imagine Tom doing the same beside me.

I'm unsurprised to find a text message from him as I climb into bed. But when I open it, it reads, 'THANKS FOR TONIGHT BUT I DON'T THINK WE SHOULD SEE EACH OTHER AGAIN. I'M SURE YOU ENJOY YOUR WORK BUT I THINK I NEED SOMEONE WITH MORE AMBITION.'

He works with James and I don't want to offend him, so I think I'm pretty restrained when I reply, 'YOU PRICK.'

One thing is certain: before I meet George, I need a new job.

8

SOFT PLAY CENTRES sum up parenthood perfectly – loud, chaotic, a little bit musty and yet for some reason they feel safe. I appreciate its familiarity and the way I blend in there. It's more than a week since the date with Tom but the shame still feels fresh. Leanne, Lucas, Moses and I take up a spot in the corner of the ball pool. The boys entertain each other by throwing the brightly coloured plastic balls at each other's heads, and Leanne tries to help me make sense of my life as we work our way through the bag of Revels she has brought for us to share.

'Why were you seeing a therapist?' asks Leanne, before waiting for a moment when Lucas is distracted to slip another chocolate in her mouth and return the packet to its hiding place underneath a yellow ball.

'Do you think it's weird?' I ask in return.

'Of course not,' says Leanne. 'You see a doctor for your body and a therapist for your mind.'

'Have you been in therapy?' I ask. I watch Leanne watching our children and reconsider what I know about the world. Is it possible that my beautiful friend, with her picture-perfect life, has been struggling too?

'God, no,' she says. 'Like I said, I don't have anything against it but I tend to just get on with things.'

'Right,' I say, and then I shove a handful of Revels in my mouth.

'We're all different, hun,' says Leanne. 'Seriously, no judgement. I guess I just wondered why you thought you couldn't come to me.' I finish my mouthful and release all the breath in my body.

'Because there wasn't anything I could come to you with really, nothing I could properly articulate.' I think about the nights when I couldn't sleep, my mind numb. I longed for tears or anger or something that could direct my sense of unease. 'I had everything I'd ever wanted but I was still so unhappy and I didn't even know how to be happy.'

'Did you talk to Alexander about it?' says Leanne. I know, for her, it would be this easy, that she and James would just speak about things, make time to work through it; have urgent, hushed conversations late at night as their children were sleeping. I try not to envy her for this.

'I tried but I just got . . .' I sweep my palm in front of my face to indicate the invisible wall that Alexander had created between us. 'He didn't get it and he got frustrated with me. It was him who suggested counselling.' Leanne looks at me carefully, as if I am something fragile and the wrong words might break me.

'Did it help?' she asks.

'Yeah,' I say. 'Look at my life now.' I wink at Leanne to make clear that I understand how crappy my circumstances are; if I didn't then I would *really* need to be in therapy.

'I know it probably all feels a bit of a mess right now. That's why you need to take control,' Leanne says. 'Don't let him make you feel like your life is over, he's taken enough.'

I start to bury my legs under the balls. 'It's not even about him,' I say. 'It's about me. I've forgotten who I am.'

Leanne turns to me sharply. 'It *is* about him. You can't

let him get away with this. Why is he still living in the flat? He's probably shacked up there with some bimbo. I'm sorry to say it but that's what they're like.'

I asked Alexander about Poppy and he told me she was there to help him organize his end of year files. He told me he couldn't even think about another relationship yet.

'His office is there,' I say.

'You're still accommodating him!' Leanne snaps. 'He has your cat, for God's sake.'

'Why are you angry with me?' I snipe back.

'I'm not,' says Leanne. 'I'm angry *for* you. You need to make him step up to the plate.' I'm unsurprised by Leanne's attitude; she has a zero-tolerance stance towards exes in general. Her own former lovers are not even permitted to have names – they are known as the tall one, the stupid one and the one with no job.

'He's called me a couple of times, to make arrangements for Moses. We decided it's probably best we don't see each other for a while.' This is not strictly true. Alexander spoke; Alexander decided. His voice, at the time, had this stoic quality that I resented deeply. As if speaking to me was a heroic act. Moses crawls over to me and lies on his back before pushing his feet towards my face.

'Stinky,' I say, and he giggles. 'He's agreed to take Moses every other weekend.'

'How good of him,' Leanne says.

'And he's still paying for nursery,' I add in a rush. For some reason I feel the need to defend him; some habits are hard to break, I guess.

'Have you thought about a solicitor?' asks Leanne. Moses rolls towards Lucas, who is arguing over ownership of a lost sock with a vengeful-looking little girl. I lie down in the balls; they feel cool against my head.

'Can't. Too scary.'

Leanne grabs my hand and pulls me back up to sitting. 'Living with your mother for ever is far, far scarier.' I feel my face contort in horror. 'Right?!' says Leanne. 'Get the ball rolling. As soon as you take action you'll feel really empowered.'

'You sound like Tashi,' I say.

'Another therapist?' asks Leanne.

'No, this girl at work. She's trying to convince me to go on a retreat with her. You know, learning how to breathe and whatnot. She's always going on about empowerment.'

'She's right,' says Leanne. She claps her hands together several times and in response Lucas stops trying to drown Moses in the sea of plastic. 'I think it's a great idea to get some headspace. You need to get a serious plan together. You remember when I moved from audit to tax?' I don't want to lie so I keep my face very still. 'I had a week in Greece and it completely cleared my head. Do you want the details for my career coach?'

'What exactly did she do?' I ask. I imagine someone screaming at me as I type up covering letters.

Leanne shrugs. 'She helped me to identify my strengths and create a two-year plan.'

'Did you achieve it?' I ask. Leanne raises her right eyebrow and I laugh. 'OK, of course you did.' I notice Moses has a trail of snot hanging from his nose. I beckon to him but he's too busy trying to bend over and look through his legs. 'So, you think that could work for me?'

Leanne pulls a face I can't interpret.

'What? You don't think I can do it?' I ask.

'No,' says Leanne. 'I know you can. I got an orange-flavoured Revel – you know I hate them.'

I laugh again; it feels good. 'Why do you even buy Revels when you don't like half the flavours?'

Leanne wrinkles her nose as she considers this. 'I'm a realist. Life is like a bag of Revels: you have to put up with the orange ones because it makes it so much better when you get a nutty one.' I try and think of my marriage as one big orange-flavoured piece of confectionery. It helps. Leanne slips another chocolate in her mouth. 'See, nutty,' she says. 'I'm sorry,' she continues. Her gaze is lowered and she is speaking so softly, for a moment I am not sure she is addressing me. 'I'm sorry,' she says again, with more conviction, as if the first time she said it was a rehearsal. 'I shouldn't have set you up on that date.' She grabs my hand. 'You need to be working on you. I meant it when I said you were brave. You've done the hard part – now you'll make your life amazing, without him, without any man.'

I squeeze her hand and then pull my own away. I was going to tell her about George – I've already felt my phone vibrate twice in my pocket and I am desperate to see if it's him reaching out – but she looks so proud of me, so sure I can make it alone, that I hold back. I sort of want to believe her too. It's not that I don't think a single woman can have a happy existence; I'm just not sure that happy woman would be me.

'I'm gonna nip to the loo,' I say. I make my way out of the pit, carefully avoiding the limbs of small children, and then I hurry to the toilet. I want to savour the moment, so I don't look at my phone until I'm seated. The messages are from Greg asking me if I want to join the work Christmas party planning committee.

'IT'S GONNA BE EPIC', he's texted in a follow-up to the question. I relax my body, and pee and anticipation drain out of me.

'THE PARTY OR THE COMMITTEE?' I reply.

Greg immediately shoots back, 'HAR DE HAR.'

The thought of Christmas is like receiving a kick when I'm already in the foetal position, defeated by blows. I'm not a fan of the holiday as it is – the jolliness is overwhelming – but to help give Moses and Alexander a proper family Christmas, I could pretend. There would be no more pretending now; Moses will never have a real Christmas again.

Back at the pit the boys have started piling balls on to Leanne and she is doing a valiant job of pretending to enjoy it. I wade over and join in with their endeavour.

'No! Not you as well!' Leanne shouts. The boys squeal with delight.

'OK, truce,' I say. I grab Lucas, who has two balls poised above his head. 'Let's calm down and go for a walk.' We gather up our children and strap them into their pushchairs. They're too tired to put up a decent fight and within a few minutes of strolling along the seafront the two are asleep. Leanne and I keep walking and when we reach the pier I suggest we get some soft scoop. Even though it's October and chilly, it's bright and if you look towards it you can feel the sun on your face; so we park the children next to a couple of deckchairs and look out to the water as we slowly work through our ice creams. Leanne bites the end off her cone and sucks the last of the ice cream out, just as she did when we were kids.

'Do these taste better than I remember?' she asks.

'Yes,' I tell her. 'I think they do.'

9

LEANNE SENDS ME the details of her career coach. Her glossy website outlines the achievements of her former clients in intimidating detail. In a video introducing herself, Grace Fermin explains how she will help me to 'rise through the ranks of my current career'. Rising through the ranks of my current career would mean becoming Bob; I don't know what I want but I know I don't want that. Grace also says a lot about investing in yourself, which I understand as code for spending money that I don't have. I'm not willing to give up, though; I know Leanne believes in me and Moses needs me and that knowledge gives me enough motivation to scour the internet for careers advice deep into the night. Just before my brain bails out on my enthusiasm, I come across an ad that reads, 'Are you stuck? Are you unmotivated? Worried you'll never achieve the life of your dreams? We can help.' I think yes, yes and resoundingly yes and so I use the online booking system to claim an appointment for the next morning.

The Live the Life You Love business mentor scheme's office is located above a hot yoga studio in the centre of town. I climb the stairs, squeezing past a couple of dozen Lycra-clad yogis on their way out of class; I can't quite believe

67

that so many people would *pay* to start their week that way. At the top I reach a tiny stairwell/waiting room with a grey polypropylene chair and a very artificial-looking plant. I sit and look for a mint in my bag. Before I locate one, a short woman with a generous bosom opens the door. She has a very sharp, expensive-looking bob, underneath which is a face so round it verges on spherical. She introduces herself as Patricia.

'I'm the scheme's founder and chief mentor. Welcome.' She offers up her hand and, still seated, I receive a firm but clammy handshake.

'Thanks for meeting me,' I say.

'Come in,' she says, before leading me into a window-less office. As she clears several carrier bags of groceries from the desk, Patricia says, 'When I say welcome I mean welcome to the rest of your life.' She gestures for me to sit before doing the same. Patricia rests her elbows on her desk and builds a little steeple with her fingers. 'What brings you here?' she asks.

'Uhm, I guess I'm going through a transition and I need some support to, uhm, support me through this, well, transition.'

'Quite,' says Patricia.

'I'm on my own for the first time in a long time and I need to start bringing in more money. I work part-time because I've got a little boy, so I want my work to be flexible. I thought starting a business could make that happen.' I know starting a business isn't easy – I watched the whole ugly process up close and personal when Alexander started his design company – but whilst I know it will be hard, life already feels hard, so what's a little more?

Patricia glances up at the ceiling before pulling a wad of tissues out of her cardigan sleeve and blowing her nose heavily. 'Sorry,' she says, 'allergies. Anyway, let me tell you some more about me. Three years ago, I had nothing.' Patricia opens her hands suddenly; I guess in case I'm not sure what 'nothing' consists of. 'Nothing at all except this' – she taps her head – 'and this.' Patricia then places her right hand over her heart. 'Then I launched and I realized I had this business inside me all along and so do you. So why don't you tell me about your business plan.' My armpits prickle. I kind of thought she would be giving the plan to *me*.

'Well, it's not quite outlined yet . . .'

'Of course,' says Patricia. 'That's why we're here.'

'I guess I want to help people.' Patricia smiles. 'People like . . . women.'

'It's an under-resourced market,' she says. We sit in silence for a couple of seconds, until I understand that Patricia expects me to continue.

'I want to help women . . .'

'A business should always be of service. Help them with what?'

I figure that what I need is probably true of everyone else, so I say, 'I want to help them meet their ideal partner, if they haven't already. Which in my experience is rare.'

Patricia chuckles. 'I hear you, sister,' she says.

I make my face smile. I think, if I can connect with this woman, with whom I can already tell I have little in common, I can do it with women like me.

'I've been invited to a retreat this weekend,' I say, 'and I think I could use the experience to work out how to set up one of my own, or maybe I could do coaching.'

I hope that Tashi can still get me a place on the retreat and that she isn't suspicious of my sudden turnaround.

Patricia opens a new notebook at the first page. 'Well,

your business plan sounds like a simple subscription model: sign them up and sell them something! And of course the dating arena is ripe for the picking. What's your social media presence?'

'Limited,' I say.

'That's no problem,' says Patricia, scribbling 'limited' in the notebook. 'I can help you develop a really clear company message. I'd suggest you start with your market research and then come back to me and we can pull together your avatar.' I didn't even see that film, so I have no idea what she is referring to, but I'm excited I'm winning her over.

'So, shall we get started?' asks Patricia.

'Sure, yes please,' I say.

'Yes!' says Patricia, making a fist.

'Yes!' I say with more conviction, but I can't bring myself to mimic the gesture.

'OK,' says Patricia, turning to a desktop computer to her right. 'I just need to take a few details and then we can get you up and out there.' She spends a minute or so tapping on the keyboard before telling me, 'The entire year costs eleven hundred pounds, which is the best value you will find for this level of input.'

I want to pick up my bag and run. I came here with the hope of making money, not losing funds I don't yet have. 'I can see some hesitation,' says Patricia, raising a finger, 'and let me tell you that's just because you don't yet believe in your vision . . . but you will. Every flight starts with a leap.' I nod. 'I can see you still have reservations, so here's what I'm gonna do for you. If you pay a non-refundable deposit of two hundred pounds today, you can pay the rest off in two instalments. Let me offer you this.' Patricia places her hands flat on the desk. 'You can think if you need to but thinking has got you where you are today; wouldn't it be nice to stop thinking and just feel?'

I'm not sure how much Patricia is right about but she's right about that. I open my bag and get out an old debit card. As Patricia merrily taps the information into her computer I say a silent prayer to the money gods. The last time I used the card a man called Kalpesh called to tell me that I was in my *overdraft's* overdraft, and pretty much implied that if I used it again, the thing would self-destruct.

'All gone through,' says Patricia, and I release the breath that I didn't realize I was holding. 'Why don't you go home and email me through a basic business plan and we can start from there.'

'That's it?'

'Oh, of course,' says Patricia. She roots around in her desk drawer and pulls out a hot pink folder, which she hands to me. The words 'The Life You Love Starts Today' are printed on the front.

'So, I should just go?'

'Yep, to wherever you feel most inspired. Here's the thing: it's really more simple than you think. Every action begins with a thought. Have you ever thought something' – Patricia clicks her fingers – 'and just like that it appears, just as you imagined it?' For the most part I have a thought and the outcome isn't even in the same family as what I had hoped. I have *never* imagined something and had it come to pass, until George.

I pop into a coffee shop on the way to work and order a latte with extra foam and expensive syrupy stuff. As I wait, I look around at the other patrons and consider Patricia's words. To these people there is no reason why I couldn't be a successful entrepreneur, taking a self-directed break at the start of her amazing day. I decide that if I think it, it is so – what is reality but a construct of the mind?

I walk into the office and straight into Greg. A little of my coffee spills on to his shirt sleeve but he tells me it's fine as I dab at the stain unsuccessfully with my napkin.

'How are your teeth?' he asks when I cease my efforts.

'My teeth?' I echo, forgetting momentarily that I fabricated an emergency trip to the dentist in order to meet Patricia. 'Yeah, good. Great.' For some reason, I feel guilty lying to Greg. He always looks so earnest. As he smiles at my response, I feel like I'm tainting him with my deceit.

'You coming to the meeting?' he asks. I nod. 'You don't know what meeting I'm talking about, do you?'

'Busted,' I say.

'It's the first Christmas party planning committee meeting.' I wasn't even planning to attend the party but I let him lead the way to the conference room.

Lisa, an administrator in the training department, is standing authoritatively at the front of the room.

'Take a seat, Greg,' she says. 'We're just talking about refreshments.' She says nothing to me. We sit down and Lisa continues, 'I'm committed to making this the best party we've seen in years, so no suggestion is too crazy, guys.' I look over at Greg but he doesn't look back at me; he's watching Lisa with a fierce concentration. I take her in properly for the first time. She has an elaborate braid in her hair and her blue shirt is precisely the same shade as her kitten heels. Everything about her screams enthusiasm. It looks exhausting.

'Salsa,' says someone to the left of me.

'Great,' says Lisa, writing the word on a whiteboard

behind her. 'Everyone loves dips and we'll need something that can last the night.' She turns back to us, her face flush. 'Any more?' The room becomes a cacophony of snack foods; Lisa looks unsettled. 'Guys! Guys! One at a time, please.' Her plea goes unheeded; two lads in the customer retainment department start chanting 'Monster Munch'. Lisa looks a little as if she might cry.

Greg stands up, cups his mouth with his hands and shouts, 'Oi! Put a lid on it!' The room falls silent.

'Thanks, Greg,' says Lisa. He winks at her in return and she appears flustered. 'Let's get into pairs and come up with a bunch of ideas,' she says. As I turn to tell Greg how stupid it all is, she reaches out to him. 'Greg, join me.' He goes to her without even acknowledging me, and then, when I look for someone else to pair with, it seems that everyone has already coupled up. I leave quietly and head to my cubicle. I have bigger things than dip to think about.

Marthashotbod: I've just had a really exciting meeting about the new business I'm starting.

Undeterred83: Awesome! What's the business?

Marthashotbod: I'm working on the vision now so I'll let you know when I've really got it down.

Undeterred83: I'm so impressed by your work ethic, I'd love to start my own thing. Can't wait to chat to you about it. Only eleven weeks till I'm back on British soil!

Marthashotbod: I know! What's stopping you? From starting your own thing.

Undeterred83: You always know exactly what to say. There's nothing stopping me. I had a challenging time a few years ago but I did the work, cut out some shit, started meditating and I feel really confident now.

Marthashotbod: It's so important to work on yourself. I'm going on a meditation retreat next week.

I'll confirm with Tashi when she comes in for the evening shift. I won't mention that when she sent me an email to let me know she had reserved me a place, I sent it to junk.

Undeterred83: Man. I swear you are perfect for me.

I don't reply because there is nothing more to say. I can't remember the last time someone wanted me, no strings attached – no trial period, no training necessary.

10

ABOUT ONCE A month I take my mother out for coffee. I think for her it's a tangible representation of a legitimate mother–daughter relationship and for me I get to have all my wrongdoings outlined in one contained hour. Nine times out of ten she picks a tearoom on the seafront; I think she likes the high footfall. It means she gets to show her friends and acquaintances what a wonderful bond we have and if I'm lucky, after subtracting all the pleasantries she stops to exchange, she only spends ten or twenty minutes engaging with me.

I really don't mind my mother's commitment to community cohesion because I love being around her when her attention isn't focused on me. She's the sort of person who draws you in from across a room; she just has this wonderful, uplifting presence that makes people (and small dogs) want to be around her. Conversely, ten seconds into any interaction with a new person, I become convinced I have a bogey on my face and then spend the entire conversation focused on how quickly I can get away to rectify this. My extraction is always forced and awkward and more than once it's been the case that my suspicions have been confirmed.

I suggest that we go and collect Moses from nursery

together and stop on the way for a catch-up. In the tea-room, I buy my mother a symbolic slice of chocolate cake. It is symbolic because my mother will not touch it. Ivy Ketch claims to have no prejudices; in fact she is fond of saying, 'I am against nothing,' and then pausing to allow any onlookers to glory in her beatific aura. She's almost right; my mother is against nothing – she is against every-thing and everyone. There is one thing, however, that she reserves a special kind of hatred for, the kind of disgust that one would usually find aimed at the far right or per-petrators of child abuse: fat. Fat on herself, fat in her line of vision and most of all fat, actual or potential, on her only daughter. My mother's personal attitude to fat is to head it off at the pass – she eats little and not very often; one of my earliest memories is sitting in a high chair watch-ing her bob along to a callisthenics video. Over the years her methodology may have changed – power walking, aer-obics, Zumba – but the aim remains: avoiding fat, avoiding even the merest implication of fat, at all costs.

I always found it slightly odd, this anti-fat stance. She was born into a Jamaican family that was large in all senses of the word. Ample curves weren't just the norm, they were positively coveted. As a child, one of the places I felt safest was in my grandmother's tiny kitchen in her retirement flat in south London. She would pile steaming white rice into a bowl before adding a generous knob of butter; this would melt into the grains, creating a satisfy-ing glaze which would coat my lips as I ate. Sometimes my mother would tut as I scraped the bowl clean but my grandmother would simply offer me a refill, to which I always said yes. Partly because, then and now, I exist in a permanent state of hunger, but mostly because I loved to see the joy in her eyes. She would pinch my cheek and say,

'What a way you fat and roun' and pretty,' and her words were like clutching a hot water bottle to my stomach.

Being with Alexander didn't do a lot to curtail my body issues. He was always very supportive of my endeavours to lose a few pounds but perhaps a little too supportive. He saw my body, obviously – how could he miss it? – but I never got the impression that he held an opinion on it, negative *or* positive. I've noticed it's become a trend for young women to complain about comments on their figures received from men in the street. I always read another article and think, it's all right for you with your peachy face and your high breasts, 'cause the thing that no woman ever admits is that they don't want men to talk about their bodies, but then again they really, really do.

Before James, Leanne briefly dated a guy (the stupid one) who was entirely unsuitable for her. Wally (I never discovered if this was a nickname or his given one) was a walking, breathing stereotype of the British working-class man. He had a job in construction and a potty mouth. Whenever the conversation became too involved he would procure a dirty, crumpled edition of the *Sun* from somewhere and become immersed in the copy until the discussion returned to safer ground. I didn't get it; I didn't want to get it. My friend was bright, refined and disciplined, and he was an oaf. Then one day we were out for a pint and apropos of nothing he said to Leanne, 'You've got such a great arse.' As I watched her pretend to be embarrassed I understood.

Not for the first time I worry that when George first lays eyes on me, he isn't going to like what he sees. The only dating advice my mother has ever given me is that 'men decide with their eyes'; she said this as she gifted me a girdle. Irritated as I was by her crassness at the time (the girdle went directly from the bag to the bin), I have to admit my father, a man whose only passion in life is the dunkability of his evening biscuit, unreservedly adores her. Whatever Mum might say, I don't think his dedication is based solely on her waistline. I was around ten when I became fully aware of the fact that my parents had a relationship outside of raising me. As much as it grossed me out, I took note of the way my father would kiss my mum as soon as he stepped in the house, before removing his coat; I would see him watching her in crowded rooms, smiling as though he had a secret. Whilst I can't imagine a life without cake, I would give it up for love like that.

A woman wearing a canary yellow tracksuit stops at our table. 'Heeeellllo, Ive,' she coos. 'That dessert is divine! You're in for a real treat.'

Mum gives a little laugh. 'I'm sure,' she says. 'We missed you at bums and tums last week.'

'Oh, I haven't got time at the minute,' says the woman. 'I'm in training for a 5k.' She bends her arms at the elbow and swings them back and forth by her sides several times.

'Oh, good for you, honey,' says Mum. 'Let me know if you want sponsors or anything.'

'Thanks, I will! Enjoy your cake.' She marches out of the cafe. As soon as her yellow posterior is out of sight Mum tuts.

'These people, you'd think she was doing a triathlon – such a bloody fuss. I do 5k round the supermarket.'

'At least she's trying,' I say. I dip my finger into the icing of the slice of cake and pop it in my mouth. Big Bird was right, it is delicious.

'Barely,' says Mum, her face briefly contorting in disgust.

'Well, I'm doing the half-marathon,' I say. I have no idea why. The closest I've ever got to a marathon is watching an entire season of *Grey's Anatomy* in one weekend. Then I see my mother's face; confusion gives way to something approaching pride and I decide that I *am* doing a half-marathon. I know at least that I want to be the kind of person who does a half-marathon.

'A project is just what you need! And with all that training, when you see Alexander he won't know what's hit him.' I open my mouth to protest but stop myself; she's actually right. I can't wait to feel lean and comment-worthy and accomplished and spiritually superior, but the person I want to impress is not Alexander but George.

11

'WHAT DO YOU take to a retreat?' I ask Tashi as I climb into her green Nissan Micra on Friday morning.

'Just an open heart,' says Tashi.

'So, I won't need my hair straighteners?'

'No,' says Tashi, 'I don't think so.'

I smack my left hand on the dashboard. 'Then I'm good to go.'

Tashi tells me she has been meditating twice a day in preparation for the weekend. 'You have to train your brain,' she says. 'Being present is like a muscle. Have you ever meditated before?'

I scour my brain. I am rarely present; I'm always thinking about how things will be better in the future, or about how I've fucked up in the past.

'I did some hypnobirthing classes when I was having Moses. I had to pretend my vagina was a flower. Is it something like that?'

'Erm, I'm sure there's some overlap,' Tashi says.

As Tashi drives, I fiddle with the radio until I find a station playing old classics. I don't think Tashi knows any of the songs but she hums along companionably. Tashi is concerned that her car won't make it up to motorway speeds

80

so we drive on small country roads. Although I barely know Tashi, I suddenly feel very connected to her. I just know the trip will be life-changing; we'll be like Thelma and Louise but with less murder and more snacks.

I've never learned to drive. Living in Brighton, where most things are walking distance, there didn't seem a point. That's what I told myself and anyone who questioned my avoidance of such a common rite of passage, but now I wonder if, on some level, I chose not to learn because I loved the experience of having Alexander drive me. He's a great driver, never more comfortable than when on the road – distance, traffic, nothing fazed him. In the early days he would often give me a ride to work or drop me off on a night out. Once, I had gone to a festival a couple of towns over with Cara. She'd hooked up with a guy, a bassist in a Danish death metal band, and being the good friend I am, I gave up my space in our two-man tent and told her I would get a cab home.

Of course, every taxi in the area had been booked weeks in advance and I was faced with a very long wait or an even longer walk home. I called Alexander with the dying embers of my phone battery; gave him sloppy directions to the edge of the field I was standing next to and somehow, through sheer will or possibly an intangible connection, he found me. I don't remember what he said to me on the drive home – I was more concerned with the way my brain seemed to be running laps within my skull – but I remember the feeling, the warmth of knowing he had been there to save me.

When 'Young Hearts Run Free' fills the car, I feel compelled to join in. I've always loved the song, mostly because so many people think it's fun and upbeat, when in fact the lyrics are desperately sad.

'I didn't know you could sing,' says Tashi. I feel myself blushing.

'I can't, not really,' I say.

'Oh, OK,' she says.

I ask Tashi how she got into Tula Shiki and request a little more information on where she's actually taking me. 'Tula is a philosophy,' she says. 'Its basis is in minimalism and self-contemplation. The retreat is based at its main centre. My ex, Guido, got me into it. He's such a centred man, so introspective. He taught me a lot.'

Tashi explains that she met Guido when he was running a workshop on her university campus entitled 'The Fast Path to Simple Living'. 'I needed to pay off, like, five credit cards but I got so much more.' Tashi tells me that she found herself blown away by Guido's presence and intensity; apparently his lack of investment in material objects gave him a sense of freedom she found highly desirable. Guido was a former model and having experienced a life of excess, he understood its limitations. Hearing about his previous profession, I wonder if it was just his freedom she desired.

'So why did you break up?' I ask. Tashi inhales slowly through her nose and then exhales loudly from her mouth.

'I guess he had too much love to give,' she says.

'Is that possible?' I ask.

'Sure,' says Tashi. 'When you have so much you need to share it around several people, it's too much.'

Tashi tells me, as though relieved to unburden herself, an age-old story of empty beds and unanswered calls and how women are so ridiculously adept at ignoring the patently obvious. She tells me that a few weeks into their courtship he had taken her to a party. She remembers taking great care over her outfit – she wanted, so very much, to live up to the moniker of his girlfriend. The party was the sort that Tashi found intimidating – a crowd of older people with interesting stories – but Guido's friends were warm and inclusive and she quickly found herself having a good time. She was listening to a guy tell her about a recent trek through Peru when she got the sense that Guido was no longer with her, not emotionally, but physically. She excused herself from the conversation and searched the apartment. She remembers opening a door to find an empty broom cupboard before she started to panic. She wanted to leave. She wanted to go home and eat ice cream and cry but to do so would be to accept the fact that he had abandoned her. When Guido returned two hours later, she confronted him. He told her she was being hysterical and that he had just stepped out for a cigarette, and she accepted this despite the fact that he didn't smoke.

When she was forced to face the truth, it was on the screen of Guido's open netbook. An email from a girl stating in uncompromising detail what he had done to her and what she would very much like for him to do to her again. The time stamp offered no escape route for him. The message, read but not deleted, was offered up to her so carelessly that it was clear that Guido either wanted to get caught or did not care if he was. When she asked him, calmly and clearly, what his explanation was, he said, 'We didn't say we were exclusive.' Tashi had given up her room in a shared house just three weeks prior to move in with him.

I sympathize with Tashi and reassure her that we've all been there because it's true. Alexander never cheated on me, not that I know of, but he had shown me in many ways that he was biding his time, and even if he was not with someone else he was certainly not with me.

Once we had taken a holiday to Ibiza. I had obsessed over it for weeks. I was so determined to make the trip perfect I even went to a travel agent, rather than picking it on some low-cost website, and had been bedevilled into paying for a load of unnecessary, barely noticeable extras. As holidays often are, it was a disappointment – we were too old for the party scene but not old enough to admit it. We spent most nights pretending we were going to hit the clubs and then getting drunk in the hotel bar. There was one day, though, that we made it to the old town. We wandered the cobbled streets for hours and I kept imagining that other tourists would look at us and marvel at how beautiful and in love we were. We found ourselves at Café del Mar, a stunning waterside bar known for its amazing atmosphere. It was one of the few places I've been to that has lived up to my expectations. The bar is the place to be at sunset, when the resident DJs play ambient sounds to complement the unbelievable view. Thirty minutes before the sun went down I asked Alexander if he wanted another beer. 'I'm kinda hungry,' he said. 'I fancy paella.' I placed my hand on his knee.

'Let's hold off,' I said. 'I think I'm happy here.'

'Sorry, babe,' said Alexander, sounding anything but. As we left, another couple eagerly scrambled into our seats. How could I have imagined I would make him stay for a lifetime if I couldn't get him to commit to a sunset?

My phone stirs.

Undeterred83: Are you OK?

I decide it's time to start being open.

Marthashotbod: I am now I've heard from you.
Undeterred83: That's great. That's exactly what I wanted to hear. What you up to?
Marthashotbod: I'm going on a journey.
Undeterred83: I'd love to be coming with you.

Marthashotbod: Maybe next year?
Undeterred83: If I play my cards right?
Marthashotbod: You're holding aces right now.

'You wanna stop for supplies?' says Tashi.

We stop at a shop in a tiny village, run by a woman who clearly wants it to stay that way. She serves us with such open hostility I start to reassess my hair, my clothes, even my gait for evidence of their contemptibility. Tashi seems oblivious to her blind hatred and babbles happily as she buys toilet roll, water and nuts.

'Hi, Mary,' she says. 'Had a lot of us coming through?' Mary's face offers nothing. 'I'm so excited to see you again; you're like the start of my awakening every time I arrive.'

I think Mary is going to comment but she simply coughs productively, leaving her mouth uncovered as she does so. I replicate Tashi's shopping, although as she leaves the shop, stating plans to warm up the car, I add three Bounty bars, and then just before paying I ask the woman to get me four of the miniature brandies she has behind the counter. This seems to defrost her, and she winks at me before slipping the bottles into the bottom of the bag. I thank her and hurry back to Tashi. As I'm leaving, Mary speaks for the first time. I can't exactly be sure what she says but it sounds like, 'You're gonna need it.'

The Tula Shiki Education and Resource Centre is located behind a small copse of fir trees. From the road it looks like an outdoor centre, the kind Scouts might frequent to learn skills they will never require in a modern world, but as we drive closer to the collection of buildings I see figures dotted about in the trees and pathways. Adults, some dressed in robes, others in fun, stylish clothes; but all wearing the same 'ready for Armageddon' smile that Tashi also sports. After parking the car, we are met in reception by a woman with waist-length grey hair who introduces herself as Sunbeam.

'Welcome, welcome,' she says breathily. She shuts her eyes for several seconds and, just as I am growing concerned she is having a stroke, she leaps back to life, like a mechanical doll. 'I've just got some medical forms for you to fill in and then I'm pleased to tell you you can have a sitting with Larry.' Sunbeam offers us two wooden chairs as she goes to fetch the paperwork.

'Who's Larry?' I whisper to Tashi.

'The guru!' says Tashi.

'A guru . . . called Larry?'

'Yes,' says Tashi, 'and we're really lucky that we get to see him so early on!'

Sunbeam comes over with the forms. It's mostly standard health stuff; I try to make myself sound like a functioning human. I pause at the emergency contact section, a place where Alexander's name used to live. I shake my head to see off any burgeoning tears and write 'I need nothing and no one' in the space, but then I cross it out and put down my mum. Sunbeam returns to take our forms.

'Can I also have your phones,' she says. Tashi is busy rooting around in her bag and so cannot see me staring at her in stunned silence. When she hands her mobile to Sunbeam I still haven't moved. Sunbeam watches me with a fixed smile.

'I can't,' I say. 'I . . . I have a son.' Yes, the child card, I think. No one can argue with that one.

'It's fine,' says Sunbeam. 'All the calls are monitored and if there's an emergency we'll get you immediately.' Very briefly I consider running and then I feel a bit ashamed about how ridiculous I am being. For the first half of my life I didn't have a mobile phone; I will be fine. I hand my iPhone to Sunbeam and in return she gives me a small bow. 'Leave your bags here and someone will take them to your room. Larry will see you now.' She gestures for us to head to a door across the reception. Tashi gives Sunbeam a bow of her own before rushing over and I quickly follow, unsure of what is scarier – going with her or being left alone.

Inside the room heavy curtains block most of the light but a few candles illuminate Larry's brown, lined face. Although it is cold he is wearing a light tunic and sandals. He nods very slightly to us as we enter. Tashi sits cross-legged on the floor in front of him and I follow suit. 'Welcome back,' Larry says towards Tashi.

She claps her hands over her mouth. 'You remember me,' she squeals through her fingers.

'All my students have a piece of me in them,' he says.

I know the enlightenment process has already started; otherwise how is it that I'm able to resist giggling at this unfortunate statement?

'You,' says Larry, his head whipping in my direction, 'you have lost something.'

'No, I don't think so,' I say.

'Yes, I think you have.' I can actually feel Tashi's eagerness radiating on to me. Clearly, she has something to contribute to the conversation. She doesn't know about Alexander so I'm keen to know why she is so confident that I'm a loser. I glance at her.

'You lost your key, remember,' she whispers.

'Right, yeah, but I found it again.' I turn to Larry. 'It was under my bed.'

'It always is,' says Larry. 'I think there's more, though.'

I can feel myself colouring. 'Not to worry, you will find something here, even if it is not what you have lost. Be open.' I nod.

'Can you show her the way?' he says to Tashi.

She grabs my hand. 'Of course,' she says.

'You should probably eat less meat,' he says. 'Your energy is stagnant.'

Tashi squeezes my hand. I look at her and she raises her eyebrows. Her eyes say, 'I told you so.'

'I must encourage you to go for replenishments now.' It takes a few seconds for us both to understand we have been dismissed and we stumble a little as our bodies try to catch up with the realization.

'He likes you!' cries Tashi as we walk towards an outhouse that serves as the kitchen.

'How can you tell?'

'I can tell,' she says. 'My first meeting with him, he didn't even speak.'

I grab Tashi round the waist. 'The problem is, I'm not sure if him taking a shine to me is a good thing or a bad thing.'

'Oh, it's the best thing,' says Tashi, reciprocating my gesture.

When we reach the kitchen Tashi asks Brett, a bearded Welshman with a gentle manner and questionable tattoos, for our 'assignment'.

'You're on potatoes,' he says. He hands each of us a small raffia sack. I follow Tashi into a vast vegetable patch.

'Just fill it, you're not supposed to talk,' she says before falling to her knees. I think about my Bounty bars. I wonder if I say I'm going to use the toilet I'd have time to go and snaffle one. I look at Tashi pulling away soil, the wind licking her hair into her face, and I decide to try to be open and embrace the process. I start digging tentatively but I quickly discover that my bag will never be full this way and so I increase my fervour, pushing my fingers into the cool mud, fearless in the face of earthworms and other mini beasts. After a few minutes some more people join us. I look up and acknowledge them but I don't break the rules by saying hello. When I've filled my bag, rather than returning my haul to Brett, I help the others fill theirs. One woman appears to be in her seventies; when her bag is full she grabs my hand and kisses it. Her lips are so cold and so rough and yet so comforting.

We all carry our potatoes back together. 'You've definitely earned your supper, sweetheart,' says Brett, taking my sack. He exchanges it for a steaming bowl of vegetable stew. Tashi, the rest of the potato pickers and I sit together on the wooden benches that line the kitchen. We eat in satisfied silence. The meal, though small and lacking in seasoning, tastes wonderful. When I try to work out why, it occurs to me that I may never have been truly, physically hungry before.

Tashi and I have been put in a room on the first floor of the centre, from which you can see miles and miles of unbroken green from the window. I could not live more than five miles from the nearest Marks & Spencer but it's nice to step outside your own life from time to time. Our room has three single beds; one is already occupied by a woman with cropped, grey hair. She is lying on top of the covers and dressed completely in white – even her socks. I cannot tell if she is sleeping or meditating but either way it does not seem like the right time to make introductions.

Tashi and I brush our teeth in the small sink in the

corner of the room before getting ready for bed. As I change into my pyjamas I sneak a glimpse of Tashi doing the same. Her legs are thin and undefined, almost colt-like. The little weight she carries has settled around her middle and although not overweight she has a rounded tummy. It's nice; it's womanly and also sort of childlike. I can tell by the way she wiggles quickly out of her clothes and aggressively pulls on her oversized T-shirt that she has no idea how beautiful she is.

We lie in our beds facing each other. 'How are you doing?' asks Tashi.

'I'm good. No, I'm really good,' I say.

'That's wonderful,' says Tashi, 'I knew this would move you.'

'I kinda feel like I'm on a school trip.' I can't quite make out Tashi's face but somehow I can feel her smile. 'Which isn't a bad thing.'

'Mmmmm,' says Tashi.

I can hear that she's only clinging to the edge of consciousness; perhaps that's what gives me the courage to pause and say, 'I wasn't honest earlier. I have lost something ... someone. I'm getting a divorce.' It's the first time I've said this word out loud in relation to Alexander and myself. I'm relieved to find the experience is like getting a jab; all the pain is in the anticipation. 'I thought I had lost my husband but I'm starting to think that maybe I had already lost myself a long time ago. Maybe he was just, I don't know, collateral damage or something ... Tashi ... Tashi?'

A voice that does not belong to Tashi says quietly but firmly, 'Shut the fuck up.'

12

I DREAM THAT ALEXANDER and I are getting married and it's our wedding day, but I cannot find one of my shoes. I search frantically for it, mussing my hair and snagging my dress in the process. I beg my friends and family to help me look but they dismiss me. The church bells chime. I stop my search, take off the other shoe and start running. My anxiety is eased by the sound of the bells fading into the distance. I can hear the wedding guests calling after me but I ignore them until . . .

'Martha, you've got to get up!' It's Tashi; I'm not getting married, I'm the furthest thing from it. When I open my eyes, she's leaning over me grinning. 'We have yoga.' Yoga, I can handle yoga, it's just lying down with good PR. I sit up. Our roommate has already gone to spread her positive karma elsewhere.

'What time is it?' I ask.

'Five,' says Tashi. I lie back down.

'That's the night, Tashi,' I mumble. Tashi pulls the duvet off me.

'It's not,' she says, 'it's the beginning of a brand new day!'

Yoga is led by Sunbeam. She sits at the front of the hall, her eyes closed and her legs folded into a pretzel. Tashi immediately takes a position at the front of the room but I hang back – I don't need a room full of people staring at my arse. Sunbeam rings a little bell which seems to be the signal for everyone to assume the same position and I do the same. She starts making a series of moaning sounds; I look round to see if anyone else is trying not to laugh but they all appear to be going to their happy places. After a few minutes Sunbeam stands and raises her arms, followed by everyone else. She then starts a series of movements accompanied by foreign phrases. Everyone else joins in with her without question and I try to recall the details of an article I once read about cults.

I stay sitting on the floor cross-legged, hoping to find a moment when I can join in successfully. I try to put together an expression that looks peaceful. I don't feel at peace, though, I feel out of step with everyone there and that's a familiar feeling. It's tense and awkward and seems unfair but I recognize it and that knowledge makes me feel unsettled and frustrated, which in my opinion is the worst combination of emotions one can experience. I know I need to cry but not sad tears; sad and angry tears, which are much uglier and generally louder. I close my eyes to try and halt, or at least delay, the process.

After a few seconds I feel a presence behind me. Above my head I hear Sunbeam: 'Carry on with the sequence, everyone. Whatever stage of your yoga journey you are in, remember that yoga means breath. As long as you're inhaling, you are in touch with your yogi.' Without request for consent, two hands clasp my belly. I have to swallow an instinct to start elbowing her in the ribcage, a move I was shown at a self-defence class at university. Her breath is on my neck. 'Just exhale all the negativity you're storing,' she whispers. 'I can feel the tension in your body, it's like it's full of static.' I'm not sure what she expects; she is essentially trying to mount me and she hasn't even bought me a drink. 'Breathe with me,' she says, and the whole thing levels up from creepy to creepy as all hell. I open my eyes and everyone is on all fours and I think I will feel marginally less self-conscious if I attempt to join in.

I wriggle free of Sunbeam, who takes the hint and continues her journey round the class. As the group moves, I try to move with them. The woman to the left of me looks very pleased with herself but if I could put my forehead to my knees, I would also feel smug. The man to my right seems to be struggling with the positions but he is enjoying his struggle, sometimes chuckling to himself as his body fails to meet up with his ambition. The class is much faster than I anticipated; no lying down at all. I have to keep looking up to see what everyone else is doing and as a result I am always a few seconds behind. At one point I stand up to see that everyone else is on all fours again and I feel like crying. The class seems like an analogy for something, something I don't actually want to think about right now. I get down on the floor just as everyone else glides into the next position and I give in. I stay where I am, heavy-limbed and cow-like.

There was a moment during my labour with Moses when I found myself in the exact same position. It did nothing to ease the searing pain of contractions but for some reason I felt safe down there. I could smell the disinfected floor and feel it cool against my palms. The midwife was trying to convince me to stand but I was immovable. Alexander returned from getting a coffee and she said, 'You're gonna have to get her up.'

'I don't know how,' he said.

Sunbeam comes over to me and places her hand on the

small of my back. 'That's right,' she says, 'just stay in the moment and breathe.' I can do that; breathing is about all I can do.

Sunbeam announces a five-minute break before chanting begins. I know that I will be tempted to chant, 'You are all frickin' loopy.' So, as the others are milling around, getting water and bowing to each other, I slip out. My intention is to sneak back to my room and eat my contraband and catch up on the four hours' sleep I was robbed of this morning, but as I approach the stairs I'm halted by a little girl, sitting on the bottom step in tears. She's a pretty, skinny thing. Her shiny, brunette curls are in sharp juxtaposition to her muck-strewn overalls. I crouch down in front of her and ask if she's OK. She collapses on to my shoulder and sobs energetically. 'What happened?' I whisper.

'He took my rooooooock!' she wails. I hold her at arm's lengths in an effort to protect my eardrums.

'Ah, I see,' I say. Not seeing at all.

'I was playing with a rock and Jack, to—, to—, took it.'

'Where's your mummy?' I ask. The girl points towards the hall door, where the groans of Sunbeam and her followers can be heard.

'OK then. Should I go and talk to him?'

'Yeah,' she says, whilst nodding violently. I stand up and hold my hand out. She grips it with a surprising force for such a small hand. My new friend pulls me into the garden and then behind the kitchen, where, in a clearing surrounded by thicket, is a small crowd of children; it looks like a scene from *Oliver Twist*. The children – a variety of ages and sizes – are shouting and chasing each other and seemingly trying to cover themselves with as much debris as possible. Sitting at some distance is a long-limbed teenage girl, tapping industriously on a mobile phone; I assume she is the allocated supervisor. Watching her, I feel a wave of irritation, partly because she has such a lax attitude to her responsibilities but also because of her access to social media. I also feel sad for the kids, left to fend for themselves as their parents chase enlightenment. I look down at the little girl. Her expression is fearful and something about her vulnerability reminds me of Moses. She deserves more than a rock.

'Is there a tiger here!' I yell. The children stop and stare at me; they look like startled woodland creatures, awaiting further gunshots. I see their shock turn to confusion and morph again to mirth. 'I lost my tiger,' I say, 'have you seen him?'

'Nooooooo!' the children chorus.

'Oh dear, oh dear,' I say, and scratch my head in pantomime fashion. 'If I don't find him, he'll get hungry and you know what he eats . . .' Some of the children giggle nervously. 'Children,' I say with a growl. The kids scream and scatter. I hold my hands up and shout, 'I'm kidding! He's a vegetarian. He eats vegetables but he'll eat absolutely everything, the whole garden, and then we'll have nothing for dinner.' The children stop and come towards me. 'But you know what he likes? Singing! Especially children singing. Do you want to help me?' The supervisor breaks eye contact with her phone screen and looks up just long enough to roll her eyes at me, but the other children come together and sit on the grass in front of me, my little audience. I sit down with them. My new friend nestles next to me, her rock seemingly forgotten. 'Are all your parents doing yoga?' I ask. They nod. 'What are your names?' All the children shout out their names at the same time. 'OK, OK! One at a time. You start,' I say to the little girl with the curls. 'Tell me your name and something you're really, really good at.'

I teach the children how to sing a round and we manage to produce a pretty rockin' version of 'London's Burning'; the supervisor is even inspired to record a performance of it on her phone. When we hear the breakfast bell ringing, the children beg me to stay and teach them another song. I remind them we should get to breakfast before the tiger does and they scatter. I feel lighter than I have in a long time as I walk back to the main building to find Tashi. Being with the children made me think of Moses and miss him even more but it also made me realize I can be something other than his mother. I had feared that without him to think about I would feel even more lost, but for twenty minutes I had felt more in control than I have in a long time.

I find Tashi in the hall, her face flush with excitement. She disengages from the man she is talking to and rushes over to me. 'Are you OK?' she asks. 'You didn't stay for chanting. Was it too emotional?'

'Yeah, I think it was all a bit much for me. I won't lie, I felt like a bit of a prat,' I say. I start towards the kitchen; everything is better with carbs. Tashi tries to reassure me that it's all just part of the process but I'm concerned it's a process I no longer want to go through. I'm feeling a little embarrassed; I had visions of massages and sitting in window seats reading. My mind flits to my brandy stash.

'It will get easier,' she says. 'When I started yoga, I couldn't even touch my toes.' She says this as if I should find it shocking, as if touching your toes is a thing you're *supposed* to be able to do. As we reach the kitchen Tashi suddenly stops.

'Uhm, go without me,' she says.

'No way!' I counter. I'm not going in alone, but also my stomach is growling an angry protest. I grab her arm and we wrestle a little in the doorway. I'm about to abandon the cause when I turn to see the source of her distress, all six feet of him. The man walks over to us and places his hands in prayer position.

'Namaste,' he says.

'Sure,' I say. Tashi says nothing. I give her arm a little tug but she doesn't respond.

'Tashi, is this . . . is this him?' Tashi nods. 'Excuse us,' I say to the man before pushing Tashi back into the garden. 'Did you know Guido was going to be here?' I say from the safety of behind a tree.

'No, no. Of course not. I thought he was in Kerala,' says Tashi, her eyes still trained on the kitchen.

'You still talk to him?' I ask.

'God, no. I just check his Facebook . . . and his Instagram and stuff.' I place my hands on Tashi's shoulders.

'Well, maybe he's here for a reason. Maybe he's been sent here so you can finally have closure, so you can be at peace with him.'

'I feel sick,' says Tashi.

'Tashi,' I say, 'you are ten times the man he is. Well, you're not a man but you know what I mean. You are so much better than him and so much better than this.' I mean the whole hiding-behind-a-tree thing but a little bit of me means the whole retreat, the whole charade. It's all starting to feel like cheap theatre and if anyone knows about pretending it's me.

'I can't do this,' says Tashi. She breaks away from me and runs back in the direction of the main lodge. I can taste my anger and, propelled by the sense of injustice, I turn and march back to the kitchen.

Guido is standing in the centre of the room, his hand placed on the breastbone of a tall blonde woman. As I approach I hear him say, 'I can feel your prana expanding . . .'

I tap him on the shoulder. 'So you're Guido?'

'Excuse me,' he says to the blonde, who bows prettily and walks away. 'I am honoured to be in your presence,' he continues. 'How can I aid you?'

'You can't,' I say. Momentarily he looks irritated, and in his face I can see the petulant little boy he once was. 'What you can do is wipe that smirk off your pretty face and go and apologize to my friend.' It *is* a pretty face, so attractive it almost becomes boring – almost.

'Who is your friend?' he asks. It is this comment that tips my anger into full-blown rage. Tashi *is* my friend – somehow this ridiculous trip has sealed us – but also she is every woman who has been dismissed by a man. Tashi is my friend but she is also me.

'My friend is someone who you should never have had the privilege of breathing the same air as, let alone been allowed to have anything close to a relationship with. She is a person that if you are clever you will remember as the best thing you never had and who will remember *you* as a brief and regrettable footnote in her otherwise amazing life. My friend is someone who is so beautiful you were blinded by her light, which must have been why you tripped and let your dick fall into some other hippy tramp. My friend is wonderful and graceful, and her name is Tashi.'

Guido lets his mouth fall open for a few seconds. He then shakes his head and says, 'You are filled with so much anger.'

'You bet I am,' I say. Then I pick up a glass of something

algae-coloured from the table next to me and throw the whole thing in his face. I think it best to quit whilst I'm ahead, so I leave to look for Tashi. I won't lie; as I walk I hear Beyoncé in my head. At the door to the kitchen a petite Asian girl smiles widely and holds her hand up, and I raise mine to meet hers in a very unzenlike high five.

Tashi is huddled on her bed in our cell. Her face is damp and blotchy, and she wipes her nose messily on her sleeve when she sees me come in. 'I'm sorry,' she says.

'For dating that nimrod, you should be.'

Tashi gives me a weak smile. 'I don't know why I let him get under my skin; we only saw each other for a couple of months.'

I sit on Tashi's bed and tuck a piece of her hair behind her ear. 'Tashi, there are some people that are put on this earth simply to steal part of our soul.'

Tashi sighs. 'I guess if I hadn't met him I wouldn't have found Tula Shiki.'

'Yeeeeah,' I say.

'At school I was such a geek,' Tashi says. 'The idea that someone like him would even look at me . . .' I want to slap her – affectionately.

'He is clearly riddled with insecurity; he sweats the stuff. You deserve so much better,' I say. 'You know that, right?'

Tashi shuffles towards me and gives me a hug. 'I'll meet someone else?' she asks as we untangle ourselves.

'You can't be serious,' I say, giving her a playful prod. 'It could be worse – you could have married him.'

Tashi laughs. 'Can you imagine?' Sadly, I can. 'I can't go back out there,' she says.

'I don't think he's gonna be bothering you,' I say. I tell Tashi about the smoothie facial I gave Guido.

'Oh my God, I love you,' says Tashi.

'I know,' I say. 'Do you want a Bounty?' Tashi nods.

Tashi and I share her bed and my chocolate until she feels ready to face the world, or at least the world of the retreat. 'I think you're right. He was sent to test me,' says Tashi. 'I'm so ready for the meditation now.'

'What does that consist of?' I ask.

'Just being,' she says.

We return to the same room we did yoga in except it's been filled with candles and cushions. Tashi encourages me to take a seat next to hers. The cushion seems to be primarily decorative because I can feel the floorboards through it. The room is filled with quiet chatter; there's definitely an air of anticipation. It amuses me a little that everyone is so excited about essentially doing nothing. The elderly woman I helped in the garden is at the front of the room; she waves at me and I smile back. I probably wouldn't admit it to anyone but I am feeling very peaceful.

Larry walks in and the room falls silent. He sits on the floor facing us all; he does not use a cushion and no one offers him one. Once settled he makes a loud moaning sound and then nothing. No one moves, no one speaks, no one does anything. I sort of want to scream. This is a habit I have – finding myself wanting to do the most inappropriate thing at particularly sombre moments; I can't even see a church without wanting to shout an obscenity. I find myself wondering what George would be doing on a Saturday morning. I picture him sitting on a sofa, flicking through the weekend broadsheets, but this is not really George; this is something Alexander would do, is probably doing, committed as he is to carrying on with his life as if nothing has happened. My leg gets an itch. I try to ignore it but it yells at me urgently. I wiggle around trying to find a more comfortable position but doing so seems to make the itch worse as well as draw the attention of the people around me. Then I want to pee – does nobody else need to pee? I cave and get up, avoiding Tashi's gaze as I creep out backwards.

Sunbeam is in the reception. 'Is everything OK?' she asks.

'Just need a water break,' I say. Sunbeam gives me another of her bows, as if she's blessing the emptying of my bladder. I examine her properly. Her face is dramatically and irreversibly sun-damaged. Her long hair, naturally highlighted with white streaks, is starting to dreadlock in the lower half. It's difficult to tell if this is intentional or the result of chronic mismanagement. If I saw her on the high street outside a Tesco Metro, for example, I would think she was deeply troubled. I would assume she was a woman rejected by a society insensitive to the needs of the traumatized or addicted; but here she looks very serene. Trite as the word seems, she appears happy.

'Can I ask you something?' I ask her.

'Of course,' she says.

'Why are you here?'

Sunbeam doesn't miss a beat. 'I'm here to welcome new followers and help them commit to their path.'

'Yeah, sure,' I say, frustrated at what I see as her avoidance of my enquiry, 'but how did you end up here; what was your life like before?'

Sunbeam laughs. I know she's not laughing at me; she's amused by a previous iteration of herself. 'I had a life,' she says, 'of sorts. By anyone's standards, I was successful.'

'What do you mean?' I ask.

'House, husband, friends . . .' Sunbeam waves her hand dismissively, as if these things are mere trinkets on the charm bracelet of life.

'And you gave it up?' I ask. 'For this?'

Sunbeam pauses. She looks up at the ceiling, searching for the right words there. 'I was playing a game,' she says, 'and I didn't know the rules; no one did. My husband, the one I had dedicated my life to, given up almost everything for, just left me. No word, no explanation. I realized that nothing in life is guaranteed; everything is so transient. What Larry and the group showed me is the only thing you can rely on is the present. You can never hope for more than this moment.' She clasps my two hands in hers. 'This very moment.'

'How long does it go on for?' I ask.

'Who knows? Time is a man-made structure. A moment could be a lifetime, if we wish it.'

I pull my hands away and try not to look afraid. 'No, I mean how long is the meditation?'

'We meditate for the morning,' says Sunbeam. She offers this as if it's a gift. I feel like a ten-year-old who's just found a book voucher under the Christmas tree.

'What's the morning?' I ask.

'Around three hours.'

'Right . . . OK . . . And how long have we been going?'

Sunbeam looks at her wristwatch. 'Nineteen minutes.'

'I feel really uncomfortable,' I say. 'It's a bit hot in here – are you hot?'

'The growth is in the discomfort,' says Sunbeam. 'We all live in a personal hell. Enduring this is the key to your awakening.'

I don't want to endure a single second more of discomfort. I hastily scribble an apology note for Tashi and tell Sunbeam to book me a cab. I don't leave her side until she confirms that it's on its way. I'm getting the hell out of hell but not before getting my phone back.

13

'YOU'RE BACK EARLY,' says Mum as I fall on to the sofa.

'I got let out for good behaviour,' I say.

'I don't understand,' says Mum angrily; she hates feeling like someone is getting something over on her. I start to describe the weekend's events but Mum has already started busying herself packing Moses's change bag, so I stop talking.

Moses comes over to me waving a plastic horse. I pull him on to my lap and make the horse dance up and down his leg, causing him to laugh uncontrollably. 'You might as well come with us to Stanmer Park,' says Mum. I don't really want to – I've just endured a cab, a train and a bus back from the middle of nowhere – I want to have a bath and some recovery time from my so-called retreat, but this isn't an option; Mum is giving me her 'dare to defy me' face and Moses is bouncing like a spaniel that's just heard the word 'walkies'. Before we leave I stop to coat my lips in red. 'Who's that for?' says Mum.

'For me,' I say.

Stanmer Park is just a few miles outside town but it feels like a different world. I have always intended to take Moses but other things seemed to come up. On the journey Moses waves his horse enthusiastically as Mum tells me what he's been up to. She insists that he knows his colours on the basis that she asked him to pick out red socks that morning and he did. I tell her that he just loves red socks. 'He is my child, you know. I know what he can and can't do.'

'Yes,' says Mum, 'but you've been distracted lately. I think he's benefited from the consistency of being with me.'

'I've been distracted by the breakdown of my marriage, Mum,' I say. Mum snorts incredulously; I'm not sure what part of my claim this is in reference to.

Mum pulls up outside Stanmer House, the stately home in the centre of the park. I love old buildings like this; I'm always fascinated by the idea people once actually lived here – that we are taking a casual Saturday stroll through what was someone's life. As I take Moses out of his car seat he makes little whinnying noises, and the simple pleasure he takes in this makes me feel a burst of joy that I had a part in creating him. 'I love you,' I say. He whinnies in response.

'We better get him to those horses before he explodes,' says Mum. We walk together through a wooded pathway, stopping regularly for Moses to pick up a stone and examine it before throwing it back to the ground.

'You used to like coming here when you were a kid,' says Mum.

'Yeah,' I say.

'You used to like playing hide and seek. You'd put your hands over your eyes and think no one could see you.'

'Fancy a game now?' I ask, smiling at her.

She looks at me and frowns. 'Why didn't you wear a coat?' she says.

When we reach the horses, it's clear that the fantasy has

not lived up to the reality for Moses and he quickly becomes restless. I try to engage him by holding him up to the fence to get a closer look at a white mare but he just wriggles furiously until I put him down; even the horse seems to be looking at me in a way that says, 'Nice try, love.'

'He enjoyed it last week,' says Mum. The mare sticks her nose over the fence and starts to sniff in my direction. I want to pet her but I can't remember how you should approach a horse; I recall something about a flat palm but nothing else. The horse sticks her tongue out and I quickly step back. She tips her head to the side, which, if there is one, I decide is the equine equivalent of a shrug, and then she backs up a little before galloping across the field. I look down, where Mum is crouched beside Moses, showing him a ladybird.

'Let's go get a scone,' I say. Mum looks up at me and rolls her eyes but she doesn't protest as I start to walk back towards the house.

We are seated at a table next to an amazing open fire. I order a scone and a slice of carrot cake for Moses and me, while Mum has an espresso. After it all arrives Mum says, 'Are you going to tell me what happened with you and Alexander?'

'Nothing happened, Mum. We got married, it didn't work out, we broke up.'

'Do you think he had someone else?' she said. Oddly this comment doesn't upset me but it offends me. It doesn't occur to her that it could have been me that had someone else, that I could have been the desirable one.

'There was no one else involved, Mum.'

'You don't know, though,' says Mum, 'men can be very

sneaky.' I think about Dad shining his shoes at exactly ten o'clock every evening.

'I think you young people give up too easily; as soon as it gets tough you're looking elsewhere,' says Mum as she brushes cake crumbs from around Moses's mouth. When she has finished, I give him another piece.

'I don't know why you're so bothered,' I say, 'you never even liked Alexander.' She doesn't correct me.

'If you had listened to me and delayed the wedding I think things would have been different,' says Mum.

To my mind the wedding was not rushed. I had been wanting it since the day we met, or perhaps the day after; Alexander had not been as sure. He had told me more than once that marriage was an institution and he was not ready to be committed to one. His escaped engagement was a sign, he felt, that marriage was not the right choice for him. I would have been happy with that, to be together but not shackled together, for an eternity. I had made the decision to be happy with that and then I got pregnant.

I knew I wanted children and Alexander had not resisted the idea. Our discussions about a family were always cut short by him making a vague statement about the right time. I think on some level I feared that that time would never come and this was probably why I took such a cavalier attitude to contraception. When the two lines appeared, it felt like a magic trick. I kept closing my eyes and thinking that when I reopened them the test would say something different. I carried the pee-soaked stick through to Alexander in his office. He stared at it for several seconds before saying, 'I'll do whatever you want.' What I wanted was to get married. Never in my life had I described myself as a traditionalist but I was a sucker; I had been sold a lie of fairy tales and Barbie princesses and I wanted my turn. It was the first time in our relationship that I had been insistent on anything and I think it may have been this, rather than the pregnancy or the marriage, that caused Alexander such concern.

I went about choosing invitations and planning guest lists, unperturbed by the anxieties he voiced. One evening I asked him to help me pick colours and it seemed he had reached his limit; he told me he didn't care, he didn't even want to care and he was going out to meet Matt. Matt is the man that every woman loves until he is friends with her partner – good-looking, charismatic and unnecessarily wealthy. The only thing matching the size of his bank balance is his ego. Matt and Alexander went to school together and appeared to have retained a childish sense of rivalry from their youth; they were always pushing each other to go faster and further, and more than once it resulted in physical or emotional injury. The first time I met Matt we were two champagne bottles into the evening when he began telling me that he could have any girl he wanted because he had the cash and connections to meet any woman's needs.

'What do you want?' he asked. 'I can get you anything.' My mind battled to come up with something suitably cool to ask for. 'I can have coke here in twenty minutes,' he suggested. I didn't want cocaine but I said yes just to see if he could actually come through, and he did. An hour later, when half of the supply had been 'tested' by the boys, Matt leaned across our small table and said, 'If Al ever fucks up, I've got a seat for you right here.' He indicated his lap. I turned to Alexander to see how he was reacting, what he might say or do to defend my honour; I'm not sure I had ever seen him look so pleased.

The night that Alexander left me at home with my aqua-marine napkins he was anything but pleased. I don't know where he went that evening because I did not hear from him or see him until three the following afternoon. I was lying on the sofa, queasy from hormones and worry, and he knelt on the floor beside me.

'OK,' he said. 'I'll marry you. If you think it best, I'll marry you. Just let's do it without all the crap. Let's do it the way we want it.' The next day he gave me Jenna's emerald and I booked the soonest available wedding date at the town hall.

It wasn't perfect but it doesn't put me off it all; if anything my previous failure has reinvigorated me – how many chances do you get for a do-over of one of life's key events? As soon as I have disposed of this marriage, I want to get married again but I want to do it the right way, with the right man. I look up at the six-foot fireplace and imagine it covered in peonies. I decide that I want to be married right here with someone who knows, to their very core, that marrying me is the right thing for them.

'Excuse me,' I say to Mum. I go to the ladies' toilets, lock myself in a cubicle and pull out my phone.

Marthashotbod: Do you want to get married?
Undeterred83: To you? :)
Marthashotbod: :) Generally.
Undeterred83: Yes. Definitely.
Marthashotbod: I'm spending the afternoon with my son. Do you want kids?
Undeterred83: That's brilliant. I really want kids.
Marthashotbod: Why haven't you had them already, if that's not too forward?
Undeterred83: It's not at all. Can I call you later? I would

rather tell you over the phone and anyway I think it's about time we spoke, don't you? What's your number?

I type the digits into the screen with unsteady fingers. Suddenly I'm nervous. Within the next few hours my list will start to become my reality.

14

MUM TELLS ME she needs to go to Waitrose on the way home. I cannot endure a turn round the supermarket with my mother right now; there's a legitimate chance I might brain her with a frozen leg of lamb. In the carpark, she asks me to fetch a trolley and as I do I call Cara.

'Can we meet?' I ask.

'Sure,' she says.

'When are you free?'

'It depends what you need,' Cara says.

'I need to get pissed,' I say.

'Meet me in Neighbourhood in twenty,' she says. I push the trolley over to Mum and she sets about strapping Moses in.

'I forgot there's something I have to do,' I tell her. She doesn't respond. 'I could take Mosey with me but . . .'

'It's fine, you go,' says Mum. 'He'll be ready for a snack soon anyway. I'll see you at home.' I don't wait for her to change her mind. I practically run to Neighbourhood, a small bar squeezed in between the charity shops on the high street. Cara and a strongly mixed drink are waiting for me.

*

'What's the update on A-hole?' says Cara. I take a swig of my drink.

'Well, first of all, we don't call him that because we're doing a thing called respect and focusing on productive co-parenting,' I say. Cara does the face you make when someone farts.

'I've heard about this co-parenting – isn't it where you don't think about yourself all the fucking time? How's A . . . sorry, it's Alex*ander* right? How's he getting on with that?'

'It's an adjustment,' I say, 'but I'm hopeful. We've agreed the days he'll have Moses and how we'll do the exchange. He's being reasonable.' I don't tell Cara that these arrangements were made over a series of sinisterly formal text messages and that Alexander has engineered things so that he always collects and delivers Moses to nursery and there is no risk of us having actual, human contact.

'Hmm,' says Cara, 'so he's getting his dick wet.'

'That's not relevant,' I say, as I push unwanted images from my mind.

'It's totally relevant,' says Cara. 'Speaking of which, how are you getting on with Linger?' I have a short debate in my head. Just say it, I tell myself, say you've found the man of your dreams and you're working towards becoming the best version of yourself so that you can meet him and fall in love and live your days out together like that couple in *The Notebook*.

'I'm a bit confused by how it works; do you have to swipe right to get a match?'

'Aren't you the one with the degree?' asks Cara. 'It could not be simpler: right for the treasure, left for the trash.'

'But it's random. You can't just get sent a match, based on your profile or something?'

'Give it here,' says Cara, reaching for my phone.

'No, no, it's fine!' I say, snatching it out of reach. 'I'm probably just not ready for it.'

Cara rolls her eyes. 'You don't have to be ready for it, it's not a German invasion. It's not like you have to marry the guy.'

I sip my drink. 'Cara,' I ask, 'have you ever been in love?'

'Sure,' she says, 'I fall in love once a week. I'm in love with the guy that made this drink. I *am* fucking love.'

'But you know,' I say, 'love, love. Can't-live-without-you love.'

Cara examines me carefully. 'Why on earth would I want to put myself in a situation where I can't live without someone?'

'Because it feels good,' I say.

'It feels good to feel like your very existence is tied up in someone else's regard for you?' She doesn't sound like she's judging me; she sounds like she genuinely wants to understand. I don't know how to explain it – it does feel good; even the lows feel good because the lows are proof that the highs are real.

Cara leans in towards me. 'You know what feels good? Knowing that your happiness is a product of nothing but your own damn awesomeness.' Her eyes are intense. I try to turn my head away from their glare but Cara gently pulls my face back towards her. 'When you get,' she says, and I have never heard her sound so serious, 'that no man or child or beast or fucking face cream will make you feel like enough; that being you is enough. That feels really bloody good.'

My throat starts to get hot. 'It's not that I want a man to make me feel good, it's that . . . I don't know . . .'

'You want a man to make you feel good?' suggests Cara and we both laugh.

113

I throw my hands up and say, 'Is that so bad?!'

'It's not bad,' says Cara, 'it's just too easy.' She reaches out and stops a man walking past our table. 'Would you like to have sex with my friend?' she says.

I say, 'Sorry,' at the same time as the guy says, 'Yeah, all right then!'

Cara turns to me. 'You see? Where was the creativity, the hustle, the magic?' The man clears his throat and Cara turns back to him. 'Did you want something?'

'Err, no,' he says before walking away.

'I believe in magic,' I say. I touch my phone before I realize what I'm doing. Cara downs the rest of her drink.

'Oh God, I can't believe you're gonna make me go all Oprah on you. You *know* how much I hate that shit.'

'What do you mean?' I ask.

She sighs. 'What have you done for *you* since the break-up?'

'Loads,' I say. I tick the points off on my fingers. 'I've signed up for a half-marathon, I've just come back from a retreat . . .' Cara makes a face like she ate something rotten. 'Also, I've got a business coach.' I try not to smile too widely but I do seem to be on a bit of a roll.

'For what business?' asks Cara.

'The one I'm starting,' I say.

'Why are you starting a business? I thought you wanted to be a singer?'

'Yes, but I'm not sure how practical that is. I mean, singing would be great but I don't have any access to that world; this way I can build the life I want.' As I'm talking Cara raises her arm in the air and holds a peace sign above her head. When I see the barman spring into action behind her I realize she's ordering us fresh drinks.

'I'm an events organizer, babe; if you want a link into

114

performing, I'll get you one. I haven't before because I thought you were kinda committed to the old married lady vibe.' Cara starts to look through the contacts on her phone.

I wave my hand no. 'It's OK—'

'I'm gonna send you to Marc,' says Cara. 'He'll look after you – besides, he owes me.'

'The thing is I'm not sure it's what I want . . .' The barman places two tall rum and ginger ales in front of us.

'Thanks, darling,' says Cara, and then she says to me, 'If it's not what you want, sack it off. You've had some practice at that recently.' I'd like to be enthusiastic but singing means travel and late nights, something that's tough to do as a single parent, and more to the point not the best plan when you're about to meet the love of your life.

I try to distract Cara: 'What's going on with you, anyway, what are you working on?'

'Don't try to distract me,' says Cara, still fiddling with her phone. 'There, I've sent Marc your details, I've told him you're kinda funky, kinda jazzy, kinda rocky cause I wouldn't know.' She swallows half her drink. 'I'm good, thanks for asking. I've not picked up any new projects 'cause I'm going abroad for a bit, see if I can get anything going in Stockholm.'

'Why?' I say.

'I've always preferred the cold and would you believe I've never been with a blond?' Cara says.

'No, I mean why are you going away and how? I mean, how can you afford it?' I ask.

'Because why not, Martha. You need to start asking yourself that more. I've got some savings but I'll probably rent out my place – actually I was going to give you first refusal.'

'Wow,' I say, 'I don't know—'

'I'll take down the pole,' says Cara.

'No, it's not that, it's just . . . I hadn't thought about where I'm gonna live or anything like that,' I say. Thinking about it now feels like turbulence on a plane; sort of exciting but also like you're possibly going to die.

'Course, I'm sure you've had more important things to think about.' As if in answer to the question my phone rings.

'I'm sorry, I have to take this,' I say.

'No probs,' says Cara, 'gotta see a man about a dog anyway.' Cara leans over and gives me a quick kiss on the cheek before dropping a twenty-pound note on to the table and sliding out of her chair. I make sure she's out of earshot before I take his call.

15

'HELLO?'

'Hey,' says George. 'How you doing?' I had expected his voice to be faint, distorted and eroded by distance but it's strong and clear and very sexy – he could do voiceovers for luxury car adverts.

'I'm good,' I say. 'Thanks for calling. Does it feel weird?'

'A little,' he says, and he sounds relieved, 'but in another way not weird at all.' It's what I've been waiting for my whole life, someone who knows exactly the words to make everything OK.

'Where are you?' I ask.

'It's gonna sound crazy but I'm sitting overlooking a waterfall.'

'Wow,' I say.

'Yeah,' says George, 'it's pretty amazing but it would be better to share it with someone.' I feel my face grow warm. 'What you been up to, you've been quiet.'

'I was on my meditation retreat,' I say.

'Cool,' says George. 'The ten-day silent retreat I did was intense. I learned a lot about myself though.'

I think about telling Guido where to go and say, 'Yeah, me too.'

117

'I can't believe how much we have in common,' says George.

'I know,' I say. 'It's like—'

'Fate.'

'Or something.' We are silent for a few seconds.

Finally, George says, 'How was your day with the boy?'

'Boy?'

'Your son.'

'Oh, of course,' I say. 'It was great.' I tell him a little bit about Moses, about how funny and crazy he is. George makes appropriate noises in response, noises that Alexander couldn't even muster up.

'What did you want to talk to me about?' I ask when I've finished.

'Oh, the children thing; a message seemed a bit impersonal.'

'That's OK,' I say.

'I was engaged a few years ago. We wanted to have children.' And here it is: after all the messages and all the longing, he's going to tell me that he's scared of commitment because he had his heart broken by some tramp. 'She died,' he says.

'Oh,' I say, 'I'm sorry . . . How?'

'She was sick,' he says. 'I knew when I met her but I was hopeful.'

'That's so sad,' I say. In fact, it's tragic. 'Thanks for telling me.'

'It's OK,' says George. 'I wanted to. You know, talking to you I feel so much less alone.'

'I know,' I say, 'it's weird.' I'm annoyed I've said 'weird' again; I'm no poet but my vocabulary is more developed than that. 'I'm sorry,' I say. 'I'm a little tongue-tied – you make me feel like I'm a teenager or something.'

'I couldn't have put it better,' he says. 'I feel like I'm about sixteen but that's the way I want this to feel.' He doesn't define 'this' because he doesn't have to. We both know what 'this' is; this is the start of our story. 'It kinda feels like our first date,' he says.

'A waterfall is quite an impressive first date destination,' I say. 'How will you top it with our second?'

'Where would you like me to take you?' he asks.

'Well, if I get a free choice, The Salt Room,' I say. The Salt Room is a beautiful restaurant on the seafront. I had dropped hints for Alexander to take me there for months and when the hints did not prove effective, I simply begged. He said it sounded pretentious, which is not something he had ever seemed to have a problem with before.

'I can do better than that,' says George. 'How about Paris?'

I don't like France. I know that's a ridiculous statement, like those people who say, 'I don't like music,' as if music is a singular thing. I know that France is a tapestry of people, cultures and climates but I have been several times and on each occasion I've felt as if everything – the people, the food, the architecture – was silently judging me. I like that George has chosen Paris, though, because of what it represents; nothing says 'I choose you' more than a stroll along the Seine.

'I could deal with Paris,' I say, and George laughs. I love the feeling of making him laugh.

'So, we've been to a waterfall and to Paris – what next?'

'A walk along the beach, obviously,' I say.

This is the sort of thing I would suggest to Alexander from time to time, lightly; very, very casually. He would snort as if I had made a wry joke. Once I described to him how a colleague's boyfriend had sent her a huge bouquet of long-stemmed roses to the office, with a note that read, 'Because it's Tuesday.' Alexander, who was watching *Top Gear* at the time, did not remove his eyes from the screen as he said, 'I'm so glad we aren't one of those couples that go in for all that obvious stuff.' It's not that there was no romance in our relationship, it's just that, as Alexander said, it wasn't obvious – you had to seek it out; you had to remain aware at all times, or risk missing it.

George says a walk on the beach sounds perfect, so I leave the rest of my drink and Cara's money on the table and walk down to the seafront.

'It's cold,' I say.

'We better get coffee then,' says George. He's quiet as I buy an instant coffee in a plastic cup from a hatch on the seafront. I settle on to the pebbles to drink it.

'This is romantic,' I say.

'It sort of is,' says George. 'I'm supposed to ask you about your hopes and fears now, right?'

'Oh God, no,' I say. 'Don't kill my buzz.'

George laughs. 'But seriously,' he says, 'what do you want?' The question shouldn't be as complicated as it is but I've spent so long denying or ignoring what I want that I struggle to find a definitive answer.

'I want to stop running,' I say. 'I feel like I've lived every day of my life waiting for it to begin.'

'I know how you feel,' says George. 'I felt the same way until Cass died. Then I realized that what I was running to or from probably didn't matter.'

'Is it time to stop running then?' I ask.

'I think it is,' he says.

'I'm really cold now,' I say.

'OK, I'll let you go,' says George.

'No, no,' I say. 'Walk with me.'

'OK.'

I get up and start to stumble across the pebbles. 'I'm walking towards the pier,' I say. 'Did you know Brighton Pier was erected in 1903?'

George laughs. 'Was it?'

'I have no idea,' I say.

'Tell me the real story,' says George, 'your story.'

'All right,' I say. 'I had my first snog under the pier; it was with a boy called Tyler. He lived in a caravan.'

'He lived in a caravan? How old was he?'

'With his dad!' I say. As I walk under the pier the smell of stale urine takes me back to the moment, the highlight of one of those endless summers of childhood. I tell George all my pier stories: Leanne and I trying our first cigarettes followed by her vomiting violently; a guy I once met and spent the afternoon with, who told me about all the adventures he had had, and only years later did I realize he had been homeless.

'Where are you now?' asks George.

'I'm walking in front of OhSo, it's my favourite bar.' OhSo is right on the beach, and in the evenings they set up environmentally evil heaters. When I drink there I always forget to go home.

'I love it there too,' says George. 'I can't wait to take you.'

I smile. 'I'm smiling,' I tell him.

'Me too,' he says.

We walk the length of the beach. It's dark by the time I get to the end and I realize I'm going to need to take a bus home.

'I should go,' I say, as I make my way back up to the road.

'I hate shoulds,' says George.

'Me too, but this is a real one,' I say.

'Thanks for a lovely date,' says George.

'Thank you.'

'I think this is where I kiss you,' says George.

'It absolutely is,' I say. We end the call. My fingers are so cold I can barely work the buttons on my phone but inside I'm burning up. That was the best date of my life and he wasn't even with me; I can't help but imagine how good it will be when he is.

'What have you been up to?' says Mum as I walk into the living room with a smile still plastered on my face.

'Walking,' I say.

'You've been drinking,' she says, narrowing her eyes, 'your face is all red.'

'No, I've just been walking.' I sit down beside her on the sofa. Mum shifts as if to make space for me, although there is plenty.

'Moses is in bed,' she says. 'You've missed him.' It's early still; I imagine her drugging him to prove a point.

'I'll see him in the morning,' I say. I pick up the remote control and start to flick through the channels, although I can't really concentrate on what is on each one. Mum takes the remote from my hand and places it on the coffee table.

'Your dad and I are worried about you,' she says. I look at Dad in his chair; he looks like a dog caught with a chewed slipper.

'You don't have to be worried about me, I'm fine. I'm better than fine.'

'OK,' says Mum, 'we're worried about Moses.'

'Why?' I ask, elongating the word with practised insolence.

'You just seem to have, what do they call it, checked out. Motherhood is not a part-time thing.'

'I know that, Mother,' I say.

'Great. What are you planning to do about it?'

'What do you mean?'

'Well, you can start by getting up with him in the morning.' I *am* up in the morning but I hear her fussing around with him and I worry about being the extra cook that spoils the broth. I can tell Mum is preparing to unleash a full litany of my errors and I don't want to give her the satisfaction.

'I agree,' I say. 'I'm on it; in fact, we've got a lovely day planned tomorrow. I'm going to get ready for bed so we can start early.' Mum purses her lips; I feel a fizz of satisfaction at having sabotaged her intervention and leave before she can come up with a response.

I go up to my room and lie on the bed. The frustration I feel with my mother becomes wrapped in a layer of anger, like one of those turkeys stuffed in a duck. The anger is directed towards Alexander, or more specifically the question, what is his part in this parenting fail? Perhaps Mum is right – I should be spending more time with my son; but I also deserve a decent break, a break that should be given to me by his father. It has always been this way, as if Alexander was just an innocent bystander in the car crash of parenthood. I remember when Moses was little, I would do all the feeding and the burping and the bouncing whilst Alexander would just eye him suspiciously. If I asked him to do anything he would express complete incredulity. Sometimes he would offer that the baby was 'too small' for him to handle. Of course, if there were ever witnesses he would be chucking Moses around like a beach ball.

One evening, completely floored by the combination of

exhaustion and responsibility, I told Alexander I was taking a bath and asked him to watch Moses for an hour or two. Twenty minutes into my soak I felt like I was beginning to regain access to who I was before my labour and Alexander knocked on the door.

'Where do we keep his pyjamas?' he said. I heaved myself from the tub, dripping water through the flat as I got a fresh Babygro from the chest of drawers in the nursery. I can't believe I handed it to Alexander and didn't shove it down his throat. I think about ringing my ex and telling him I'm dropping off his son for a week but the thought of doing it makes me feel outraged on Moses's behalf. Alexander can disregard me if he wants to but my child should never feel anything but wanted. Instead I ring Greg.

'Hey, buddy!'

'Are you doing anything fun with the girls tomorrow?' I ask.

'Yeah, we're going to the zoo. Wanna come?'

'Yes please, we'd love to.'

'That's great,' says Greg. 'Have you got a car seat? We'll pick you up.'

I give Greg our address and he says he'll be with us at ten. Moses needs two parents, and if necessary I'll parent for two.

16

GREG HONKS HIS horn at precisely ten. I tell Mum to watch Moses for a second whilst I run out with the car seat. Greg gets out of the car to meet me. We haven't seen each other outside the office before and it feels slightly wrong; I don't know how to greet him. I lean in to give him a kiss on the cheek and, at the same time, he tries to give me a hug; immediately I try to convert my kiss to a hug and he tries to redesign his hug into a kiss. We untangle and smile at each other stupidly.

'Need help with that?' asks Greg. He nods to the car seat on the pavement.

'Nah, it's tricksy,' I say. I open the car door and heave the seat inside. Greg's two daughters stare at me as I do so.

'Hi,' I say, 'I'm Martha.' They remain silent. I strap the seatbelt into the car seat but I struggle to latch the belt into the clip.

After watching me grapple with it for some time, the bigger of the girls says, 'You're doing it wrong.' She takes the belt and smoothly clips it in.

'Thanks,' I say. She returns to silence.

Mum carries Moses out. 'Have you got extra clothes in the bag?' she asks.

'Of course, Mum,' I say. Greg extends his hand; Mum hands Moses and the change bag to me before shaking it.

'Lovely to meet you,' Greg says.

'Hello,' says Mum. She has this ridiculous coquettish look on her face. Mum thinks every man is a heartbeat away from falling in love with her.

'Let's move!' I shout. I bundle Moses into his seat. He chuckles at the girls who, unable to resist his charm, laugh back at him. Greg tells Mum to have a nice day and climbs back into the driver's seat. As I go to get in myself, Mum gives me an awkward and unaccustomed hug.

'Have a lovely day,' she says. 'If he likes it maybe we can go next week?'

'Sure,' I say.

In the car I clap my hands together. 'Where are we going!' I cry. No one says anything. 'To the zoo!' I answer myself.

Greg laughs and pulls away. 'The zoo it is,' he says.

Greg introduces me to the girls. 'This is Charlotte and Lyra,' he says. They don't say anything. He makes pleading faces at them in the rear-view mirror but they won't concede. 'They're shy,' he says. I twist round in my seat to look at them. They don't look shy, they look mean. 'Charlotte just lost a tooth so she's self-conscious,' says Greg. Charlotte folds her arms and breathes out heavily. I can tell she is furious at her father's indiscretion; I fear for her future partners.

'Ugh, is it sore?' I ask. She looks at me but doesn't respond. 'You know what helps with that,' I say. She doesn't speak but I sense a slight shift in her energy. 'Singing.' I turn up the radio and Taylor Swift's 'Shake It Off' fills the car. 'The bakers gotta bake, bake, bake, bake, bake,' I sing.

'Noooooo!' squeals Charlotte. 'That's not how it goes.' She is smiling broadly now and I can see the space where her front tooth used to be.

'Oh no, how does it go?'

Charlotte sings along with Taylor. Her sister joins in for the last part of the chorus. I love watching them express themselves so freely and joyously. Moses tries to join in, clapping and wiggling from side to side. I look over at Greg and he looks back at me for a second and winks.

Even though it's drizzly the zoo is quite crowded. By the time we get to the front of the queue the kids are fractious and eager to get on with it. Greg chats to the guy at the ticket booth for a couple of minutes and then waves us through. 'How much do I owe you?' I say.

'It's OK, I had a voucher,' says Greg. 'What first, girls?'

'The monkeys!' they shout in unison.

It's only when we're standing in front of the primate enclosure that I remember that sometimes zoos depress me. They're so sad. I imagine the animals all knowing that their peers are somewhere living it up in the jungle or wherever. I find the attempt to recreate their natural habitat the most upsetting part. The concrete rocks can't compare to anything in the great outdoors; it kinda makes me think they should just give up and go in a completely different direction – base the enclosure on a New York cityscape or something. The girls press their noses up against the glass, and the apes look back at them with very human expressions of tedium.

'They're not monkeying,' says Lyra. She thrusts her bottom lip out and looks to her father. Oh, how I miss those days, when I still held the belief that my dad could fix anything.

'Oh no,' says Greg, 'do you think they've forgotten how to monkey?' Lyra nods sadly. 'I better show them then,' he says. Greg takes on an ape-like stance and starts to side-step along the glass, scratching his head and his armpits and making monkey noises. Lyra begins to giggle. Greg exaggerates his actions further, pretending to sniff other families and beating his chest. Both girls and Moses are in hysterics.

Lyra looks up and points. 'Look, Daddy, you showed him how to monkey!' A large ape is swinging down from a branch at a pace that its size belies. Once on the ground it picks up even more speed, charging towards us with bared teeth. When it reaches the spot where Greg is putting on his show, the ape stretches up to full height and bangs on the glass. The girls both jump back, and the crowd takes in a collective breath.

'Hmm,' says Greg, 'maybe he's not in the mood for a lesson today.' He gathers up one girl in each arm. 'Shall we go, ladies?' The girls nod yes. 'Good day to you,' says Greg to the ape before leaving the enclosure. Once outside we all look at each other and dissolve into laughter.

'Remember when the monkey ran, Daddy?' asks Lyra.

'Yes, princess,' says Greg, before giving her a kiss on the forehead. He then crouches down so that he is eye to eye with Moses and says, 'I think you should choose what's next, buddy.'

Moses throws his hands up in the air and says, 'Fish!'

'The master has spoken,' says Greg.

The aquarium houses not only fish but also a collection of intimidating-looking lizards and snakes, which the girls take turns pushing each other towards while squealing. 'They're pretty rad kids,' I say to Greg as we watch them.

'Aren't they,' says Greg. 'They're the best thing I've ever done.' I feel like if anyone else had said this it would sound cheesy but he really means it.

'It's hard being a single parent, though?' I ask.

'It gets better,' says Greg. 'You'll be OK.'

'How do you know? I . . . I mean, what makes you think I need to be OK?' I think I ask this a little too aggressively because Greg holds his palms up in a gesture of surrender before speaking.

'You've just been out of sorts lately and then the change in shifts and the whole retreat thing and picking you up at your mum's. I assumed . . .'

I almost tell him to mind his own business but I look at how much fun Moses is having chasing the girls round a pillar and I say, 'It's shit, isn't it.'

'It's the worst kind of shit,' says Greg, 'but then it's a little less shit and then it's even less shit than that and then one day you wake up and realize it's only slightly shit.'

'A soupçon of shit,' I say.

'Just a light smattering of shit,' says Greg, and we smile at each other. The girls run over to us, with Moses following, and proclaim abject boredom.

'Ready for some grub?' says Greg to cheers all round.

The restaurant has an animal theme and a menu of basic foods with exotic names – crazy cobra chocolate cake and lion's tail pasta. Greg tells the girls to pick a sandwich each but they have already caught the scent of chips and make it clear that they are unwilling to compromise.

'Come on, girls,' says Greg. 'We've had a lovely day, let's not ruin it. We had chips yesterday and chips aren't a healthy food.' I recognize his voice as a 'parenting in public' one. To many people it might sound like a calm, reassuring tone but other parents can detect the slightly sinister edge to it. Sadly, Charlotte and Lyra don't. Lyra starts to wail and Charlotte begins kicking a wall with a surprising amount of ferocity.

Greg starts to blush. 'If you keep behaving like this we will have to go home and you will not like that and it won't be fair on Moses,' he says. I look at Moses; having forgotten his buggy he has done more walking than he's ever done in his life and he looks like he'd be well up for going home, but I don't say anything. 'Girls, I mean it,' he says.

I step forward and place my hand on Charlotte's shoulder. She stops kicking the wall and I think for a second she's going to redirect her aim at me but she simply looks at me. Her sister stops crying and does the same.

'Your dad's right,' I say, 'chips aren't healthy. So if you want them you have to eat something healthy with them to balance it. How's this for a deal? If you want chips, you have to have a serving of vegetables first, a big one.' The girls both tip their heads to the side to ponder my offer. I steal a glance at Greg; I'm worried he might be offended at my heavy-handedness but he looks as if he might kiss me.

After a couple of minutes of deliberation and several rounds of eeny meeny, Lyra decides to play it safe with a ham sandwich and Charlotte chooses chips along with a serving of broccoli. We find some seats and settle down to eat. Charlotte immediately starts shovelling broccoli into her mouth, eager to get to the main attraction. Greg tells her to slow down but she shoots him a look that makes clear that eating slowly was not in the contract.

'When we've finished this, I've got a great idea about what we should do,' I say.

'What?!' shouts Lyra.

'Go and watch the penguins have *their* lunch!'

Lyra cheers and her sister nods, her mouth still filled with greenery. Greg reaches a fist across the table and I give it a little bump with my own.

The penguin enclosure is quite a walk from the cafe so Greg offers to put Moses on his shoulders. Moses finds this to be the most exciting thing that's happened all day and I wonder if taking toddlers on day trips is a waste of time and effort. When we reach the pool I lead the way to the best spot, a small ledge on the far side, from where you can see every angle. I remember my dad bringing me here when I was a kid and sitting with him for hours watching the birds. Every now and then he would say, 'You ready to go, love?' And I would usually say no and we would sit in silence for another twenty minutes. When I was around twelve my mum adopted a penguin in my name, which I think meant I had my name on the wall somewhere and I paid for his fish for the year, but by that time I was kinda over penguins, so I never went to visit him.

The zookeeper is telling us about how penguins hunt in their natural habitat. 'This bit's rubbish,' I whisper to Charlotte. She wrinkles her nose with pleasure at an adult saying something naughty. The zookeeper picks up her bucket and the penguins all do their little Charlie Chaplin waddle over to her. She then starts to throw the fish into the water and they dive after them. I remember why I loved the penguins so much; on land they seem silly and ungainly but then they hit the water and they're so agile and grace-ful you realize you were wrong to laugh at them, because underneath it all, they're badass.

Lyra tugs at my hand. 'I can't see,' she says. I put my hands under her armpits and haul her on to my hip. There, she wraps her legs around me and nuzzles her head into my shoulder.

After the penguins, we decide to call it a day. Greg carries Moses back to the car and Charlotte and Lyra each hold one of my hands. On the drive back the kids all fall asleep so Greg and I sit in silence so as not to wake them. I watch him drive, shifting smoothly between gears and lanes; it feels nice to be with someone so in control. As I watch Greg's broad, smooth hands work the steering wheel I am reminded of the phrase 'a safe pair of hands'. I think with Alexander I just wanted to feel safe. Not feeling safe is exhausting. I message George.

Marthashotbod: I miss you.

My phone rings out an alert when he replies and I whisper, 'Sorry,' to Greg.

Undeterred83: I miss you more.

17

LEANNE KNOCKS ON Mum's door at 7 a.m., a plan that I felt so positive about the night before but now every cell of my body is rejecting. I try to lure her in with coffee but she won't be distracted; she stays bouncing up and down on the doorstep, her bobbing ponytail exhibiting more enthusiasm than I can muster. 'Have you got those endorphins I keep hearing about?' I ask as I shrug into my hoodie.

'Honestly, babe, it feels like shit for a bit but then there's this point you just break through and get this rush.' She stops bouncing and pulls her left foot up to her bum, and then repeats the move with the other leg.

'It sounds like losing your virginity,' I say.

'Only so much better,' says Leanne, returning to the bouncing.

'It'd better be better than that German exchange student slapping my arse like I'm a horse struggling up a hill,' I say.

'Exactly,' says Leanne. 'If you could pretend to enjoy that, this will be a piece of piss.'

It's not. By the time we get to the newsagent's round the corner, my shins feel like they're on fire. Leanne tries to tell me about warming up and lactic acid but I can't run and listen and breathe so I don't take it in. I think about stopping and getting a Cherryade and a packet of Flamin' Hot Cheetos from Mr Chaudry, the ever-present proprietor, but as Leanne pulls ahead it occurs to me that this experience is like so many others I have had. So many times I've had a goal or an opportunity and I've given it up before I've really got going; I've watched everyone else get ahead as I sat at home and ate Cheetos.

We reach the park and I think this seems like an apt juncture to turn back but Leanne is just getting started. 'We'll only do two laps of the park,' she says. 'At this stage it doesn't matter how fast you go, just don't stop moving.' Leanne sets off at a pace I would use to flee a pursuing assailant, and even if I wanted to try and stay with her I know it wouldn't be physically possible. Instead I move at a speed that isn't walking but could not truthfully be called running; it's a kind of trot and I'm sure it looks ridiculous. It doesn't feel completely ridiculous, though; it feels kind of good. I'm enveloped in a peculiar feeling, a kind of fizziness in my tummy, and it takes me a few minutes to recognize it for what it is: excitement. The second lap feels harder; the knowledge that I am only halfway through becomes a weight on my back. I repeat Leanne's words in my head – don't stop moving. This seems to help and I speak them quietly; then louder, the rhythm of the words matching my steps.

When I finish the lap, Leanne is sitting on the ground with her legs stretched out in front of her and her head bowed forward and resting comfortably on her knees. I fall on to the ground beside her, breathing heavily and trying to focus on the cartoonish, fluffy clouds above my head. Leanne sits up and looks down on me. She has a slightly troubled expression. 'How you doing?' she asks.

I close my eyes for a second and when I open them she's leaning in towards me. I give her a weak smile and say, 'I feel all right.'

Leanne springs up and holds out her hand. 'That'll do for me,' she says.

When I get home I can hear that the flurry of morning activity is well underway. I sit on the stairs and message George.

Marthashotbod: Just completed a few laps of St Ann's.
Undeterred83: I love running there.

This makes me decide I'm going to do it again tomorrow and it's the first time I feel grateful that I'm living with Mum and Dad. Moving back to your parents' in your thirties would be a soul-destroying experience were it not for all the free childcare. When I was in a partnership I thought single parenting would be nothing but toil and turmoil, but compared to the casual efforts at fatherhood made by Alexander on a day-to-day basis, and having Mum to get up with Moses, ferry him to nursery and make him nutritious meals, single parenting feels quite freeing.

It also means I've had no further encounters with my soon-to-be ex-husband. It's not that I don't want to see him; I do. At least, I think I do, but I want him to come to me. I want him to realize the colossal hole I have left in his life and seek me out. We've still managed to avoid contact with each other. He's collected Moses from nursery or I've asked Mum to drop him off. Mum always gives me a little description of Alexander after an encounter, however brief – he looks so tired; he's a broken man; he didn't say it but he misses you. That I believe, but I'm sure what he

135

misses most is the way I magically created clean, folded laundry from dirty clothes. My mother's continued advocacy for Alexander angers me no end; what happened to being on my side? Moses would have to murder several innocent strangers in cold blood before I would even think to utter anything that suggested that I was not completely on his team.

Mum comes into the hallway and pours some water into a flower arrangement on the sideboard. I think I may have let my frustrations with her show, that they may have seeped out, despite my best efforts, through the suspiciously loud crunch of toast or a smile held for just not long enough. I think this is why, as I sit on the stairs, clammy but triumphant, she casually informs me that she has landed me right in it.

'I've agreed to go and visit Mrs Jenson – you know, the lady that lived next door but one? Now she's in one of those wretched facilities. I mean, would you ever do that to me?' She stares at me as I pull off my trainers. When I look at her, it's clear she's waiting for me to respond.

'No, Mum.' She wrinkles her nose. Right answer but too late, so still wrong.

'She hasn't got anyone to see her there. I mean, she's got children and grandchildren, but the son is so cold; he was always giving me those stiff little waves. I've made her some of my famous banana cake.'

I rub my feet. I can already tell I'm going to get a blister on the back of my right heel. 'That's nice of you then, Mum.'

'Are you being sarcastic?' she says.

'No,' I say clearly, careful to ensure an even tone.

'Well, I can't tell with you. Everything sounds like you're taking the mickey. Some things in life are serious, you know.'

I stand up quickly and turn to go up the stairs as I say, 'That, I know.'

'Anyway,' she says. She speaks quickly, sensing she's losing me. 'You can't stay late at work as you'll have to be here when Alexander collects Moses. He said he'll keep him and take him to nursery in the morning.' I've already started up the stairs and it's as if my brain takes a few seconds to translate the sound to words. By the time I've understood I'm halfway up. I rush back down to the bottom, so that I'm eye to eye with my mother.

'Can't Dad watch Moses?'

'Don't be silly, he's driving me. What, do you think I'm going to drive there on my own?'

I want to shout, 'Yes, Mum, do something on your own, it might be good for you, you might learn something. Some of us don't have the choice!' Luckily, I'm exhausted by the exercise, or my circumstances, or both, and instead I say, 'You should have checked with me; I can't just tell them I'm not working late.'

'For God's sake, you've put in loads of hours there recently, don't they owe you? Anyway, you're one of the ones in charge – just give yourself some time off.'

I may have let my mother think I have more responsibility at my job than I do. I may have intimated to her that I manage some things and possibly some people. I've never said it outright, but I've never disabused her of any beliefs she may have had along these lines and now does not feel like the time for honesty. Mum takes my silence as acceptance, which I suppose it is.

I arrive in the office ten minutes early rather than with seconds to spare. The knowledge that I am going to be face to face with Alexander again has given me a burst of

137

adrenaline. I power walk from the bus stop, then become impatient waiting for the lift's slow descent and take the stairs, two at a time. When I reach my floor, I see Greg standing in the little square of carpet between flights. His eyes are trained on his phone and both of his thumbs are working across the screen. He is so engrossed in the task he doesn't seem to hear me coming and doesn't look up until I'm inches away from him. When he does he breaks into a smile and shoves his phone into his pocket. 'You shit the bed?' he asks.

'What?! No!' I say sharply. This day is stressful enough without my workmates accusing me of incontinence. Greg looks shocked and reaches out as if I might trip and he wants to be there to steady me.

'Sorry,' he says, 'just something my mum used to say. You're not usually early.'

'It's hardly early,' I snap. 'And it's not like I'm always late, not all the time anyway. And just because someone behaves one way for a long time, doesn't mean that that's how it's gonna be for ever, you know.' Greg withdraws his hands and opens his mouth but doesn't speak. He takes a step back and gestures towards the door, like a butler. I feel a prick of anxiety that I have treated Greg – who is always on time, always helpful, possibly (very sadly) the most reliable thing in my life – in such a derisory way, but I also feel completely justified. As a woman, as a mother, I'm expected to be soft and nurturing and agreeable all the time. Not any more.

I sit down at my desk. I've never been here with time to spare before and I feel a bit at a loss. I straighten up the stationery and give the grooves of my keyboard a quick excavation with the tip of a pen; as I'm doing so a mug slides into my peripheral vision. I look up and see Greg with a drink of his own and, even though I still feel a bit indignant, I offer him a closed-mouth smile. It's not just Greg I'm angry with; it's all men, every one that gets to wander about the earth basking in his own privilege, but especially Alexander. I want to know that he's as agitated by the thought of seeing me as I am of seeing him. I want to know that he is affected by me and not just inconvenienced. I deserve that.

On the inside of my handbag is a small pocket. I've never been clear what it's for. It's too small for my phone and until recently had served as a stray-gum-and-pennies receptacle. However, now it holds The List. I pull my bag up from its home next to my feet and smooth the list out on the desk in front of me. As I read I pause at 'long conversations'.

I think I've avoided looking at the fact that these guidelines, as well as being a representation of what I need, are a reminder of a lot of the things I didn't have. Alexander has always been conservative with his words. One day I told him about an article I had read which reported that the average woman says three times more than the average man on any given day, and he responded, 'OK.'

When I first knew him, I was naive enough to think this trait made him enigmatic and that his silence – as counter-intuitive as this may seem – was because he was *more* thoughtful than most. Once, not long after we had met but before we were a couple, I told Cara that we had an understanding that was unspoken. We were at a gig, so I had to shout a little. I told her that so much of what was said between us was in gestures and mirroring and just a connection that wasn't entirely understandable. Cara's face bunched up. I remember thinking she hadn't heard me and was going to ask me to repeat myself, so I leaned in and as

I did laughter exploded out of her like a misfiring machine gun. The people around us started to stare and I pulled her towards the side of the room to minimize my embarrassment. Even with my hand vice-like on her arm, she maintained a steady stream of mirth. Once at the side of the room, she managed to regain control of herself. She pushed her hair from her face and met my eyes. I looked at her steadily. I wanted her to know it hadn't been a joke, that just because she hadn't experienced it with anyone, it did not mean it wasn't real for me. She wiped a couple of stray tears from her eyes and patted me on the shoulder gently, like she was offering sympathy to a recently fired colleague. I never really forgave her for that but she was probably right; perhaps Alexander didn't share his thoughts with me because he had nothing to share, or worse, nothing he wanted me to hear. I won't make that mistake again.

'What's that?' I hear Greg say from beside me.

'Nothing,' I say, and quickly fold up the bit of paper.

'I've not got a lot of education but I know what nothing looks like,' he says. 'Is it a secret plan to kill us all?' He sits down in his chair and loads up his computer. 'Actually, don't tell me 'cause then I'll be forced to push the button.' I'm still a little annoyed with him but I can't resist biting.

'What button?' I ask.

'You know, the button you press when you find out people are doing something untoward. We did that training.'

I laugh. 'It's a whistle, Greg, you blow the whistle.'

'Yeah, but that's a bit naff, innit. Makes me feel like a Boy Scout leader or something. Pressing a button, that's more dramatic. You know, like, boom!' He slams his hand on his desk.

'Shut up, Greg,' I whisper. 'You'll get us both in trouble and you better know that before that happens I will throw you under the bus so fast.' Greg turns to me and narrows his eyes as if he's trying to measure a distance.

'Really?' he asks. 'Just like that?'

'No question,' I say lightly.

'Really?' repeats Greg. His face looks searching now and, unexpectedly, I feel self-conscious. 'Are you gonna blow my whistle, Martha?' He holds my gaze for a couple of seconds before his mouth betrays him with a twitch that is clearly an effort to conceal a smirk. I smack him hard on the arm. He bats my hand away with his, ineffectually – an imitation of schoolgirl fighting. I pull my hand back and take a sip of the coffee he brought me; it's good. I put on my headset.

'You know I wouldn't push the button though, Martha,' says Greg. 'I mean, I know we're supposed to but you might have a good reason to want to top us all. I feel like you'd rather I asked you about it, right? Sat you down and said, "Martha, you seem a little maniacal. Is there any way I can help?"'

Just as he finishes speaking my first call comes through, so my response to him is, 'Hello, Martha speaking, how can I help you today?' Greg winks at me and puts on his own headset.

'I want to know why I keep getting all these charges when I int bought nuffin?' says a gruff Bristolian voice. And so it begins.

The day goes by quickly and for once this doesn't feel like a good thing. At lunch Greg asks if I want to go and grab a sandwich with him. He tells me he's planning a trip to Peppa Pig World with the girls and that Moses and I should come. To be honest, it's bad enough having to experience that wretched, porcine brat for five minutes every day; a whole afternoon sounds like a pig-themed hell, but also, I'm not completely sure when I will be free to go with him; what my long-term co-parenting arrangement will be. I tell Greg I'll take a rain check on the sarnie because I have to run to the high street. I need something – a crutch, a talisman – that will give me the strength not to blurt out all the questions in my head when I see Alexander.

In Boots, I wander up and down the make-up counter, waiting for something to jump out at me, some magic fix that I've missed despite a twenty-year commitment to women's magazines. The woman behind the counter offers me her counsel and I tell her, 'I need something that will make me feel like myself again.' She ducks behind the divide for a few seconds and then stands holding a gold tube, a lipstick.

'It's just been released,' she says. 'It's really natural but it's got these little gold flecks that make it shimmer just the right amount. It's basically you but better.'

'That's exactly what I need,' I say, and put it on my credit card.

I can tell Moses is a bit confused when I change his clothes after nursery.

'I know,' I say. 'I'm confused too.' I put him in a clean pair of jogging bottoms and a polo shirt that Mum bought but I've never put him in because I think it makes him look like a tiny golfer. I want Moses to look like he is being parented by someone strong and capable, someone who owns an iron.

As my parents leave, Mum tells me she didn't cook but there's pizza in the freezer. I feel irritated that she thinks I can't fend for myself and simultaneously annoyed that I

have to, so I mumble goodbyes to her and Dad and pretend
to be preoccupied with packing Moses's bag, even though
I can tell she's waiting for more from me. When I don't
supply it she leaves wordlessly, and I go to the big mirror
in the hallway to apply my new lipstick. It doesn't look like
me but better; it looks like me with some slightly shim-
mery, beige stuff on my lips.

Alexander rings the bell at exactly ten past the hour.
His lateness was one thing I couldn't bear about him, even
when I was tits over arse, can't see the wood for the trees
in love with him. He is never anywhere on time; it's as if
he's physically incapable of it. Even on our wedding day I
had to circle in the car, which was in fact a taxi clocking
up minutes on the meter, so that I could arrive after him.
At times it felt like a message, never to forget that, whatever the occasion, his time was more important than mine.
Not any more – he is no longer entitled to any of my time
and I open the door prepared to let him know that.

'If you can't be on time, you're gonna have to be early,'
I say. 'Don't ever keep our son waiting.' I finish before the
door is even fully open. Alexander's face is crimson and he
nods his head with a nervous energy.

'I know,' he says. 'I'm sorry. I was in this meeting and
the director kept banging on. I should have just said something but you know what I'm like, I was being all British
about it and just sliding my chair across the room, hoping
no one would notice.' I really don't want to but I smile
because I know this is exactly what he would do. I recall
all the dinners where he battled his way through over-
cooked meat or stone-cold vegetables, never willing to
draw attention to his unhappiness. 'It won't happen again.'
I believe him and I don't know if it's because I don't have

all the doubts about our relationship clouding my thinking or because he's started being honest.

'It's OK, come in,' I say, and step aside to allow him space to walk through. Moses waddles up to him and Alexander picks him up and holds him over his head. Moses giggles and kicks his feet and I feel a spark of joy that is quickly extinguished with a bucket full of cold grief. From now on Alexander and I will each revel in Moses's happiness but we will never share it. Alexander settles our son on to his hip and pulls at the collar of his shirt.

'What's this,' he says, 'channelling Tiger Woods's son?' Alexander smiles at me but I don't return it.

'Bring it back, it's new,' I say.

'No problem,' says Alexander in a businesslike tone. 'Anything I should know?'

My stomach jolts. 'About what?'

'Food, poos, you know, the usual.' I feel a bit disappointed. The moment, the one where Alexander tells me all the ways he's hurting and why not having me in his life is tantamount to torture, is not coming. Not today, not ever.

'No, he's been great. How are you?'

'Yeah, good,' says Alexander. 'I've got this new account and they are sucking me dry but they've got three offices in the UK so I'm hoping if I can get my foot in the door . . .' It's like a time machine, Alexander banging on about his work as if it's the most significant thing going on in the world. I swear there could be a sudden outbreak of war and all Alexander would care about would be submitting his invoices before getting to the bunker. 'I'm bringing in someone part-time,' he continues. 'I've got help, obviously, but I'm getting a freelancer to do some of the artwork.'

I grip the sideboard and focus on not screaming, 'I don't care, no one fucking cares!' I hate that he wants to just pick up where we left off and the hate is glazed with a coat of rage, that in mentioning 'help' he is referencing Poppy the anorexic intern, however obliquely. I pick up the backpack that gets passed between us along with Moses and say, 'That's brilliant, just wonderful. Have a good night.'

'Hey, you asked me,' says Alexander, with the audacity to look wounded.

'Right, but you were late and I've got stuff to do. I don't have time for the whole song and verse.' Alexander looks at me with an expression en route from confusion to amusement.

'What stuff?' he asks.

'Stuff, stuff. My stuff. Stuff that's none of your business.' Alexander doesn't move and I'm forced to walk past him and open the door.

'OK, OK, I'm going,' he says. 'I'll let you get on with your stuff.' He says this with a half smile he does, a smile that has always been an instant aphrodisiac. I'm horrified to discover that even though I hate him in this moment (I hate him in the way a proud, retired man hates the foxes that shit on his lawn) if he kissed me, I would kiss him back.

Alexander moves past me and I shout to his retreating back, 'I will! I'll enjoy doing my stuff a lot, thank you!' And then I throw the door closed behind him. Afterwards, I feel like the door slamming might have been a bit much.

When I'm alone I can feel my tears are close to the surface and I dig out the list to remind myself of what I'm waiting for, because despair can't live in the face of hope.

I message George hello and a few minutes later he replies:

Undeterred83: HOW ARE YOU? WHAT ARE YOU DOING? TELL ME, I WANT TO BE ABLE TO SEE IT. SORRY DON'T KNOW WHY MY PHONE IS DOING CAPS.

2) <u>Must be intrigued by me.</u>

His words are like a virtual hug. I swear, if men asked women how they were doing seventeen times as much as they currently do, the divorce rate amongst heterosexual couples would plummet.

Marthashotbod: Just getting ready to go out.

It's a small lie, a white lie, because God help me, I'm going to find something to do. Alexander thinks I have nothing in my life because I gave up what little life I had to cater to his needs. If a man is going to be intrigued by me, I must do some stuff that makes me intriguing. So I put on another coat of my more-me-than-me lipstick and make a call.

18

Is it ironic that I work in a call centre but hate making phone calls? If it's someone I know and trust, I can cope, but when I have to reach out to someone new and by default intimidating, I always imagine they're in the midst of something terribly important and my interruption only serves as an irritant. Unfortunately, Cara's gig contact 'doesn't do internet' so ringing is my only option. And however much my pits are sweating, I'm going to call him because people with stuff to do pick up the phone and make that stuff happen.

'Marc Billingsworth,' he says after a lifetime of rings.

'Hi,' I say. 'This is Martha Ross.'

There are several seconds of silence in which I think we may have been disconnected and then he suddenly barks, 'Good for you, love. What do you want?'

'Oh,' I say. I hadn't really planned beyond this point. 'I think Cara messaged you about me . . . ?' Marc coughs, seemingly without moving his mouth away from the phone. 'I'm . . . are you there?'

'Yes, love, spit it out.'

'I'm . . . I'm a singer.' Now I've said it, I suppose I am.

'I gather that. Yeah, all right, anything jazzy will do. You'll have to do all the standard stuff but at the end of the night we mix it up a bit. Can you come down about half nine and let me hear a number? If it goes all right I can get you on for a full set next week.'

'Tonight?' I manage to squeak.

'No time like the present, darling,' he says.

After our call I go into what can only be fairly described as complete meltdown. The problem with my singing goals is that they have pretty much only manifested in my head. When I was eight my mother, father and I stayed at a self-catered apartment somewhere in Greece. The holiday itself was a bit of a disappointment; the resort appeared to have a concrete theme and my father got second-degree sunburn on our first afternoon there. On our final evening, in a desperate attempt to rescue our disastrous trip, my mother made us all attend the dinner and cabaret put on at a local restaurant each night. As we sat in front of rubbery chicken and watched a string of failed musical theatre students leave their souls on the stage, I felt increasingly tired and fidgety and full to bursting of that end-of-holiday feeling when all you want to do is return to the damp comfort of home.

Maybe it was because I was feeling so despondent that the headline act had the impact that she did. She was tiny, so small that at first glance I thought she was my age or even younger. Then I clocked her tight purple dress and deep red nails and, to me, she was the epitome of womanhood. Little as she was, her presence filled the room and had she simply stood there I would have been in love. But she didn't only stand; she released the purest, most moving sound I had ever in my short life experienced. She sang an old Whitney Houston song, and the themes it covered – sex, infidelity – I knew nothing of but the feeling she sang it with, that I knew. That was universal. I told myself that when I was a grown-up, I would be *that* woman, or as close to her as I could be.

It might seem strange but from that evening forward I knew singing was something I would eventually do; it was only a matter of when. According to Marc, my when is now; the panic I feel is induced by years of longing and not an ounce of preparation. I don't even have a song ready, and more importantly, what will I wear? I spend thirty minutes pulling all my clothes out of my wardrobe and rejecting them as too old or too sad or too trashy. Eventually I settle for a black dress I bought for a funeral – not that exciting but clean and vaguely flattering. I find an old songbook from my piano lesson days in a cupboard. It's filled with wartime songs but I figure I can jazz them up a bit. I sing the opening lines of 'A Sentimental Journey' but it doesn't feel right. I think maybe it's because I don't have music, so I find a video of Doris Day singing the song on YouTube and try to duet with her. This only serves to emphasize how far from competent I am and my head starts to itch as the sweat collects in my hairline. I call Cara and tell her about the audition.

'I can't do it,' I tell her.

'Sure you can,' she says. 'You book an Uber and get your butt into it.'

'No, no, I mean I'm not ready,' I say.

Cara tuts. 'Martha, I do not have time for your histrionics.'

'I just need to relax a bit. I can't curb my nerves.' I hear what sounds like Cara getting into a car.

'Relaxing I can do,' she says, 'gimme five.' And then she ends the call. I sit on my bed, staring at my phone. The problem with having a soon-to-be boyfriend in Africa is it's not really convenient to ask him for a hug.

A number I don't recognize flashes on the screen and when I answer a voice says, 'You want a twenty-five bag or a forty?'

'Uhm, I think you have the wrong number,' I say.

'Nah, Martha, right? Cara said you needed me to hook you up.'

'Hook me up how?' I ask.

'With weed, right? It's good stuff. So, twenty-five or forty?'

'Twenty-five or forty what?'

'Pounds, lady.' I'm silent for a few seconds whilst I contemplate the madness of this call. Like many things Cara does, it's crazy but also a little genius. I realize that being a single parent could be kind of like living a double life. I can spend part of my time being a responsible parent and my child-free evenings enjoying a life of glamour and debauchery.

'Twenty-five, I guess,' I say.

'Safe, let me know your address and I'll be over in thirty.'

I stand up. 'No, no, no.' I imagine my parents' neighbours watching me open the door to the friendly local drug dealer. 'Can I meet you somewhere?'

'Whatever you want, lady. Meet me outside the cinema on London Road in thirty.' He hangs up.

'OK,' I say to no one in particular.

I am completely clueless as to what one wears to meet a drug dealer so I put on the funeral dress. When I reach the cinema, there is no one to be seen and then I realize I don't know who I'm looking for anyway. What does a drug dealer look like? It's not as if they can wear a company T-shirt. I'm starting to think the guy's not coming when I hear a voice behind me call my name.

'Oh, hey Martha!' shouts Greta as she waves energetically.

Greta attends the same mother and toddler group as I do, when I have the mental strength to attend. Her partner goes for the odd pint with Alexander and we've had dinner at their elegant Victorian terrace on several occasions. Greta has sharp but beautiful features and always looks harassed but in a smug way, as if she's only flustered because she is consistently running from one fabulous thing to another. When Greta reaches me she briskly kisses me on each cheek. As she withdraws she slowly looks me up and down and says, 'You look good,' because what else are you supposed to say after you've examined someone in this way?

'Thanks,' I reply.

I'm about to return the compliment when she says, 'I'm sorry about you and Alexander.' It's strange, hearing about the split from outside my own head. Whenever someone else brings up the separation, the outline of the concept becomes more solidified.

'Oh, thanks. It's OK, though,' I say.

'Between you and me,' Greta says conspiratorially, 'I think it's really tacky, him taking up with that Poppy girl. Men are so lazy sometimes, they'll just take the first thing in front of them.'

I nod voicelessly. It becomes very important in this moment not to convey that this is the first time I am hearing this information. It comes as a blow, even though, if I'm honest, it was knowledge I already had on some level. I knew it the way that suspicious partners know the truth before they check their lover's phone; my heart knew it but my head was holding out until the bitter end. Before I can think of a response we're interrupted by a short, pale young man wearing wire-rimmed spectacles.

'We speak earlier?' he asks.

'Excuse me?' says Greta, with haughtiness practically oozing from her pores. 'Are you lost?' The guy looks from her face to mine quickly.

'Who's Martha?' he asks.

'I'm Martha,' I say quietly.

'So are we doing this?' He begins tapping his foot self-consciously. I look at Greta.

'You want the weed, lady?' he says.

'Drugs!' shouts Greta, as if she wasn't gurning her tits off every Friday in her pre-baby days.

'I'm sorry, I—' I say.

'Lady, this ain't how I like to do business,' says the boy.

'I'm sorry . . .'

'I'll see you around,' Greta says, still looking at the boy. Then she grabs my forearm and says to me, 'Look after yourself.' She speeds off, clearly eager to find someone with whom she can share this stellar piece of gossip.

'Here.' He looks around before handing me a small plastic bag full of what looks like dead parsley. 'Get me next time. I don't usually run tabs but, yunno, it's Cara.' He turns and jogs out of sight. I stuff the package in my bra and walk home quickly.

Back at home I lock myself in Dad's office, which is actually a very large shed in the garden, and since he recently retired, is more or less functionless. In the shed I set about rolling my first joint. I've smoked cannabis before – there was a semester of university when I was more often stoned than not – but it was always a guy procuring the drug and preparing it for consumption. I'm not sure how much to put in and I forgot to purchase tobacco when I self-consciously asked Mr Chaudry for Rizlas, certain my intentions were clear on my face. I take about a quarter of the bag and pack it in to the paper. I look back at the house to check my parents haven't come home before lighting up and taking the first drag. I'm hit by a familiar light-headedness and almost immediately I think that maybe, possibly, I can do this audition; so I take another deep inhalation.

I hold my breath for as long as I can and when I finally release it the sensation takes me back to a moment with Alexander. Shortly after we became a couple he convinced me to go to a world music festival in Spain. My taste in music falls more into the category of pop than progressive but at the time I carried a feeling that having snagged Alexander I should not let him out of my sight. On day two of our trip Alexander managed to buy a batch of brownies, baked with an extra special ingredient. We spent the afternoon sitting on the grass, chasing our treats with warm beer. By the time the evening had set in, I was done. Alexander tried to encourage me back to the tent but I just settled down on to the cool grass. I felt very sure that if I attempted anything vertical I would vomit or worse.

'It's OK,' I murmured. 'I'll just stay here.'

Alexander tugged at my vest top. 'You can't stay here, baby, we have to go to bed.'

'We don't have a bed,' I said very logically.

'Well, tent then.'

'No,' I said firmly, 'here.'

Alexander lay down and spooned me on the grass. 'You are so mashed, my beautiful, so very mashed.'

'Hmmmmm,' I said.

'Whatever my little mashed princess wants she will receive. We will make our bed on this Spanish soil and I will protect you from the beetles.' I know he said that last

153

bit to inspire me to move but I didn't care, I kinda liked the idea of it. When my only response was to pull his arm tighter around me he laughed.

'So we're really gonna stay here then?' he asked.

'If that's OK.'

'Whatever you want; we'll stay here all night,' he said. I think he was trying to be dramatic but that's what we did. I woke in the morning to discover that my neck no longer had a full range of motion and my mobile phone had been stolen but I was so very happy.

After my second toke everything starts to feel a bit furry. My body feels too heavy, particularly my head. I lie down on the tatty two-seater sofa Dad rescued from Mum's last home makeover and close my eyes. That feels terrible so I open them. It's times like these that you need a boyfriend, for when you get disastrously stoned by accident and need someone to remind you that you're probably not dying. Also for when you can feel something strange on your back and you need someone to check if it's a zit or something more sinister; or for when you want to call in sick but you know if you do it yourself you'll fake-cough a suspicious number of times; or for when you bump into Chloe Leonard, who used to terrorize you at school, and you want her to believe that you are loved, that you are capable of being loved.

Apart from these things, being single isn't as bad as I thought it would be; it's like a whole drawer of my brain has been cleared out of Alexander and is now available to hold so many other cool things. Like maybe I will learn to waterboard or maybe I will keep bees. I think maybe I have confused waterboarding with something else but it's the concept and not the details that is important. The freedom to explore who I am, without the annoyance of having to manipulate the experience to accommodate someone else's wishes. Not having to consider someone else's feelings every minute of every hour is good, but I must admit it is nice to know there's a person thinking about you. Little updates from George are what get me through the day at the moment; for example, he'll message me to say he had some chicken and he didn't think it was cooked through. It's uplifting to know that I am the one he needs to tell him he might get the shits.

This, I realize, is a brilliant idea for a business. I'll provide a service that messages single women with cute, affirming messages throughout the week. I'll get them to create their own list of the perfect man's attributes and base my communication on it; a kind of virtual boyfriend. He will tell you he loved last night's dinner and he thinks you're beautiful; he will never forget your anniversary or start sleeping with his barely legal personal assistant. I haul myself to sitting and grab a piece of paper and pencil from Dad's desk to scribble down my business idea. I can already see the logo – an outline of a man sitting on a moon. Maybe I will call it Man in the Moon or maybe To the Moon and Back. Maybe I won't go with the whole moon thing but the rest is gold. I sink back on to the sofa. I'll just have a little nap, go to my audition and then take over the world.

I wake up an hour later, fifteen minutes into my audition. A piece of paper beside me says, 'Fake . . . Messages . . . All the pretty things . . .' I call Marc and tell him my son is unwell and I can't leave him.

'Little fuckers,' he says. 'No worries, I trust Car. She knows her talent. I'll put you in for a full set in a couple of weeks.' I can't feel my legs but I have my first singing gig.

19

WHEN I READ the email, I think I'm still high. It's so
unreal I print it out so that I can actually hold it.
I then keep it in my pocket for the entire afternoon
and it plays on my mind like a backing track throughout
the day.

Collecting Moses from nursery, I take on the role of an
engaged parent. I ask about his day and praise the artistic
talent displayed in his haphazard splodges, but despite my
efforts I pull on his coat a little too briskly and push him
into the buggy hurriedly because I know my mind will not
quieten until I have addressed the contents of the message,
which reads:

> *Martha,*
>
> *I want to apologize for how things with us ended.*
> *Don't feel bad, it was absolutely my fault. I thought*
> *I was ready to move on but being with you made me*
> *realize that I was still in love with Rhiannon.*
>
> *We've reconnected and I knew that I couldn't let*
> *her get away from me again so I'm pleased to tell you*
> *we're engaged.*
>
> *We'd both like you to come to our engagement*
> *party on 4 November, at OhSo from 8 p.m. You are*

an important part of why we are able to celebrate the
occasion.
  I hope you are well and have been able to make
positive decisions of your own.
  Kind Regards,
  Tom

I must have read it a dozen times and at every reading the structure and content is the same. It's enraging and also completely baffling – for a start, how did he get my email address? I guess it's true that with a little time and effort he could have investigated me online but Tom is not that guy. Tom would only have my contact details if they were right in front of him.

Leanne opens her front door. I have Moses in one arm and with the other I hold up the email like it's a search warrant. 'What the hell is this?' I demand.

Leanne lifts her left eyebrow. 'A piece of paper,' she says.

'Where's James?' I say. I hand Moses to Leanne and push past her, leaving the buggy on the porch.

I walk straight through to the kitchen and Leanne follows me with Moses, saying, 'Hi, Leanne, how are you doing? Oh, I'm fine, yeah the kids are great.' I ignore her; I have no time for pleasantries. James is sitting at the kitchen table, his slippered feet resting on a chair. When he sees me, he swallows the biscuit he's eating guiltily.

'Hi, Martha,' he says, but his greeting is a question. I give him the answer.

'What moved you to talk about me to Tom?'

'Huh?' says James. I slam the email down on the table. James looks at it and then back at me and then behind me to his wife. I push James's feet from the chair so that I can sit down and force him to look me in the eye.

'This is an invitation to Tom's engagement party. One that he has sent me as some sort of charitable act.'

'Right,' says James. Leanne places Moses in front of a wooden toy kitchen in the corner and comes and stands between me and her husband. She puts her hands on her hips, fully embracing the role of referee.

'James,' she says. 'Did you and Tom talk about Martha after their date?'

'No,' says James. 'Well, not really.'

I slam my palm against the table, sending the family hamster into a flurry of activity in his cage. 'You did or you didn't: there are no "not really"s in this scenario,' I say.

'Erm, OK, so yes.'

Leanne covers her face with her hands.

'I mean, barely,' continues James. 'Obviously he asked me if you were OK – he said you seemed a bit angry after your date.' James's eyes flit wildly between the two women before him.

'And . . .' says Leanne.

'Well, I said no,' says James. 'I said you were having a hard time, you . . . with . . . you know, stuff. I thought it might help to explain things . . .' I smack my forehead with my hand several times. I consider that if I seriously injure him right now I could offer a very reasonable defence. Leanne crouches down beside her husband.

'Honey,' she says, 'it almost never helps to explain things, OK?'

'OK,' says James. 'I'm sorry—'

'Just stop talking,' I say. Millie comes into the kitchen. She's wearing a Batman costume and holding a small plastic handbag.

'Mummy, can I have a snack?' she asks.

'Yes, darling,' says Leanne. She prods James in the thigh. 'Go get them something to eat.' James gets up and pats me on the shoulder before rounding up Millie and Moses. Leanne takes his chair.

'Don't worry, if Tom mentions you at the party I'll set him straight,' she says.

'Oh, I'm going to the party,' I say. 'Thanks to your husband I have to.' I look at James, who has the grace to look embarrassed.

'But . . . I don't understand . . .' says Leanne. I hope I wasn't this ignorant when I was in a relationship.

'I have to go to show him that I am, and look, amazing,' I say.

'Let's go see if Dora is on,' says James, ushering the kids out of the room.

'Why do you care what he thinks?' asks Leanne. 'Move on with your life; he clearly has.'

'Ouch! Let's just run that one in a little deeper,' I say, and then, 'Whatever. I don't care what he thinks.'

'You clearly care what he thinks,' says Leanne.

'OK, I care, but only in the most time-sensitive, transient way.' Leanne gives me an unconvinced face. 'Really, I just don't want him to think all women are helpless little walkovers – it's a feminist act really.' Leanne opens her mouth to say something, something I know will be a chastisement, so I interrupt her and say, 'Anyway, I'm kinda seeing someone.'

Leanne closes her mouth then asks, 'Who?'

'His name is George,' I say.

'Like the list George?' Leanne asks.

'Exactly like the list George. He's got red hair and everything.'

'Where did you meet him?' she asks.

'On Linger,' I say. I can feel my blood pumping faster as I gear up to spill the beans. Leanne stands up.

'I'm gonna need wine for this,' she says. Leanne pours out two large glasses of shiraz and I tell her all about him. I downplay the overwhelming sense that we are destined to be together but she clearly feels the significance because when I finish talking she remains silent for a few seconds.

'So his name isn't George, it's Nathan,' she says. I understand this is why I didn't want to tell people about him; because it's human instinct to want to taint things. I remember going to visit a butterfly house at primary school. Before we went in we were told under no circumstances were we to touch the butterflies and we all nodded our heads solemnly, but of course as soon as we were ushered in, those beautiful but forbidden wings were far too inviting.

'Well yes, but you're missing the important bit!'

'Which is?' asks Leanne.

I smile. 'That he gets me, that he wants me. I'm so excited about meeting him and I'm nearly ready, I just need to lose a few pounds and get the work thing sorted . . .'

Leanne shakes her head as if she's trying to empty it. 'What's the point of him wanting you if you're just going to change who you are?' she asks. Leanne is really annoying sometimes.

'You know, you're really annoying sometimes,' I tell her.

'Annoying or right?' Leanne asks.

'Definitely annoying,' I say.

20

LISA HAS PROCURED a clipboard from somewhere. I've never noticed one in the office before, so I suspect that she has purchased this specifically for her role of Unpaid Christmas Party Planning Dictator. Lisa informs us that the theme of the party will be tapas and almost everyone nods agreeably. Lisa's hair is styled in a very intricate arrangement. Waves muddle with plaits and meet in a glossy ponytail at the nape of her neck. It's the sort of style that should be impressive but makes me feel a little bit of second-hand embarrassment, because I know it has taken three YouTube videos and a can of hairspray to achieve the look and that the whole thing was contrived in the hope that just one person would say, 'Ooh, that looks nice.' That makes me feel a little sorry for Lisa because it's a hope I recognize – that something I have achieved, however minor, will be acknowledged. That's why I feel a little guilty when I raise my hand.

'Yes?' asks Lisa, with a glare that says, 'Who let you in?' I lower my hand, conscious of the other people in the room waiting for my response.

'Uhm, it's just I'm pretty sure tapas isn't a theme.' Lisa rolls her eyes and throws me a smile that could be given no other description than patronizing.

'A theme is just a feeling, Marsha,' she says.

'Yeah, Marsha,' says Greg from beside me, 'it's just a feeling.' I can hear the catch in his voice, where I know a laugh is lurking. I stare at my knees so that I can't look at him and fail to keep my composure.

'See,' says Lisa, 'Greg gets it.' I raise my head, expecting to see him pulling a face or sneaking me a sideways look, but he is winking at Lisa and for a minute I'm unsure if he was joking and that uncertainty makes me feel uncomfortable.

'Let's all decide what area we're going to cover,' says Lisa enthusiastically. I am given olives. I think it's a punishment. I decide not to care. As we're leaving Lisa asks me to stay behind, as if I've been caught passing notes in the back of her class. I really want to walk out but my feet are politer than my mind.

'Everything OK?' I ask. 'I really got behind the tapas thing in the end.'

'Don't worry about it,' says Lisa, and I'm annoyed she thinks I was. 'I just wanted to ask you something.' She stops and her mouth twists to one side. She's assessing me, checking if I'm a worthy source of information.

'Of course,' I say.

'You sit next to Greg, right?'

'Right,' I say. For a second I think she's going to make a complaint about him and I want to run. The thought of pushing the button on Greg makes me nauseous.

'I was wondering if he's single?' She lowers her eyes bashfully as she says this and I'm glad because it means that she doesn't see my own widen with surprise.

'Yeah,' I say, after too long a pause. 'I mean, yeah, I think so.'

'And you'd say he was a good guy?' she asks.

'He's the best guy,' I say, and I mean it. Her body relaxes and she lets out a pretty laugh.

'I know he's not the tallest but he's so funny and, I don't know, he's sorta got something about him. He's really kind, you know.' I do know this and I feel embarrassed because I realize that, in a vague, unformed way, I had believed his kindness had been inspired by me.

'He's tall enough,' I say, a bit offended on Greg's behalf. Lisa smiles.

'I guess so. I mean, I usually wear flats so it'd be OK.' Even in her kitten heels, the top of Lisa's head only reaches my nose. I don't know why she would want a tall guy. What exactly would she do with all those extra inches? Put them into storage? Share them with her friends? Lisa's response is jarring; I didn't intend to communicate that he was tall enough for her – I meant tall enough for someone, tall enough for anyone – but I can tell that my throwaway comment has greenlit whatever fantasy Lisa has been concocting in her head.

'OK, thanks then,' says Lisa, and then she turns to start tidying the room, carefully collecting abandoned pieces of paper with sketches of sombreros and lists such as 'Best Cheeses'. I don't say anything to her before leaving, which is my way of expressing disapproval, but by the time I reach my desk I worry that leaving without speaking might be like a disgruntled customer not leaving a tip. The waiter doesn't understand you're unhappy, they just think that you're a twat.

Greg is packing up and doesn't stop as he says, 'The theme is definitely not cultural sensitivity, then?'

I laugh and feel a rush of relief. 'You know what's really awkward?'

Greg looks up. His face is eager and I wait a beat, so I can enjoy this.

'Lisa just asked me if you're single.'

Greg's eyes widen for a second and then he does a little swaggery jig. 'Still got it,' he says in an American accent. He returns to packing his bag with no further comment and I worry that I've made a faux pas by informing him of Lisa's crush.

'Sorry,' I say. 'I didn't mean to embarrass you or anything.'

Greg removes his jacket from the back of his chair and slips it on. 'No problem,' he says. 'Why would I be embarrassed? Lisa's a cracker.' He grabs his backpack and swings it over one shoulder.

'Catch you soon, amigo,' he says with a chuckle.

'Bye,' I say, and then watch him walk away, his bag bouncing with every step.

8) Has to be tall.

Lisa's comment about Greg's height makes me think that it might be wrong to have a personal requirement based on physicality but then I recall a string of messages in which I asked George to describe himself and he told me he is tall, so tall he rarely fits completely on a standard-sized bed, and he told me that he had been on the rowing team at university and that the discipline had left him with defined arms, even though he no longer found the time to train that much. I could not resist – although I admit I did not try – imagining myself being enveloped by him, for once feeling dainty and for ever feeling protected.

Rather than getting ready to leave work myself, I message George.

164

Marthashotbod: I can't wait to feel your arms around me.
Undeterred83: Be careful what you wish for. Once I get hold of you I might not let go.

To myself I say, 'I think I'd like that,' but I reply:

Marthashotbod: What're you up to?
Undeterred83: Setting up camp. Climbed a mountain today. The altitude effect is crazy.

What's crazy is that he climbed a mountain. For fun.

Marthashotbod: Mountain?! That's awesome.
Undeterred83: Maybe we can bag a peak together some day. I love Grasmoor.
Marthashotbod: Sure.

And I feel, as I often do when I interact with George, a sense of optimism that makes me a little breathless. He is healthy! He is mountain-climbing healthy, which by my standards is exceptionally healthy. The idea of hiking and climbing and exploring with him is wonderful in theory, although it doesn't jibe with my lifestyle to date. When I wrote the guidelines I failed to take into account that a successful, tall, exceptionally healthy man may want a mate who matches that. It doesn't seem fair to offer this perfect specimen of a man a woman made of poorly stitched together scraps. I want him to meet someone whole and happy, someone who deserves to be his equal.

Even though I'm getting concerned looks from the rest of my shift teammates, who are racing to the exit, I remain at my desk and pull the list from my bag. I can recite it from memory but I read it again and then I turn it over and start another list on the back. A list of what he might want, but more importantly a list of what *I* want – for me.

1) <u>Must be healthy in mind and body and have an outside form that is representative of her inner worth.</u>
2) <u>Has plans and ambitions and must be taking steps to ensure they are achieved.</u>
3) <u>Always bold, assertive and unwilling to accept bullshit in any of its presented forms.</u>
4) <u>Speaks French.</u>

I cross out the last one. Even a woman with ambition can't commit to learning French in a few weeks. I feel like I should write more, create a list for myself that equals the one I have outlined for my mate, but it's so much harder doing it for yourself. Still, I like this girl I've described. And I know that a girl like her wouldn't slug home and watch two episodes of *Hollyoaks* and feel sorry for herself. She would play with her son, eat dinner with her loved ones, go for a run and reward herself with a long bath. So that's what I choose to do.

21

IT CLEARS MY head hearing the thump of my feet on the pavement. I can't really think about anything except the burning in my throat and that comes as a bizarre reprieve. I feel a bit of empathy for the crazies I met at the retreat; pain is a short holiday from the incessant whirring of my mind.

When I get home and go inside, I fall back against the front door and wait for my legs to remember what they're for. Mum pokes her head around the living room door and eyes me with a mixture of suspicion and contempt. 'Be quiet,' she hisses, 'you'll wake Moses.' Any warmth created by our family dinner earlier flies out of the building.

'He's my son,' I remind her firmly, assertively, 'I know what level of noise would wake him.' Mum retreats without comment. I slowly climb the stairs to take my bath and I hear Moses making the low groaning sound that's usually a prelude to crying. I swear under my breath and creep into his room. His blanket has been kicked from his body. His eyes are closed but he is twisting his head from side to side; he's on the edge of awakening but putting up an admirable fight. I carefully place my hand on his chest and start to sing, slow and very low. It's a Stevie Wonder song that I have used as a lullaby since Moses was safe in my belly and would keep me up with his nocturnal disco dancing. After a few bars I can feel his breathing start to slow and then return to his little snorting snores.

As I take off my clothes, I catch myself in the mirror. I have a body that would be aptly described as sturdy. It would probably be good for living on a farm in 1923 but it doesn't fit with any modern-day goals of womanhood. After I had Moses my body didn't, as they say, 'bounce back' – my stomach hangs lazily over the waistband of my pants and my breasts have been left sad and empty. Exercise is several steps in the right direction but, obviously, I have to go on a diet. I have a gig, an ex's engagement party and a real-life date with the love of my life to prepare for.

Diets and I have a weird relationship; we're sort of frenemies. I hate them, I talk endlessly about removing them from my life, but then as soon as I'm in trouble I run right back to them. I have been on various iterations of the following diets: low calorie, low sugar, low fat, low carbs, no carbs, no meat, no wheat, no dairy, no food, no fun. I have failed at them all, evidenced by the fact that I have to keep going on a new one. This time will be the last time, though; I'm ready to start a new life at a new weight. I think in the past it wasn't that I didn't have the right diet, but the right motivation.

After my bath I write out a diet plan of one thousand calories a day. It includes a couple of treats a week but most of the good stuff has been removed. I kind of like that, though; I don't deserve good stuff right now. I never understand it when people try to sell diets by saying they don't feel like a diet. I think the punishment is part of the process. If I don't feel like I can never go through this again and want to die, what will prevent me from putting on all the weight again? When I'm done, I feel a bit more at peace. I have a plan for my body, for my life and for love.

I gather a family bag of crisps, two Kit Kats, a slice of Victoria sponge cake and a bottle of pinot grigio, because before every diet there must be a really big blowout. You have to eat so much of the wrong kind of stuff that when you wake up in the morning you don't actually want to eat again anyway. As I work my way through my stash, I do what I always do – I revisit all my Facebook photos, analysing my body throughout the years. There's a period in 2012 when I definitely look a lot thinner than I thought I did. As I scroll I get a message from George.

Undeterred83: I'm bored. Entertain me.

I pour myself another glass of wine before replying.

Marthashotbod: How can you be bored, you're in Africa.
Undeterred83: I'm bored because I don't have you.
Marthashotbod: Good point. What are you doing?
Undeterred83: Nothing. In my cabin, having a beer. What you wearing?

There it is. The text message that every guy sends at some point and every girl, depending on how drunk or horny or needy she is, can choose to embrace or ignore.

Marthashotbod: Wouldn't you like to know?
Undeterred83: I would actually. That's why I asked.

I am wearing a pair of my dad's old pyjamas. The elastic is all but gone from the waistband, which is partly why they were chosen.

Marthashotbod: Knickers. Black ones.
Undeterred83: And?
Marthashotbod: A smile.
Undeterred83: Awesome.

I relax now as I realize there isn't much to this sexting business, just suggesting you're semi-naked and up for it. Alexander and I started dating at a time when mobile phones were basically a tool for logistics and not the actual method of dating.

Marthashotbod: What are you wearing?
Undeterred83: Cargo shorts. I'd rather be wearing you though.

OK, I recognize this juncture. This also happens in the physical realm. The moment when the man tries to push his luck and the woman grants or denies him access, a dance performed since the dawn of time.

Marthashotbod: I have a feeling you would wear me well.

Access granted.

Undeterred83: I would. I would wear you out.
Marthashotbod: How long would that take?
Undeterred83: As long as you needed.

I unwrap a Kit Kat whilst I think about my reply. It could be a good opportunity to educate him, but if the universe has listened he won't need direction and men hate being told what to do in bed. I eat a finger of chocolate to see if the sugar helps to kickstart my creativity, and he writes:

Undeterred83: And as long as you needed again.

OK, that works for me. To the point, without being totally, obnoxiously obvious about it. There was a guy in my university halls like that; we called him the cheerleader because he would announce every act as if you both hadn't just been there to experience it – 'Yeah, grab my arse! Whoo, condom on!' I lick some chocolate off my fingers before typing:

Marthashotbod: I can't wait to get you out of those shorts.
Undeterred83: You can't! I can't wait, I think you're lucky
    I'm not there now.
Marthashotbod: Not long to wait though.
Undeterred83: Too long, please let me have a preview.

And here we have it: the question every girl must also answer. To send pictures or not to send pictures? I've heard all the horror stories and I know all the rules – no identifying features, nothing too graphic – but still, I've never sent a risqué picture to a guy, not even Alexander. The concept doesn't offend me; I get it – the teasing, the anticipation. It's like how I sometimes look up a restaurant's menu online and choose what I want to eat the day before I visit. What scares me is offering a guy solid, undeniable evidence of my flaws, something he can refer back to. The mind is fluid and creative; it will airbrush cellulite and stretch marks from a memory. A picture does not lie.

Everything with George feels like an adventure, though. I get the sense that if I do everything differently maybe this time will *be* different. I take off the pyjamas and then wrap myself in a bath towel. I take twenty-four different pictures of myself lying across the bed. It takes me quite a few minutes to find one that has enough skin showing to be considered sexual, if not sexy, which also hides enough of my body for me to feel OK sending it. Once I have selected the shot, I crop and edit it to the point where I can almost look at it comfortably, and then I send it before I lose my nerve. George doesn't reply for four terrifying minutes but when he does he says the only thing I wanted to hear.

Undeterred83: Wow.

22

AFTER THE ENGAGEMENT invitation from Tom, I have been avoiding my emails, which is why I missed three from Patricia. Three on top of the two I had previously ignored. When I still don't respond, she switches her weapon of choice to the phone and I slip up one morning when I answer a call from a withheld number.

'I'll assume that it's because you're off living your best life that you haven't been in touch,' says Patricia. Her tone is curt, rather than full of its usual frothy exuberance.

'I'm sorry,' I say, 'my kid's been sick.'

'Kids get sick all the time,' she says. 'The world of business doesn't stop for a head cold.' I tell her I'll be in to see her as soon as I can. I take the folder she gave me and also a leather-bound notebook I bought to fill with all my business ideas, which both remain empty.

When I arrive at her office Patricia starts speaking before I even sit down. 'You're late on your next instalment, so I'm sorry but I'll have to charge you a fee,' she says. When she says this she does actually sound sorry, as if she has no control over the appearance of this fee; the fee, capable of independent thought, has simply turned up, determined to ruin my day.

'I guess I've spent longer on the research period than I thought I would.'

'OK,' says Patricia, the bounciness back in her voice, 'what have you got so far?'

I fumble with the hem of my T-shirt. 'I guess I'm not much further than where I was.'

'Right. Let me just pull up your details.' Patricia taps briskly on her keyboard. 'OK, you want to set up a support service for lonely women.'

I wince. 'I want to help women. I guess I want to support women to find something better than they have had in the past.'

Patricia types as I speak. She hits the 'enter' button with a flourish and then turns back to me. 'And what experience do you have of this?'

'Of what?' I ask.

'Well, what have you experienced in past relationships?' This is the big question; moving forward is not just having a list of what you want but having a sackful of non-negotiables too, all the things you will never again tolerate.

'Nothing,' I say. Patricia looks confused. 'I mean, no passion, no joy. A relationship should be two amazing people coming together to become two really amazing people together. In my past relationship it was like two average people coming together and making the other less than average.'

Patricia nods slowly. 'So you're saying you have to work on yourself before you commit to a relationship?'

Am I saying that? 'Yeah, I guess so.'

Patricia takes off her glasses and smiles at me conspiratorially. 'Let me tell you a little secret. My partner, Phil, adores me.' As Patricia says the word 'adores', she elongates its vowels and rolls her eyes. 'I mean, he literally worships the ground I walk on. That definitely happened because I had my house in order before I took up with him.' I glance down at Patricia's chest. On her red blouse is a small stain, toothpaste I think. 'Also, he gets a bit of the other, whenever he wants. No questions asked.' I have questions, but this is not the time. 'So, tell me about your current relationship,' says Patricia.

'I'm not in a relationship right now.' I think of George. 'Not quite.'

Patricia puts her glasses back on. 'Well, this is a problem,' she says. 'How can you educate others on something you have not done yourself? I mean, where's your test model?'

'That makes sense,' I say. I feel a familiar hot sensation behind my eyes, and noticing what is threatening to occur, Patricia hands me a couple of tissues from her sleeve. I take them and dab at my eyes before blinking a few times to try and stem the flow.

'Listen, this is what I'll do,' says Patricia. 'Just get me this instalment and I'll put your account on pause. You need to invest in yourself right now. Get some therapy, get a bit of a makeover, find your dream guy and then teach other women how to do it.' Patricia is smiling and nodding as if this is the most revolutionary idea ever conceived.

'I don't know. I've already tried therapy . . .' I say.

'OK, I see what's happening here: you need a clear-out. A soul clear-out. You can't become the phenomenal businesswoman I know you can be without saying cheerio to this scared little creature.' As Patricia says this she waves her hand in my direction. I think the comment is sort of mean but I'm pleased that she referred to me as little. 'Let's go on a field trip – this one's on the house.'

Patricia takes a minute to pack her belongings into a vast tapestry bag and apply another layer of lime green eyeshadow. She leads me out on to the main road and sets off purposefully.

'Can I ask where we're going?'

'You should always ask where you're going,' says Patricia, 'but I'm not telling you.' Patricia and I weave through tourists in the Lanes as we walk; she seems to be giving me a guided tour of the city. 'I got my engagement ring fixed in that jeweller's. Phil gave me something that belonged to his mother; they got me a new stone and a new band and now it's perfect ... The empanadas there are literally to die for; I mean, you have to take a first-aider with you because it's literally to die for.'

I feel like telling her that I've lived in Brighton almost my entire life and that if you tried to tell a Spaniard that the food in that restaurant was to die for, they'd probably kill you. I don't say anything because I'm not sure that Patricia would care. I wonder what it takes to be so sure of yourself and if, after I have finished being mentored by her, I too will have this self-assurance.

Patricia leads me to a groyne on the seafront. A doughnut-shaped piece of art sits on the end of it and it is a place I have always loved. I harboured a secret hope that Alexander would ask me to marry him here, as it would be such a romantic spot for a proposal; perhaps hope is not lost. I say a silent prayer that Patricia won't ruin the place for me. She leads me to the edge of the groyne. The wind crashes against us and I have to concentrate on staying upright.

'OK,' says Patricia, 'let her go.' I feel a little bit anxious; I mean, I really don't know this woman. 'Send everything you no longer need out to sea. Scream it into the surf and let it carry it all away.' When I don't react Patricia faces the water and shouts, 'A belief in scarcity!' She then turns and looks at me. After a couple of seconds I shout the same.

'Very good, but you have to choose your own things and also you need to be about ten times louder.'

I think for a few seconds and then I shout, 'Fear!'

'Good,' says Patricia.

'Low self-worth!'

'Yes. Good, good.'

I glance behind me. 'People are looking,' I say.

'People will always be looking,' says Patricia.

I exhale deeply and shout, 'Disconnection from the world! A feeling of inadequacy! Alexander Eric Ross! Shame!' I'm on a roll now. 'Disorganization! Procrastination! Self-loathing! Unhealthy habits! Low motivation! Indecisiveness! Bullshit!' I stop. I'm smiling. I feel free.

Patricia pats me on the shoulder. 'Excellent. Now does that sound like a woman who doesn't pay her debts?'

I promise Patricia that I will get her money to her as soon as I can, and she leaves me standing looking out to sea. I really want to be a woman without all those negative things – my biggest fear is that George thinks I'm already that woman. It would be nice to think he would love me *and* my flaws but I've tried that and it didn't work out so well.

I lost my baby before the wedding. Not 'lost'. Before my wedding day, my baby died. I remember the precise moment my symptoms shifted from 'commonplace' to 'concerning'. Alexander said something along the lines of 'what will be will be', definitely something that belonged on an Instagram post and not in the mouth of my soon-to-be betrothed. The wedding day was a haze of pain, both physical and emotional; the only bit I really wanted was to fall asleep with my new husband but sadly I was unconscious before he made it up from the bar.

My parents sent us to the Algarve on honeymoon. The

first morning we had tea and toast on our balcony over-looking the coast and I thought, I might be willing to try again, or at least to take the risk of looking forward and not back. Apparently, Alexander was thinking the same. He told me he'd been considering it for a while and he wanted to give birth to something big.

'When we get home,' he said, 'I'm going to set up my own business.' Alexander had been working for a small design company for years, but like every employee on the planet he thought he was ridiculously undervalued and woefully underpaid. I wasn't sure it was the best idea; you can throw a stone in Brighton and hit a graphic designer. Also, new businesses and newborns don't really mix.

'It means you're gonna have to hold the fort for a while,' said Alexander. I agreed because sitting in that gentle morning light I didn't know what that meant; I didn't know that it meant a year of anxiety as I fell deeper into debt.

As soon as we got back on British soil, Alexander Ross Design was born. To his credit, he made it work. He sought new clients with a determination I had never seen in him before; I took this to mean he was committed to building something for us. Almost exactly a year to the day after Alexander told me his plan, his business was turning a profit and he celebrated by buying a classic MG – soft top, two seats. Now it's my turn. I'm going to create something out of nothing, and I may not have someone supporting me financially but I have someone behind me emotionally, which is priceless.

Marthashotbod: Just had an amazing session with my business mentor.
Undeterred83: Because you're amazing.

23

HOWEVER QUIRKY I find Patricia to be, I respect what she is saying. I want to invest in myself, I'm desperate to create change, and desperate times call for desperate measures. It's out of pure desperation that I offer to work a night shift. I hate them. The office is full of the lost and lonely, the people with no one who cares where they are at three in the morning. It's like corporate purgatory. You get time and a half for working after ten but you pay for that with a little bit of your soul. You have to man the phones even when no one calls and the majority of the time no one does. When you do get a call the customer falls into one of two categories – drunk or mad.

My line is particularly quiet tonight. It leaves me alone with my thoughts, which is not always a fun place to be. When my phone rings I'm relieved. I ask how I can help and I mean it.

'Where's Darren?' asks a woman.

'Hi,' I say. 'I'm Martha, I'll be helping you today.'

'Well, I don't want you. I want Darren.' Mad.

'I'm not sure who you spoke to earlier but I'm sure I can help you.' I hear some shuffling, after which the woman recites the customer hotline.

'Is that the number?' she asks.

'Yes, it is,' I say.

'Well, it's supposed to be Darren.' She says this as if she has caught me out in a lie. 'Can you get me him?'

'What is it you would like to discuss?' I ask.

'None of your beeswax,' snaps the woman. 'Darren told me I could have all this stuff but I ain't got no stuff.'

'What were you expecting, Madam?' I ask.

'I don't know – that's why I need to talk to Darren. He told me with the gold plan I get all this stuff . . .'

'Well, the stuff isn't actually physical,' I say. 'I mean, it's not tangible stuff.'

'Eh,' says the woman, 'you calling me a liar?'

'Listen, lady,' I say, 'I don't know what's going on here but it feels like you've got more problems than your preferential customer plan.'

There is silence on the line and then the woman says, 'I have half a mind to—' I cut off the call. I have no desire to hear what she plans to do with her half a mind. When I'm angry I want to cry; it's one of the traits I like least about myself. It's so ineffective, and you end up communicating completely the wrong message. Often it results in an awkward hug with someone I hate.

I escape to the break room before the tears arrive. When Greg comes in shortly after me my head throbs with irritation. I really want to be alone but then he hands me a Twix and I soften. I'm probably more hangry than angry. I thank him and experience a brief moment of guilt about the chocolate's impact on my diet before cramming both fingers in my mouth at the same time.

'Yeah,' says Greg, 'You just had this kind of wild, low-sugar look in your eyes.' I hope that my face tells him I'm not amused, because my mouth is too full of biscuit and caramel to speak. 'And from what I understand chocolate solves every female problem, right?' I finish my mouthful.

'With beliefs like that I can see why you're divorced,' I say.

Greg laughs. 'That's not why I'm divorced.'

'Why then?' I ask, popping the last bit of Twix in my mouth.

'It's a long story,' says Greg. 'We didn't appreciate each other and wanted different things, et cetera, but the radio edit is she started shagging the guy upstairs.'

I make a noise like I've been punched in the gut. 'That's harsh, Greg.'

'Yeah, I know,' he says, 'I was there.' Greg clocks my astonished expression and clarifies: 'Not literally there but, you know, I experienced it. The weird thing is the long story is true too, but I don't know if it happened before or after she . . . you know.'

I lean forward and pat Greg on the knee. 'It's obvious you wanted different things,' I say. Greg smiles weakly at me. 'She wanted to shag the dude upstairs and you didn't want her to.' There is a moment of silence before Greg collapses into laughter. Watching him makes me feel much less tired. 'What about Lisa then?' I ask, keeping my voice light, letting the words slip out quickly. I've seen them a couple of times having earnest-looking conferences in the hallways. When I walked past them once, Greg stopped and said hello, feigning politeness to keep their conversation under wraps. He never mentioned it afterwards and for some reason I hadn't wanted to bring it up until now. Greg's face grows serious. He's quiet but I can tell he's not being evasive, just seeking out the most honest response.

'I've only really been in relationships. Even at school I

didn't do dates; I was committed. I'm not sure I know how to play the game. It's not about my ex – honestly, I'm over it. It's just that sometimes the idea of dating seems tiring.' I smile, even though Greg isn't looking at me as he speaks.

'Do you want a coffee?' I ask. 'I brought in the posh instant.'

'Yes, definitely,' Greg says.

'On another double shift?'

'Bills to pay, yunno,' he says with a tired smile.

I go and make us two milky coffees. As I make them I realize I don't know how Greg takes his so I don't put in any sugar. I tell Greg this as I hand him the mug and he insists he is 'sweet enough'.

'So how did you get over it?' I ask, clutching my hands around my mug like I'm sitting beside a camp fire.

'If I'm honest, I didn't really,' says Greg. 'Maybe I won't ever. It wasn't even the sex. I mean, some guy putting his penis in my wife: *not* on my bucket list, obviously, but I think I could have dealt with that. It was all the lying; all the messages; all the bullshit that went with it.' I nod. 'She didn't even tell me – he did. He came straight up to me one day when I was bringing in the shopping. I felt like such a prick. Her face when I confronted her. I almost laughed – she looked like a cartoon character, you know.' Greg uses his index fingers to mime his eyes coming out on stalks. I laugh, and he smiles.

'So you didn't end it straight away?'

Greg takes a sip of coffee and shakes his head. 'I couldn't. My dad left when I was eight; I couldn't do it to the girls.'

'What changed?' I ask.

'Me,' says Greg. We both drink our coffees in silence for a bit before Greg asks, 'What's happening with you?'

I wave my hand dismissively. 'It was done before it was done.' Greg nods. 'I'm just looking to do it again and do it right this time.'

'How will you know when it's right?' asks Greg.

'When I can relax,' I say. 'When I know I have what I've been waiting for.'

'Which is?'

'Everything,' I say.

'Obviously,' says Greg.

'I mean all of it: the mixtapes, movies in bed, home-made soup when I'm ill and giving me his coat even when it's not that cold, even when I've already got a coat on.' Greg laughs but it's not a 'you're hopeless, I'm so glad I'm more evolved than you' laugh; I think it's a laugh of recognition. 'If I can't have all that, I just want someone who would step in front of a train for me. You know, your standard to-hell-and-back, dragon-slaying stuff.'

'You don't want much then,' says Greg, 'just your standard dragon-slaying stuff.'

'Right,' I say, and he winks at me.

'I know what you mean,' says Greg. 'You'd think we'd be more cynical after divorce.'

'I'm not divorced yet,' I say.

'Aww, well maybe when it comes through you'll wanna forget all this romance business. You'll probably just want to stick all the men on an island and forget about us.'

'Could I visit the island?' I ask him. Greg grabs a flyer for the inter-office football team from the coffee table, screws it up and lobs it at my head. It bounces off and lands in my lap. I pick it up and raise my hand.

'Don't even think about it,' says Greg. 'You don't know what you're starting here.' Before I retaliate, Anekwe, the IT supervisor, walks in.

'Having fun?' she asks, raising her eyebrows.

'We'd better get back to work,' I say. Greg has his back to Anekwe and makes a face at me. 'Come on,' I say, before pulling him up from his seat. 'You can stop me from traumatizing any more customers.'

24

I ONLY MANAGE TO grab a few hours of fitful sleep when I get back after the night shift before Mum walks in unannounced with my fractious toddler in her arms. She deposits my son on my stomach and says, 'I know you've been working but, may I remind you, motherhood is a full-time job and I've got water aerobics.' I grunt in response. Moses starts to smack me in the face so I sit up and give him my phone to play with.

'Morning, baby,' I say to Moses. At the same time the phone rings out an alert. I prize it from his fingers and he looks like he might cry so I get my laptop from the floor and put on *Thomas the Tank Engine*.

Undeterred83: Hey! How are you?
Marthashotbod: I'm OK.
Marthashotbod: Can we talk again? It's important.

George tells me he'll try me in half an hour, which leaves me with thirty long minutes to fill. I run a bath with loads of bubbles for me and Moses. I set Moses between my legs and as I do I notice the pedicure Leanne got me a month ago has grown out and chipped. I scoot down so that the warm water can start to work on the tension in my back.

'Duck,' says Moses. I forgot his bath toys. I give him a loofah sitting on the side of the tub.

'Duck,' I say. He looks at it, only slightly doubtful, before pushing it under the water.

'Quack! Quack!' he shouts as it bobs back up again. If only all men were so easy to please.

I was so anxious about becoming a mother. I probably spent more time on the internet researching childhood diseases than asleep that first year. It's strange because the reality of babies is that they're very easy. They need to be warm, they need to eat, and they need to be cuddled. Everything else is just frills, stuff to make you feel good. I wonder if things would have been different if I'd invested more time into what Alexander needed? I was so worried about whether I could be a mother, the most natural thing in the world, but a relationship with another adult I expected to just excel at. I believed it was my right to be in a happy marriage. I wanted a singing career, I wanted a baby, but I never believed it was guaranteed that I would have those things. A relationship, on the other hand – of course I would because, well, everybody gets that.

'You have me,' I told Moses. 'Don't assume you'll get more than that unless you work really hard on being a really good person who deserves it.' Moses tries to eat the loofah. 'Don't eat that,' I say, and take it from him. He looks like he might cry so I give it back.

I pull myself out of the bath and dry off. When I've finished I look at myself in the full-length mirror. I have no memory of looking at my body and being happy with what I saw. I often hear women talking about their favourite and least favourite parts of their bodies but I don't have either; I hate it all just a little bit. I think I was one of the only women in the world to actually look forward to having a post-baby body – at least then I had an excuse. I put on Dad's bathrobe and as I am lifting Moses out of the bath I hear my phone from the bedroom. I run down the stairs, clutching my son under my arm like a sandbag. In the kitchen, Dad is watching a programme about people trying to buy houses in Spain; I shove a dripping Moses in his lap.

'Can you take him? I have a call,' I say, and I don't stop to hear his reaction. In my room, I fall on to my phone, convinced the ringing will stop as soon as my hand reaches it; when it doesn't I'm surprised and I fumble as I try to take the call.

'Hello?' I hear George say.

'Hi! Hi! Hello.' My breathing is heavy; I hope it sounds sexy.

'It's good to hear your voice,' he says.

'You too.' It feels like we've never been apart, rather than on two separate continents.

'What was it you wanted?'

'Oh yes, that.' I sit on the bed. 'This is the thing. I'm concerned you don't realize . . . I mean . . . The thing is . . . I need you to know I'm a bit fucked up.'

'Aren't we all?'

'No, but like, I mean . . . I'm worried you don't understand I'm a mess. I mean I'm going through a divorce, I think.'

'You were married?'

'Well yes, exactly!'

'Don't worry – we all have stuff going on, just ask my therapist.'

I play with the cord of the dressing gown. 'I know, it's just . . . I'm not quite the person I want to be, maybe not the person you want to be with, if you want to be with me.'

George pauses. 'I'm pretty sure I do,' he says, and it feels like I've solved a riddle. I've done the one thing I've always avoided doing when getting to know a guy – told the truth.

'As long as you know that things are kind of up in the air right now. I'm in transition at work. My ex isn't great, he hasn't really stepped up with childcare. He's kinda left me to work things out. I'm doing all the hard work and nothing's changed for him – he's still got his work, he's living in our flat, he still has my cat, for God's sake.' George doesn't respond; maybe I got carried away with the honesty thing. 'I'm sorry,' I say. 'I shouldn't offload on you like this.'

'You should,' says George. 'I want to know what you're thinking. He sounds pretty pathetic – who keeps someone's cat? That's just evil.'

I laugh and I swear I can hear him smiling. 'Well, he was our cat, Moxie, that's his name, the cat. He was our cat but, you know, not really. He was *my* cat, you know.'

George laughs softly. 'Break-ups are hard. Don't worry about it. You can tell me anything.'

I lie back on the bed. I feel like I'm a teenager again, or I guess what I would have felt like if any boys had called me.

'I guess I just don't want to feel like I'm overburdening you.'

'But isn't that what I'm for?' An interesting concept. I spent a lot of time with Alexander trying to make sure that I didn't burden him in any way. I kind of thought that was my job; I never considered another option might be to share the burdens.

'OK. Actually, that sounds really good.'

'So hit me . . .'

'What do you mean?'

'What's the worst thing you've ever done? Burden me.'

'Ha ha!' This seems so wrong; this goes against everything I know about being a woman trying to attract a man, but I guess this is the ultimate test. If I give him my worst and he can take it, then maybe he deserves my best.

'I went through a period when I was in my teens of stealing stuff from shops. Nothing big, stationery mainly, but then I felt too guilty to use it and stashed it all under my bed.'

'Ha ha! So you didn't commit to a life of crime?'

'Also, I once told a bride she looked fat on her wedding day.'

George laughs again. His laugh is so deep and even. 'Who?'

'My cousin.'

'How old were you?'

'Six.'

'I think we'll let that one slide.'

'OK, also' – I'm sort of warming up now; I think I'm kinda getting the whole Catholic confession thing – 'I let someone take the blame for setting the chemistry lab on fire at school.'

'And arson. Nice little catalogue of evil there. I'm going to have to take all this under advisement.'

'OK, fine,' I say. I feel a bit foolish for starting it all but I also feel wonderful that I did. 'What's the worst thing you've done?'

'I killed a man once.' For a second, time stops, until I hear him chuckle down the line. 'No, the worst thing I've done is let too many opportunities pass me by.' We both pause to let his words sink in. 'Don't worry about not being whole; it's a journey. And go get your cat. I'd never let someone keep Marley from me.'

'Who's Marley?' I ask.

'My cat – she's with my mum at the moment.'

9) <u>Has to like animals</u> and will have a cat called Hendrix.

Marley. Close enough.

25

DETAILS MATTER. THE fact that George has a cat might seem trite, a bit silly, but it says so much. It says that he's kind and nurturing and that he can commit to something. I see now that I've been approaching the task of changing my life in a big-picture way, when I need to be working on making each day different, working on the individual minutes. I find a running schedule online, one that outlines a weekly target of circuits. The first session is walking for twenty minutes at a steady pace. I know I can walk; I do it every day. I just need to walk with intention.

When I go out for the first time, the park is almost empty. A woman with an overexcited terrier says hello as we pass and I love the interaction – two independent women, doing something productive with their evening. As I walk away I imagine she is saying to herself she might do a bit more tomorrow – put on her trainers, take Fido for an extra-long run. I see her reasserting her promise to herself that she will finally get started, because she has seen me and I already have.

I sit down with Mum and work out a proper routine for our new living situation. I let her know I'll be getting up with her and Moses in the morning and will give her and

191

Dad some money for keeping us. To my surprise she's accepting of this and when we've finished our chat she leaves the room and returns with a large cardboard box.

'I've saved some of your books,' she says. I wonder why she has waited until now to bestow them upon me, but as I pull out the yellowing hardbacks, I am taken back to long afternoons curled up on the sofa with my dad and I push aside any analysis of my mother's motivations.

'You loved that one,' she says, as I flick through *Fanny and May*. It's the story of two elephants who build a house out of cake and then one of them eats it and they are left homeless. I recall the fear I felt as the young elephant couldn't stop herself from eating the roof and the walls, a helpless victim of her own gluttony.

Moses is playing with some bricks on the kitchen floor and I take him and the book into the living room. We settle together into the armchair and I tell him a story I know by heart and my heart knows. He's so still as I read, and even though I'm not sure if he understands what's going on, he's with me every step of the journey. When I finish he shouts, 'Again!' and it's music to my ears.

I decide to spend half an hour reading with my boy every day. Together we rediscover my old friends. He loves the playfulness of Dr Seuss and the naughtiness of Peter Rabbit. Often, he comes home from nursery and calls out, 'Book! Book!' as if he is summoning a pet. If I am not too tired after I have put him to bed, I go for a walk around the park. I can feel it getting easier, feeling less like something *other* people do.

'I'm doing really well,' I tell Leanne over coffees and babycinos with the boys one Friday. 'I'm moving past stuff. I'm just . . . moving.'

'I'm really pleased for you,' she says. 'I want nothing but the best for you.'

'You sound like a greeting card,' I say.

'I don't mean to,' she says, and then takes a sip of her coffee. 'I'm just wondering what's got you so fired up?'

'If I'm honest, I think it's George,' I say. 'You were so right about the list thing. If you ask the universe, it will give you what you need.' I pick up a biscuit that Moses has abandoned and then change my mind and place it back down.

'I was sort of worried you would say that,' says Leanne.

'Expand,' I say, maintaining my smile in an effort to hold on to my positive outlook.

Leanne licks her lips and says, 'You invested so much of your happiness in Alexander. I don't want you to be let down by another man.'

'I'm not going to be let down. That's the point. He's not the sort of guy who would do that. The list was your idea, Lee. Why would you build me up just to shit on my disco?'

Leanne gently places her cup on its saucer. 'I'm not' – she clears her throat and glances at Lucas – '*pooping* on anything. We were drunk; coming up with that list was a laugh. I don't want you to think it means anything.'

'Everything has meaning,' I say, and I realize I sound like Tashi.

I don't try to convince Leanne but I don't let her doubt derail me either. If I have found a fire within me, what does it matter who created the spark? I still check in with George most mornings. He continues to be the first thing I think about but now I have something to share, little tit-bits from the previous day – things that have lifted me up. I start to feel closer to being a whole person and not a fragile Kinder Egg, with a missing toy. Having George to share my day with helps me to think about my actions. I don't want to tell him that I stayed in bed all day, that I ate a ready meal and cried myself to sleep, so I don't. I keep my head down at work, I read to Moses, I call Marc and confirm my gig. I work on the minutes and change my days.

26

THE DAY OF Tom's engagement party I go to a boutique just off the high street. I need to find a dress, specifically the most fabulous dress I have ever worn in my life. My dream is that Tom will see me and wonder why he ever let me go. Failing that, I want him at least to wish he'd had the chance to spend the night with me before he did so. I'm greeted enthusiastically by the saleswoman, who asks me if she can help. 'I need something that's going to make me feel amazing,' I say.

'Amazing I can do,' she says. 'What size are you?'

'A fourteen,' I say. She pauses – not for long but long enough that I know she is reconsidering whether making me look amazing is something she can achieve.

'I have the perfect thing,' she says. She goes out back and returns holding an emerald green dress in front of her. I take it into the fitting room. It's a great choice – knee length and close fitting with a large bow at the neck. I take off my clothes and wiggle into it. It takes some effort. Standing in it I still think it's a great choice but perhaps for someone else's body. There is some ruching around the stomach that is definitely not part of the design and I don't usually go for sleeveless because I've always thought my arms are a little sausagey. I stand on my toes to try and simulate heels and turn slowly from left to right. When I inhale the dress looks better; can I hold my stomach in for two hours?

'How are you getting on?' asks the saleswoman. I open the curtain and look at her questioningly. 'Oh,' says the woman, and then claps her hand over her mouth. She adjusts the bow a little and steps back to review me again. 'It looks perfect,' she says. I like how the dress looks through her eyes, so I go back into the changing room, put my clothes back on and take it to the till.

'It doesn't have a price on it,' I say.

'Yes, it's just come in, literally this morning. It's a hundred and eighty-nine pounds.'

I don't speak. I have to pay Patricia. I have to think about finding somewhere to live; I can't spend that much money on a dress. I also can't say no now; I can't have this woman look at me and see me for the failure that I am. I get out my debit card and force a smile on my face as I place it in the machine. As I head home, I console myself that a woman in a dress like this couldn't possibly have a bad night – and also that, as it has no price tag on it, I can wear it and return it.

Mum has taken Moses to a miniature railway, so I sleep for an hour before throwing back a fortifying vodka and forcing two pairs of Spanx over my thighs. On the way to the party I stop by Cara's flat. I had tried to persuade her to come with me – crashing the engagement party of the guy who rejected your mate seemed like the kind of subversive act she would enjoy, but she refused. I hope that I can convince her – Cara would make it fun; she'd help me to find the punchline to this joke – but as she leads me to her living room, she repeats what she told me on the phone: 'I won't be part of this sadness.'

'Not everything has to be achingly cool, Cara.' She pours us both a glass of rum from her drinks trolley and tops each of them with a splash of ginger ale.

'Not that kind of sad,' Cara says as she hands me my drink, 'although I do find the concept of an engagement, let alone a party for it, pathetic. The literal sadness. Whatever sadness is in your soul that makes you think this is a good idea.' I take a sip of my drink and Cara's generous measures make me cough a little. Cara drinks half of her own glass and waits for my response.

'It's not that I think it's a *good* idea,' I say. 'It's just something I have to do.' Cara dismisses this idea with a shake of her head.

'That's the thing. You don't have to *do* anything. I guess besides raise your kid, but that's your fuck-up.'

'I suppose I want to feel empowered. I want to show him that he doesn't affect me.'

Cara looks thoughtful. 'He doesn't affect you but you're going to celebrate him shackling himself to some other human?'

'OK, that he doesn't affect me, like, negatively.'

Cara finishes her drink and says, 'Why don't you show that by coming with me to a house party at Julie's? I won't try and force you to play naked Twister this time.' She nods towards my glass. 'Top up?'

'No, Cara, I'm going. I bought a dress.' Cara takes in my outfit without comment and shrugs. 'It's going to be good. I'm going to show him what he missed out on.' I hand Cara my glass and prepare to leave. She shakes her head.

'Don't say I didn't warn you,' she says as I gather my things.

'I appreciate it,' I say, 'but I know what I'm doing.'

Cara lifts my half-full glass in a toast. 'I'm glad someone does, babe.'

On the walk, I repeat uplifting mantras to myself – I am beautiful, I am confident, I am free. It sort of works and then I arrive at OhSo. Fairy lights are strung up and jazz music is playing and it is exactly as I would have had it. A woman ushers me in.

'Hello, my darling,' she says. 'Green is obviously in fashion.' I look at her lime green skirt suit and nod wordlessly. 'Are you a friend of the bride or groom?' she asks. I can tell that saying this tickles her.

'The groom, I guess,' I say.

'I didn't think I recognized you,' she says. 'I'm Rhiannon's mother.'

I need another drink. We stand in silence and the awkwardness starts to set in. When another woman approaches us, I am relieved at first but then I see the joy on the face of my companion, and I want to cease existing.

'Rhi, Rhi!' My new friend squeezes her daughter around the waist. 'I'm going to go and powder my nose. This is one of Tom's people.' As her mother leaves, Rhiannon gives me a hug and flashes me a model-perfect smile. She is wearing a dress of ivory lace that embraces every inch of her body and I can't take my eyes away from her perfect stomach, a stomach that looks like it has never held more than a salad, let alone a baby.

'Thanks for coming. Do you work with Tom?'

I am too wounded to lie. I say no. 'I'm Martha,' I tell her. I think she will look angry but her smile becomes even more pronounced.

'Thank you for coming and *thank you*,' she says again. She gives me a wink, as if we are co-conspirators.

'Well, I never turn down a drink,' I say. Rhiannon throws back her head and laughs wildly. As she does so her waist-length auburn curls bounce around her face. I have a vision of cutting the lot off in her sleep.

'There's plenty of that,' says Rhiannon, 'and if you don't mind me saying, lots of lovely single guys.' I search her face for evidence that she is aware of the cruelty of her comment. I find none and decide that she is simply an imbecile.

'That's fine,' I say. 'I'm seeing someone.'

'Oh, great!' she says. 'Where is he?' She looks behind me as if my boyfriend could have been hiding behind me all this time.

'He's not here,' I say. 'He's in Africa.'

'Cool,' says Rhiannon. 'Where's he from?'

'Uhm, Brighton,' I say.

'Oh right, why is he in Africa?' Her brow furrows and I realize that because I am black and my boyfriend is in Africa, she has completed a mental equation that results in him coming from the motherland.

'He's not African,' I say. As I say this I hope she will look a little embarrassed. She doesn't, though; she's either too confident or too happy for such a negative emotion to touch her. More people arrive and she looks distracted.

'The bar is over there,' she says, indicating behind her. She doesn't have to tell me twice. The bar is staffed by two young guys wearing bow ties. They're probably students; they look like they're in fancy dress in their starched, white shirts. One asks me if I want a cocktail or some prosecco.

'What's in the cocktail?' I ask.

'Pretty much vodka and pomegranate juice,' he says.

'Yeah, but how much alcohol?' The bartender shrugs. 'Maybe one shot.'

'OK, give me prosecco,' I say. 'Two glasses.' The barman

dutifully does so and I down the first glass. I'm about to start on the second when I feel a tap on my shoulder. When I turn Tom is standing there. He's red-faced and breathing audibly; he looks like he's been running.

'Hiiiiii!' he says. He tries to draw me into a hug but I'm still holding my drink and he ends up just crashing into me. 'Thanks so much for coming,' he says. He's actually smiling at me, smiling as if we're friends.

'No problem,' I say. 'I wasn't doing anything anyway.'

'Good, good,' he says. 'You look . . . great.' I can feel my dress bunching around my waist and I'm not sure I believe him.

'Whatever,' I say, and finish my drink.

'Two more,' says Tom to the barman. 'It's a free bar,' he says to me. The barman places them in front of us. Tom holds up his glass; I assume he wants me to toast.

'What am I doing here?' I ask.

'You were the one who made me realize what I had lost,' says Tom, still smiling like a loon.

'Well, that's great. That's dandy. Good for you.'

'I just wanted to make things right between us,' he says.

I laugh and then Tom laughs and I say, 'You're a psychopath.'

Tom stops. 'I think you need to relax,' he says. He puts a hand on my shoulder. It feels like a lead weight resting there. I down my drink and reach for another glass, shrugging my shoulder as I do so, so that his hand slips off. 'I'm not that great a catch,' says Tom. He smiles again; I guess that's his way of apologizing.

'I'm fine,' I say. 'I'm relaxed. Thanks for this.' I tip my glass at him and walk away. I try to move in a way that looks purposeful, although I have no idea where I am going. I walk towards the toilet but before I get there I spot

Leanne arriving. She looks amazing; her blonde hair is in a neat bun and she's wearing a yellow shift dress and nude heels, the quintessential colleague's wife.

'You were supposed to be here before me,' I hiss at her.

'Lucas wouldn't settle,' she says. 'You OK?'

'Yeah, yeah,' I say, but I feel really light-headed. In part because of the booze and the lack of food and the underwear cutting off my circulation, but also because of the injustice of it all. 'How does it work?' I ask Leanne. 'How do some people get this?' Leanne looks confused but before she can speak James pulls me in for a hug.

As we part he looks at my face and says, 'Let's get pissed, eh?'

James gets us all fresh drinks and we sit together as he tells us stories about his colleagues. Apparently Tom doesn't have any friends outside work, so almost the entire office is there. 'That's Mike,' says James, pointing to a tall, thin guy with acne scars and a scowl. 'We call him Crazy Mike because he eats the same lunch every day – one egg sandwich and a packet of salt and vinegar crisps. Never plain, God forbid smoky bacon.' Although there is no way Mike can hear us he looks over and we all giggle. James tells us off. 'You two are gonna get me in trouble,' he says. It occurs to me that I'm starting to have fun. I probably shouldn't have waited this long to go out with Leanne and James. I hope that George and James get on and we can go on double dates and then on holiday together.

The jazz has been replaced by a DJ playing nineties music and Pulp's 'Common People' comes on.

'Oh my God,' says Leanne. 'We have to dance!'

'I can't dance,' I say; I literally can't in this dress.

James holds out his hand. 'Can I have this dance?' he asks his wife. She accepts, and he leads her to a small clearing between the tables. Soon most people are dancing, including Tom and his wife-to-be. Although the song is uptempo they have their arms wrapped round each other and are swaying gently. A small pit of loneliness starts to jostle around in my stomach and I look for someone to distract me from it. A few chairs away I see Crazy Mike sitting alone. Although ale is not being served, he has acquired a pint from somewhere. I admire his resourcefulness and I go and sit next to him.

'You having a good time?' I ask.

'Does it look like I'm having a good time?' he asks back. He says this in a friendly way, though. He has a nice Yorkshire accent.

'Not really,' I say.

'Shit, and I was trying so hard,' he says.

'Why have you come then?' I ask him.

'That's what I've been trying to work out,' he says.

'Well, you've met me now,' I say. He smiles a little. 'You have no excuse; this is my ex's party and I'm having a great time.'

He studies me closely. 'No, no,' I say, 'I've found someone else now. He's perfect, literally perfect. I asked the universe for what I wanted.' Crazy Mike looks a bit concerned. 'I know it sounds mad, no offence. You should try it, though, if you want someone who will accept you for you; who won't ask you to change.' Mike takes a sip of his pint. I put my hand over his. 'If you like egg sandwiches you will find someone who appreciates that.'

Mike removes his hand from mine and says, 'There's someone I've got to say hello to.' He gets up and crosses the room and takes a seat next to no one. Whatever, I think.

Marthashotbod: What're you doing?

202

No response. I head back to the bar and sample the cock-tail. It goes down like squash. I tell the bartender to keep them coming and, although he looks at me suspiciously, he obliges. The music stops and Tom's voice fills the room. I look round and see him standing by the DJ booth.

'Thank you all for being here,' he says. 'My wife-to-be and I—' His words are then drowned out by a drunken cheer from the crowd and he starts again. 'My wife-to-be and I want to thank you for being a part of today and of our future. I'm so happy I've found her.' He gestures to Rhiannon, who walks over and stands beside him. He wraps an arm round her waist and says, 'Now that I have her, I'm never letting her go.' The crowd cheers again. An elderly version of Tom walks over to him and takes the microphone.

'Hello, hello,' he says into the mic and everyone laughs. 'For those of you I haven't met, I'm Thomas's father. I want to say I hope you're all enjoying yourselves and I hope Rhiannon and Tom have a long and happy life together. I'm so pleased to have her in my family. She really is the most elegant, beautiful girl I have ever known.'

'Why don't *you* marry her then,' I mumble, and a couple of people turn to look at me.

'I don't know how Tom has done it,' he says. Everyone laughs, I think in agreement. 'I hope everybody here can have what they have.' He raises his glass and everyone cop-ies his action. 'To Tom and Rhiannon,' he says, and the crowd parrots it back before giving applause. When the party is quiet again Tom's father asks if anyone else has any words to say. I have a lot to say. As I approach him I can feel the anticipation of the crowd. I can hear whispering voices questioning who I am as I take the microphone.

'Hello,' I say to a rapt audience. 'I just want to say that

everyone deserves love, whether they're young, old, thin or a little bit chubby but more or less in proportion.' At this point I catch sight of Leanne in the crowd. Obviously, I have no definitive proof of this but I'm pretty sure her eyes are the widest they have ever been. Her face sobers me a little. I glance at Tom and Rhiannon, who are looking at each other with similar expressions. 'Anyway, to Tom and Rhiannon,' I say to continued silence. I hand the microphone back to the DJ and he quickly starts playing 'Build Me Up Buttercup'.

Leanne rushes over to me.

'What the hell was that?' she asks.

'My speech,' I say. I decide I will just brazen it out, I will brazen the whole thing out.

'You need to go home,' she says. As she says this she links her arm with mine and starts to move towards the door. I wrestle from her grip, causing us both to stumble a little in the process. Leanne looks upset.

'What I need is another drink.' I march back to the bar, leaving her alone.

'More prosecco,' I tell the barman.

He folds his arms. 'I think you've had enough,' he says.

'I'm so sick of people telling me what to do,' I spit at him. The barman starts serving someone else; my body feels almost overwhelmed by the shame of his dismissal. I walk away from the bar and I decide to keep walking, to walk away from the whole thing. I leave OhSo, struggle up from the beach on to the road and hail a cab.

'Where you going, love?' says the driver. And I give him the address. My address with Alexander, the address my bank statements still get sent to.

27

As THE CAB pulls away from the apartment building it seems like an appropriate time for me to work out why I'm there, what it is I hope to gain, and then I see it, crouched underneath a fir tree – Moxie. I walk towards him and he mews softly. I feel a stab of guilt that he may have been missing his mummy. I put my hand out and he licks it but when I try to pick him up he struggles. 'Shhhhh,' I say. 'We need to go home.'

He does not comprehend my Human and hooks his claws into the front of my dress. I sit down on the damp grass and try to wrap him up in my cardigan. He does not like this. I don't know if it's my wailing or the cat's that wakes them but I suddenly find myself bathed in the glow of the security light, and standing silhouetted in the doorway of the flat entrance are Alexander and Poppy. Poppy is wearing one of Alexander's T-shirts. I remember he bought it from a market in south London and I laughed at him for paying forty pounds for a crappy T-shirt. I still think it's crappy but Poppy does not look crap in it; even tousled hair and a scrunched-up sleep face can't detract from her long tanned legs and flawless complexion. Alexander has on his dressing gown. I know he has nothing underneath it because that's how he sleeps. When we first got together he would walk round the flat naked in the mornings, making toast and tea and swinging his penis to make me laugh. At the end he was always in that tatty dressing gown and there was no penis swinging of any kind.

Alexander returns indoors briefly and comes back wearing a pair of trainers. He stops at the door and says a few words to Poppy. She looks over at me sadly and nods. Alexander kisses her on the nose and she disappears inside. He then walks over to me. Without helping me up or bending down he says, 'Martha, what the fuck are you doing? I mean, seriously, what the fuck are you doing?'

'This is my cat,' I whisper.

'What?' asks Alexander.

'This is my fucking cat!' I shout.

Alexander gives me a lift back to my mother's, Moxie huddled with me in the passenger seat of the MG. We drive in silence; even the cat seems to understand that now is not the time for conversation.

After he's parked Alexander says, 'What is going on with you?'

I stare out of the passenger window of the car. 'I'm getting a divorce,' I say.

'And what about me?' says Alexander. 'You act like this is a good time for me.'

'Isn't it?' I say. 'Shacking up with your child bride. You look like you're having fun to me.'

Alexander smacks his hand against the steering wheel. 'You dumped me!' he shouts. 'You decided on a whim you were over being married to me and now what? I'm supposed to support you through it?' I look at Alexander. He looks hurt and angry.

'We're supposed to support each other,' I say. 'And Moses, what about him? He needs to see more of you.'

Alexander closes his eyes. 'Yeah, I want him to stay more often but I don't want to confuse him. I worry I'm not good to be around him. I'm feeling pretty shaken up.' I look at Alexander, strong and sober in the driver's seat, always in the driver's seat.

'He needs you,' I say, and then quietly, 'I need you.'

Alexander rakes his hand through his hair. 'Don't say that,' he says. 'It doesn't help. We both need space.'

I look at Alexander's profile as he leans back against the headrest. When Moses was born, I was taken aback by how much he looked like his father. When I was pregnant I would imagine my tiny, new child and in my mind he was a smaller version of me, but from day one I could see Alexander's big eyes and strong chin. I don't get to have space; I see Alexander every day. I begin to cry.

'I'm sorry,' I say. 'Can we just start again?'

Alexander laughs bitterly. 'From when? From tonight? Yes, let's do that and try you not turning up in my garden, mad and drunk.'

'What about from the beginning?' I ask. 'If we could start again from the beginning what would you have done differently?' This is what I would have done differently: I would have told him how I felt about him sooner; we would have gone travelling; I would have worked harder; we would have danced together more often; I would have asked him what he wanted; I would have told him what I needed; I would not have had the calamari that time; I would have told him I loved him every day, even if I didn't feel it, but I *would* have loved him every day because love is about actions and not words.

'I wouldn't have married you,' says Alexander.

I get out of the car. It takes some time because I must negotiate keeping hold of Moxie as I do but after I succeed, I slam the door behind me and I don't look back.

28

I OPEN MY EYES and try to put together the pieces of the previous evening but they won't fit. Mum comes in carrying Moses. 'Do you plan to lie in bed all day?' she asks.

'No,' I say. I can't. In my wisdom I confirmed my gig for today, believing I would be boosted by my triumph at the party.

'Why is there a cat in my kitchen?' asks Mum.

'I'll sort it,' I say. Mum looks like she has more to say but thankfully she leaves and takes Moses with her.

After I drag myself from the comfort of my bed, I spend the afternoon curled up on the sofa watching cartoons with Moses and drinking Dad's secret stash of full-fat Coke. I text Leanne an apology and a carefully selected 'I'm sorry' GIF but she doesn't reply; maybe she wishes she didn't know me too.

As the evening draws in the last thing I want to do is sing and only the thought of George makes me feel like I can do it. I know you're not supposed to say that; you're supposed to pretend that all your strength comes from within, manufactured from a little inner strength factory located in your gut – but that's bullshit. Everything good I've ever done has been with the encouragement or approval of someone else – my mother, my friends or a man. That's why I achieved so little with Alexander; he never gave me strength. I think he was scared of what I might do with it. Once I told him I was thinking about a career in talent management. I thought I could partner with Cara; we could manage artists and put on events. He didn't say, 'That's great!' or, 'Tell me more!' He said, 'Why?' George knows that it doesn't matter why; what matters is me. I know it is this thought that gives me the motivation to put on my make-up and iron my funeral dress. I even manage to push my anxiety to the edge of my consciousness as I walk to the club, until I see Cara. She is standing with someone who must be Marc in the club's dressing room and seeing her familiar face makes every-thing real. She gives me a kiss on each cheek.

'Ready, darling?'

'I think so,' I say.

'Not quite,' says Cara. She gets a lip gloss out of her bag and indicates that I should open my mouth. I do so and she carefully applies it to my lips.

'Now you're ready,' she says.

Marc pats me on the bum. 'Looking good, darlin', I hope you sound as good as you look.' Marc is at least three inches shorter than me and from my vantage point I can see the light bouncing off his head through his thinning hair. Despite our obvious incompatibility he is looking at me like I'm a plate of baby-back ribs. I guess having the power to offer people what they want gives a man a decent dose of self-confidence.

'What have you got?' he asks.

I give him my sheet music and he looks over it.

'It'll do – a little vanilla but we can work on that. As soon as you're settled can you come and sound check?'

'Sure,' I say, and he leaves. 'I didn't know you were coming,' I say to Cara.

'How could you think I wouldn't come?' she asks.

'I guess I just thought you might have something better to do.'

'Something better than this? You're ridiculous.' She turns to face the mirror and pushes her fingers into her hair, wiggling her hands around to lift her roots. 'Besides, have you seen Curtis on the drums? Hands off.'

I laugh and say, 'Don't worry.' I take off my coat and as I slip it on to a coat hook I say, 'Actually, I'm seeing someone.' I try to say this casually. I hope my tone makes clear that this is just an aside, nothing to dwell on. Even though I want to tell her about George, I instinctively know I don't want Cara to ask any questions. Cara, however, is very skilled at doing the exact opposite of whatever someone wants her to do.

'No, you're not,' she says. 'So what's really going on?'

'What do you mean?' I ask.

Cara straightens out the hem of my dress before saying, 'You're not seeing anyone because if you were you would have told me already. You wouldn't have been able to resist reliving the romance and regurgitating all the tawdry details. So what are you really telling me? Are you back with A-hole?'

'No, God no. I actually have a boyfriend.' We haven't confirmed this officially but it's one of those unspoken things we both know.

'How did you meet him?' asks Cara. She does not sound happy; she does not sound like a friend eager to share in her buddy's joy. She sounds dubious.

'I met him on the app. On Linger.'

'Right, so you met him on the app and now . . . he's your boyfriend?'

210

'Yes,' I say. I say it with a finality that Cara ignores.

'Has he met Moses?' she asks.

'No, not yet,' I say.

Cara's face relaxes. 'Is he good in the sack?' she asks.

'I . . . er . . . I don't actually know yet.'

'Ooh,' says Cara, 'playing coy.' She shrugs as she says this and then leans in towards the mirror to check her eye make-up. 'Good kisser, though?' she asks.

I watch her for a few seconds before saying, 'I don't know that either.' Cara stops preening and looks at me via my reflection in the mirror. 'We haven't met yet.' Cara stands up straight and turns around so she is facing me.

'So you *don't* have a boyfriend,' she says.

I shake my head. 'You have no idea what you're talking about,' I say.

'Mate, you're the one with the make-believe boyfriend.'

I feel my arms get tense. 'Can't you just be supportive or pretend to be supportive or does that go against your moral code or something?'

Cara presses each thumb and forefinger together and moves them up and down to emphasize each word, as if she is conducting a tiny orchestra. 'You. Have. An. Imaginary. Boyfriend,' she says.

'What is it?' I ask. 'It's like if you're not being a bitch you don't have a reason to exist.'

Cara narrows her eyes. 'You're right, babe, I don't have time for this.' She gives me a kiss on the cheek and leaves the dressing room, but just before she closes the door she says, 'Break a leg.'

Having Cara go like that is something of a relief. I'm tired of having to hold on to things. In truth I think I prefer doing things on my own – being with other people, even

211

people you like, requires constant assessment of their wants. It's not possible to keep doing that without damaging yourself in the process. I don't have the energy any more. I have a little cry and then I redo my make-up. It's time to accept that I need to start doing stuff without anyone to support me.

> Marthashotbod: I have a gig tonight, wish me luck.
> Undeterred83: That's hot. What sort of gig?
> Marthashotbod: A little jazz club.
> Undeterred83: Wow, you have so many talents, I'm feeling inadequate.
> Marthashotbod: You are anything but that.
> Undeterred83: Well, good luck. Not that you need it, you're amazing.

The club is small and made to look smaller by the black and red decor. There's a handful of patrons dotted around the room, along with a full table at the front. Marc is at the bar drinking a short. 'Was that as quick as you could be? Women for you, I guess,' he says. He slips an arm round me and rests his hand on my hip. 'If you don't mind, can you go straight into your set? I have some special guests in.'

'Uhm, the band—' I say.

'Don't you worry yourself about the boys, they're tight. These folks have just signed up for my premium member scheme – the stuff people will pay if you include a glass of cheap fizz, eh. I want you to charm them a little for me.' He leads me over to a table at the front of the room. Two men and two women, I assume couples, sit looking pleased with themselves.

'Meet the talent,' says Marc to the table. They smile and

nod. Marc turns to me and I realize I'm supposed to say something.

'Have a wonderful evening,' I say. It takes Marc a few seconds to work out that I don't have any more. He shakes hands with the gentlemen and then leads me to the side of the stage.

'Take it easy on this set,' he says. 'You can go on again later and bring it home.'

'Definitely,' I say. My throat feels tight, as if it's fighting to keep hold of my voice. I know that professionals do vocal exercises and, since I'm getting paid, I'm a professional now too. I stand at the side of the stage and gently run up and down a scale.

'Fuck, fuck, fuck, fuck, fuck, fuck, fuck, fuck, fuck,' I sing. The room around me goes into soft focus. I understand that it's just a tiny club with an audience smaller than the average coffee shop line but, however low-key the event is, its symbolism is huge. It's a gig, a real solo spot. It's the first step in the direction of a new life.

I've never even performed in public before, but there was another occasion when I was supposed to. Aged ten I was cast as Mary in Stanford Junior School's musical version of the nativity. I don't remember how I was given the role; I can't imagine I put myself forward for it. Perhaps a bright-eyed teacher was hoping for her *Dangerous Minds* moment and tried to give the shy, awkward girl her day in the spotlight. However it came about, the decision was controversial. I was the first Mary of colour Stanford had seen and my classmates made it clear I was not the popular choice.

The scene is tattooed on my mind, Mrs Baker playing my introductory chord over and over until it rang in my ears, and even then I think I might have been OK, but then

I caught my mother's eyes, narrowed in anticipation, and I did the unthinkable. I wet myself. The warmth of the liquid was almost comforting and Mary's robes were concealing most of the evidence. Mrs Baker skipped to the next song and it would have been fine – my humiliation might have remained personal – if Christopher Nagle, my nativity husband, had not noticed the puddle and shouted, 'She pissed herself!'

There was an impromptu interval whilst I was cleaned up and bundled into our car. My mother didn't even comment on the event; it was obvious to all that her judgement was not necessary. When I ended up attending secondary school across town, the official reason was because of the school's excellent GCSE results, but the move was really to escape the ghosts of Christmas past.

Standing next to the stage now, I'm taken back to that moment. I can even smell the hall – wood polish and boiled veg.

'Ready?' the drummer mouths to me. Cara was right, he is good-looking. He's got a shaved head and two full tattoo sleeves; he looks like he might keep me safe up there. I lift a finger to indicate that he should give me a second. Then I walk slowly to the bar and ask for a glass of water. As I drink I scan the room. I can see Marc still sweet talking his golden table but his eyes are trained on me. Bile rises to my mouth – nerves with a side of hangover. I ask for a second glass and drink this one more slowly. I concentrate on the sensation of the liquid sliding down my throat and on the cold firmness of the glass. I place it on the bar and turn to face the stage. The six band members are looking at me with a variety of 'what the fuck' expressions. I walk over to them and as I climb the steps they seem to shake. I look at my knight on drums and he just looks bored; none of the band members speak to me. I stand at the microphone and as I adjust it I survey the crowd. There's a handful of people either deep in conversation or smiling at me encouragingly; I should be fine.

From behind me someone says, 'Shall we go from the top?' I nod and the band starts to play without even counting me in. As Marc promised, they're tight, so tight I can't breathe. I clear my throat and hear the sound ringing around the room. I open my mouth to sing the first words of 'My Baby Just Cares For Me' and nothing emerges but a croak. The band keeps repeating the intro; I try to start again and the same thing happens. One of the ladies at the front table holds out a glass of water. My bladder couldn't take any more liquid and that thought drags me back to that terrifying school stage and a hundred tiny heads bobbing with laughter. I reach out to take it anyway but my hand is shaking so much I can't be sure I'll be able to hold it. I stand with the mic to my mouth and my hand outstretched, like a confused zombie. The band keeps playing. I try to smile but moving my face unleashes the tears that have been working their way to the front of my eyes. I apologize and drop the microphone. It shrieks in protest as it hits the ground. I apologize again even though no one can hear me now and walk carefully off the stage.

I try to pack my things up quickly but I'm not quick enough. As Marc enters the dressing room his face glistens from the effort of coming to find me, or perhaps from rage. 'What the fucking fuck was that, missus?' he asks.

'I'm so sorry, I've had a lot on my mind,' I say.

'You've lost your mind, more like,' he says.

I put on my coat. 'I'm not feeling well,' I say. 'I'm sure I could do better a bit later or maybe tomorrow.'

'There ain't no tomorrow for you, love, you're dead to me.' That seems slightly dramatic.

'I'm sorry,' I say. He seems to soften; perhaps this happens to a lot of people. 'I won't expect full payment.'

Marc laughs. He actually clutches his stomach as he leans over and lets the mirth overcome his body.

'Payment! Payment? You've got some cheek. You should be paying me!'

'OK, I'm gonna go then,' I say, and walk past him towards the door.

'I thought Cara was your mate,' he says, without turning round. 'You've made her look like a dick.'

I don't respond. I think, no one can make Cara do anything.

29

THE NEXT MORNING I call in sick. I don't even have to do the calling-in-sick voice because I feel so despondent that every word I speak sounds like I'm in pain. 'Try an enema,' says Bob, 'works wonders.' I promise to look into his recommendation.

I manage to sleep through most of the day and my lethargy convinces Mum I have a lethal strain of flu she read about in the local paper. She leaves me to myself, save to pop into my room in the late afternoon with a bowl of chicken stew in her hand and a floral chiffon scarf wrapped around her mouth and nose. 'I'll go and collect Moses and keep him away from you,' she says. I want to say no because I think that Moses is the only person who won't judge me right now, but I don't want to blow my cover and have to explain that I'm not physically sick, just sick of life.

Leanne calls me shortly after seven. I can hear a car door slam and the start of the engine and I know that she's just left the office. 'How's things?' she asks. 'Sorry we didn't get a chance to catch up properly after the party.'

'I feel shit,' I say.

'Hmmmm,' says Leanne, 'is it work?'

'No, work is always shit, it's a bit of everything, a

smattering of shit.' I leave a gap for Leanne to laugh but she doesn't. 'I don't know. I've just got a lot going on.'

'I know, babe,' says Leanne, 'but we all have.' I hear the clicks of her indicator. 'How's the running going? That usually clears my head.'

'Yeah, I'm not in the mood.'

'You've got to push through that, hun,' says Leanne. I recognize her tone. It's warm but distracted; it's a voice she uses with her children. 'They have been busting my arse at work but I can't take it home. I don't have a choice.' I'm not sure how supportive this is, bringing up her cosy home life when I'm clearly struggling.

'You wouldn't understand, Leanne,' I say quietly.

'I understand tough times,' she says sharply. I feel like she's telling me off and I don't know why. 'Anyway, you've got good stuff going on – how was the gig?' I just can't say it; she's my best friend but I feel as though telling her how horribly and suddenly I watched my dream fall to pieces would break me.

'It was fine,' I say.

'Well, practice makes perfect,' says Leanne. The sentence makes me wince. I want to tell her that not everything has to be perfect. 'I'd stop by but I really need to go straight home tonight.'

'No, that's OK,' I say.

'I better run, I'm at the gym now. Speak soon, yeah?'

'Course,' I say.

Honestly, I think it was because of Leanne that I first went to Jacqueline. Motherhood was and is wonderful but it can be bloody hard. The initial fuss and excitement was so intoxicating but then everyone went back to their lives and I was left to try and understand mine. The ads for mild washing powder and unperfumed shampoo, featuring plump, laughing babies and clean-haired mothers – they lied to me. Finally, I was playing a role I had coveted for so long but I felt guilty every moment my heart wasn't filled with gratitude, and there were a lot of those moments. What hurt the most was how untouched Alexander's life seemed to be. He still took on new projects and went out with his friends; if anything he went out more as he always assumed I would want to stay home with Moses and go to bed early, and the fact that he was right didn't make it any less annoying.

One evening he had gone to a really important five-a-side meet-up, and no matter where I went in our home, I couldn't run away from the feeling of loneliness. I called Leanne and begged her to come over and she did. She arrived twenty minutes later with fresh cream cakes and even fresher highlights and seeing her, polished and in control, contentment leaking from her invisible pores, I felt more isolated than ever. I held it together for her visit. She talked me through a list of courses and activities that she was sure Moses and I would 'absolutely love' and to say otherwise would have seemed like a betrayal of my boy. I clutched him to my chest because he served as a reminder of why I should bother to keep going; Leanne cooed over him and told me that he was making her think about having another. Her admission was overwhelming – how could she possibly think about having three young children; why did she believe she would cope?

Leanne left and I couldn't stop my grief escaping. Alexander returned, flushed and loose-limbed, and found me lying in a damp patch of tears on the sofa. He sighed. I could tell he was irritated that I was killing his vibe, but as a wife, wasn't that my right? He sat gingerly next to me and told me about his day. I knew he was avoiding asking me what was wrong. I interrupted his chatter to say, 'I don't know who I am.'

Alexander squeezed the bridge of his nose. 'OK,' he said.

'OK, just OK? That's all you have to say?'

Alexander threw himself back on to the sofa. 'What else can I say? I can't tell you who you are.'

'Who can?'

'I think you need to talk to someone,' Alexander said.

'I'm talking to you!' I cried, pulling my knees up to my chest.

'Someone who can help you,' said Alexander, gently but firmly.

The following morning I still feel like a pile of crap that's been put through a NutriBullet but I make the decision to go to work. At least there, I know who I am and what I'm doing, even if I don't like it.

When I arrive, Bob is giving the room one of his 'motivational' speeches.

'. . . and some of you may not be used to winning, but let me tell you, when you get into the mindset you don't want to stop, and that's why I want this team to be top performing for the second year running.' As I take a seat Bob starts to walk up and down the room, sporadically tapping the back of someone's chair. 'You wanna know what I do? I look at myself in the mirror every morning and say, you are amazing. Not you – you lot need to pull your socks up if you wanna get back on track before end of year. *I* am amazing. Try it tomorrow. "I am amazing." It'll put a rocket up your arse.' No one responds, and Bob leaves us to take in his words.

'Don't know about you, but I'm feeling pumped now,' says Greg.

'What do we even get if we win?' Tashi asks him from across the desk divider.

'That,' says Greg, pointing towards the wall behind her. Tashi turns to look at the glass plaque awarded to the team last year. She turns back to face Greg and nods her head.

'I better get to work then,' she says.

It's a slow morning – thankfully, because I can't focus. A customer even manages to come through to me a second time, his voice full of indignation that he had been passed to 'entirely the wrong person'. Even though I start each call by stating my name, I pretend to be someone else and ignore his protests.

I plan to use my break to hide in reception and eat at least two Mars bars, and so as I see Lisa walk towards me as I end my last call, I think momentarily about ducking under the table. I know she's going to want to engage me in some inane prattle about paper plate colours or tapas-themed music. I prepare myself to be polite but boundaried or at the very least not to tell her to piss off. Lisa doesn't start with her usual pleasantries, though; she licks her lips before saying, 'I need to know if you've done any work on the olives?'

I look at Lisa. She's maybe twenty-two, twenty-three, and I understand that olives are the sum of her problems.

'What exactly did you want me to do with the olives?' I ask.

Lisa lets out a noise of complete exasperation. 'Well, work out numbers, ask about preferred colours, think about bowls . . .' She marks each item by tapping a finger of her left hand with her right forefinger. I understand I have drastically underestimated the amount of olive-based admin there is.

'No, Lisa. I haven't had time.' Lisa glances at my desk,

221

perhaps thinking it will reveal the source of my lack of focus. I am aware that a half-eaten packet of Jelly Babies lies there and I'm too tired to even work up the energy to feel embarrassed about it.

'If this is too much for you, let me know so I can hand it over to someone else.'

I let my eyes drop. 'Yes, I think it's too much.'

Lisa doesn't speak and when I look up I expect to see her angry, but what I see is worse: she's staring at me sympathetically.

'It's not a problem', says Lisa, in a tone an octave higher than her standard speaking voice. 'I'm sure it can be reassigned.'

Greg, who has clearly been listening, although he has given no indication of this, stands up. 'I can help, Lisa. To be honest we can probably knock it out over break.'

'God, thanks G!' cries Lisa. She reaches out and for an awkward second I think she's going to kiss him but she simply places her hand on his forearm. They walk away together, already deep into olive chat.

I'm still watching them when Tashi says, 'Do you want to try a healing mantra with me?' And I feel so desolate, I agree.

Tashi and I go to the multi-faith prayer room, which as far as I know has never been used in any spiritual way, although a temp once claimed she had sex there with a guy who works in the canteen, which is pretty close. Tashi opens the blinds and the light that streams in throws a spotlight on hundreds of pieces of fluff dancing through the air. She clears up a few Styrofoam cups and tosses them in an already overflowing bin.

'Not the most inspiring environment,' she says, 'but

that's good, that will show you that it's about using your mind to transcend your circumstances.' I smile weakly at her. I know that the only way my mind will be able to transcend my circumstances is if I help it along with a litre or two of vodka. 'OK,' continues Tashi. 'We just need to make an altar out of something.'

'Like in church?'

'Similar, but, like, less Goddy. Just something to focus your mind.' Tashi pulls a chair into the centre of the room and then removes a string of beads from around her neck and places them on the seat. 'I had this made to attract more creativity into my life.' I make an agreeable noise but I'm thinking it looks like something gleaned from a cut-price Christmas cracker. 'Now we need something from you.'

'My cardigan?' I suggest.

Tashi shakes her head. 'It's got to be more personal.'

'This is personal, it's on my body. You can't get more personal than that.'

'Yes, but it doesn't really mean anything to you.'

'I disagree, it means I haven't frozen my tits off today.'

Tashi's face wrinkles in concentration. 'What about that?' she asks, and grabs my left hand.

My engagement ring. I pull my hand away and at first I think about refusing but I can't come up with an honest reason why. I ease it off my finger and put it on the chair next to Tashi's beads. Tashi grabs her long, dark-blonde curls and twists them into a rope over her shoulder. We both sit on the floor in front of the chair. Tashi says, 'Let's do "ra ma da ma", it's totally cleansing.' She then begins to chant the phrase in a low, sinister voice. She sounds possessed; perhaps this is the explanation for the fact that she is completely bonkers. After a minute she stops and looks at me.

'Is it not working?' she asks. 'Do you not feel anything?'

I feel my knees starting to ache. 'It's just the chanting. It's a bit . . . ridiculous.'

'It might be a bit advanced,' says Tashi, and I know she doesn't intend to sound offensive. 'Just tune into what's happening outside you. Listen to the sound of a silent room.' Tashi closes her eyes; I do the same and for fifteen minutes I listen to the sound of my growling stomach.

I decide to walk home from work; not for exercise, just to lengthen the amount of time between being in one place and another, to have some space to be nowhere. As I walk, I think about Tashi, how serene she looked sitting on that scratchy carpet. Perhaps I'm the one who has it all wrong. I used to describe myself as a spiritual person but what I think I meant by that was my life was kind of OK and I was content to attribute that to some unknowable force in the world. When my life began to lose the shape I was comfortable with, any affinity with the universe was lost. When I was a child my grandmother would sometimes take me along to her church. My mother would take me to her flat the day before and I would sleep alongside my grandma, staying awake as long as I could so I could listen to her snoring, loud and strong. In the morning we would take two buses to attend the service in a chapel that looked not dissimilar to three others we would pass along the way. One Sunday I asked my grandmother why she went so far. Was the word of God not the same word at the church round the corner? Grandma said she liked the pastor's sermon, which was only more baffling because his weekly offerings were so dark – full of sin and damnation, never failing to remind us all that we were one misstep from the fiery pits of hell. 'Remind me why I need 'im,' she said. I guess I get it now; she wanted to be assured that she had something to protect her from all the fucked-up shit in the world. I wish I could go to her now, so she could protect me.

Mum and Dad are watching a show set in a hospital when I arrive back, neither of them looking up when I enter the room. I watch them for a few moments, enthralled by a clumsy romantic scene. I'm struck by how comfortable they are, with their lives and themselves. I chastise myself for wanting more, for harbouring such ridiculous dreams for so long and letting the inevitable implosion shake me so much. I should have aimed for so much less – trust and companionship. So much less but so much more. I whisper that I'm going upstairs and close the living room door behind me.

4) <u>Must be spiritually aware.</u> Not necessarily religious but have values and a belief system.

> Marthashotbod: Do you believe in God?
> Undeterred83: Nah.
> Marthashotbod: What do you believe in?
> Undeterred83: I've never thought about it.
> Marthashotbod: No time like the present.
> Undeterred83: Maybe but I'm a bit pissed.
> Marthashotbod: OK, have a great night.
> Undeterred83: :) :) :)

I can't judge him for that. We can't always be in touch with our spiritual side and who doesn't like a drink? In fact, I would quite like to be drunk right now. Dad has a pretty decent collection of whisky stashed in the back of the larder. I can't find anything to mix it with so I chuck a good few measures and a carton of apple juice into a pitcher and discover it makes a reasonably palatable cocktail. On an empty stomach I feel the effects quite quickly and I wonder if this dinner choice means I have a 'problem'. I decide that I'm the problem and within this jug lies the solution. I once read that drug addicts of any variety aren't seeking oblivion but connection. And if this is true it makes sense that ever since the invention of the telephone excessive drinking results in one common occurrence – drunk dialling.

He answers just as I am making the decision to end the call.

'Hey,' I say.

'You good?' Alexander asks.

'Yes, I'm fine,' I say carefully.

'Why are you ringing?' he asks, and I remember I have to have a reason to now.

'I'm just ringing to check on Moses. I miss him.' It's true.

'Yeah,' says Alexander, and I hear his voice relax, 'took ages to get him off. He kept saying horsey.'

I smile even though he can't see me. 'That's the little plastic one; it's in his bag. He takes it to bed now.'

'Really? That sounds uncomfortable.' I am enjoying Alexander's amused confusion. I can imagine him scrunching up his nose as he does when he's trying to understand something or someone.

'If it ain't broke,' I say.

'Whatever the man wants,' says Alexander. 'I'll get one for mi—, here. In case we forget it one day. You were right about him staying over more often. We'll make it happen.' I nearly miss the last part, I'm so floored by the fact that he nearly said 'mine' for our flat, by how easily it came to him.

'I feel a bit lost,' I say. Alexander is quiet and I want to take the words back. I'm reminded of trying to pour wine back into a bottle and then I remember my cocktail and serve myself another glass.

'You'll find your way,' he says eventually. I'm happy he has faith in me. 'I think you can do anything you can put your mind to. You just have to put your mind to something.' I laugh and Alexander says, 'Anything,' and I know he's taking the piss out of me and it feels really good because he's taking the piss out of me in a way that only someone who really knows you can. 'I'm sorry about what I said in the car the other day,' he says. 'I didn't mean it.' I nod, forgetting for a second he can't see me.

When he doesn't fill the silence, I whisper, 'Yeah.'

'I mean it,' he says, 'I wouldn't change anything.' My breath shortens but then he adds, 'Moses is the best thing that ever happened to me.'

'Yeah,' I say, 'Moses, yeah, of course.'

'I better go, though,' Alexander says. It takes me a few seconds to understand the conversation is over because nearly all our conversations are over. He's there for me but he's very much not.

'Is it Moses?' I ask.

'No, he's fine. Gotta go.'

'Bye,' I say, long after he has disconnected.

I have a sensation, sort of like I'm falling. I lie down to try and steady myself. I had been so focused on the ending of our relationship that I didn't realize the magnitude of what I would have to take on – creating a new home; forging a stable career. Had I truly understood the path I was setting out for myself, I can't be sure I would have made the same choice.

I am unaware of the process of completing this thought, falling asleep and then waking up again, but this must be what has occurred because I find myself lying in the dark, my clothes twisted uncomfortably on my body and my stomach calling for attention. I change into Dad's old dressing gown and creep downstairs. I think I spotted a pavlova in the fridge earlier. The light switch isn't quite where I remember it to be and it takes me a few tries to illuminate the room. When I do, thoughts of pavlova vanish and all the air leaves my body to force out a noise in the same family as a scream.

'Bleurrrrrgh! Yeurgh! God! Why?' Sitting at the kitchen table, face calm, rollers still in, is my mother. 'For fuck's sake, Mum, are you trying to kill me?' My mother doesn't move.

'You'll wake your dad, and don't say fuck,' she says. I sit opposite her. She looks so much older than I remember. I feel a flutter of fear that I've been asleep a very long time.

'Mother, neither of those things would be an issue if you weren't hiding in the dark like a deranged person. What's going on? Is this early dementia? Sorry, I mean, you can't ask a person with dementia if they have dementia.' I feel sick. I'm not in a position to take on the care of my deteriorating mother, although it would explain some things. Mum tuts.

'I'm not mad or senile. I just couldn't sleep.'

'Why not?' My mother is so happy, at least with herself. I can't think of a reason why she wouldn't be able to fall into a tranquil, dream-filled sleep each evening.

'I don't know. It's been that way since you were born.' Fabulous, I think, another thing I've fucked up. Mum reaches across the table and squeezes my hand. 'Nothing to do with you. You were perfect, slept through from about six weeks, but I still couldn't rest. Felt I always had to be ready for something.'

'What?' I ask, hoping perhaps she will impart something that will give me wisdom or at least understanding.

'I don't bloody know,' she says. 'If I knew I'd be ready for it.' I feel so tired I want to weep. Even my mother, a woman who makes an art form out of self-satisfaction, is looking for something. I'm devastated by the possibility that maybe I'll never find the answer; maybe there is no answer. It might just be the case that life, love and all the rest of it is just some omnipotent force's huge practical joke.

'Are you happy, Mum?' I ask.

'Yes,' she says. 'What other choice do I have?'

I pull my hand away from her. 'Loads,' I say, 'life can be really, really shitty.' As I say it, I feel it, and a hard knot forms in my throat.

'I know,' Mum says softly. 'You know what I do when I think that?' She leaves her chair and goes to the little digital radio that lives by the sink. I watch her play with the buttons until she is satisfied and I hear a man, with the low, smooth voice that all eighties DJs were required to have, introduce, 'Another great tune from the time when tunes were great.' Cheryl Lynn's 'Got To Be Real' starts to play and Mum walks towards me with her arms outstretched. I shake my head, embarrassed, even with an invisible audience. Mum refuses to accept my protest. She grabs my hands and pulls me to my feet. Still holding my hands, she starts to step from side to side, pulling me into her rhythm as I remember her doing with me when we would attend family weddings in my childhood. It doesn't take long for me to succumb to the music and her mood and I start to match her pace before spinning her under my arm, causing her to laugh and lose her balance and cling on to me for support. Mum regains her composure and

229

starts to roll her shoulders and tap her heels; I can imagine her thirty years ago, lost in music, owning a dance floor in a sweaty club. I do a few body rolls and Mum cocks her head at me.

'Oh, you got moves, have you?'

'Looks like it,' I say. She clicks her fingers along to the beat and I join in. Then we both strut around the kitchen, pulling poses when the lyric inspires it. For a few minutes, it's just my mother, the music and me. And that's how the sunrise finds us, barefoot in the kitchen, dancing to funk in our dressing gowns.

30

Patricia has restarted her phone campaign. She leaves me several voicemails reminding me that I can only have my mentorship deferred if I stump up the cash and finally she sends me a text message that reads, 'UPDATE ME ON YOUR PERSONAL DEVELOPMENT. HAVE YOU GONE BACK TO BEING THE TYPE OF GIRL THAT DOESN'T PAY HER DEBTS?' I call Tashi and beg her to swap a shift with me. She tells me that she needs the cash to attend a karmic cleansing workshop but I convince her that her karma will be far improved by giving me her shift.

The evening shift is much livelier than any other; many of the staff in are students making extra beer money, and you can tell they're under the misguided belief that amazing things await them. It helps being somewhere where I know what I'm doing, and I breeze through the clients and even manage to sound something approximating chirpy. Towards the end of my shift Bob comes over to tell me he has noticed the additional hours I've been putting in. 'It's great when staff don't have a social life,' he says, which I think is the closest I will ever get to a 'well done' from him.

After he has strolled off to find someone else to torment,

Greg says, 'Let's show him who doesn't have a social life – wanna go for a pint?'

'You don't have a social life, Greg; you're always here.' Greg colours a little. 'Anyway, I'm exhausted,' I say. I am and also I haven't heard from George for three days. This fact is like a toothache, taunting me throughout the day.

'Just one,' says Greg. When he says this he bats his eyelids in an exaggerated way that makes me laugh.

'OK,' I say, 'let me clean up.' I go to the ladies' and send George a quick message asking how he is. I don't get a response, so I wash my hands and leave. Greg is waiting in the hallway with his head leaned back against the wall and his eyes closed; he looks as tired as I feel. I tap him on the arm and he springs to life.

'Are you sure you wanna go? You look knackered.'

Greg rubs his face. 'I'm a dad. This is how I look.'

I link arms with him. 'Right, let's do this.'

We walk to the Foragers, where a pub quiz is in full swing. 'We should start a team,' says Greg. 'Stop us from going brain-dead.' I think about how pedestrian it would be to finish up at the call centre and then go to a pub quiz every week and shudder. 'What you drinking?' asks Greg.

'Surprise me,' I say.

Greg goes to the bar. I can't hear the conversation he has with the bar lady but at one point she reaches over the bar and slaps him playfully on the arm. She looks happy. I don't know her, I've never seen her in my life, but I'm envious of her ease. She may be crawling through the depths of a metaphorical hell but if she is it's not evident. Maybe it's that simple. I make a little promise to myself that I will be happy and if not *be* happy, look it.

Greg comes back and puts a drink in front of me.

'What is it?' I ask.

'Gin and tonic,' he says.

'That's not much of a surprise,' I say. I rest my chin against my hands. 'Is that how you think of me?'

'What do you mean?' asks Greg as he settles in his seat. He looks pleased; I can tell he's gearing up for a debate. I recognize the excitement – when you spend a lot of time conversing with children some adult banter is light relief.

'Well, gin and tonic, it's so, I don't know, so obvious. It's predictable.'

Greg takes a sip of his own gin. 'Sometimes that's nice though, right? Sometimes it feels good to know what's coming.' I think about this as I have a bit of my own drink. It tastes good – familiar.

'I want a combination, I think. A bit of the expected but something to keep you on your toes.'

'All right, gin and Coke next time?' asks Greg.

'Bleurgh, no way.'

'See,' says Greg, 'unpredictable isn't always as good as it sounds.'

'Is that why you work at Fairfax?' I say. 'You like saying the same thing over and over again?'

Greg makes a face like he's smelt something really bad. 'Sometimes I have to count the minutes in pounds. Like, two hours: that's school lunches for the week.'

'But you always sound so into it,' I tell him.

Greg shrugs. 'It's not the customers' fault I don't know what to do with my life.'

'What did you plan to do?' I ask.

'I never really had a plan,' says Greg. 'My mum was – still is – an alcoholic. I was focused on making sure the younger ones were OK and then as soon as I could get out, I got out.'

'I'm sorry,' I say. I am. Greg's a nice guy, the sort of guy that deserves to have a dream. 'What would you do if you could do anything in the world?' I ask.

'Be Beyoncé's foot cushion.'

'Foot cushion? Aim higher, love! Not even pillow?'

'Thanks for your encouragement,' says Greg.

'Any time,' I say.

'What about you?' asks Greg. 'What would you do if I could wave my magic wand and make it happen? Hang on.' Greg pats his pockets. 'Shit, I left it at home.'

My car crash of a gig comes back to me in high definition. 'I have no idea,' I say.

'Well, you know that's the best place to be,' says Greg. 'You're free to do anything. I could put a word in with Beyoncé; you could be her flannel or something.'

'Not sure I have the skills,' I say.

'Aw well, you'll work it out,' says Greg, in a way that makes me think he believes it. We both fall silent and after a few seconds Greg leans over to a guy on the next table and says, 'Aha, mate.'

'What?' says the man, which is exactly my sentiment.

'The answer. It's a-ha, the band.'

'Oh, right. Of course it is. Obvious when you know it,' says the guy. 'Cheers!' He turns and tells the other men at his table and they all smile and give Greg thumbs up.

'Maybe you could build a career out of knowing obscure pub quiz answers,' I say.

'Been there, done that,' says Greg. The next question starts a furious debate from the guys at the next table, and it's my turn to lean over.

' "Fight For This Love",' I say, and the men turn to me. 'Cheryl Cole's first number one single.' The men cheer.

'We need you,' a large blond guy says to me. 'If we get all the answers from you and you don't join our team, we'll be cheating.' Greg and I look at each other and silently agree. The blond pulls out a chair for me and the two other guys pat Greg on the back as we sit down.

'I'm Jimmy,' says the blond. 'We've been coming here for years and haven't won so much as a lollipop.'

'Come on then,' says Greg. 'Let's do this!' He puts his hand in towards the centre of the table; we each pile one of our own on top of his and, instinctively, all make a caveman-like grunt.

We storm the music round; Greg has an encyclopaedic knowledge of the eighties and I have the cheesy pop artists covered. Up next is sport so I offer to get the drinks in; when I get back from the bar our new teammates are all completely entranced by Greg, who's telling them a story about a time he performed a citizen's arrest on a cricket team mascot. 'I had to keep smiling so the kids would think I was hugging Fergy and not catch on that he was a violent cokehead.' The guys all laugh; I can tell they really like Greg.

For the first time I consider Greg as a potential romantic candidate, or more specifically I wonder if he finds me attractive. I subtly undo another button on my shirt. The guys all say thanks for the drinks and Greg winks at me. The final round is about Brighton. Greg and I are both born and bred, an anomaly in this transient town, and we impress the table with our local know-how. It feels good to be the one in control for once.

There's a buzz of excitement as we wait for the results and I find myself caught up in it; maybe all this time a good pub quiz was what I needed. The quiz master draws out the announcements and each time he says a team name that's not ours we cheer.

'Annnnd the second runners-up ... The Accrington

Stanleys!' Jimmy stands and beats his chest. Greg reaches over and gives me a high five and one of the other guys hugs me.

'We couldn't have done it without you,' he says. Our prize is another round of drinks, which we claim immediately.

'To victory,' says Greg, after the bar lady brings over five brimming pints.

'To victory!' we chant together.

Greg offers to walk me home. 'I'll get the bus,' I say.

'You sure?' asks Greg. 'You seem pretty squiffy.'

'I'm fine,' I say, and then a few steps down the road, I trip on a bit of cracked pavement. Greg catches me by the elbow. 'I'm fine,' I say again, and laugh.

At the bus stop Greg says, 'We showed Bob, then?'

'What do you mean?'

'We were social.'

'We were totally social,' I say.

'We're fun,' says Greg. 'Our exes are idiots, right?'

'Well, *I* dumped *him*,' I say to Greg.

'Aw, he still let you go,' says Greg.

My bus arrives just as we reach the bus stop and I'm still smiling as I take my seat. Even when life chucks you a load of lemons, you can take a slice and make a strong gin and tonic.

31

WHEN I WAS really little, I would wake up almost every day feeling excited. Most days I wouldn't even know why. I'd have to claw through my memory for the source of my joy until eventually I'd locate it: ah yes, chips for lunch! And the excitement would then be amplified. I wake up today feeling a fuzzier version of that but it's a good fuzzy, a feeling I want to sink into. It's so nice, I'm a little irritated when my phone alert sounds, but when I look and see it's George this dissolves.

> Undeterred83: Sorry for the gap, I was moving between cities and had no reception. Good luck for today!
> Marthashotbod: No problem, no problem at all. Good luck with what?
> Undeterred83: The half marathon.

I shuffle downstairs; somehow I think moving quietly and slowly will make the situation less real. I hear my mother in the kitchen and brace myself before going in.

'You're up!' she cries. 'I've made you porridge – it's got these seeds from the health shop. I read they're good for runners. I don't think you can taste them.' She places the bowl on the table and looks at me. Her face is questioning;

I know she wants me to say I'm not doing it, that I'm failing at yet another thing. I won't.

'Thanks,' I say, 'this is perfect.' Mum waits until I start eating before making breakfast for Moses.

'Mummy run!' cries Moses.

'Yes, honey,' I say.

My sports bra and leggings are in the bottom of the wash basket where they were abandoned, so I pull on a tracksuit I bought for sleeping in on cold nights. Dad finds a parking space near the start line in Hove Park. Mum is full of advice.

'Remember to pace yourself at the beginning,' she says.

'I will,' I say. I stare out of the passenger window. I'm looking for a sign but I'm not sure what I want it to say.

'I haven't seen you doing much training,' says Mum.

'I've been using the treadmill at the gym in my lunch hour,' I tell her. This seems to please her.

'You know, it's very different running on the road. I hope you don't get injured.' I try to distract myself from my frustration with her by reading the event welcome letter again. It doesn't say much – basically, run. Run really far. 'I read about a woman who did a marathon and tore something in her ankle so badly she couldn't walk again.'

'That's not very useful,' I say, 'pointing out the potential for terrible injury just before I do something.'

'I'm just trying to help,' says Mum. 'That's your problem, you always want to have your head in the sand.'

We pull into the allocated parking and I watch the other runners, clad in Lycra and dripping with anticipation. I can feel a knot starting to tie itself in my stomach. I go to the registration tent and a woman talks me through the process. I recognize what is coming out of her mouth as words but I don't take in the content. I'm fairly sure it's just run, run really far.

Mum tells me that she and Dad and Moses will wait for me at the finish line and then I'm by myself. I mean, I'm not, I'm surrounded by hundreds of people, but I feel set apart from them. This isn't a new experience; I often feel as though everyone else has had an email that I missed. I make my way to the centre of the crowd of runners, where they look a bit more light-hearted than the steely-eyed people at the front. Around me people are folding them-selves forward and jumping up and down, so I imitate them, more to blend in than because I believe it will have any benefits.

'Hey,' says a petite Asian girl beside me, 'you ready?' I recognize her voice but I can't place her face. She obviously sees my hesitation and explains: 'I work on reception. You're in customer care, right? I've seen you in town with your son, he's so cute.' As she says this she is bouncing from one foot to the other.

'Yeah, right . . . uhm . . .'

'Nisha,' she says. 'Martha, right?'

'Yeah, sorry,' I say. 'I'm pretty nervous.'

'Me too,' she says, although she doesn't look or sound it. 'Is your boy gonna be at the end?'

'Yeah,' I say.

'How cute!' I don't think it will be cute, for a boy to see his mother limp towards him, her fat face contorted with exertion. I think it may well be traumatizing and I wish I had my phone to tell my parents to save him from the hor-ror. 'It's really good for him to see you doing stuff like this. What's it called, modelling?' Nisha prattles on. I can't respond to her words because of the screaming in my head. 'When he goes to school, you'll be like, "I'm not a regular

239

mom, I'm a cool mom."' Nisha looks confused at something she sees in my face and says, 'Haven't you seen *Mean Girls*? It's great.' I'm in awe of her ability to casually reflect on teen movies in the face of such a personal trial. 'Anyway,' she continues, 'see you at the finish . . . probably.'

She bounces away through the crowd and as I watch her disappear I know that I won't make it with my current mindset. I can't see this as a torturous, ridiculous mistake; I must view it as a rebirth. As I stand I am scared, lost Martha Ross, but I will emerge as a cool, single mother who runs half-marathons. Nisha believes this already so there's no reason why I shouldn't.

It's a disarming feeling as an adult to realize that you can't do something extremely basic, some would say ingrained. I realize, at perhaps the most inopportune moment ever, that I don't know how to run because I've never truly run, not even for a train. I assume I ran in childhood but I don't recall it. As soon as what I was informed would show up as buds appeared as fully blown breasts, I unofficially retired from running.

In secondary school we had a sadistic physical education teacher who would force us to jog the length of the sea-front. We would set off from school and be collected three miles along the coast. If I hadn't found a creative enough reason not to partake I would duck out early on and use my dinner money to get a bus to the end of the course, such was my commitment to not breaking a sweat; that was when I thought you could get away with taking shortcuts.

I take Mum's advice to pace myself and move only slightly faster than walking pace. I think of my tentative park runs and Leanne's words to just keep going. This, I tell myself, is just an extension of that. I think if I stay at

240

this pace, I'll make it, and I repeat the phrase under my breath – I'll make it, I'll make it. I start to believe I can do it; these strangers lining the route believe I can. But dozens of people overtake me – young, old, inconceivably old and at one point a camel. I imagine myself finishing behind such a ragtag bunch and increase my speed. Maybe I accelerate too quickly – maybe every individual has a definitive ceiling to their physical capacity and I have reached mine – because alarmingly quickly my chest starts burning. I stop and lean over, hoping it will ease the pain, but it seems to make it worse. As I straighten up I see a small child waving. He gestures for me to come towards him. When I do, he hands me a sweaty little pile of Jelly Babies.

'You can do it!' he shouts. I hobble away with my head held high; I don't want to let the little tyke down. I try to distract myself from the pain in my thighs by thinking about George. I believe strongly that there is a finite amount of love in the world and the reason he has come into my life now is because I have created room for him; I have stopped giving myself to people and things that don't deserve me, like Alexander and Cara. I was just a mirror in which they could see themselves reflected; neither of them really wanted me to succeed because if I had my own life I could no longer be their adoring audience. I feel a burst of anger which helps to power me along for some time. I love the energy that surges from the spectators; I feel more support from them than I have felt from my friends and family in a decade.

I feel like I'm flying. I can hear the blood pumping in my head and little flashes of light appear before my eyes. Trees and people blur into a Monet beside me. I try counting my paces and for a while it makes me feel calmer. The landscape starts to become less green, more urban; I can't remember the route but I think it means I'm making progress. Then I see a sign that says we have gone four miles, only four miles. I feel all the exuberance drain out of me, exiting through my feet. Also, I really need to pee. I had noticed several toilets along the course but now, obviously, there isn't one to be seen. Everything I look at is assessed as a receptacle to hold the contents of my insistent bladder.

When I spot the next set of toilets I relax in anticipation a little too soon. I make it, but only just. It's a desperate scramble to get my tracksuit bottoms and pants past my knees. As I do, relief floods through me. Most of that relief is down to the fact that I am no longer running. I think it might be feasible to stay right here, to sit on this chemical toilet until the whole thing is over, and then there's a pounding on the door. The urgent banging of someone clearly worried about getting a good time, as opposed to just surviving. 'In a minute!' I shout. I hear the hushed, clipped tones of British people grumbling from outside. I get up and straighten myself out. I open the door to a tiny pensioner, still jogging on the spot. She beckons for me to hurry and the instant I'm out, she scrambles up the steps without a second glance at me.

Starting again is even harder than getting going in the first place. I wonder if Mum and Dad and Moses have got to the finish line early to get a good place. When I first signed up I had meant to tell Leanne to come down with James and the kids. For once my flakiness has been to my advantage. Thank goodness for small mercies. Whatever miracle seed was in my porridge has worn off because I'm extremely hungry and my legs feel like lead. I've no idea how long it will take me to run the remainder of the course and that thought makes me feel like I'm having one of those dreams in which you're falling and falling yet never reach the ground. Sweat is pouring in a sheet down my face; I try to claw the moisture from my eyes with my hands and somehow manage to impede my vision further.

'You all right?' asks a man passing me. I don't have the voice to respond and he seems to take this as confirmation that I'm OK. I'm not OK. I'm fairly sure I'm going to have to stop, certainly within the next five minutes. I decide I'm definitely going to stop, I'm making the decision to stop. And then I look up, and leaning over the barrier about a hundred metres ahead I see George. He's wearing a blue beanie and waving at me. He's showed up for me in a way that even the list could not predict. I keep going; the moment I am in his arms will make it all worthwhile. As I get closer I speed up and start to push my way past other people. The crowd notice my triumphant return to form and egg me on. This is not how I wanted to meet him – damp, exhausted and wearing a lumpy tracksuit – but even so, he's the only thing I want to see. I'm less than a few feet away when I understand it's not him, it's not even close to him, and it's the final blow to my psyche. I stop, my body folds in on itself and I find myself heaving forcefully. Everyone around me jumps away in horror, but they needn't bother because I don't have enough in my stomach to bring anything substantial up. A light pebble-dashing of oats leaves my mouth before I collapse on to the road.

32

WHEN PEOPLE SAY their life has flashed before them, you imagine this montage consists of poignant moments – wedding days, the birth of a child – but it's not like that at all. You start thinking that you definitely left your winter jacket at the dry cleaner's and about how you never got round to watching *The Wire*. I must have lost consciousness because when I regain awareness of my surroundings I can make out people already in the throes of conversation.

'Just get her out the way, she's gonna get trampled on.'

'We're not supposed to move them until the paramedic gets here.'

'Stop being such a jobsworth, Caroline. We're *supposed* to make the area safe – having her sprawled out like this definitely isn't safe.' I try to speak to reassure them that I'm more or less OK, but I just feel a stream of drool trickle from the corner of my mouth. I sense several sets of hands pulling on me; even in my semi-consciousness I cringe at the sound of the effort they have to make. The hands are removed.

'Yeah, leave her here,' says one of the voices. The next voice I hear is one I recognize, that of my mother.

'No,' I hear her telling someone. 'She doesn't have any health problems, she's been training for weeks. Someone needs to find out why this happened. Do you think she may have had a heart attack? I've read about that.' I think I probably could open my eyes at this point but I decide against it.

'She's unresponsive,' says a new voice. 'We'll have to take her to general.' They shift me on to something soft and I feel myself rise before being wheeled away. As I move I can hear Mum shouting instructions, I presume to Dad. It feels nice to have someone else in charge of what's happening to me and where I'm going. I love listening to the paramedics discuss my condition in calm whispers.

The smell of the ward is so familiar. This hospital is the site of my most immense pain and my greatest joy. Perhaps it's fate that I find myself here, and I'm supposed to come out the other side as yet another incarnation of myself.

'I'm going to help you move now,' says a soft voice. I open my eyes and look into the gentle, shining face of a nurse. For no reason I can identify, the African lilt in her voice is a comfort to me. She stands ready to catch me as I shift awkwardly from the gurney to the bed. Even though I'm still in my tracksuit bottoms the nurse pulls the covers over me, tucking the stiff sheets into the sides of the bed so that they stretch across my legs in a tight embrace.

'I'm Precious. Do you want a cup of tea?' she asks, and I have never wanted anything more in my life.

Precious leaves and is replaced by my mother. She has a concerned expression and fresh lipstick on her face. 'They have no idea when you will see the doctor,' she says. 'Did you get that private health insurance I sent you the details for? We can have you moved within the hour.'

I shake my head no. 'Where's Moses?'

'Your father has taken him home. I didn't want him to see you like this.'

245

I close my eyes again. 'That wasn't your decision to make, Mum.'

She tuts. 'I think it was, because I made it. It was bad enough that he had to see you rolling around on the ground like that, in front of everyone.' I look at her now and search her face for the warmth I imagine I would exhibit if my child was in a hospital bed before me.

'I'm sorry I didn't think to collapse more privately,' I say. Mum looks around, clutching her bag to herself as if the ward were a city centre underpass.

'These places are full of disease,' she says. 'You know you'll come out worse than when you came in.'

Precious returns with a plastic cup, which she hands to me. I take a sip and it's grainy but hot and very sweet.

'I just need to take your blood pressure, dear,' she says. She helps me out of my tracksuit top and straps the gauge to my bicep. We all stare at the reading as the numbers rise and fall before settling on something that means nothing to me. 'It's a little high,' she says. 'How do you feel?'

'Tired,' I say, and glance at my mother. Only very briefly but long enough, it seems, for Precious to understand my plea.

'I think we should leave her to have some rest, Mum,' says the nurse.

'No, I—' says my mother.

Precious places a hand on her back as she says, 'I need your help with some information about her medical history – it would speed things along.' Mum allows herself to be led away. I feel that surge of appreciation you only experience when you witness someone being really good at their job. A lot of people don't like hospitals and I understand this; they house so much suffering. But sitting in this bed I feel sheltered from the world; it's a similar sensation to the one I have each time the door closes after I've boarded an aeroplane. The sense of calm that comes from knowing that no one can expect anything of me is reassuring. I adjust my bed and fall back into the pillows. I am hungry and sore but, for the first time in weeks, I feel safe.

'Hey,' someone whispers. I open my eyes and see Greg poking his head through my curtains. 'Is the coast clear?' he asks.

I shuffle up in the bed. 'Sure,' I say. 'What do you mean?'

Greg steps in and shuts the curtains behind him. 'I came earlier and your mum started quizzing me about how hard we're pushing you at work.'

I laugh. 'I think you're safe.'

Greg holds out a bright pink gift bag, inside which is a copy of *Grazia*, a bag of white chocolate buttons and some posh hand cream.

'The girls wanted to get you flowers but I wasn't sure how useful they would be.'

'This is wonderful,' I say.

'Yeah, you're always using that goop on your hands at work,' he says. Greg sits in the chair beside the bed and starts to help himself to the chocolate buttons.

'How did you know I was here?' I ask.

'Your mum rang to say you wouldn't be back on shift for a while. What's wrong?'

I lean back against my pillows. 'I'm dehydrated and very, very stupid.'

Greg smiles and says, 'How do they treat stupid?'

'With lots of rest,' I say.

'It's not contagious, is it?' he asks.

'Yes, I'm afraid it is,' I say. 'How was work today?'

'Same old,' says Greg. 'People called, I put them through, yunno, life and death stuff. Something's going on with Bob, though.'

'This is news?'

'Nah,' says Greg, leaning forward and lowering his voice, 'I mean he's weirder than usual. When I told him I was leaving to come see you, he said something about changing company policy. I thought he meant about me taking time off but he started muttering something about employees not being allowed to get sick.'

'Bloody hell, I need to get out of there.'

'Is that what this was all about? You didn't want to come to work? You know they have annual leave for that.'

I lean over to try and swipe Greg but he moves back quickly and I miss. 'I'm trying to change my life. I need to. I know it might sound stupid but I just wanted to do something impressive.'

Greg gives me a chocolate button. 'It doesn't sound stupid. I get it. I mean, that happens to me all the time. I meet someone who kitesurfs or climbs mountains or whatever and I think, I want to be like them. I don't want to *be* them because they're usually smug twats, but I want to have something they have.'

'Money, usually,' I say.

'Wise words.'

I shift so that my body is turned towards him. 'Do I just need to grow up? You can tell me. Is it too late; should I just be happy with my lot?'

'No way,' says Greg, and there's no trace of his usual joviality. 'It's never too late, never.'

'I don't know,' I say. 'I'm feeling really, really old.'

'You don't look old,' says Greg.

'How old do I look?' I ask.

'Not a day over forty,' says Greg. I reach into the bag of buttons and throw one at his face.

'I'm starting to think you have a problem with violence,' says Greg solemnly.

'I assure you, it's a Greg-specific problem.'

'Maybe that's my thing,' he says, 'protecting others from all your seething rage.'

'You're doing a very good job,' I say.

Greg stays for another half an hour. He tells me about his daughter Charlotte's school play. It's great watching him talk about his kids; his love for them fills the room. Eventually Precious appears and tells me I have to see the doctor, so Greg says he'll leave me to it. 'Don't run any more marathons,' he says before he goes. I promise him I won't.

The doctor says I'm fine but it's too late to discharge me. They'll give me fluids and let me rest overnight. I'm not unhappy but I try to look like I am. When he leaves I sit and listen to the sounds around me, families whispering news from home and nurses offering reassurance. What I love about hospitals is how everything is stripped back to the basics. You only receive what you need; you only see the people who truly care. When Moses was born I lost a lot of blood; they made the two of us stay until I was strong enough to be a mother at home. On my second day, I called Alexander, crying.

'How am I supposed to get better when they're feeding me this crap?' He arrived thirty minutes later with a Subway sandwich and a thermos of coffee, the really good kind. He climbed on the narrow bed with me and we shared the food together and watched our baby sleep in his little Perspex cot. Just the three of us and processed meat; it was everything I needed.

*

I must have drifted off because I am suddenly aware of Leanne standing beside me. 'Visiting time has just finished. They let me come in as long as I promised to be five minutes,' she says. Leanne is the type of woman people want to give five minutes. She sits on the edge of the bed and strokes my leg through the hospital blankets. 'What were you doing?' she asks.

'Running a marathon,' I say. 'Well, half of one.'

'I know, but why?'

'Why not?' I ask. 'Why can't I be a woman who runs half-marathons?' And then I start to cry. Leanne hands me a tissue from a box on my bedside table and I use it to mop up my face.

'You can be a woman who runs half-marathons; you can't *wake up* and decide to be a woman who runs a half-marathon without proper preparation. You just ran round the park with me for the first time the other week. Are you doing all this to avoid the separation?'

'No,' I say. 'This is nothing to do with Alexander, I almost never think of him. I had already let go of him long before we broke up.'

'Even if that's the case,' says Leanne, in a tone that suggests she doesn't believe this for a second, 'maybe you're not over the idea of him, the fantasy of being in a perfect couple.'

'Why would I get over that? You're in the perfect couple. Are you saying I'm not good enough to have that too?'

Leanne laughs. 'James and I are far from perfect – there is no perfect. There's basically trying as hard as you possibly can every day.'

'That's what I don't think you understand,' I say, grabbing Leanne's hand. 'I am trying, I'm trying so hard. I'm so, so sick of trying.'

Leanne squeezes my hand. 'I know you are, honey, I know.'

33

HOSPITALS ARE SO easy to get into and so terribly hard to get out of. I need to wait until the doctor discharges me but all the next morning there's not a doctor to be seen. I don't mind it except that the longer I stay the more stupid I feel for ending up here, and Precious has been replaced with a stern Irish woman called Anna, who consistently makes me feel like I'm interrupting her Sunday dinner. When I call her to ask yet again when I will be seen, she tells me to be a patient patient. 'There are sick people here, you know.'

I go to the TV room for a change of scene. There's no one in there save for an older woman watching *Jeremy Kyle*. She's wearing two cardigans and a felt hat.

'Hello,' I say.

'All right, you waiting for someone to pick you up?'

'Yeah,' I say, 'are you?' The woman laughs as if I have said something extremely funny.

'I'm not getting out for a long time, if at all. I just like to get up every day. Even if I did get out, got no one to pick me up. Got no one.' She laughs again; I can see the gaps where her teeth should be. I sit in one of the plasticky chairs and message George.

Marthashotbod: Hey, are you there?
Marthashotbod: I really need to talk to you.
Undeterred83: It's tough today.
Marthashotbod: Please.
Undeterred83: I'll do my best.

I rest my phone on my lap.

'Are these people for real?' asks the woman, I think to me, but her eyes don't leave the screen. I scroll through my contacts to avoid engaging with her. I pause at Cara's name. I should message her; she would force me to see the funny side. I know she'd say something about the dangers of cardio but I'm still upset with her – for leaving me, for not believing me or believing in me. 'Of course 'e's lyin',' the woman says, 'they're always lyin'. Men, who'd 'ave 'em?'

I feel relieved when my phone rings.

'Yeah, what's up?' asks George.

'Nothing really. I just wanted to hear your voice.'

'Ah,' he says. 'It was quite difficult to call you.'

'Oh right, sorry. What are you up to?'

'I'm rafting today,' he says. He sounds happy. I wonder who he is rafting with.

'I've been ill,' I say. 'I'm in hospital.'

'Oh wow, sorry,' he says. 'Hang on.' I hear him moving. 'What happened?'

'I kind of collapsed at the half-marathon.'

'After?'

'During.'

'Crap. You OK now, though?'

'Better for speaking to you.' George doesn't say anything and then I hear him talking to someone. It's muffled, as if his hand is over the phone.

'Sorry, they're calling me,' he says.

'No, it's OK. I just wanted . . . I wanted to know if we could get a date in for when you're back?'

'Yeah, of course. I don't have my diary on me at the minute though.'

'Oh right, I guess you don't need it on a raft.'

George laughs but it sounds a bit forced. 'I've really gotta go,' he says.

'OK, have a great time and let me know how it goes.' I hold the phone to my ear long after he has gone.

'Man trouble?' asks the woman.

I put my phone in my pocket. 'No, not really,' I say.

She laughs again – I wonder if she's on drugs.

'I 'ad an 'usband once. You know what 'appened?' I shake my head. 'I killed 'im.' I glance at the closed door of the room. The woman waits for me to make eye contact with her before saying, 'I did, though, I picked, picked, picked until 'e was dead.' Each time she says the word 'picked' she jabs at the air with her forefinger. 'This is what I know. I don't know much but I know this: 'ave a man an' leave 'im be or don't 'ave one at all.' She says this with a nod of her head; this is the final word on the subject as far as she is concerned. Times have probably changed since she was a young woman; husbands have changed.

I remember my father's mother talking about her husband as if he wasn't in the room. 'Tell Grandad his tea will get cold,' she would say, and I would walk over to him and repeat it, worried that my mother's whisperings that she would 'lose her marbles' had come to pass. This wasn't the case, though; she had every last one of her marbles until the bitter end and each and every one rolled around in a small pool of bitter resentment. I don't want that; I don't want to leave my man be or have him leave me be. I want to exist together; I want us entwined irreversibly even when it's boring, even when it's hard – especially when it's hard.

Anna the nurse bursts into the room. 'You're here!' she scolds. 'You're at me all morning and as soon as the doctor appears you're nowhere to be found.' I stand up to go with her. Before I leave I look back to the woman, who's engrossed in her show again. To be honest, she looks perfectly content.

34

Returning to Mum and Dad's from hospital is like arriving home after a holiday, both a relief and a disappointment. Mum tells me she has made me some soup but all I want to do is get out of my tracksuit, burn it and have a long shower. When I get to my room my stuff isn't there. It's as if I have been the victim of an extremely orderly robbery.

'Mum!' I shout, and she appears behind me.

'I've moved you to the extension, so you won't be disturbed by Moses,' she says. A small bead of pain forms at my temple.

'I want to be disturbed by Moses,' I say carefully, 'because he's my son. Where is he?'

'Alexander came and got him; I wanted the time to get you settled.'

I sink down to the floor and lean back against the wall. 'How hard is it to call me and ask? How hard is it to treat me like an adult?'

Mum goes over and sits on what used to be my bed and says, 'I do want to treat you like an adult but you don't always act like one.'

'How am I supposed to do anything?' I whisper. 'How am I supposed to do anything if the one person who's meant to be behind me every step of the way isn't there at all?'

'What are you talking about?' asks Mum. She sounds impatient. Whenever I have a conversation with her I get the sense that she's eager to get off and do something more interesting. Even as a small child I felt this. I think this is why people often comment on how quickly I speak; I was always aware that I had to get out as much as I could before I was dismissed.

'Could you not *ask* me what I need rather than patronizing me and stealing my son?'

'I'm not trying to steal him. I did not see myself raising a child at this stage in life but you need to get yourself together.'

'I'm getting a divorce, Mum,' I spit at her. 'It's one of the most stressful life events you can experience; I'm doing pretty well. I'm working, I'm looking into new opportunities, I'm seeing someone . . .'

Mum looks up at the ceiling, where I assume she believes God is hiding. 'You can't be seeing someone already. This is how you get a reputation.'

'Mum, it's not 1803, and Alexander is already shacked up with someone!'

'It's different for men,' says Mum unapologetically.

'Why can't you just want me to be happy?' I say. I look towards her but not directly at her, and in my peripheral vision I can see Mum fold her arms.

'Because happiness is a cop-out. Any idiot can be happy.'

I roll my eyes. 'Apparently not.'

'Do you know how hard your grandmother worked? On weekends, I used to go with her. I'd watch her iron piles and piles of white people's clothes. She never let me help; she always told me to read my books. When I met your dad and he earned enough to keep us both, I thought I had won but . . .' I wait. The moment feels so heavy. I understand that what is said next could change things for us for ever. 'I know you can do better than this,' Mum says finally. She waves her hand in my direction on the last word.

My emotional scale teeters between anger and acceptance. On one hand I'm so sick of her constant criticism; on the other I am sitting on the floor of my childhood bedroom, a failed half-marathon runner and almost divorcée.

Mum says, 'I know *I* didn't raise you like this.' And the scale tips. My rage propels me from the floor and I am quickly standing looking down on her. She tries to hide it but I can see she's shocked; I might give her some lip now and then but I've never stood up to her in a real or metaphorical sense.

'This is *precisely* how you raised me. What? You think your gold star parenting gave me all the tools I need to excel but I, stubborn little wretch that I am, was just determined to be a fat fuck-up?' Mum opens her mouth to respond but I continue, 'Newsflash: that's not the case. In fact, I'm starting to think living with you might be a big part of the problem.' I turn and walk away and formulate my plan as I do so.

My stuff has been put away neatly in the loft conversion. I repack it into the bags that Alexander sent it to me in and then haul each bag downstairs, one by one. I allow every load to bounce heavily on all the steps of the two flights to the entrance hall. When I'm finished I'm sweating but I feel good; perhaps these are those endorphins that they talk about. I walk into the living room, where my mother and father are sitting in silence. Mum turns away as she sees me enter the room so I leave her to it. My father looks at me, his face full of apprehension.

'Dad,' I say. 'Can I get a lift?'

35

Leanne reacts to me, my cat and all my bags showing up at her door with an admirable level of calm.
Most friends say that you can always call on them. They
clutch your hand and murmur, 'If there's *anything* you
need.' But they say this safe in the knowledge that you will
never, ever actually call on them. Leanne isn't this person.
If Leanne says she'll be there for you, she'll be there, early,
with muffins. She puts me in her guest bedroom, which is
always ready for guests. It's quite small and it's only after
I bring up my belongings that I remember that I will need
to fit Moses and all his toddler paraphernalia in here too.
I sit on the bed and look at the contents of my life in hold-
alls. I have so very little and it still has nowhere to belong.
Moving to Leanne's is like unwrapping another layer of
pain; I actually feel a dull ache in my belly. The little
nicotine-like hits I had been getting from George's increasingly sporadic messages are no longer enough.

Leanne comes in with extra blankets and joins me on
the bed. 'Wanna tell me what's going on?'

I pull one of the blankets over my legs. 'I just reached
the end of my rope with Mum.' I don't have to say anything else. As a teenager I would spend many a weekend
hiding from my mother at Leanne's family home. I loved

her mother Tanya so much – a wiry redhead who, contrary to the stereotype, was always quiet and measured. She rarely offered more than the blandest of small talk. After which she would make us chip sandwiches and huge mugs of tea and sit in the kitchen as we lay sprawled in front of her television, watching soaps for hours. Leanne always swore that her mother's passivity came with its own disadvantages but I just think she was trying to make me feel better.

'So, shall we talk about boys?' asks Leanne. I smile. Leanne and I have clocked up hours and hours lying on her bed discussing boys over the years; usually boys who didn't know we existed.

'I feel like he's pulling away,' I say.

'I didn't know you were talking,' says Leanne.

'Not *talking* talking, but we message every day.'

'About Moses?' We both look at each other in confusion. 'We're talking about Alexander, right?' Leanne asks.

'No! Of course not. George.'

'Oh,' says Leanne. 'Nathan George.'

'Shut up,' I say. I show her our conversations on my phone. This is something we used to do years ago, analyse the syntax and frequency of his messages in order to ascertain just how quickly a guy was falling in love.

Leanne reads in silence. When she's had her fill she says, 'He sounds nice.'

'Don't get too excited,' I say, snatching my phone back from her.

'I'm worried it's too soon.' George's profile says he's online but I decide to wait to see if he sends me a message first.

'Weren't you the one telling me to ask the universe to hook me up and setting me up on hideous dates?'

'I still want that for you – not the hideous dates, but finding the right guy,' says Leanne. 'Anyway, what do I know?'

'Exactly,' I say, 'what do you know with your amazing marriage and your beautiful house and your adorable kids?'

Leanne purses her lips and then says, 'Yes, but you know I'd give it all up for your eyebrows.' I scoot across the bed and rest my head on her shoulder. I'm shocked at how good it feels to have her body against mine. I wonder how long it would take to get used to not being held – a month? A year? A decade? Sometimes I see this old woman in the Co-op. As I queue up behind her, I watch her fumble for exact change in a small coin purse and I hear the cashier humour her as she offers embarrassingly unnecessary commentary. I want to stop her before she leaves the store and ask, 'When was the last time you were touched – I mean, really touched?' When Leanne says things like 'it's too soon', she says this from the position of someone who knows she will be touched in a few hours and again tomorrow and most probably every day after that. When I think about George I know that it's very much not soon enough.

'OK, tell me more,' says Leanne. 'What's he like?'

I sit up so she can see my face. 'He's perfect.'

'Just perfect, not extraordinary?'

I grab Leanne's arm so she will focus and hear my words. 'No, you don't understand – he's literally perfect.'

'OK, but what's his flaw?'

Leanne and I made an agreement when we were in Year 10 that every guy has a flaw and as a woman you must find it as fast as possible. It happened when she fell deeply in lust with Troy Adeyemi, the new sixth-former transferred from somewhere mysterious and exotic like Kent. He was really quiet, bordering on mute, but Amy Mitchell had told us that she had seen him with his mum in Tesco and that he could definitely speak. What he lacked in conversational skills he made up for in aesthetics; he had impossibly high, almost feminine cheekbones set into a perfectly symmetrical face. He stood a good head above most of the other guys and had arms so strong that, even at fifteen years old, I couldn't look at him without imagining him throwing me on to a bed; not that I would have had any idea what to do when I got there.

Leanne and I plotted for months about how she would secure him. She was allowed to claim him because we had come to an agreement that anyone who said they 'actually, truly' fancied someone would earn the right to pursue that person indefinitely. I was a bit miffed in this case. When Troy started I thought that our shared status of 'token mixed-race kid in class' would propel us together. It didn't. He looked at me the way you would examine a torn cuticle.

Leanne didn't fare much better but had a significant weapon in her arsenal: her grandparents had recently moved to the outskirts of town, into a house ordinary in every way aside from one key detail – an outdoor pool. Leanne's grandfather had been plagued by arthritis for many years and thought a daily swim and the coastal air would heal his ailments. We thought a pool party with amazing bikinis might lure in Troy.

We had to wait until the weather was appropriate to mobilize. Leanne endured eight long months of watching Troy from afar before the longest winter ever ended. She was unwilling to do anything without parental permission, so we had to work within the parameters of what her grandmother was willing to accommodate. That would be no adult supervision for the time it took her to do her big shop and have a slice of cake and a cup of tea in the garden centre. Leanne managed to invite Troy and a few of his friends with the promise of an empty house and perhaps the implication that there would be alcohol; I think this was when I really started to understand how determined Leanne could be. Of course, there was no alcohol; in fact I had to hide the jug of squash left out by Leanne's gran. The boys did not seem too disappointed by the lack of booze or birds – they were happy to raid the fridge and throw each other into the pool. I remember one moment when, stepping out of the house after returning from the loo, I looked at the scene unfolding before me and thought, I will never be happier than this.

As the afternoon drew to a close the lads became restless and Leanne started to worry about her grandmother's return. When Troy told Leanne that they were leaving to attend another party (our invitation apparently got lost in the post) she told him she had to show him something in the kitchen. Troy's friends deftly ignored me as Leanne went inside to complete her master plan. When they emerged five minutes later Troy looked as handsome as ever and Leanne looked miserable. She was silent the entire time we cleared the garden and mopped the water from the tiles around the pool. She was silent even after her grandparents came home and I had to speak on behalf of both of us when they asked if we had had a nice time with our friends.

Later that evening as we both climbed into her queen-sized bed she let out a long, low moan. 'It was awful,' she said, 'it was so, so awful.' I could feel her body grow tense, simply from the memory of whatever horror she was about to share. 'He just sort of licked me,' she said. 'I mean, he licked my whole face! How can he be so beautiful and such a bad kisser?' It was after this night that we decided that every man, however wonderful he may appear, however beautiful or cool, has a flaw, and as a woman it is your job to find it and find it fast.

'He's gotta have a flaw,' says Leanne now.

'Well, his fiancée died—'

'Oh God!' cries Leanne.

'I know,' I say.

'You can never compete with a dead ex.'

'He seems pretty together about it,' I say.

Leanne looks thoughtful. 'As flaws go, it's not that bad,' she says. 'What did we say Alexander's flaw was?' I don't like that she has changed the subject from George but I have to admit I was thinking the same.

'I think that he's a bit self-absorbed,' I say.

'Sounds about right,' says Leanne. 'That's quite a big one; why did I let you get away with that?'

'I didn't give you a choice. I'd fixed him so firmly in my sights, an articulated tank couldn't have pushed me off course.'

'So what makes it different this time?'

'This time is *so* different,' I say. 'This time I have the list.'

She makes me get it out. 'We were quite drunk, you know,' she says. I pass her the now thin and grubby piece of paper and she carefully examines each point. 'So, he's meeting the criteria?'

'He's more than meeting them; he's surpassing them.'

Leanne nods. 'Well, he's got the looks. Job?'

'He's a freelance researcher working in international development.'

'Nice.'

I point to the next thing on the list. 'He's really in touch with his emotions; he went on a ten-day silent retreat.'

'He's in touch with something,' says Leanne.

'I won't lie,' I say, jabbing at the next point, 'I don't really know what his relationship with his family is like, but I know he lives alone. He wants kids but he doesn't have them because—'

'Dead ex,' says Leanne matter-of-factly.

'Exactly, but it's the rest that's really amazing. He listens to me, I mean *really* listens, and asks questions afterwards. I don't have to debate with myself about whether he likes me or whether he wants to be with me.'

'That's nice,' says Leanne softly. 'What about the cat, though?'

'He has one! He's called Marley,' I say.

Leanne shrugs. 'Close enough.'

36

As leanne helps me to unpack, Dad calls to tell me he's bringing Moses over from Alexander's. He adds, 'Can you sort it out with your mum, she's been crying.' Which has as much authenticity as a Louis Vuitton bag on a Hackney market stall.

I choose to ignore him and say, 'I'll see you soon.'

When Dad drops Moses off, Millie is so excited by the impromptu sleepover that her bouncing and shouting prevents him from addressing the issue again. He gives me a big hug instead. I am reminded of being a child and falling asleep in his lap as he watched old, black-and-white films into the early hours of the morning. As he holds me I think, you fucked me up, Dad. You made me think I could find a guy who would always be there.

Once we've managed to sedate the children with snacks and Disney, I suggest to Leanne that we get into our PJs and open a bottle of wine, but Leanne says, 'Let's finish getting you organized.' As we return upstairs she says, 'We should definitely review things. I called Cara the other day. She said to ask you if you'd finished having your tantrum.'

'Review? I'm not a project. I just want to hang out with my friend.'

'What did she mean?' asks Leanne, ignoring my admonishment. 'I take it you had a falling-out?'

I hand Leanne a pile of clothes and she starts to arrange them in colour-coordinated piles. I shake my head, perhaps too emphatically.

'A disagreement,' I say. 'She can be so up herself sometimes. It's as if she thinks she's superior to everyone.'

'Really?' asks Leanne. She tilts her head, as if examining an object from a different angle. It makes me angry. Leanne always gave me the impression she was keen to have a bitch about Cara.

'I didn't even think you liked her?' I ask, trying and failing to disguise my outrage. *I* didn't like Cara when I first encountered her at work. When we spoke, which was rarely, it was in brief, instructive missives (from her). I told myself, and anyone who might be interested, that she was 'very self-focused' and 'not my kind of girl', which is sort of true but also a lie, the sort of lie we tell to protect ourselves. I was intrigued by her and I was intimidated by her, both much more impressive than being likeable; as soon as she offered me an invitation into her world, I RSVP'd yes.

'I admire Cara's spirit,' says Leanne thoughtfully. I want to know if Leanne admires my spirit but I'm scared to ask.

'You don't need to call a friendervention every time I have a minor crisis,' I say.

'As if I'd have time,' Leanne says under her breath, but not under her breath enough that I don't hear it, which seems careless.

James's voice floats upstairs. 'You've got a Moses coming through!' My son runs in and stands next to the bed.

'Up!' he shouts with his arms raised. I pull him up, scattering Leanne's folding in the process. Moses squishes my face between his small palms and says, 'Bisbik.'

'No biscuits, darling,' I say.

'Bisbik peeeeease.' Leanne smiles at Moses and I think that maybe she believes I've done one thing right.

'Shall we get our wine o'clock on?' I ask her.

'Actually,' she says, 'I was hoping since you're here that James and I could go out.'

It's an affront – I'm a friend in need; I feel like she should offer the evening to me. To leave your newly single mate to go out on a hot date with your husband seems callous, but Leanne's giving me a roof over my head so what can I say but, 'Of course. Of course, I'll do something fun with the kids. We'll bake cakes.'

Leanne gives me a 'like heck you will' glance but she says thank you. With that she's gone to get ready and leaves me to potter around aimlessly. I take Moses downstairs and leave him playing cars with Lucas, who is clearly basing his game on a recently witnessed incident of road rage. I go to the kitchen to make a cup of tea and try to source some biscuits but turn up nothing. Millie wanders into the room and watches me for a few moments.

'What you doing, Auntie Marfa?' she asks. I continue to root around in a cupboard of saucepans.

'I'm looking for biscuits.'

Leanne comes in and stands behind her daughter. Seeing them there together, the same half-quizzical, half-judging expression on their faces, I am struck by how similar they look. Millie has her father's colouring but her mannerisms are pure Leanne. I always think Moses looks nothing like me but in this moment I wonder if it's something you can only see from a distance.

'She's looking for biscuits,' Millie says.

'We had a clear-out,' says Leanne. I look at Millie, who shrugs.

'No worries, we can make them,' I say. 'Wanna make biscuits with Auntie Martha?' Millie whoops.

Leanne gently pushes me aside and gets out baking stuff.

'We won't be long,' she says after she has laid it all out. She gives Millie a kiss on the head. 'Daddy and I are going to get pizza.' The word pizza causes my stomach to growl; all the drama distracted me from dinner.

'Let's start now,' I tell Millie. 'Go get the boys.' Millie runs off.

'Thanks for this,' says Leanne.

'Any time, and thanks for letting us stay – I promise I'll get something sorted soon.'

'No problem.'

Leanne leaves and it's only when I hear the door slam that I realize that she's *gone* gone. The kids run in, hyped up by the promise of sugar. Seeing the three of them there is a little intimidating, but I know I've got this.

When all the children are covered in flour I realize I have no idea how to make biscuits. I've eaten a lot of them though, so I can guess the basics – flour, sugar and loads of butter; what doesn't taste better with loads of butter? I get Millie to be head stirrer and ask the boys to sort the raisins. They dump the entire bag on the floor. Millie is taking her job very seriously; the tip of her tongue pokes out of her mouth as she focuses on not letting anything spill from the mixing bowl. 'Do you ever make biscuits with your mum?' I ask her.

'No,' says Millie, 'she doesn't really like a mess.' I feel a bit smug that I'm introducing her to this quintessential bonding activity. The boys grow bored before the biscuits are ready and I have to abandon the project to build them a den under the dining table. When I return to Millie she has created a dozen mismatched biscuits. She looks so proud and I don't want to take this away from her so I put them in the oven as they are.

It's a little way before bedtime but with three kids to get ready I decide to get started. The boys seem to sense that they are being short-changed and both begin to protest. Lucas begs for his mother and Moses chooses his preferred method of resistance, violence. Every time I try to pick him up he struggles and kicks like a wild animal. 'Millie, can you be a big girl and look after Moses whilst I put Lucas to bed?'

'Yes,' she says confidently. As I carry a mournful Lucas upstairs I hear her say, 'Moses, do you like jam?'

Lucas bleats pitifully as I get him into his pyjamas. I want to tell him that if he thinks life is bad now, he's got a big shock a-comin'. I carry him to bed, where he lies down but raises the volume on his crying. If he were Moses I would leave him to it and get stuck into wine time but this seems a bit inappropriate with someone else's child. I kneel down beside the bed and stroke his hot little head.

'One day,' I say gently, 'there was a little boy called Lucas. He had a lovely mummy and daddy but what he didn't know was that his mummy was a princess.' Lucas grows quiet. 'When she was little she lived with the king and queen in a little castle in Saltdean.'

'Like Grandma and Grandad?' asks Lucas.

'Of course,' I say. Lucas pops his thumb into his mouth.

'Princess Mummy liked being a princess but she thought it was really boring. Princesses have to wear big, big dresses and really heavy crowns and they can't climb trees or swim in the sea, so one day she went to her daddy and said, "What do I have to do if I don't want to be a princess

269

any more?" Her daddy said that princesses need to look after the castle so that princes can catch dragons, and that if she didn't want to be a princess any more she needed to go and catch her own dragon. So, one day the princess walked to the scariest, darkest part of Saltdean until she found a massive, scary dragon called Henry. She said, "I need a favour. Can you come back to my castle?" So, they both went back to the castle and the king and queen told her, "Well done, you don't have to be a princess any more," and they all had a big party.'

Lucas has closed his eyes and his breathing is starting to slow; I take the opportunity to slip out. In the kitchen the scene before me makes Mardi Gras look like a tea party. Millie has decided to introduce Moses to a variety of condiments and he is creating food art on the tiled floor. 'OK, both you guys need a bath now!' Millie looks happy but Moses stares at me as if I have committed the deepest of betrayals.

In the bathroom Millie tells me her dad lets her have loads of bubbles and tips about half a bottle of Matey into the water. 'Does your daddy give you a bath every night?' I ask.

'Yes,' says Millie, 'it's "daddy time".' As she says this she makes quotation marks in the air with her fingers.

'Do you know what that means?' I ask, imitating her action.

'No,' she says happily. After undressing she leaps into the foam with so much excitement I suspect I might have been had. I take off Moses's clothes and nappy and put him in beside her. He is still scowling. Millie tries to cheer him up by putting bubbles on her head but he is unmoved.

'Why doesn't he like baths?' says Millie. 'Baths are the best!'

'I guess everybody's different, baby,' I say.

*

After their bath, I tell Millie to go and put on her pyjamas and then I tuck Moses into the bed we will share. Despite his earlier refusal he is obviously knackered and falls asleep almost instantly. I watch him for a couple of minutes; I wonder if all the change is too much for him. Perhaps settling down with someone quickly and providing him with a good male role model is the most important thing I can do right now.

I go to Millie's bedroom, where she is lying in bed with her pale pink duvet pulled up to her chin. As I'm giving her a kiss on the forehead she says, 'I love you staying.' It feels so good to hear it. 'What will we do tomorrow?' Millie asks.

'Whatever you want.'

'Can we make friendship bracelets?'

'Sure,' I say. I pat the duvet around her, making her giggle. 'Millie, what's that smell?'

Millie's eyes stretch open. 'The biscuits,' she whispers.

I race downstairs, which is futile because it's clear from the acrid scent making its way up the stairs that the few seconds I save will not rescue these baked goods. I pull twelve lumps of coal out of the oven. I guess I'll never know if I had the right recipe. I feel more let down by this than I should. In search of something to help me hide from my own disappointment, I find a bottle of red wine. It looks quite nice but I know that Leanne bulk-buys wine from Costco, so it won't be missed.

I sink the first glass quickly, too quickly; the effects of the alcohol are immediately felt in my head and extremities. I pour another glass and then break a big chunk of cheddar from a block in the fridge to line my stomach. I walk round the house nibbling on my cheese, taking in little details that I've never noticed in all the years of

271

coming here, like a small bowl of mints on the kitchen counter and a large vase filled with umbrellas by the door. As I head upstairs I realize there's another reason I'm here. I want to study them – Leanne and James. I might get some insight into what it is that makes a marriage work.

I start in the bathroom; the best questions are answered in the bathroom. The cupboard is full of very expensive cleansers and at least five different moisturizers, so perhaps the secret to a long-lasting relationship is very good skin. The only thing that looks like it might belong to James is a dusty bottle of aftershave. Alexander is metrosexual when it comes to products. Perhaps the answer is letting your wife have more space in the cabinets.

The half a bottle of wine I've consumed has emboldened me and I decide it's perfectly OK to go into the master bedroom. The room is all soft and creamy and not the sort of place secrets could hide at all. I peek into the cupboards and in the bedside cabinets; not a break-up letter or a sex toy to be found. I start to feel desperate. I look under the bed and deep into the sock drawer, and then under the dresser I find a battered old shoebox. I open it gingerly and as I do a photo slips on to the floor. It's a picture of Leanne and James circa 2014; I know this because Leanne still has a tragically severe crop that she got in a bid to be taken more seriously at work and then spent a year growing out. In the picture James has his face squeezed up against hers; his eyes are closed but his face still bursts with pleasure. Leanne looks irritated by him but if you know her, as I do, you can tell that she's loving it. I start to look through the photos, dozens of terrible, blurred selfies from a time before selfies were a thing; photos of a wet-eyed James holding a tiny, wrinkled Millie. I scoop up the box and take it to the living room, retrieving the rest of the wine on the way. The box is a journey through Leanne's life. Unlike her Facebook it's unedited; photos featuring her with no make-up or with sneaky rolls of flab showing sit right alongside shots of her looking radiant in her youth.

Towards the bottom of the box are a collection of Leanne and me throughout our school days together, including a photo of us standing awkwardly in our school uniforms and looking ridiculously young. I remember feeling like I knew so much and that my troubles were so weighty; looking at the pictures we were clearly babies. There's another picture of us in swimwear, which I'm sure was taken on the day Leanne discovered Troy's fatal flaw. There're photos of trips and events that have long since deserted my memory bank. I would never have kept evidence of a time when I felt so ugly and unfortunate. Looking at the pictures now, I regret this. I don't look ugly, I look wonderful, and between the two of us this past version of me is far more fortunate. The secret, I think, is in this shoebox. The secret is cherishing everything, even the things that feel hideous at the time.

I must fall asleep because light streaming through the window is what wakes me. The photos have gone, and I have been covered with a throw. My mouth feels dry, so I get up and go to the kitchen to find something to drink. Any evidence of last night's carnage has disappeared and on the counter, covered in cling film, is a plate of twelve identical biscuits. I take one and bite into it. It's light but still chewy. It's honeyed and full of fruit and there's also a touch of spice. It's perfect.

37

I GO UP TO the spare room and get into bed beside Moses. Shortly afterwards, Leanne comes to the door in a skirt suit and grey T-shirt. 'See you tonight, I guess,' she says. 'The spare key is on the hook in the kitchen.' She doesn't mention the fact that I trashed her house or went through her personal belongings or got drunk when her children were supposed to be under my care; so I don't either. 'Do you want me to take Moses into nursery when I drop off Lucas?' They don't actually go to the same nursery but it's sort of on the way. I know I should say no – I should tell her that she's done enough – but I nod my head. She leaves the room and I wake Moses and get him ready. This is when I love him most, when his body is warm and uncoordinated.

Leanne comes back up to get him. 'Should I give him a breakfast bar?' she says, looking at him anxiously.

'No, it's OK,' I say, 'they give them breakfast.' Leanne narrows her eyes at me. For once I can't tell what her expression is saying but I think she basically believes I outsource my parenting. I'm too tired to try and challenge this so I let her reach out for Moses's hand.

Millie appears behind her and says, 'Fanks for making the biscuits, they're 'licious.' Leanne and I look at each other but she doesn't say anything. When they're gone I climb back into bed and lie there until my bladder won't let me any longer. I need a plan. My doctor's note from the hospital has a couple more days on it and the hours stretch ahead of me intimidatingly. I need coffee and then a plan. I message George.

Marthashotbod: Good morning x
Undeterred83: How are you? Sorry I've been MIA. Just found out I've got funding for a new project. Been doing some research.
Marthashotbod: No worries. I'm better thanks. Good luck with it.
Undeterred83: Thanks. I'll message you later.
Marthashotbod: OK.

I wish I had some news of my own to share with him. I try and work out how to make coffee in Leanne's fancy machine and end up with a mug of dirty lukewarm water. I find a jar of decaf instant in the cupboard and add loads of sugar. As I drink it I look out to the garden. I've never really understood gardens – they're like a whole extra room to maintain and clean but one that, in this country, you can only use two and a half months of the year. It does look very peaceful out there, though. I remember digging up potatoes on the retreat and I contemplate going outside.

I decide against it because I know it won't be the same doing it alone; I've never felt more alone. I meant to walk away from Alexander leaving everything else intact but it's like ripping him out has frayed the edges of the rest of my life. Despite being an only child, I've always been shit at going it alone – I need someone else to validate my decisions. Leanne has done that for me for almost as long as I remember.

We didn't immediately become friends at school. I'd noticed Leanne but had written her off. I thought she was the kind of girl one would describe as perky, someone who wouldn't have allowed my presence to dull their shine. For the first year of secondary school I hung out with a couple of girls I'd vaguely known at juniors – a mouthy brunette called Janine, who even at that age it was apparent would lead me down a path of destruction and promiscuity; and a meek, mousy girl, Sophia, who had the unfortunate affliction of frequent, unannounced nosebleeds. If I'm honest I wanted an upgrade.

During a geography test I got one. I was stuck on a question on the formation of cliffs. We had attended a field trip to Seven Sisters but I had spent the day worrying about the fact that my new jeans didn't fit right around the crotch. I couldn't remember anything that we had been told and was chewing on my purple gel pen, hoping for divine inspiration, when Leanne, who was sitting next to me, hissed, 'You need to write in black.' She slid a biro across the desk and I quickly exchanged my purple pen for her offering. She finished the test long before me, and left the room before I could return her property. I carried it with me for nearly a week, until I found myself behind her in a long lunch line.

'How did you do?' she asked as I handed her the biro.

'Crap,' I said.

'Me too,' she admitted. I didn't know at the time that Leanne's 'crap' and my 'crap' were entirely distinct entities.

'You wanna study together for the next one?' she asked.

'Yeah,' I said. She grabbed my hand and used the pen I had returned to write her number on it. Even when the most attractive guy I have ever met gave me his number (a Trinidadian basketball player I met in a club in Soho, whom I never saw again because he either typed his number incorrectly or offered it insincerely), the thrill was not matched by the moment Leanne took hold of my hand and extended hers in friendship. From then on, I stopped feeling alone. There was always someone to bounce off and to reassure. We remained that way until after university, when I met Alexander. It's like he was a virus killing off other parts of my life, making me weaker. And somehow, he was still managing to do it.

The ringing doorbell startles me. I try to pull my tunic, crumpled from a night's sleep, down my thighs before I open the door. Behind it is a handsome man, sort of surreally handsome. Blond, windswept hair; slow, sexy smile; and, despite the low temperatures, thick, brown biceps, gripped by the almost-too-tight sleeves of a brilliant, white T-shirt.

'Hi,' I say.

'Hi,' he says absent-mindedly, rubbing his abs with his hands. 'I'm the window cleaner.' I can't help but think of a really bad porn film Leanne and I once watched after she stole it from her older half brother. This makes me blush and then the fact that I'm embarrassed makes me flush even more.

'Just looking for this month's payment.'

'What is it?'

'Fifteen.'

I run upstairs and grab my purse. When I'm back at the front door I try to count out fifteen pounds but only find eleven pounds sixty-three, a piece of chewing gum and a kirby grip.

'Sorry,' I say. 'Do you want a tenner and then you can get the rest from Leanne later?'

'Don't worry,' he says. 'Give her my card; she can pay me next time or do a transfer.' As he reaches up the step to pass me the card the bottom of his T-shirt rises up to unveil a thick stripe of taut skin. It takes me a few seconds to remember what to do with my arm before I reach out and take it. I watch him walk away. The business card is beautiful. In thick, gorgeous typography it says 'Dean Halpin, Windows' and his contact details. I feel a bit sick. Everything in Leanne's life is aspirational; even her hot window cleaner has his shit together. If I want to be a woman to be reckoned with I can't hang about in gardens, I can't expect anyone to hold my hand. I need to face up to my problems and make things happen and I have to start today. I send a message.

'MEET ME IN BILL'S AT 12 P.M.'

38

S HE ARRIVES NINE minutes late. She's completely bare-
faced and when she takes off her leather jacket I see
she's wearing a soft grey T-shirt, so lived in that it's evident that what she isn't wearing is a bra. Her look says, 'I
try not to be sexy but, God damn it, I just can't help it.'

'Thanks for coming, Poppy,' I say.

'No, no! Thanks for asking! I wanted to message you
but Alexander said you'd need some time.' And there he is,
casually coming out of her mouth within a minute of meeting. Fortunately, we are interrupted by a waitress.

'Can I get you anything?' she asks.

Poppy flashes her a brilliant smile before asking me,
'Are we drinking?' I want to slap her. My right hand actually itches.

'No,' I say.

'Ooh, OK,' says Poppy. She plays with a lock of hair as
she looks at the menu. 'I'll have a hot chocolate, please. Do
you have any marshmallows?' She looks back at the
waitress.

'No, I don't think so,' she says.

'No worries,' says Poppy. 'You have amazing cheekbones, by the way.'

The waitress touches her face. 'Thank you,' she says.

'Would you like some cream or something with your hot chocolate?'

'Oh, you're amazing,' says Poppy. The waitress looks at her like she's a little bit in love. When she leaves, Poppy turns her attention to me. She creates a little ledge with her hands and rests her chin on it as she appraises me. 'You're looking really good,' she says.

I fold my arms. 'Let's start by getting one thing clear,' I say. 'We're not gonna be friends.' I feel grateful that I have never liked her. I remember the first time she was introduced to me and stood there with this expression of faux humility, as if silently apologizing for being so attractive.

Alexander, sensing my apprehension, would often try and sell her to me. 'Poppy has started an ironic cross-stitch group for young professionals; you might like it?' The fact that he stopped doing this several months ago should have alerted me to something. From what I understand, Poppy started as an intern, which meant fetching Alexander sushi and tidying up, and then her role stretched and morphed into a PA, which meant the same with the occasional email. She was studying interior design or visual merchandising or something that made me think, yeah, you probably don't have to be able to read to do that. When our paths crossed at the flat she would often try to ingratiate herself with me by offering a macaroon or a used magazine, but I resisted her charm offensive. Today I see that all those little gestures were silent apologies for her betrayal. I take a sip of my water.

'So, when did you start fucking my husband?' I ask. It's a bit soap opera but it feels so good saying it.

Poppy coughs. She leans back and places her hands in her lap. 'It wasn't like that,' she says.

'No? You haven't slept with him?'

280

Poppy clears her throat. 'Neither of us saw this coming. It wasn't like we planned to . . . It was more of an emotional relationship, I guess.' Make me gag. 'I know things have been hard for you two since Moses was born and so I . . . I just don't think this had anything to do with me, really. Perhaps it made what was already there clearer.'

Did Alexander cheat on me? I don't know and the reason I don't know is because, as many couples fail to, we did not lay down the groundwork and agree with each other, or even ourselves, what cheating actually was. Was it cheating to walk to the expensive coffee shop because the barista has a cute smile? Was it cheating to give up your seat on the train to a perfectly able-bodied woman simply because you want her to think of you as gallant? Was it cheating for your knee to be pushed against your new colleague's thigh when having lunch in a crowded pub and to leave it there just a few seconds too long before moving it? If yes, then I suppose Alexander did cheat, but then so did I.

'Did you ever think that maybe he was just spinning you a line? "My wife doesn't understand me" – it's like king of the clichés.'

'I don't think so,' says Poppy. 'He wasn't telling me to get anything from me, he just knew I could meet him where he is. Anyway, I had a boyfriend.'

'And he had a wife.'

The tips of Poppy's ears turn red. She is so young and for the first time I don't think about this with envy. I look at her and I see me ten years ago, seduced by Alexander's insistence that I was the only woman that could save him.

'You know why you can meet him where he is? Because you're not fully formed; you're basically amoebic in your

281

emotional development. You can meet him where he is because you don't know who you are. Let me tell you now – not as his ex or your rival or whatever – as a woman to a, well, almost woman. Get out, don't make the mistake I did. However shiny and pretty he looks now, it's all just an illusion.'

'He said you'd say that,' says Poppy. She looks sad, as if she's disappointed that I'm so predictable. The waitress brings out her drink; I want to stand up, put my hand on the back of her head and push her face into the cream on top of that hot chocolate. Maybe Greg's right; perhaps I do have a problem with violence. 'People grow apart,' she says. 'I can't help that.'

'So when you two grow apart, or more specifically you grow up, it will be OK if some floozy takes him away from you?'

'If that's what he wants,' she says.

'How very big of you,' I say.

'That's the thing: we just give each other what the other wants.'

'I agree,' I say. 'He wants to pretend he's a kid. He wants to act like he has no responsibilities but he does.'

'Oh, he knows that,' says Poppy. 'He adores Moses and so do I.'

'That's cute,' I say, 'but he can't raise *our* child on adoration alone.'

'Look, Moses has nothing to do with this – he still loves Moses.' Implication received. He no longer loves *me*. I move my chair closer to the table, so that she can see the seriousness in my eyes.

'Tell him from me I want you nowhere near my child.'

'That's not reasonable,' says Poppy.

'It's perfectly reasonable. Moses has been through

enough without someone else playing Mummy to him. You'd know that if you had kids.'

Poppy smiles and I am filled with horror. She is smiling because she doesn't have kids but she is thinking, as most women at the start of a relationship do, that she could. She could have a child with the father of my child. We would be linked for the rest of our lives and Alexander would have to parent two children when he does such a sloppy job of parenting one. Poppy glances around before she speaks, as if checking for witnesses.

'I'm in Alexander's life, so I'm in Moses's. I appreciate you might not feel comfortable with that but please accept it. It will be so much easier if we're friends. I'm actually really nice.' I think this is meant to be a joke but nothing about its delivery indicates this. Also, I get the sense that she's loving this; she's soaking up the drama of it all. How exciting to play the role of the measured mistress. I can see her later, recreating the scene for her friends. I know she'll shake her head and say, 'It's insane!'

'I know this is all fun and games for you, your little adventure with an older man, but this is my life; this was a family. You don't know half of what we've been through. You weren't there when his mum passed away or when our dead baby was dragged out of my body. You don't know how devastating it all was.'

'I know,' says Poppy, 'he told me.'

'He told you what?' I ask.

'Everything,' she says. She makes a sweeping gesture with her hand as she says this, a gesture that is meant to represent the beginning and the end of my marriage and all the gruesome bits in between. Alexander never once spoke about the baby after we lost her. Except for one occasion when he mentioned that he had found some 'stuff' in a drawer (baby books and tiny clothes) and put it in a bag to take to the charity shop. Now he's telling this flat-chested woman-child all the gory details. I should be angry, I should be outraged – instead, I cry. If there is a humiliation greater than crying in front of your soon-to-be ex-husband's much younger, much hotter girlfriend in Bill's cafe, I don't want to know what it is. Poppy moves towards me and I look up sharply, giving her a gaze that I hope communicates in no uncertain terms that if she touches me I will remove all her fingers. It clearly reads this way or near enough because she recoils.

'I'm gonna go,' she says, pushing away from the table. She takes a few steps and then looks back and says, 'Take care of yourself.' I picture her and Alexander curling together like vines in bed tonight, expressing artificial concern for my well-being. I didn't even get to slip in any details of George. If anyone was going to walk out it was going to be me, preferably after covering her with milkshake. Instead she gets to glide away like a model, leaving me to pay for her untouched hot chocolate with my eleven pounds sixty-three.

39

'SHE'S SUCH A bitch,' I tell Leanne when she's home from work. Leanne continues to spiralize courgettes. 'I suppose we knew she was a bitch but we didn't know the levels; we didn't understand the depths of her bitchiness.' This doesn't even raise a smirk from Leanne. 'What's wrong? Tough day at work?' Leanne starts to crush garlic without answering me. 'Coz, yunno, I've had a coffee with my husband's mistress and you're supposed to agree she's a bitch. That's like best friend 101.'

Leanne puts down the crusher and says, 'It's a waste of your energy focusing on her. You've had an afternoon to yourself. An afternoon that you could have spent doing something useful.' Leanne gestures to the baking stuff still in the sink. 'Instead you fill your time creating drama.' Leanne and I once made a rule that we would always be honest with each other. It happened the morning after I drank too many blue WKDs and asked a boy on the bus to be my boyfriend; when he refused (repeatedly) I cried and then covered the seat and my new dress in blue vomit. The next morning, I chastised Leanne for not making clear to me that it was a terrible idea to proposition a stranger on the number 5 and we promised we'd offer each other honest counsel from that day forward; we pinky swore on it. But telling the truth doesn't mean spewing negativity all over your friend, especially when that friend is processing the fact that her ex has a hot, young, new girlfriend.

'I already have one mother,' I tell Leanne, 'I don't need another one.' Leanne washes her hands and doesn't comment. I say her name to let her know the conversation is far from over. She stands across from me and places her palms flat on the island.

'Maybe you do. We're not kids any more – we *have* kids. The little scrapes you get yourself into are no longer cute.' Her words sting, as was their intention. She looks at me pityingly and I decide it's time that Leanne heard some truths of my own.

'We can't all be perfect, Leanne, and you know what, some of us don't want to be. You think you've got it all figured out, don't you? Well, here's something you haven't figured out. We can see it, we can all see how hard you're trying and how much you care what people think of you. It doesn't look that perfect, it looks exhausting. It looks sad.'

Leanne curls her hands into fists before leaning forward and saying, 'I'd rather be sad than a mess. I'd rather be someone my daughter can look up to.'

I rise from my stool. 'Are you saying my son shouldn't be proud of me? Are you really saying that?'

'If the shoe fits,' says Leanne.

I jab my forefinger on to the counter. I can feel the tenseness in my jaw as I say, 'My son will be proud of me. Because I may be a mess; I may not have chrome doorknobs and Ocado deliveries and all the other shit you think is so important, but I'm a good person. I care about people. I'm a loyal friend.'

Leanne laughs and the sound shocks me. 'Of course

you're a loyal friend!' she cries. 'If you weren't you wouldn't have anyone to clean up your little accidents.'

'Fuck off, Leanne,' I say. 'I've never asked you to fix anything. All I've asked is for you to be there for me, to show a bit of interest. You barely listen to me these days.'

Leanne and I have fought before – there was the time she and Rebecca Grayson from the year above went to see Peter Andre in concert and didn't even ask me; when she ditched my birthday celebrations for a first date with a bloke who only talked about *World of Warcraft*; and when she went to bed on my wedding night, when what I needed her to do was sit with me and hold my hand until I passed out, stone-cold drunk. Leanne covers her face with her hands and when she takes them away her expression is hard and unreadable.

'I listen,' says Leanne, 'but I don't know why I bother because you say the same things over and over again. And you don't seem to want to hear any solutions. I'm here for you, I really am – may I remind you that you're living in my house? – but when are you going to fucking start being there for yourself?'

I shake my head. She's just being cruel. 'What is this about?' I ask. 'It's not all about me. I think it's because, even if I'm fucking everything up, I'm trying to make changes. I'm moving, I'm not living the same boring life day after day until I die.'

Leanne just looks at me, her bright green eyes shining with anger, and then she starts to cry. I feel panicked. I was angry; I didn't really mean to hurt her.

'Martha,' she says, as she drags her hands across her face. 'James has cancer.'

I wait for the punchline. It doesn't come.

'What?'

'He's been diagnosed with prostate cancer.'

'Oh, honey,' I say. 'Oh no. Oh, Lee . . . I hear that's the best one to have, though.' Leanne looks shocked and then starts to laugh and then I laugh and then we both start to cry. I grab her hands across the island and I don't want to let go.

'It *is* the best kind,' she says eventually. 'Everything should be OK, but it's just the thought, the thought of being without him . . . I don't know if I could do it.'

'It won't happen', I say, 'but if it did, of course you could do it.'

'Yes, I know,' says Leanne, 'but I wouldn't want to.'

I force Leanne to abandon the garlicky courgetti concoction and order pizza. When James comes in we are sitting on the bar stools next to the island eating it out of the box. When I see him and his little, smiling eyes, my own fill with tears.

'Aw,' says James, and then to Leanne, 'you told her.'

'I'm so sorry, James,' I say.

'Yes,' says James. 'I'm dying, but then again, aren't we all.' He comes over to me and gives me a hug. I've never noticed before but James is the best hugger. He doesn't just tentatively place his hands on your back; he really squeezes so that the air rushes out of your body and your feet leave the floor. When he releases me, I tell him that I will move out as soon as I can.

'Don't worry,' says James as he lifts a slice of pizza from the box, 'I like your influence.'

'He will be having surgery soon, though,' says Leanne, although she is looking at James.

'I'll be out of your hair as soon as possible,' I say. Then, after a pause: 'When did you find out?'

James takes off his tie. 'Martha, do you mind if we just . . . don't. I've been with HR all afternoon. I want to be the man without cancer for a minute.'

'Sure,' I say. 'In fact, why don't you guys go out again tonight? They have sofas at the cinema on London Road; it's so cosy.'

James shrugs. 'That'll probably take my mind off cancer.' He looks at Leanne. 'Fancy it?'

'What's a cinema again?' she asks.

'Dark place, no kids, snogging in the back,' says James.

'Definitely,' says Leanne. 'Thanks, Martha.'

'Any time,' I say, and I really mean it.

When James and Leanne have left in a taxi, I gather the children on to the sofa. I am not making the same mistake as last night; I am employing the support of a trusted friend – the television.

'Today, kiddos, we are going to watch the greatest film known to man.'

'*Frozen*?!' shouts Millie.

'No, better than that.'

'*Frozen 2*?!' shouts Millie. I ignore her.

'It's *Mary Poppins*!'

Lucas and Millie stare at me in silence. God, what is Leanne teaching these kids? I put the DVD in. They're bored by the start of it and I have to admit there's a lot of build-up so I fast-forward to when the adventure begins. Moses recognizes 'Jolly Holiday' from his previous exposure to Mary and starts to clap his hands. Lucas and Millie also get into the spirit of things and Millie makes a gallant effort to join in with the songs. I have loved Mary from the moment I met her; so strong and capable, and of course beautiful, but her beauty is the least interesting thing about her. We four snuggle up on the sofa and it seems I am not the only one entranced by her magic, but I forgot how long the film is and halfway through the children are sleeping. I carry them upstairs one by one. I take Millie last and as I lift her she wakes up.

'I'm angry with you,' she says.

'Why, darling?'

'You never did friendship bracelets.'

'Oh, Millie,' I say, 'I'm so sorry. Why didn't you say something?'

'I just 'membered,' Millie says, and smiles.

'You silly sausage,' I say, and tickle her. 'How am I supposed to remember if you forgot?'

Millie curls up her body so that my fingers can't reach her tummy. 'It doesn't matter if *I* didn't 'member – you're supposed to 'member cause you promised,' she says.

I think about my wedding vows and say, 'You know, I think you might be on to something there.'

Downstairs I watch the rest of the film. Usually it makes me really happy but I feel a little overwhelmed when Mary flies away. How can she leave so readily? How can she go like that when Bert is clearly so in love with her? I want a bit of Mary for myself, to be able to leave before everything turns to shit, or better yet, I want my own Mary – someone to work her magic and show me how to make myself happy. And then I realize that maybe I do have one.

40

'I<small>T'S CALLED</small> "<small>SORRY</small> I'm a defensive, insecure cow who has never appreciated how much you've done for me"' I tell Cara as I put a cocktail down in front of her.

'Interesting name,' she says.

'It's called "Sorry" for short,' I say.

Cara takes a sip. 'Mmmm, what's in it?' she asks.

'Basically booze.'

'I love it. And I'm sorry too.'

'What for?' I ask.

Cara puts her hand on my forearm. 'If you want to have a fictional boyfriend by all means go ahead.'

I shake her hand off my arm. 'You bitch,' I say.

Cara shrugs and I have to laugh.

'And Leanne told me you weren't well,' Cara says. She drops her head. 'I should have come to the hospital. I can be . . . stubborn.'

I point at her and feign confusion. 'You?'

'Shut up,' says Cara sharply. 'Listen, I had to bite my tongue so much when you were with A-hole pretending to be happy. I'm not good at it and I don't want you to do it again. The idea of you hiding in some virtual love affair makes me fucking angry and I don't get angry about shit I don't care about. I want you to show the world who you

291

are. Open the door, shake those amazing tatas and say, "Look out, here I come!"'

'You think my boobs are amazing?' I ask, grabbing them.

'Come on,' says Cara, 'you know you've got great baps.'

'Well, no actually, I don't. Don't you think you could have mentioned that before?' I look down at my chest. My left boob is definitely bigger than my right but I suppose they are pretty good in a lopsided kind of way.

'They're stuck on the front of your body; I didn't think you'd need it pointed out to you. If you wait for someone to tell you how fabulous you are, you may be waiting for ever. Anyway, that's enough talk about your tits. How are things going?'

'Well, actually . . .' I take a fortifying inhalation. 'I wanted to ask if I could take up your offer to stay at the flat. If you're still willing to let me and it's still available?'

Cara takes a sip of her drink. 'Of course it is. I was just waiting for you to come to your senses.'

I lean over and kiss her on the cheek. 'How soon can I move in? It's just there's a situation at Leanne's.'

'Too much limescale in the kettle?' asks Cara.

'James has cancer,' I say.

Cara puts down her drink. 'Fuck. Fuuuuck. Fuck that. Fuck cancer. I mean, he's a boring little fucker but he doesn't deserve that.'

'It's pretty shit,' I say.

'Which one is it?' she asks.

'Prostate.'

'That's the best kind,' she says.

'That's what I said.' We both sit in quiet contemplation. I wonder if Cara's thinking what I'm thinking: that we're too young for our friends' husbands to be dying.

'How's Leanne?' asks Cara.

'She's doing OK. To be honest, she seems a lot less uptight than usual.'

'Well, she couldn't get any more uptight.'

'That's mean,' I say.

'That's honest,' says Cara.

'It's not necessary to be honest all the time.'

'No, it's not, but I am,' says Cara. 'It's my thing. And – honestly – you need to get laid so why are you messin' about with this fantasy guy?'

'He's not a fantasy, he's so real it's untrue. And he's back in about five weeks.'

'What's so real about him?' asks Cara.

'I'm not going to tell you because you will mock me,' I reply sternly.

'I promise I won't mock you,' she says.

I take another deep breath. 'You know the list we wrote, the one to the universe?'

'Vaguely.'

'The universe answered and sent me George.' Cara doesn't react. 'I don't just mean a guy called George, I mean everything on the list. It's him. I mean all the things I asked for in one man. And I know it sounds crazy and it feels crazy but, you know, good crazy. I even tried to ignore it myself because it seemed so mental. You know I went on that date with Tom, and it was awful, and then I thought, what the hell, because George really is everything, *everything* I ever wanted. I've barely thought about Alexander because it's like I let go of what I didn't need and created space for what I did.' Cara sits in silence.

'The thing is, I think it's been better this way because George has been in Africa and we've got to know each other and we haven't let sex or expectations get in the way.

We've established that we can trust one another and that's what I was missing the whole time I was married – trust.' Cara remains perfectly still. I look up to the sky. 'Fine, go on then,' I say, and Cara collapses into giggles.

When she has recovered she says, 'Let me get this straight: you're in love with a dude you've never met, who says whatever you want to hear, and he's in *Africa*.'

'Yes.'

'One word – catfish.'

'No, no,' I say. 'He's not African and I think that might be a bit racist, by the way. He's from Brighton, he's just working out there.'

'Fine,' says Cara. 'You've got a boyfriend. You've got a boyfriend that lives in the internet. I'm very happy for you.'

'Thank you,' I say.

'I just want you to have what you want. I get my kicks from flesh-and-blood guys but if virtual is your thing, I'm behind you every step of the way. I will totally attend your Skype wedding.'

'You know I hate you.'

'I do,' says Cara sweetly. 'Look, you can move in whenever you want. I'm going away next week, then I'm back for a few days, and after that I'm in Stockholm.'

'Where are you going next week?'

Cara pauses to have some of her drink. As she does, something very odd happens; a band of colour rises up her neck. It takes a few seconds for me to comprehend that Cara is blushing.

'I'm going to see Rico.'

'In Brazil? But you hate the heat!'

Cara shrugs. 'Sometimes we do crazy things for love.'

I clap my hands over my heart. 'Oh my God, you love him!'

'Jesus Christ, don't wet your pants. I don't know if I love him yet, but I like him a lot and I think it might be worth going out there to, I don't know, investigate some stuff.'

'What stuff?'

'Mainly his penis, granted, but to see if I can handle being with someone for an extended period of time, I guess.' I can't believe that Cara has met a guy she's willing to let her hair frizz for. 'OK, we're done with that. So, the flat.'

I really want to push for more details but I know it's pointless. 'I'll try and sort myself out for next week. How much is the rent?'

'I'll get you the keys. The rent is free for the first three months.'

'No, Car,' I say, 'I can't do that.'

'You can and you will. Your payment to me will be getting on with your life, because I can't always be the one with the stories at cocktail hour – it's exhausting.'

'No, it's not right—'

'What's not right is you pussying about in a shit marriage for years and never doing anything for yourself. What about this business?'

'I kind of put it on hold,' I say.

Cara slams her palm on to the table, causing me to jump and several punters to look over at us. 'Stop putting your life on hold, Martha. It's getting really fucking boring.'

'OK,' I mutter.

'I've got a ticket to this event tomorrow night, it's kind of a networking thing. You'll meet a ton of people and you'll be inspired and then you'll move into my fabulous flat and then you'll take over the world.' She holds up her glass and doesn't move until I join her in her toast.

'OK,' I say. 'OK, fine. What's the event?'

'It's some women's thing.'

'The business I was thinking about was for women, women looking for love.'

'That's cheesy as fuck but this will be perfect for that. I'll text you the details.'

'Thank you, Cara. Thanks for everything,' I say.

'Thank me by living your life,' says Cara.

'Cara, I'm sorry about messing things up between you and Marc,' I say.

'Forget about it, he owes me about a million favours.'

'Why?' I ask.

'You don't know how many Saturdays I sat waiting for him to come and take me to the bloody park.'

'Wait! What?!' I shake my head as if it might lodge the information into place. 'Marc's your—'

'Dad, yeah.'

'Cara,' I say, 'this explains *so* much.'

41

LEANNE IS HAPPY to babysit so I have no excuse not to go. I'm not sure what to wear to a networking event so, despite the lack of luck it's brought me, I decide on the funeral dress. When I arrive, the other women look like they're dressed to go to a nightclub; one even has a bustier on. It makes me realize how much I have to learn.

We're given a champagne cocktail on arrival and I think I could get used to this being in business malarkey. A lot of the people here seem to know each other; I realize I'm opening myself up to a whole new social circle. I once read that you become who you associate with; if I hang out with these women maybe I can get some of what they have. We're ushered to some seats set up in rows. It takes a few minutes for everyone to settle but finally the crowd falls silent and a woman walks to the front of the room. She's wearing a tight-fitting, black trouser suit and impossibly high heels. She introduces herself as Agnes.

'Thanks for having me back,' she says. The audience gives her a round of applause. 'Today I'm going to be talking about reclaiming your feminine power.' I take my notepad out of my bag. 'How often throughout your day do you honestly feel like a woman?' she says. As she says the word 'woman' she grabs her crotch with her right hand

and everyone cheers. I write 'how often do you feel like a woman' on my pad. I can feel the person sitting to my left watching me. She seems amused by my note taking. I look around and no one else is writing so maybe it's not the done thing. I slip the pad under my chair.

'First time?' whispers the woman.

'Yeah, you?'

'I've been coming for years.' She places her hand on my knee. 'Just relax, everyone's great.' I smile a thank you. For years, I've been trying to find somewhere I really belong and perhaps I've finally found it. I don't understand much of the rest of what Agnes says – she spends a lot of time talking about chakras – but I like just being in her presence, feeling her energy and the reaction she elicits from the group.

'Enjoy!' she shouts when she finishes, and everyone cheers again. I guess this is when the networking starts. Most of the women go to get more drinks, and around me ladies greet each other enthusiastically. I see an older woman standing alone and approach her.

'Hi,' I say, and reach my hand out. She looks at it for a few seconds before shaking it. 'What's your business?' I ask. She laughs, and her face, which had previously looked quite serious, softens beautifully.

'Design,' she says.

'Oh, I used to be married to a designer,' I say. I say this lightly, like it was a lifetime ago, which in some way it feels like it was.

'Guy or girl?' asks the woman. I love this, how cosmopolitan my life is becoming. That I'm hobnobbing with the type of people intelligent enough not to assume.

'He was a guy,' I say. 'Still is.'

'Well, I'm sorry he put you off,' she says.

'Designers?'

She laughs again and I feel pleased I'm such a natural at this.

'I'm just going to get us a drink,' she says. 'I'm Moira.'

'Martha,' I say.

'M and M, I like that,' Moira says before walking away. As soon as she's gone a black girl with a big afro grabs my arm.

'Don't let Moira get her teeth into you, she's such a predator. Seriously ruthless. You're far too sweet.' I'm a bit disappointed that my inexperience is so obvious. 'Here, talk to Annie, she's a newbie too.' The woman pulls me towards a girl with a gorgeous head of blonde curls.

'Hey, Annie,' she says to the girl, 'this is . . .'

'Martha,' I say, and offer my hand. The girl shakes it and, satisfied her work is done, the woman with the afro leaves.

'It's Áine, actually,' says the girl with a soft Irish accent. Her skin is flawless and she doesn't have a lick of make-up on.

'You look kind of young to be starting your own business,' I say.

Áine frowns. 'I'm not starting a business, I'm a student. I want to be an animator.' I guess I didn't establish the exact purpose of the event. I suppose it's just a general female empowerment thing.

'So, is this your first time at a sex club?' asks Áine.

'A what? I'm not at a sex club!' I say. Áine giggles and then stops when I don't.

'Excuse me,' I say, and run to the reception. As I do I see so much that I didn't previously. The low lighting and scantily dressed bar staff, all women. It's like one of those optical illusion pictures that looks like a boat or whatever, but then someone points out that if you focus on it in a different way it looks like a fox playing table tennis, and you just can't unsee it.

I step out on to the pavement and call Cara. 'You sent me to a sex club!' I hiss.

'OK, hun,' she says. She sounds distracted.

'This is so inappropriate!'

'You need a new perspective,' she says.

'I feel violated!' I shout.

'OK, darling, talk to you later. Byeeeee!'

I'm fuming. This is the most disrespectful thing that has ever happened to me. I feel a hand on my shoulder and turn to see Áine.

'You're not leaving, are you?' she asks.

'Yeah, I think . . . I don't think . . .'

'Don't go,' she says. 'I'll be honest, you're the only girl I've seen that I like tonight.'

'It's just, I don't . . . I mean, I'm not . . .' Áine takes my hand; the action silences me.

'I know,' she says, 'but live a little.'

And even though I am livid with Cara, I did promise; so I let her lead me back in.

I wake up with Áine's curls covering my face. They smell like almonds. Had you asked me before this morning, I would have told you that it would be weird to wake up next to a woman, but it isn't. It feels a bit like the mornings after I have bunked in with Leanne, safe and cosy; although with Leanne I have never had an orgasm the night before, let alone three. I think Áine is asleep but then she reaches behind and slaps my thigh.

'Morning, beauty face,' she says.

'Good morning,' I say.

300

'You want eggs?'

'Yeah.'

Áine's place is stunning. She has the penthouse flat in an apartment building; out of the French windows the sea looks close enough to step into.

'Student accommodation has come on,' I say as I sit at the breakfast bar, and Áine places a cup of coffee in front of me.

'My dad's loaded,' she says. 'When I got accepted on my course he bought this place as an investment.'

'Wow,' I say, looking round again, 'lucky for some.'

'Maybe,' says Áine. She returns her attention to the frying pan. 'I'd rather have a dad with no money that wasn't a bigot.' I drink my coffee.

A few minutes later, Áine places a plate of creamy scrambled eggs in front of me.

'Wait,' she says, then picks a sprig of parsley from a pot on the counter top and sprinkles it over the eggs.

'This is brilliant, thank you. You're good at this.'

Áine sits opposite me with her own plate. '*You're* good at this,' she says. She eyes me meaningfully and I fight to hide my smile. 'I can't actually believe this is your first time.'

'Well, it is,' I say. Last night was my first time at many things.

When we went back into the club, music was pumping and most people were on the dance floor. The DJ was playing these amazing dance tracks imprinted on my muscle memory from my university days, and even though I was trying to stay angry with Cara, the mood pulled me in. Áine made me go to the centre of the dance floor and it felt like I was being consumed by the music and the crowd. Sweat was dripping down my entire body and I felt my hair sticking to the back of my neck. Ordinarily I would be mortified by this but I barely noticed.

When the intro to Christina Aguilera's 'Dirrty' filled the room, the energy lifted even more. Áine flapped her hands in front of my face to cool me down and I returned the favour. When I did, the woman with the afro spotted me and thought I was waving at her. She waved back and then beckoned me over to the stage where she was standing. No chance, I thought, at the same time as Áine screamed, 'Yes!' She pushed me over and it just felt easier to let her pull me up with the other half a dozen women dancing there. I froze for a couple of seconds, looking out at all the people staring back at me. They were dancing but they also seemed to be encouraging me.

I started to shake my hips and a woman in a cat suit shouted, 'Go, sister!' I raised my arms over my head and let the song work through me. I tried to embody the sassiness of the lyrics, dragging my nails up my thighs and swinging my hair around. Áine started smacking me playfully on the bum and I wiggled it in her direction to calls for more from the crowd. She wrapped an arm round my waist and we rolled our bodies in unison. I've danced with girls like that before but only for boys; this was for me. As the song climaxed we broke apart and I did a series of vigorous chest thrusts, throwing my head back with each one, and at the last line I opened my arms as if receiving an encore and shouted along with Christina, 'It's about time for my arrival!'

Áine asked me if I wanted another drink and I told her that I was actually pretty hungry, and I should be getting home.

'Home! As if. Have you been to Incognito Burrito? It's fantastic!' I had not.

Incognito is a tiny takeaway on a side road near the beach. The place was packed; apparently it was not so Incognito any more. Áine said I had to have the pork – I'd only ever had chicken before so I had to say yes. We found a place to stand in the corner and eat. When I bit into it my teeth glided through the meat like it was marshmallow.

'Right?! Right?!' said Áine with her mouth full. She told me she moved to Brighton not long after coming out. Her family, but her father particularly, had told her it was a phase, a phase he would not tolerate. Up until that point she'd been his golden girl.

'He's such a tool. He didn't realize that all the shite that made me such a good girl, yunno, no interest in the boys and going to the footie with him, was screaming lesbian.' I laughed. 'Brighton seemed like the holy land to me. I like animation enough but to be honest if I didn't study it I couldn't have justified coming here.'

'But your dad must know that Brighton is one of the most gay-friendly places in the UK?' I asked.

'People see what they wanna see,' she said. Áine quizzed me about growing up in Brighton, about the clubs I had been to and if I had ever seen Nick Cave.

'To be honest, I'm not the best Brightonian. I've never even swum in the sea.'

At this point Áine dropped the remainder of her burrito. 'No way!' she said. 'That's not possible. We're going.'

'Going where?' I said.

'The sea, obviously. You can't live by the sea and not go in; it's disrespectful.'

'Áine, can I point out that it's winter and the night,' I said, but I still let her drag me down the narrow street towards the water. As we stood on the pebbles I pulled my coat around me as Áine took hers off.

'We won't swim, just get in the water. Make it official. Come on: are you a man or a mouse?' she said.

'Actually, I'm a woman,' I told her. She stopped then and turned me towards her.

'That you are,' she said, and she kissed me. The heat from her mouth contrasted deliciously with the cold air and although it was a very sweet kiss there was just enough pressure to tell me there was much more where that came from. It was a risk kissing me like that, and it made me think I should take one too.

'OK, before I change my mind.' I dropped my coat to the ground and ran into the sea in the funeral dress. I had imagined that it would be cold but it was even colder than I had imagined. I wasn't sure that I would be able to keep moving forward; my breathing had become shallow and my teeth were chattering. I could hear Áine shouting beside me but I was so frigid I couldn't even shout back. As soon as the water had hit my chest, I considered it official and retreated to the shore, where Áine helped me into my coat before putting on her own.

'You poor thing,' she said.

'Why . . . are you . . . OK?' I asked.

'The Irish Sea, I guess,' she said. 'Now, we better get you to my place to dry off.'

'Where's your place?'

Áine smiled and raised her eyebrow before pointing to the building in front of us. 'Right there.'

'You're obviously a natural then,' says Áine. She scoops up the last of her eggs and wrinkles her nose at me as she chews them.

'Thanks, I guess. You too,' I say.

'Well, no, I've had a lot of practice,' she says.

'How? If you've just come out,' I ask.

'Boarding school,' she says with a smirk. 'And you're sure I can't tempt you away from men?' she asks as she clears up our plates. I shake my head. Last night before we went to bed I made sure that she understood it couldn't be more than a one-off. I didn't want to be responsible for any more hurt in the world. Áine said she would rather be with me once than never at all. All evening I had known that spending the night was a possibility but it was only when she said that, that the coin finally settled on heads. We had a shower, which led naturally to more kissing. Áine moved beyond that very slowly but I still panicked a little.

'Just do what *you* like,' she said, and I simply didn't know. When she noticed my hesitation she said, 'Do what feels good.' And it seems that what felt good to me also felt good to her. Rather than sex seeming like a performance, method acting for a piece entitled 'Skinny, Kinky Girl Satisfies Man', it felt like a game, a shared experience, not two separate ones that happened to be occurring at the same time.

'Thank you though, it was great,' I say.

'It was, wasn't it,' says Áine. Then she asks, 'What do you do?' It should feel weird going back to basics after sleeping together but it doesn't.

'Nothing,' I answer. 'Nothing I want to talk about.'

'What do you want to do?' asks Áine, unfazed by my negativity.

'I don't know any more.'

Áine looks at me as if I haven't finished speaking, so I continue. 'I thought I wanted to be a singer, but it's not me. I don't have the drive or the talent. I don't even know why I let myself believe I could do it for so long. And I kidded myself I could start a business but I can't even run my own life.'

Áine pushes out her bottom lip and then says, 'I'm the queen of fooling myself. I mean, I always knew I wanted to be with women but the idea of having a girlfriend in my backward parish with my idiotic father, it didn't fit. So, I thought I couldn't do it at all. Broke a million boys' hearts being who I didn't want to be. The thing is, you *can* do what you want to do – you just have to get over the fact that it's not gonna look exactly as you thought it would. Who knows, maybe it will look better than you even imagined.'

'Maybe,' I say. 'You never know.' Áine smiles at me encouragingly. 'Look,' I say, 'I better go.'

'So soon?' She says this uncritically; she wants me to stay but she's willing to grant me my freedom.

'Yeah, I'd love to stay longer but I left my kid with my best friend.'

'You have a kid?' Áine looks at me as if she's meeting me again for the first time.

'It's a long story.'

As I leave, Áine gives me a kiss on the cheek and a scrap of paper with her email address written on it. 'In case you need any design work, for your business,' she says.

'I don't think I'll be doing that,' I say, but I put it in my pocket.

Áine leans against her door frame and watches me walk towards the lift. 'Aw, but you never know,' she says. 'You never know.'

42

I KNOW IT'S TIME to let go of my dream. It's time to let go of a lot of dreams but this one is overripe and ready to fall from the tree. I return to work and ask Bob to give me a permanent nine-to-five contract because people who are not going to become singers do not need to work shifts. Bob seems mildly impressed by my decision. 'I knew you had a Debenhams voucher in you,' he says. Fairfax gives a Debenhams voucher to anyone who works at the company for ten years or more. I grip the seat of my chair after he says this. I sense I need to physically hold myself on to it. 'I'll get a contract for you ASAP but you can start working the hours now.'

'Thanks,' I say, and get up to leave.

'Welcome to the team,' says Bob.

'I've been working here for months, Bob.'

He leans back and puts his hands behind his head. Two perfectly spherical sweat patches shine at me like headlights.

'Yes,' he says, 'but now you really work here. Now you *work* work here.'

I go back to my desk and stare at the blank monitor. Greg is on a call but he keeps glancing at me between sentences. After he says goodbye he swivels his chair towards me. 'You all right?' he asks.

'Greg,' I say, without looking away from the computer, 'do you want to go out tonight and get very, very drunk?' I look at him; I can tell he's amused. 'I mean excruciatingly, can't see your hand in front of your face drunk.'

'There's nothing I'd like to do more, but I'm taking the girls to the panto. You should come; bring Moses.' In response, I start to cry. 'Shit, sorry mate. I can probably move the pantomime . . .' He pats me on the back.

'No, no, it's fine. I'm fine.' I try to dry my tears with a Post-it note. Greg hands me a handkerchief and I wipe my face with it before blowing my nose. 'Thanks,' I say, handing it back to him. He takes it gingerly and puts it in his pocket. 'Who has handkerchiefs anyway?'

'Is it divorce stuff?' asks Greg.

'No, not really. It's just . . . do you ever feel like no matter what you do, your life won't get started?'

Greg takes off his headset. 'Let's go for a fag break,' he says.

'You don't smoke,' I say.

'I won't tell anyone.'

We sit on the fire escape and watch the pigeons in the car park fight over a discarded muffin.

'That's what I feel like,' I say.

'Like a pigeon?'

'Like the muffin.'

Greg puts his fingers in his mouth and lets out a long, sharp whistle. The birds quickly disperse. 'Is the nine-to-five life so bad?' he asks.

'It's not the nine-to-five, it's just . . . It's the giving up. When I separated I thought I was just letting go of my relationship but it really means letting go of everything.'

'Yeah, but giving up stuff is sometimes creating space to let good stuff in. Like, aren't you seeing someone?'

'Yeah . . . how did you know?'

'You're always on your phone under the desk,' says Greg. 'I figured it was a new bloke or a serious addiction to Angry Birds.'

I laugh and say, 'No one plays Angry Birds any more.'

Greg nudges my foot with his toe. 'So what's he like?'

'He's perfect,' I say into the floor.

'Don't sound so happy about it.'

'I'm just worried—' The words catch in my throat for a second. 'I'm worried I won't be good enough for him.'

'How can you think that? You're great.' I look at Greg to see if his eyes will reveal the lie. 'You're funny and you're clever and you always have Polos.'

'I take fresh breath very seriously,' I say.

'See, funny,' says Greg.

'I don't wanna be funny. I want to be hot. I want to be fascinating.'

'Hot's overrated,' says Greg. 'What are you gonna do with hot when you're in a nursing home?'

'You really know how to flatter a girl.'

'No, I'm not saying you're not hot; of course you're hot. I just mean—'

'Yeah,' I say. 'Moonwalk out of that one.'

'I just think people place too much importance on hot,' says Greg quietly.

'George is hot.'

'Is that your guy?' asks Greg.

'Yeah. I kind of wish he wasn't so hot. Like, stop me if this is TMI, but I'm scared he's gonna turn and run the second he sees my saggy mum tum.' Greg chuckles and shakes his head. 'Thanks for that,' I say, 'that helps.'

'No, it's just that . . . I'll let you into a secret – and you need to know I'm breaking the bro code to tell you this – but guys don't care about that shit.'

'Sure, sure, that's why all those magazines are filled with girls in polo neck jumpers reading Joyce.'

Greg ducks down so he can see my face more clearly. 'Really, we don't. I mean, a lot of the time we're too busy worrying about our own shit, but most of the time we're just thinking about how fucking lucky we are to be there.'

'Is that how you feel about Lisa?' I ask.

'Lisa?' Greg looks a little confused.

'Does she make you think about how lucky you are?'

'Martha,' says Greg in a serious tone, 'Lisa would be lucky to have me.'

I laugh. The sensation is like stepping into a warm bath. 'We better go in,' I say.

'You sure you're OK?'

'Yeah, anyway I'm getting cold.'

'You want my jacket?'

'Nah, you're good.' I stand up and square my shoulders. 'Come on. I have to get on, I *work* work here now.' I look down at Greg, still sitting on the escape. 'Move it, this attitude won't get you your voucher.'

Greg jumps up. 'And what a travesty that would be,' he says.

Bob meets me at my desk. He's smiling, which is what he does when he's about to sack someone. Only I could go from getting a new contract to getting fired within the space of a few minutes. 'Can I speak with you, Martha?'

'Sure,' I say. He walks briskly towards his office and I have to jog to keep up with him. I turn to look at Greg

310

before I go into Bob's office. He puts his forefinger under his chin and uses it to lift his head a couple of inches.

'Take a seat,' says Bob. I sit on the edge of the chair. 'I want to talk to you about your request earlier today.'

'OK,' I say. I wonder if that mad woman who rang looking for Darren called back and reported me.

'We've had a problem with Carlos.' Carlos is the shift supervisor. His problem is that he's a functioning alcoholic, and everybody knows this, but Bob is implying a new, more recent problem. 'Porn.' Although we're the only people in the room, I look round for help. This seems like a very odd subject change, even for Bob. 'He's been watching a lot of porn. *A lot* of porn.' Bob gets up and walks round to lean against the front of his desk. 'Look, I don't mind – boys will be boys – but some of the girls don't like it. And you know, with all that sexual harassment business out there. We just can't afford a lawsuit.' I nod yes; that sexual harassment business is rather a hassle. 'So, I had to let him go. Shame, great guy,' says Bob. He's silent for a moment, clearly lost in some special memory he and Carlos shared.

'Which is where you come in,' he continues. 'I'm offering you a promotion.' It should be a joyous moment, being offered advancement at your job; a spiritual feast of recognition and validation. Instead I feel like someone's seen me standing on the edge of a cliff face, snuck up behind me and given me a little push. 'Carlos had to go and then you ask for this new contract and I realize it's supercilious.'

'I— I don't think that's what you mean.'

'Yeah it is, love, look it up. Anyway, I'm saying we wanna see your contract and raise you a brand-new contract with one pound forty extra per hour and your own parking space.'

'I don't drive.'

'But you'll know it's there,' says Bob earnestly. When I don't respond he adds, 'You won't get a better offer than this.' I believe him.

'Can I think about it?' I ask. Bob looks at me as if I've been given a winning lottery ticket and used it to wrap up chewed gum.

'Not much to think about in my opinion, but think away,' says Bob. 'Let me know by six.'

I don't even thank him before I stand up. I know I should – even a douche like Bob deserves gratitude – but I can't. I'm afraid that if I open my mouth to speak a scream will escape. When I leave his office I can see Greg staring at me; his eyes are asking a question I'm not ready to answer. I turn and walk out of the floor and I keep walking – down three flights of stairs, past Darryl sat on his chair in the reception area, and I don't stop until my legs ache. Even then I want to keep walking, I want to keep walking until I know where I'm going.

43

THE NURSERY WORKER looks startled when I arrive to collect Moses. 'Is there a problem?' she asks.

'I felt like getting him early,' I say.

'Sure thing,' she says. She turns to the room and calls, 'Momo!' To my knowledge no one has ever called him that in his life, but he pops out from within a Wendy house and toddles over. It brings home how removed I am from him; these strangers are raising my child. 'He hasn't had his lunch.'

'It's fine,' I say as I pull on his coat. I kneel down in front of him to do up the buttons. 'We're going on an adventure,' I tell him.

It feels like the train to London might be enough for Moses. He bounces tirelessly in the seat next to me, shouting 'Thomas!' each time another train passes. I remember taking the same journey with my own mother; she always brought homemade sandwiches, informing me she wouldn't be a victim of London prices. We don't have a picnic, so we create a makeshift one out of two Marks & Spencer sandwiches and a packet of crisps.

'What did you do at nursery today?' I ask Moses.

'Nursery,' he says solemnly.

'I love you,' I say, and for the first time he says back, 'I lull you.'

This was always the sort of stuff I thought we would do as a three. Take the train, share the baby's delight. It's odd how you convince yourself that you will do these things, that you will eat dinner together every evening and create pedestrian, but poignant to you, traditions. Why would you manage as three what you could not do as two? For the first few years we were together, Alexander and I would alternate Christmas at each other's family homes. Well, that was the agreement, but it was only a verbal contract and more often than not we had Christmas at the Rosses'. Initially Alexander convinced me with the undeniable truth that his parents lived further away and therefore could see us less, and then his mother was dying, and then his mother was dead. That year we tried to piece together some semblance of a holiday but every activity was punctuated by her absence and any moment approaching joy was seasoned with guilt.

The following year I convinced Alexander to invite his dad to our flat. Alexander's sister, Meghan (an amiable but nervy secondary school teacher), had just had a baby and I thought it might be helpful for her not to have the stress of cooking for us too. Also, I hoped that it might be an opportunity, perhaps my best opportunity, to win over Eric Ross.

Alexander's parents had always made it clear that I wasn't welcome. They weren't openly hostile; that would probably have been easier, that would have given me something to push against and an excuse to stay at home. No, they just communicated through their demeanour that they were only barely tolerating me. In fairness to Alexander's mother, I'm not sure anyone would be good enough for her darling son; in the case of his father I think he mistrusted any person who wasn't as hateful as him.

I had been preparing for two days – cleaning the flat, securing the goose they always ate, and watching dozens of online videos to learn how to cook it. Eric arrived long faced and empty handed. He removed his stiff suit jacket from his portly frame and positioned himself in the only armchair. I didn't spend much time with the men in the morning; I was standing guard at the oven, determined to get the dinner ready for their immovable 1 p.m. serving time. I paused only to give Eric his present, a cashmere scarf I had bought on credit. He thanked me before placing the gift on the floor beside him, unopened.

At ten minutes to one I emerged from the kitchen, sweaty but triumphant. 'Dinner will be served at one,' I chirped.

Eric took a long slug of his Scotch and said, 'I'm not hungry.' Alexander said nothing. I remember leaning against the kitchen counter, arguing with myself over the benefits of holding in my anger. Eventually I picked up the bird and threw the whole thing in the bin, and instantly regretted it. I told Alexander that Moxie got to it and we ate the veggies on our laps. Since that day, Eric may have said a few hundred words to me, and I like it that way. We learn how to be from our parents, either by emulating them or distancing ourselves. Alexander is charming, sometimes to a fault; he often makes promises he cannot deliver. A boy with excess charm could only be raised by a man with none.

I guess, given these beginnings, it might have been unfair of me to expect Alexander to be able to create traditions for our son. The work of parenting should be split equally but each job description doesn't have to look the same. I kiss the top of Moses's head, the only bit of him that still smells like baby. He nestles into my chest as I do so. I hope this means he has accepted my application as chief parent in charge of new discoveries.

5) <u>Must be close to his family.</u>

> Marthashotbod: Are you close to your mother?
> Undeterred83: Of course.
> Marthashotbod: Why's that?
> Undeterred83: Because she's my mother. That's enough.

I agree.

'Ooh,' says Moses. We are standing in the entrance hall of the Natural History Museum. The skeleton of a blue whale towers above us. I look at Moses and I know that's what I want, the rush of experiencing something new; excitement so immense it verges on fear. I take his hand and he looks at me and says 'ooh' again. I remember seeing a model of the blue whale in the museum as a child and being unable to accept that something that big could exist in reality. I became obsessed with the creatures; I remember Mum and I spending hours at the library researching them and her getting hold of some obscure documentary on their migration, which I watched until the tape in the video became mangled in the machine one day. I decided that, despite my lack of almost any mathematical skills, I could be a marine biologist. Luckily this was the same year Take That released 'Could It Be Magic', so I ended the year focused on a seventeen-year-old lad from Stoke-on-Trent and not the world's largest mammal. Holding my son's hand, with so much discovery before us, I am immediately taken back to a time when anything was possible.

'Come on, mate,' I say, 'there's so much more.'

We cover the dinosaurs and all the mammals. I'm so impressed by how patient and well behaved Moses is, or perhaps he is often patient and well behaved and I don't take the time to notice. We stop for tea and chocolate cake. I decide there and then that this is a fine tradition. As Moses works away at his slice I think about how much I want to protect him and how outlandish a task that is. 'Moses,' I say, 'I want you to know that, whatever happens, Mummy loves you and Daddy loves you, and, even if it doesn't always seem like it, Mummy and Daddy love each other.'

'Juice!' shouts Moses, pointing at his carton of orange from concentrate.

Exhausted by all the sights and sounds of the city, Moses falls asleep almost immediately on the train home. I lean back against the window and let him nestle into me. He fits perfectly, as he always has, no matter what his size. A woman across the aisle watches us and smiles a smile that makes me know she is remembering a small boy that was once in her own life. She catches me watching her, watching us, and her smile widens. I know she sees me as reliable, responsible, loving and loved, and I know that I have to be the person she sees. Careful not to wake Moses, I ease my phone out of my bag and call Bob. It's quarter to six.

'Greg told me your son was vomiting blood,' he says. 'It's not catching, is it?'

'No, it's all good. I'll be in tomorrow. I'm just phoning to say I'll take the job.'

'Course you will.'

317

44

E VEN THOUGH MOSES is still drifting in and out of
consciousness I take a bus in the opposite direction to
Leanne's house. The skies are black and the probably eco-
logically sound but basically ineffective street lighting
leaves me almost blind. It's OK, though; I would know
this walk in my sleep. I paused after every step the last
time I made the journey; I don't know what or who I was
hoping would intervene. This time I scurry. Moses is growing heavier with each second and I want to arrive before
the guilt about keeping him out so late stops me.

I hear something soft and foreign, possibly Indian, playing from inside the house. It's such a blatant indication
that someone's real, actual life is happening behind there
that my hand hovers for a few seconds before I thump my
fist against the door four times. I'm reaching for another
round of knocks when it swings open, causing me to lose
balance and fall forward a little and making Moses, resting on my left hip, shake his head, as if showing his
disapproval before settling back to sleep.

Jacqueline watches this with a blank expression, a kind
of therapist magnolia in the paint chart of emotions. Her
long blonde bob is tousled in a way that any man observ-
ing her would assume was the result of violent lovemaking

and any woman would know was the result of at least an hour with a full head of hot rollers. She has on a navy and white striped Breton top and a pair of faded blue jeans. Her feet are bare and perfectly pedicured.

'Martha? Are you OK?' she asks. It comes so readily that it makes me think that maybe I was not the first nor perhaps the last client to turn up unannounced.

'No, no, not really.'

'Have you had thoughts about harming yourself?'

'What?! No! At least I don't think so . . .' Jacqueline seems to relax a little. As long as I don't top myself on her doorstep we're good, I guess. 'I want to know why you told me to end it with Alexander. It's just that everything has got so much worse since then.'

'I'm not sure that I told you to end your relationship, but of course it wasn't a formal session, so I don't have notes.'

'You seemed so sure,' I say, and Moses murmurs so I whisper, 'You seemed so sure that I should end my relationship and since then, my life has been in tatters.'

Jacqueline bites her bottom lip and then ushers me in. 'Get that child in from the cold,' she says. She shows me into her therapy room. I put Moses on one of her squidgy leather armchairs and I sit on the other. She sits on her swivel chair between us. 'You want some water?' she asks.

'No,' I say. I feel ashamed now, now I am in her home, stealing her heat and her time. I really wanted someone to blame and Jacqueline, with her questions to answer questions and her exquisite soft furnishings, seemed like such a great choice.

'I'm going to book you a cab,' she says. 'Will he need a seat?' I shake my head. She picks up her phone and presses a button; obviously she has a cab firm on speed dial. 'Yes,' she says. 'Yes, to . . .' She looks at me questioningly.

'Windlesham Road,' I say, and she repeats this.

Then she puts the phone on her desk and says, 'Have you been doing any work on yourself?'

'Yes! Loads! I mean, I've been trying to . . .'

'Have you been speaking to someone?'

'Sort of,' I say quietly.

'Well, that's good and, Martha, sometimes progress doesn't look neat and linear; it's like a cut healing – at one stage it's a nasty, ugly scab but that means things are getting better.'

'It doesn't feel like things are getting better.'

'It won't always; you have to look for the good sometimes.' She glances at Moses, nestled in her chair. 'Look for it and if you can't see it, create it, and if you can't do that . . .' She stops as if remembering something before continuing briskly. 'In any case, there's little in the world that can't be undone. Tell him you were wrong and that you want to make another go of it.' I think about this, about putting back together what has been unpicked, and I think there is quite a lot that can't be undone actually.

A man sticks his head round the door. He is older than Jacqueline but he's attractive; certainly he was very attractive at one stage in his life, and something about the way he carries himself suggests he is still cruising on the fumes of this time.

'Do we have guests, Jac?' he says with a hint of mirth in his voice. Jacqueline excuses herself, which seems excessive given that she didn't really invite me. Even though she shuts the door behind her I can make out the clipped sentences of a whispered argument. Odd words and phrases float into the room. 'No . . . Never stops . . . Outrageous . . . One night . . . You always . . . Absolutely not . . .' I've been looking to Jacqueline for answers but it seems she's just as messed up as the rest of us.

There's silence and then some shuffling and then Jacqueline opens the door and says, 'Your car's here.' She stands in the doorway and watches me climb in, holding Moses. I look at her before we pull away. Her face seems to say, 'We're not that different.' Either that or, 'Thank God that crazy bitch has gone.'

Cara steals another piece of chorizo from the pile on the chopping board and chews it thoughtfully. 'What's this for again?'

'It's a celebration of life,' I say. James is playing with some Lego on the floor with the boys and as I say this he looks up at me and smiles. 'And a chance to say thank you to my beautiful friends. I'm recognizing the good in my life.' I pinch one of Cara's cheeks and she makes a gagging noise.

'If you're going to be pulling out that mushy shit, I'll need to drink a lot more,' she says.

'I promise I will keep the *mushy shit* to the bare minimum,' I say. Cara grabs another piece of chorizo. 'If you stop eating the ingredients,' I add. 'Why don't you make yourself useful and lay the table.' Cara rolls her eyes but she sets about creating a lovely dinner setting, even going into the garden to pick some holly to make a small centrepiece. Only an hour after the anticipated start time, Leanne, James, Cara, the kids and I sit down together to eat.

'This must be when we say grace,' says Cara in a singsong voice.

'Well, actually,' I say, standing up, 'I do sort of want to offer thanks.' Six pairs of eyes are trained on me; I clear my throat. 'I made this dinner to say thank you to you all. Leanne and James, obviously for putting me up, but all of you for helping me almost keep it together recently.' Leanne smiles and Cara gives me a wink. 'Not long ago,' I continue, 'with the help of my friends I wrote a list. A list of the things I thought I wanted.' James looks at Leanne with furrowed eyebrows and she dismisses his silent question with a quick shake of her head. 'What I failed to realize was all the wonderful things I already have. I have amazing friends, some of whom have beautiful children, and I have a man in my life who lights it up every day.' I bend down and give Moses a kiss in the middle of his curls. 'So, I want to write a new list. I want us to write it together. A list of all the things we're happy to have in our lives. We're not going to say grace; we're going to give gratitude.' I sit down. 'Leanne, can you start?'

'I'm grateful to have this wonderful man beside me,' says Leanne, and James drops his head coyly. 'I'm grateful for every day we've spent together and every day we will spend together going forward.' She looks at James until he looks back at her.

'I'm not going to cry,' he says, and Leanne laughs.

'Your turn, babe,' she says.

'I'm grateful for all the laughter in this home,' he says, 'from my wonderful, crazy children and my wonderful wife and her crazy, wonderful friends.' James looks to Millie.

'I'm happy for Barbie and butterflies and *Star Wars* and pizza and Mummy and Daddy and sometimes Lucas, and I'm happy that Moses and Auntie Marf are having a sleepover and Grandma and sometimes Ruby but sometimes not because sometimes she takes the pink felt tips and—'

'Honey, the food will get cold,' says Leanne.

'I'm happy for all the things,' says Millie with a firm nod of her head.

'Thank you, darling,' I say. After some coaxing, Lucas says he's grateful for his scooter, and when asked what he loves, Moses simply says, 'Horsey.'

Cara says, 'I'm grateful that you lot let me study how the normal live and, you know, it's not so bad.' I blow her a kiss and she points a warning finger at me.

'I am grateful that I have everyone in this room together and for the realization that that may be enough.' I raise my glass and everyone except Moses and Lucas follows suit. 'To love and laughter and Barbie and butterflies and scooting and horses and normality and having enough,' I say. 'Let's eat.' Everyone takes a drink and starts the food.

'Why is the pasta crunchy?' asks Millie.

As we're clearing away the dinner plates the doorbell rings. Leanne is picking food out of Lucas's hair and James is debating with Millie about the size of her dessert, so I go and answer it. He's facing away from me when I open the door, so he doesn't see my surprise. Greg turns around and puts his hands in his pockets. 'Hey,' he says casually.

I laugh and ask, 'What are you doing here?'

'Nothing. I mean, I just wanted to see if you were OK. I was driving by your mum's and thought I'd stop in. She said you were here.'

I lean against the door frame. 'Yeah, I needed some space.'

'So, everything's OK?' Greg says this intently, as if to make sure I understand it's not just a platitude.

'I'm really good. Thanks so much for checking, Greg.'

'No problem,' he says, 'anytime.'

'I'm doing a thing,' I say, gesturing behind me.

Greg takes a step back. 'Oh, of course, sorry to interrupt. Better get back. I was just on my way home. See you.'

He starts to walk down the path and I say, 'No! Come in for a drink.'

'Yep, you should totally come in,' says Cara from behind me. She wedges herself in next to me and appraises Greg coolly. A small hand prizes my legs open and Millie's head appears between them.

'Come in! Auntie Marfa's friend, come in!' she shouts.

Greg turns back and looks slightly afraid. 'No, I'll get off. Early start. See you soon, though,' he says, and then gives me a little salute.

I return to the kitchen, where the strawberries and ice cream are on the counter, and Cara follows me, stopping at the island to top up her wine glass.

'Who was that?' she asks.

'Greg, from work,' I say, indicating that she should pour me a glass.

She does so and takes a sip of her own before saying, 'Does that mean that the other boyfriend has been kicked to the kerb?' She smiles into her wine glass and I narrow my eyes at her.

'Nothing's going on with Greg, he's a . . .' I pause and try to locate the right word. 'Friend. But OK, I accept that I have to meet George, get to know him first before anything can be official. I haven't even sent him a message today because I'm holding back a bit.'

It's kind of true. I want it to be true. Cara nods as one would to a small child who has finally accepted that the stove is hot.

45

IN THE MORNING I wake full of the warmth created by an evening earmarked as a great memory, but underneath the joy, anxiety begs for attention like a mosquito bite. Being with Áine was wonderful – maybe even necessary – but I realize that in spending the night with her I have betrayed George. And maybe not – maybe he's the type of guy that might like his girlfriend indulging in that kind of experience – but it's definitely too early to ask. That's the problem with guidelines; no matter how comprehensive, they can never cover every eventuality. You'll never get to, 'If I accidentally have lesbian sex whilst trying to discover who I am, he will react in the following ways . . .' I don't think George will be keen, though; my list guy wouldn't want to share me, and it just seems so very me to find something perfect and then fuck it up before I even get to experience it properly. I message him to say I want to talk but he doesn't respond. As I wait for him to get back to me, I feel the cold finger of panic tap me on the shoulder. I need to know I can reach him, not just practically but emotionally.

One summer Alexander had gone on a design course in Copenhagen. I remember when he told me he had been accepted, his voice growing more and more excited with each sentence. As his eagerness grew so did my terror; I was utterly convinced he was going to abandon me. My belief wasn't that he would find someone else but something else – something better, more exciting, less me. I really wanted to go with him but he was insistent that if I went it was to be for myself; whichever way I tried to spin it I could not find a way to make that true. When he left I really thought he was leaving me for good and so when he called a few days later to say that he was miserable, perhaps the most miserable he had been in his life, I was moved to tears of unabashed joy.

Alexander started to write me emails – long, meandering missives without purpose. He told me about the silly little occurrences of his days. He wrote a whole message about the museum he went to that had an entire wing dedicated to chairs; he told me that he was desperate for Marmite and related the crazy conversations that ensued when he tried to describe it to supermarket staff; he told me he had a pass to the theme park and that on some mornings it was so quiet he would have a whole roller-coaster to himself. He didn't say much about the course itself; broad strokes about the content (stuff he knew) and the people (polite but boring). I wasn't really interested anyway. I craved the minutiae, the things that if he didn't share with me he would share with no one. They were so intimate that, although his emails contained no expressions of love, I considered them love letters.

I want to write to George but I don't have his email address so I send him a message through Linger, composing it first in the notes section of my phone.

Marthashotbod: My friend's husband has cancer. Leanne and I have been friends for ever and it's so

strange, really scary. I guess you know what that's like. I'm scared for him obviously but it makes everything seem scary. Like you never know when something is going to end or start! I'm just really feeling like I want to hold on to things.

It's early. I'm getting ready for work. I should tell you I work in a call centre. It's not what I wanted to do and it's not what I want to do but it is what I do. It's OK. I can do it. It feeds my kid, that's the important thing. I'm looking for something bigger, not that I know what that is yet. I got a promotion at work and I should be really pleased. Anyone normal would be really pleased but I guess you know by now that I'm not normal. I'm starting to think that might not be a bad thing. I'm weird but I'm me.

Anyway, holding on to things, it's probably good. Like, I don't really want this job but maybe I should hold on to it anyway. Maybe the secret is in the holding on but I held on to my marriage and maybe I shouldn't have . . . I guess everything has a lesson? I suppose you found that out with Cass.

When I was at the retreat they told me that I had to learn to sit with discomfort. I think I get it now: no matter what you do there's gonna be hurt and pain and shit. You've got to love that as much as you love the good stuff. I think there's good stuff here with you and me, I really do, even though we haven't met yet! The other thing is though, you can't really enjoy the good stuff unless you're honest about the crap and I want you to know there's a lot of crap. I've done some stuff I'm not proud of and I want to be able to share that stuff with the person I'm with. That's why I'm writing to say that I really want to share that with you.

I have a confession. Before I met you I wrote a list. On the list I put all the things I want in a man, not things I think I deserve – I promise I'm not a diva – but just the things that I think I might need. It's important that you know that so much of what was on that list I see in you. You are my list and I want to be yours. So, let's meet as soon as we can. Let's start this, let's be perfect for each other; let's be imperfect for each other perfectly.

George responds almost immediately.

Undeterred83: Well, I'm just about to go on safari, so meeting soon might be hard lol. I'll be in touch.

I stare at the message for some time. I guess I hope if I stare at it long enough it will make me feel what I want to feel, but it doesn't; nothing he says to me ever will. Nothing any man ever says to me will.

I want to break something. I tear through my bag until I find the list and every word on it now seems to be taunting me. I rip it to shreds in a frenzy, making the pieces smaller and smaller until my fingers hurt. The resulting pile of scraps doesn't quell my anger and so I pull them into my cupped hands and carry them downstairs. The only available receptacle is Leanne's huge Le Creuset casserole dish. I throw the pieces in and then drag through the kitchen drawers for a match. I find a packet, procured from an Indian restaurant, light one and throw it in. The pitiful flame it creates is deeply unsatisfying, so I run to the booze cabinet and pull out some brandy to use as an accelerant. It works; it works a little too well. The resulting flames shoot a couple of feet out of the pot and I am engulfed in fear – not of the danger but of Leanne's reaction if I burn her house down. I grab the pot and practically lob it in the sink. Then I throw on the tap as far as it will go. The fire is extinguished and I fall to the floor, sweat and relief pouring from my body. I'm still sitting there when my phone rings, up in the bedroom. I panic that if my accidental bonfire hasn't woken up the whole house, my jarring ringtone will. I fly up the stairs and somehow manage to reach it before the voicemail kicks in. Unbelievably, after everything, his is the only voice I want to hear.

'Sorry it's so early. Is now an OK time?' asks Alexander.

'It's the perfect time,' I say.

46

'CAN WE MEET today?' Alexander asks.

'Of course.'

'Let's meet tonight at the cafe on the corner. Eight OK?'

I remember how lovely it is to have a cafe on a corner that needs no further specification.

After work I take Moses to Mum's and ask her to have him. I think she may be able to say no to me but she won't be able to resist him. She's steelier then I give her credit for, though. She leads us through to the kitchen in silence and when I ask if she will have Moses overnight she says, 'You can't just waltz back in here and expect me to have him, no questions asked.' I put Moses on the floor and he immediately runs from the room, returning a few seconds later with his little dump truck, which he settles down to play with. I sit at the kitchen table.

'OK, ask away,' I say.

Mum continues to stand by the kitchen counter. 'Where are you going to live?' she asks. 'You can't stay at Leanne's for ever.'

'Cara's given us her flat for a bit while she's out of the country.'

'Money?'

'I've got a new contract at work. And a promotion.'

Mum sits down. It's the first time in my life I've had answers and I think we're both a little in shock.

'Am I too hard on you?' asks Mum.

I'm stunned. How can she be asking me a question that I've been screaming the answer to my entire life? I sit up in my chair and speak very clearly; I want to make sure that every word I say is heard.

'Mum, you're *absolutely* too hard on me.'

Mum straightens a place mat so that it runs in line with the edge of the table.

'When I was pregnant with you, I ate four oranges every day. I think I read an article somewhere about it. I drove your dad mad, making sure we had them in. It's not like it is now, when you can get whatever you want, whenever. I drank so much water. You know how much you pee when you're pregnant anyway. Those days, you could have a little drink when you were expecting. Not me, not a drop passed my lips.'

'I get it, Mum, you're a saint,' I say, slumping down in my seat.

'No, no,' says Mum, holding out her hand to ask for more time. 'No, not a saint: scared. I had lost two babies – I wasn't going to let you go and I was going to do everything in my power to make sure you were perfect, and you were. They said I mollycoddled you, that you were going to be spoiled. I don't think I put you down for two years. I didn't care.' Mum looks past me, towards the hall. 'I don't mean to push you; I am just so scared for you and you've always been such a timid child. I need to know that you're tough enough to keep yourself safe when I'm not here, when I can't be here.'

I feel like it's all hot air, another lecture whitewashed in sentiment. I really just want her to say she'll take Moses so that I can get on with my life.

'I'm sorry,' she says. So small and so ordinary, I almost miss it. The thing I had been waiting for without knowing I was waiting for it. I don't even know what she's saying sorry for but I am willing to take sorry for anything.

'Thanks, Mum,' I say.

'And thank you. Thank you for letting me support you through this; you never ask for help.' I laugh. I feel like all I do is mess up and flounder and cry for help. 'Of course I'll have him; I'll always have him. He can move in again, if you like. You, I'm not so sure.'

I try to suppress my smile but, as with most things, I'm unsuccessful. 'You'll be happy to know I'm meeting with Alexander this evening.'

Mum chews the inside of her mouth, as if she is actually trying to clamp it closed with her teeth.

'What?' I say.

'I am happy you're meeting him – you need to talk – but I don't want you to rush back into anything.'

I cover my face with my hands and speak through my fingers. 'Jesus, Mum, I can't win with you.'

'No, no,' says Mum. 'Don't get angry again! I just . . . I see how much you've been trying to do since the break-up. You have this, I don't know . . . energy. Maybe you should be together but maybe not for a while. And it can't hurt to make him stew a little.' She pulls Moses into her lap. 'I know I gave you a bit of stick but maybe I don't know everything.'

I stand up and then lean down and give her a kiss on the head. 'You're a nightmare,' I say, 'but you're my nightmare.'

47

I WONDER IF THE universe has one last coupon for me to cash in. If everything has been a test or a dream and Alexander and I must meet for one final, Technicolor ending. I consider this as I choose my seat in the greasy spoon he has asked me to meet him in. I pick a table by the window; it feels quite romantic with the drizzle running down it. I know that, whatever I've been through over the past few weeks, Alexander has had his own journey. I forgot for a while what I knew from the start: that his journeys before always led back to me. He may not be perfect – he may never be perfect – but maybe he is something much better than that: mine.

It seems Alexander's latest journey didn't involve him getting a new battery for his watch because he is five and then ten and then fifteen minutes late, and then just before I'm about to call it a day and accept that I have been stood up, he pushes through the door along with a gust of cold air. He stands on the entrance mat and runs his hand through his hair, before looking around for me. When he sees me, he assumes an expression of calm, one that I have not seen in months or perhaps even years. He walks purposefully towards me. I stand to meet him and for four, maybe five seconds I think he is going to kiss me and I panic a little about how to react to it. He just says, 'Hi,' though, before sitting down, and I am left standing.

'I'm going to get a coffee,' I say. 'Do you want one?'

'Er . . . yeah.' I go to the counter and ask them to bring two mugs of the stuff they have sitting on the warmer all day and night. As I walk back to the table I watch Alexander biting the skin on the inside of his right thumb, something he only does when he's nervous and that he hates about himself. I never knew whether it was the act itself he hated, or what it represented – his fallibility.

'It's coming,' I tell him.

'Thanks for meeting me,' he says.

'Of course, why wouldn't I . . . ?'

'It's just how things have been . . . It hasn't been the smoothest, for Moses or for us. I was hoping we could be friends.' Friends. This word is meant to be a gift to me but it's like a bucket of water on the very last embers of a dying fire.

'And what would that look like to you?' I ask. I try to hide the anger and humiliation but I'm not sure I do because Alexander tips his head to the right, which is what he does whenever I am being 'unreasonable'.

'You know . . . how we used to be.'

'How we used to be?' I laugh. It's comical how desperately out of touch he is. 'How we used to be was me listening to you bang on and on about what you're doing and what you need, and who I am or what I want to be never being a factor.'

Alexander looks up and I notice the waitress has brought over the coffee. She puts two mugs of grey liquid in front of us before walking away. Alexander smiles cordially until she is back behind the counter, then says, 'Does everything have to be so dramatic?'

Alexander used to hate it when I made displays of emotion in public. He said it made him feel vulnerable, as if feeling vulnerable was an entirely bad thing. We once went to a wedding in Birmingham – some girl he had been at university with – and we were wandering towards the station the next morning when we came upon the Hall of Memory, a memorial to the people of Birmingham who had given their lives in service. Only when I saw it did I remember standing there, clutching my grandfather's left hand as he saluted his fallen compatriots with his right. People would watch him as he stood, stock-still, shoulders back, and it was my first memory of feeling pride. Of course, as an adult, I realized they were probably just trying to piece together how this little brown girl belonged to this old white man, but that knowledge didn't taint the memory. I stopped for a few seconds and the tears rushed to my eyes – not for the ones who hadn't made it, but for the one who survived them all but still didn't survive long enough for me. Alexander, not realizing I had stopped, had gone on ahead and was now doubling back on himself to jimmy me along. 'We have a train to catch,' he said. 'We don't have time for your drama.'

Today there is time. I will make time because my drama deserves as much attention as anything he has to offer. I rest my chin on my right hand.

'You know, I thought for a minute, actually for more than a minute, for quite a while . . . Imagine me brushing my teeth, getting on the bus like a fool . . . Thinking that you were gonna meet me here today and ask me to get back with you!' Alexander doesn't respond, and I clap my hands together like a child with a new toy. 'You know what my biggest fear was, all this time? My fear was that you would show up unannounced on your rented white horse and sweep me off my feet, and even though in the back of my mind I would know it would be the wrong thing, I would go. I would go back to you, only to end up in the same place in two years, five years, ten years, fifty years.'

'I'm pretty sure one or both of us will be dead in fifty years,' says Alexander. I pick up a fork and slam its prongs into the Formica table between us.

'Why the hell did you try and make me feel so bad when you clearly don't give a shit?'

'That's not fair, I—'

'You forget, I've watched you go through break-ups, and you never go out without a fight or at least a last shag. What is it you used to say?' I click my fingers several times. 'Break-up sex is the WD-40 that stops the door creaking as it closes.' Alexander smiles at his own wit and it is with this smile that I understand how self-serving he is. 'So, the only reason you wouldn't have had one last hurrah with me is if you already had someone filling the gap.' We look at each other. I like to think we're having a silent conversation, and obviously I can't read his mind, but I'd like to believe he's saying something along the lines of, 'I'm sorry, I'm a piece of shit. I don't deserve you anyway,' or thereabouts.

'I don't think there's any point in wading through everything.' He sees me open my mouth to protest and holds up his finger. 'I actually asked you here to try and move things forward.' He gets some documents out of the leather portfolio he has brought with him and hands me several pages.

'What is it?' I try to look through what he's given me but the letters seem to float above the page.

'It's my financial statement. Then there's one for you to complete and return to me and there's also a parenting agreement, which I think we should meet again and discuss when you're less . . . well, less . . . heightened.'

I look up from the pages. 'We've hardly spoken, Alexander. Don't you even miss me?'

'I feel like it's easier . . . cleaner . . . if we just get everything sorted. Better for Moses too,' says Alexander, which is not quite answering the question but answering it all the same.

'Better for you and Poppy, more like,' I say, and I mean this to be hurtful but Alexander nods his head.

'It's serious with Poppy, yes. I want to move things forward.'

I ask the question that I didn't have the stomach to ask when I was a girl. 'Why her and not me?'

Alexander looks down at his lap. I think he's not going to answer but then he speaks quickly, as if he might change his mind. 'She's so open – she accepts me for what I am. I always felt like you were stuck in this fantasy world of what should be or what could be; I could never compete with it.'

'Did you try to, though?'

'Maybe not, but also you didn't give me a chance. You were always lost in the future.' Alexander leans across the table towards me. 'Do you have any idea how hard it is running your own business? Do you know how many nights I was awake with stress and worry?' He sits back in his chair. 'Poppy gets it. She doesn't try and put even more pressure on me.'

'I know – I know what it's like,' I say, 'but I also know there's more to life than work.'

'Spoken like an irresponsible brat,' says Alexander. I couldn't have been more surprised if he had spat in my face.

'What the fuck are you talking about, Alexander? Your

girlfriend probably doesn't even have the training wheels off her bike.'

'I'm talking about your bank statements, which still come to the flat because you couldn't even be bothered to change the address. What have you been spending all the money in the savings account on?'

'You've been opening my post?' I ask. Alexander doesn't open post, he just leaves it in a pile on the kitchen table.

'Don't change the subject,' he says. 'That money was for Moses.' He taps the table to emphasize the key words. 'That money' – tap – 'was for your son' – tap – 'and you've blown it on shit.' Tap.

'It wasn't shit,' I say. 'I bought a business course and—'

'More pie-in-the-sky crap,' says Alexander.

I think about when he was starting his business and I was getting loans to keep the lights on. I think about the MacBook I bought him for his birthday. Spending money was fine when it was for his gain.

'No, you don't get the right to an opinion,' I say. 'What I spend my money on is *my* business.'

'Yes, do what the fuck you want – spend it on ponies and sweeties and whatever it is you think will make you happy – but I want to make sure that my money is well and truly out of it.'

'Fine,' I say.

'It's not just that.' Alexander fixes my gaze and lowers his voice. 'Drugs, Martha?'

I let my head loll back in exasperation. I can imagine Greta gleefully retelling my fall from grace.

'For God's sake, Alexander, it was a bit of weed.'

'I know you've found being a mum hard,' says Alexander, 'but there's a limit, and buying drugs in the middle of the afternoon goes way past it.'

338

I can't accept what he says; I refuse to. 'What about the time you went to that stag do and took so many mushrooms I had to travel halfway across the country, so I could hold your hand on the train home?'

Alexander doesn't say anything; he knows it's the ultimate weapon against me. I want input, I want emotion, even if it's negative; his silence is another attack. I shove the papers into my bag and tell Alexander I have somewhere to be.

'That's cool,' he says, as if he has not just eviscerated my character. 'Call me when you've gone over it. We'll speak in a few days.'

I can't even respond – the way my life is at the moment, a few days feels like a lifetime away.

48

THE FAIRFAX 'END of Year Tapas Extravaganza' is an event you go to when you have nowhere else to go. I had thought it was called an 'end of year extravaganza' to be non-denominational and inclusive, but Bob told me the directors thought that people would expect less booze if they left out the word 'Christmas'. I'm not sure there is anything sadder than going to an office party actually *at* the office – it just drives home the message that this is all you have – but alcohol is definitely the answer to my encounter with Alexander, and *free* alcohol is always the answer. Walking to the door, I have exactly the same feeling I do before I go on shift. Darryl is sitting in the reception, as he always seems to be. 'Happy End of Year, Darryl,' I say.

'Thanks, love,' he says. He has swapped his security cap for a Santa hat, which seems to have the opposite effect to the one desired in that it just makes him look sadder.

'Darryl, do you have a family?' I ask.

'Oh yes,' says Darryl. 'Missus and three girls.'

'Is it hard being away from them? You work here a lot.'

Darryl's shoulders start to shake and for a terrifying second I think he is crying, before I realize that he is laughing. He leans forward and says to me, 'Hear that?'

I hold my breath and pay attention but all I can hear is the soft swoosh of traffic outside. 'No, I can't hear anything.'

Darryl leans back and folds his arms. 'I rest my case,' he says.

'Have a good night,' I say.

'Oh, I will,' he says, before chuckling again. I can tell he means it. I suppose it's wrong of me to assume that a place means the same thing to different people.

The party is on the second floor. Usually home to the canteen and several meeting spaces, it has been made into a Christmas fiesta, courtesy of a job lot of maracas and a truckload of cheap tinsel. Tashi is just by the lift entrance and squeals when she sees me. I let myself be swept up into an embrace by her, and even at this point the squealing doesn't stop. 'So, so pleased to see you! How are you?!'

'Better for seeing you,' I say.

'Congrats on your promotion.'

'Ugh, don't,' I say.

'Why would you say that?' Tashi asks. She holds me away from her and examines my face.

I twist away from her hands and her enquiring eyes and say, 'Well, it's not exactly celebratory. Congrats, you've won yourself another five years working here!' I lean against the trestle table set up by the lift. It was a bit ambitious to think I could come to a party at my workplace and not think about work.

'Some people would kill for the opportunity. If someone offers you something you should be grateful. It's a gift, even if it's really hard to see right away. If you're negative about it, the universe will hear that.'

I laugh. 'The universe and I aren't really on speaking terms.'

'Fine,' says Tashi, coming and sitting next to me. 'What about me? Be positive for me. Someone who's a bit lost and wants to know what to do with their life and might be looking to you for some guidance.'

I put my arm round her shoulder. 'You want guidance?'

She nods.

'You've come to the wrong place on so many levels.' I pick up a leaflet resting on the table. It depicts a weary-looking donkey, carrying a load of bricks. 'Is this yours?' I ask.

'Yes!' she says. 'It's to support working horses and donkeys. Make sure they're being cared for properly.'

'You're collecting?'

'Well, it's a raffle. There's a hamper and a trip to a sanctuary in Dorset.'

'Had any interest?'

'Jim from IT gave me a carrot.'

The lift opens and three lads from the post room step on to the floor. They spot Tashi's leaflets.

'Collecting money for your mum, are you!' shouts one, and the others cheer and applaud him.

'Tashi,' I say, 'these aren't your people. That's my guidance: get out whilst you still can.'

'Well, actually,' she says, and she stares at her shoes, 'I was thinking about volunteering with the charity.'

'The donkey people?'

'Yeah, Brett says—'

'Who?!' I suddenly realize why she's being all sheepish.

'Brett, you know – from the retreat.'

'Yes, I know! Lovely, brawny one. Massive, actually.' I try to make a measure of his breadth with my hands. 'Massive!'

'Yes, that one. After you'd gone, we ended up talking

loads, and then we kept in touch afterwards and he got me into the Working Horse and Donkey thing, and now a space has come up on this trip he's taking and—'

'Go!' I stand in front of Tashi and hold both her hands. 'Take it from someone withered and cynical; please, just go. Go now.'

'Now?' asks Tashi, looking at her stand.

'Yes, now.'

Tashi grabs her bag and shoves her leaflets and the carrot into it before dashing towards the lift. 'Thanks,' she says as she waits for it to arrive.

'You go get your happy ending,' I say, because who am I to burst her bubble?

Bob spots me standing alone and pushes me into the throng with a firm hand against the small of my back. He stops at a group of three women standing near a drinks table. 'Ladies, this is Martha, our latest addition to the senior team.' He then leans uncomfortably close and whispers in my ear, 'Welcome to the inner sanctum; try the punch.' He pats me on the hip and then backs away, telling me he's got babies to kiss.

'Tool,' says one of the three women, a statuesque brunette. 'I'm Hope, HR.' She sticks out her hand and I accept a solid handshake. 'Don't drink the punch – it's laced with some dreadful coconut liqueur. Here, have some fizz.' She pours me a serving into a plastic cup. 'This is Helen and Anekwe.'

'Hi,' I say to both. 'Yeah, we've met,' I say, addressing Anekwe.

'Yes, you're the girl that's always flirting with that boy in the break room.'

'Flirting? Boy?' I say, as if these words have only just been introduced to my lexicon.

'Yeah, this one.' She thrusts her chin forward and I turn to see Greg dancing towards us, a sombrero on his head.

'They've turned the boardroom into a disco and it's carnage in there,' he says. 'I can get you in, though.'

'It's OK,' says Anekwe. Hope and Helen shake their heads.

'It's you and me then, bud,' he says.

I put down my drink as he takes my hand to lead me away. I manage to stop his trajectory towards the boardroom by dragging him behind the giant yucca next to the recycling bin.

'I've had the shittiest day, Greg. I'm not in a disco mood.'

Greg removes his hat. 'What happened? Is Moses OK?'

'Yeah, yeah, it's just . . .' Greg watches me, his face willing to receive whatever I will say. 'My marriage is over.' I start to cry. I try to blink back the tears because it feels too much to be both 'woman who cries at work' and 'woman who cries at parties' simultaneously. Greg puts his arms round me and he does this kind of scooping thing so that I feel safe and supported, and I stop worrying about being a 'woman who' and focus on what I am, which is really sad.

After a minute or so, Greg releases me. He then holds me at arm's length as if checking for injuries and says, 'My diagnosis is not enough alcohol. I could be wrong but it would be a first.' He leaves me by the plant for a bit and returns with four shots in hot pink, plastic shot glasses.

'What is it?' I ask.

Greg shrugs. 'Dunno.'

'I don't know if I should,' I say. 'Alcohol is a depressant, right?'

Greg hands me two of the shots. 'And that's the beauty of divorce: it feels so shit, the only way is up!'

344

I can drink to that. We both throw our heads back and inhale the first shot; it's definitely, probably tequila.

'Anyway, there's karaoke starting now – you're gonna need a bit of a buzz on to watch Bob up there.'

'Jesus, yes!' I say, and raise my second tiny shot glass. Greg carefully taps his against mine before we drink. It's definitely, probably vodka.

The boardroom is filling up fast and Greg snags us some space sitting on a table to the right of what I assume is a makeshift stage. An older man I don't recognize is standing at the front, holding a microphone.

'That's Pete,' whispers Greg. 'He's one of the accountants. He does karaoke at Paddy's on Tuesdays.'

'Welcome!' says Pete. 'And for your delight and deliberation we have Bob, head of customer caaaaaaare!' Bob appears from somewhere within the crowd and whips the microphone out of Pete's hand.

'Thanks,' he says. 'Can I just say, this has been an awesome year!' Bob raises his arm to encourage audience participation, but the only result is someone in the back shouting, 'Can someone tell my payslip!'

'I, for one,' Bob continues, 'want each and every one of you to know that you have played a vital role in making a good company great!' Bob does a semi-squat and makes a growling sound.

'I don't understand,' I whisper to Greg. 'Is that Tony the Tiger?' Greg claps his hand over his mouth a little too late to stop his laughter escaping.

'Anyway,' says Bob, shooting a dark look in our direction, 'I appreciate all of you. Except for you, Marina. Should you even be here? I mean, are you allowed in the building? Can someone deal with that . . . But for the rest of you, this one's for you . . .' Bob adopts a wide-legged

345

stance, one that his trousers seem unqualified to accommodate, and bounces unsteadily to the introduction of 'Sex On Fire'. As the song progresses it becomes clear that he has partially choreographed the whole thing; his voice is not too bad but he completely negates the impact of this by constantly thrusting and looking so pleased with himself. I cover my eyes with my hands.

'I can't watch,' I whisper. Greg grabs my wrists from behind and pulls them away from my face. Bob holds his final pose for several seconds. I suspect in the version he had rehearsed in his head there would be applause. I'm not sure how Pete is as an accountant, but when it comes to karaoke he is a pro at covering up; he plays some jolly incidental music to mask the silence and starts some playful banter with the crowd. Bob leaves the stage and the room.

'Damn!' I say.

'Damn indeedy!' says Greg.

'Why would anyone do that?' I ask him, just as Pete is saying, 'Next up, we have Greg from customer care.'

49

GREG DOESN'T LOOK at me as he bounds towards the stage. Pete continues to read from a clipboard: 'Greg says that he wants to dedicate this to someone he thinks is really hot and who he hopes will appreciate it, but he also says that it's important that you know that he would rather stand in front of a train than do this. He says by the end of this song he will have been to hell and back and feel like he's slayed a dragon. Whatever the heck that means.'

By this point Greg has taken position centre stage. He thanks Pete warmly as he is passed the mic and, whilst he keeps his eyes lowered for the entire introduction to Aerosmith's 'I Don't Want To Miss A Thing', when he sings the first line he looks up and directly at me. He is really, truly awful and he doesn't get better. He literally murders every note of the ballad. Within the audience there is a small enclave of people from customer care who know and love Greg and cheer him on just for being him, but to everyone else he's a dude who's completely tone-deaf. Most of the crowd are laughing and the rest are jeering; the guys from IT start throwing Twiglets at him. The further into the song he gets, the higher and more fervent the notes become, and we all know that approaching is what *should* be a glorious crescendo. I can feel the anticipation in the room and I have to rescue him. Just before he reaches the end of the bridge I storm the stage, grab the microphone and kiss him, and as I do the backing track soars and the crowd erupts into cheers and applause. It's all pretty dramatic.

Everyone is still cheering when we pull apart. I look at them all and they get louder. I lean in and whisper to Greg, 'Shall we get out of here?'

'I thought you'd never ask,' he says.

He guides me through the room; guys whack him on the back as we pass but he doesn't stop or let go of my hand. We ignore the cries from people to stay as the lift doors close behind us, and as soon as it starts to move Greg is kissing me again. His hands feel like they have known my body my whole life; it feels safe and sexy at the same time, very sexy. I'm surprised by how pulled to him I feel, how my body responds so readily when I have only just realized how I feel about him – maybe it knew before me. The lift doors open and we both try to rearrange ourselves.

'Evening,' says Darryl, doing little to hide his amusement.

'Night,' we both mutter, as we scramble past him self-consciously.

Outside Greg tries to hail a taxi but several speed past him. As he raises his arm to try another one, I pull it down. 'Let's walk,' I say. 'We're in no rush, right?'

Greg smiles. I've never noticed the dimple that appears in his left cheek when he does. 'No,' he says, 'we're not.' Greg tells me he lives about fifteen minutes away. He fusses over me, making me reassure him several times that I can walk the distance in my boots.

'These boots were made for walking,' I tell him.

'That was terrible,' he says.

'Not as terrible as your singing,' I say.

'What's a man to do? I had to get your attention,' he says.

I can't really respond to that. I don't know why I had never properly noticed Greg, right beside me all that time. I guess because with him it was easy, too easy. Somewhere in the dark recesses of my soul I had decided that if he accepted me, no questions asked, there must be something wrong with *him*.

Greg's place is on the top floor of a dilapidated building. As we climb the stairs he apologizes for the smell. 'The people downstairs seem to eat the same fish stew every day.' The flat itself is charming, a bachelor pad crossed with a fairy princess castle. The black leather sofa is strewn with fluffy pink pillows and a Bambi snow globe sits in the centre of the glass coffee table.

'It's nice,' I say.

'You don't have to tell me that,' says Greg.

'I know,' I say. After taking off our coats we start kissing again, this time firmer, with more intent.

Greg stops and looks at me seriously and says, 'Do you want a Spanish omelette?' I smile and say yes. It's nice watching him work and so I sit in silence as he chops the potatoes and seasons the eggs. Ten minutes later he places a perfectly browned slice in front of me and the first bite warms my stomach in the way that only true comfort food can.

'This is really good,' I say. 'Who knew you were so good with your hands?'

Greg chuckles and puts a liberal serving of barbecue sauce on his own slice. 'Well, Mum was always in the pub or sleeping off being down the pub; I had to feed the kids and I learned a handful of staples. Most of them are some variation of egg and potato. I didn't even know this was called a Spanish omelette till I met my ex, so she gave me that at least.'

'What about your dad?' I ask. 'Couldn't he help?'

Greg snorts. 'You'd have to find him to ask him, and if you did you'd have done better than me.' He doesn't say it angrily; it's just a truth for him.

'How are you such a good dad when you haven't had one?'

'I don't know that I'm a good dad, I do my best. I do what feels right – what else can you do? And I love it. Don't get me wrong, the girls do my head in sometimes. But even then I feel so lucky it's my head they're doing in.'

After we've filled our bellies, Greg pours us some wine. As we settle on the sofa to drink it he asks, 'What about your fella? The one you're seeing.'

'I don't know how much I'm seeing him.'

'And the ex?' asks Greg. 'I don't want to step on any toes and you seemed quite upset earlier.' I put my legs across his lap and he gently strokes my shins as I speak.

'No, no, it's fine. I don't know if I was upset about him, actually. To be honest he's a bit of a tosser. I think I was upset about losing *it*, not him.'

'It?' asks Greg.

'The knowing someone's there, the having someone to call when you're alone and pissed. Being able to go home and tell someone all the shitty little petty things that happened to you that day and they, like, have to listen, they're contractually obliged. I'm just scared I'm not going to have that again.'

Greg pulls me on to his lap. 'You can have that again,' he says.

'Yeah?'

'You can have that again,' he repeats, and he kisses me. When we stop, Greg says to me, 'I want you to know that I want you to stay the night, and that doesn't mean I want us to do anything – I mean, I do, I really do want us to do stuff – but we don't have to. I mean, I want whatever you want.'

350

'It's OK,' I say.

'Cool,' says Greg.

'Shall we, then?' I ask. Greg looks surprised. 'Show me where the magic happens.'

Greg takes me to his bedroom. His bed is a mess and he hastily tries to pull up the covers. As he does I notice a photo frame on the table next to his bed, turned to face the wall. I brace myself before I pick it up; I'm prepared to see a picture of his ex and I want to be ready for her beauty. Instead the picture is of Greg and his girls – they look like they've been caught in the middle of a pile-on. I know it's recent because Charlotte is smiling and I can clearly see the gap where her tooth had been.

Greg sits on the bed. 'You OK?' he asks.

'Yeah,' I say as I join him. 'Why was this turned against the wall?'

He takes the frame from my hand and looks at the photo. 'It's a shit picture,' he says. It is, to be honest; the shot is totally out of focus and they all look sweaty and red. 'I just like to know it's there.'

He puts the photo down on the other side of the bed and he's still looking at it when I say, 'I thought it was going to be a picture of your ex.'

Greg scoots closer to me so that our bodies are side by side and we can't see each other's faces. 'Why would you think that?' He bumps his leg against mine.

'Something you should know – I can be a bit cynical.'

'No!' says Greg. 'I seriously never noticed.'

I hear the smile in his voice and I shimmy down the mattress so I can look up at him. 'So, what's she like?' I ask.

Greg sighs. 'She's a woman.'

I poke him in the leg with my finger. 'Come on, indulge me,' I say.

Greg lies down beside me. 'OK, I don't know . . . She's a woman, she's small. She's really clean, she likes dark chocolate.'

'What made you fall in love with her?'

Greg exhales loudly. 'You know, I can't remember. I'm sorry; that sounds like a cop-out but it's true. I guess she was reliable. I'd never had that. My mum was such a mess and here was this girl, who was . . . She was together. I knew she'd look after any kids we had.'

'And?'

'And she did,' he says. 'I won't lie, I picked a great mother. I just did a shitty job of picking a wife.'

'I'm not sure the guy I picked was a great father *or* husband,' I say.

Greg props himself up on one elbow and looks down at me. 'That can't be true,' he says. 'Look at you, you're so amazing – there must have been some good in him.' I try to think but I can only recall Alexander's face in the cafe, the way he dismissed me and his obvious eagerness to get back to his new life with his new girl and forget about everything that we had.

'You know, I think you're right,' I say. 'I mean, he's fine, he has his own business, he's clever. I think he probably has a lot of good in him. I think maybe I just wasn't the one to bring it out.'

'Maybe,' says Greg, 'but also that wasn't your job.'

'Oh right, what was my job then?'

'To be you.' He kisses me. 'That's all I'll ever want from you: for you to keep being you, and I want that for as long as you'll let me hang around.'

'Greg,' I say, 'I know you said we didn't have to do anything, but I've got to tell you something . . .' He watches me, his big brown eyes unblinking. 'I want to.'

352

It's strange that until this time I hadn't realized that sex is a conversation. It can say 'I hate you' or 'I need you'; it can be a shout or a whisper. With Greg everything feels so familiar but also really new and exhilarating. I am a little scared by how much I want to have sex with him, and not because I think it will make him like me more; because it will add another dimension to how we like each other. Greg explores every part of my body – the creases behind my knees and the tips of my elbows – and not because he has to, but because he wants to. I feel like what Greg is trying to say is, 'I want to know you, all of you, because I like what I know already.'

Afterwards he pulls my back to him so that we're spooning and every inch of our bodies is touching. I've heard people say that they fit together before and secretly judged them for being so pathetic, for trying to create something where there is nothing. Of course bodies fit together – that's what they were built to do – but I understand now what they meant. The ease with which we lie together . . . it doesn't feel like a compromise to be so close to him. I'm not, as I often have been in the past, biding my time until I can slip away and return to being just me. It feels like, why haven't I been sleeping this way, with this person, the whole time? And so that's what I do.

I wake up alone and I'm less disappointed than I thought I would be. What makes life hard is the constant unknowing. If I accept as fact that everyone is going to let me down, maybe things will be a little easier. I sit up in bed and consider whether to get dressed when Greg walks in, still in his boxer shorts. He is holding two mugs in his right hand. He bows gently from the waist as he holds them out so I can take one. 'And the pièce de résistance,'

353

he says, pulling out a packet of chocolate chip cookies from behind his back, 'biscuits, the good kind.' He places them on my lap and then climbs in the bed beside me with his own tea.

'I bet you give these to all the ladies,' I say.

Greg blows on his drink before saying, 'Nah, the last bird only got rich-teas.' When I don't respond he adds, 'That was a joke; there was no last bird.'

'I know, Greg,' I say. We both drink our tea and Greg warms his feet on mine under the covers. 'You got work?' I ask him. He shakes his head. 'So, what do you want to do today?'

Greg takes a long intake of breath and strokes his chin as if he is giving the question great thought; then he kisses me and his kiss answers many of my questions: Did he really mean everything he said? Is he happy I'm here? Will he still want me here tomorrow? His kiss tells me this is the beginning of something or the end of something, or perhaps that they are one and the same. I hear my phone offer up a notification from somewhere in the living room; I keep kissing Greg. I'll get to it later, maybe.

Epilogue

One year later

THERE'S A CAFE around the corner from our home, a three-bedroom cottage a couple of roads back from the seafront. On Sundays when the girls are staying, Greg will often take the kids there for breakfast, leaving me to enjoy an hour of silence. It's a necessity; I spend my weeks listening to the cute but chaotic compositions of the three- and four-year-olds who take my class, 'Music with Martha'. I love it but even love can become overwhelming. Greg adores these breakfasts and when he gets back later in the day, without fail he tells me he's going to reduce his hours at work and spend more time at home. I just smile and nod because I know he won't.

When I left to start my business, Greg took my job. Then, when Bob was fired after being overheard by a customer calling someone something very much out of line with company policy, Greg took over running the department. He wants to leave the office at six but he's so committed to his team it's always an effort to pull himself away, but it's an effort I know he makes and that's all that matters to me.

Cara returned to Rio for an extended visit and let Moses

and I stay on in her flat at very much mates' rates, so I was able to save enough to get together a deposit for the cottage. Mum and Dad come over for dinner at least once a week. Mum hates my curtains but she thinks Greg's fantastic and he seems to like her too.

James's surgery was successful and Leanne took a sabbatical to spend time with him during his recovery. She was surprised how much she appreciated a slower pace of life, so they're planning a move to rural Sussex. I hate the idea of her not being around the corner but I know how important it can be to move on.

Alexander and I had mediation and he agreed to give me a lump sum, which I used to get the business off the ground. We talk occasionally when he's dropping off Moses or if we bump into each other out and about. We're not friends but we're not *not* friends and that's enough. He and Poppy got engaged a few months ago; I didn't attend the party.

The sun is beckoning me so persuasively through the bedroom window that I decide to abandon my lie-in and join Greg and the kids. When Moses spots me in the cafe doorway he shouts, 'Pancakes, Mummy!' Greg and the girls look up and wave. I mouth 'coffee' and Greg gives me a thumbs up.

I stand at the counter behind a guy shifting impatiently from foot to foot. When he is passed his drink in a cardboard takeaway cup he lifts the lid and peers into it. 'Are you sure this is soya milk?' he asks.

'If that's what you wanted,' says the cafe owner.

'Yes, but people have made mistakes before.'

'Not this time,' says the owner carefully. The man turns and collides with me. A generous amount of liquid from the still-open cup falls on to my sleeve. Although I am the innocent party, I start to apologize.

'Why don't you look where you're going?' says the man. I look up and into the eyes of George; eyes that are as startlingly blue as I remember from his profile picture, looking back at me from within his list-perfect, redheaded six-foot-something frame.

I smile and say, 'I think I might retract that apology.' I say this to give him an opportunity to start again, to recognize me and be the George I once knew.

He narrows his eyes, I think at first in realization, but then he mumbles, 'Idiot.' He pushes past me and leaves the cafe without looking back.

I return to the counter and the owner asks me if I'm OK. 'Yeah, I'm great thanks,' I say. I order my coffee and a stack of pancakes with extra bacon.

'I'll bring it over,' he says.

When I slide into the booth next to Greg, he pecks me on the lips. 'Morning, buddy,' he says.

'Ew,' says Charlotte, but she's smiling. I poke my tongue out at her and she does the same, spraying toast crumbs in the process.

'What was that about?' asks Greg, nodding in the direction of the counter.

'Nothing. Someone I thought I knew.' I can feel Greg looking at me, waiting for more. When I don't speak he pushes my leg with his knee and I mime elbowing him in response. Greg chuckles and starts rearranging his sandwich; he likes to try and have the perfect ratio of bacon and egg in every bite.

'There's a craft ale festival on at Stanmer House today,' he says. 'Do you wanna go? We could let the kids have a run round and grab a sneaky ale.' I watch as Greg is finally satisfied with his work and sighs happily as he takes a large bite.

I squeeze his thigh under the table and say, 'Yes. Yes, yes, and yes again.'

Acknowledgements

Enormous thanks to everyone involved in the Penguin Random House WriteNow mentoring scheme, particularly Siena Parker for holding my hand and Sarah Rigby for giving me the confidence to jump! To all my WriteNow cohorts, you've made my life brighter. I want to know you and read your work for the rest of my days.

Thank you to all my Transworld teammates, especially, of course, my mentor and editor Francesca Best. Still wanna see more of you on Insta but in every other way you're killing it!

Mum and Dad, thanks always for showing me the benefit hard graft and for only ever wanting me to be happy. Rachel and Shellon, independent studies show you are the best sisters on the planet and, undoubtedly, I couldn't have done this without my much better-looking brother James.

Shout out to my big, beautiful, crazy family who have taught me that there is never an inappropriate time for humour. Special mention to my cuz Nadine, without whom this book would have no ending.

To my amazing, unwavering cheerleaders – Adele, Anna, Ceri, Chloe, Chris, Rhiannon, Gemma, Nicola, Sharon, Troy, Natalie, Varsha and Martin – you all keep me sane, or an approximation of it.

Graham, I'll be forever grateful for your advice, friendship and stellar fathering skills. Indeed, thank you to all the Allcotts. It has been a privilege to start this new chapter of my life with your continued support (and name).

And most of all thank you Roscoe, for giving me a reason to get up and start again, each and every morning.

Born and raised in London and now living in Brighton, **Charlene Allcott** works part time with young people in a residential care home as well as caring for her three-year-old son who has autism. She writes a parenting blog at www.moderatemum.co.uk.

The Single Mum's Wish List is her first novel.

You can follow her on Twitter @charleneallcott or on Instagram @moderatemum.

Great stories.
Vivid characters.
Unbeatable deals.

**WELCOME TO PAGE TURNERS,
A PLACE FOR PEOPLE WHO JUST LOVE TO READ.**

In bed, in the bath, at the dinner table.
On your lunch break, at the gym, or while you wait for
your kids at the school gates. Wherever you are, you love nothing
more than losing yourself in a really great story.

And because we know exactly how that feels, every month we'll choose
a book we love, and offer you the ebook at an amazingly low price.

From emotional tear-jerkers to unforgettable love stories,
to family dramas and gripping crime,
we're here to help you find your next favourite read.

**Join us on Facebook at
facebook.com/ThePageTurners**

**And sign up to our FREE newsletter for amazing monthly ebook deals at
penguin.co.uk/newsletters/pageturners**

DON'T MISS OUT. JOIN PAGE TURNERS TODAY.